A

JUST RECKONING

A

JUST RECKONING

A Tess Alexander Mystery

Joan Merriam

Darkness dwells within even the best of us.
In the worst of us, darkness not only dwells,
but reigns.

~ Dean Koontz
Strange Highways

A Just Reckoning

Printed in the United States of America

Visit the author's website at www.joanmerriam.com

Dedication

For my dearest friend Karen, who has never wavered in her love and support for me.
Or for Wheat Thins

Acknowledgements

I can't begin to thank all the people who were so instrumental in the creation of this book. If I've left any of you out, please know it's not for lack of appreciation.

Starting in London, thanks to Alex Constantine, Transport for London Customer services, for helping me understand the ins and outs of the London Underground, and Andy Leach with the Bethnal Green Underground Station for giving me so much invaluable information about the history and layout of the station. As well, a big thanks must go to Farzad "Faz" Kootyzadeh of the Metropolitan Police Department.

Former Placer County Sheriff Ed Bonner and Sergeant Scott Alford were incredibly helpful in guiding me toward a deeper understanding of the pervasiveness of sex trafficking in America, and the difficulties that law enforcement faces in dealing with the perpetrators of these horrific crimes.

My dear friend Galina Androchnikova-Imrie came to my rescue in translating names of some of the streets and landmarks in the Ukrainian city of Koktebel, and making sure my own translation of Russian words and phrases was accurate.

Galina, Jody, Carla, Jan, and Karen, I hope you can all

tolerate my brazen purloining of your names for some of my characters. At least none of you were branded as axe murderers.

And on the subject of my dearest friend Karen, thank you for enduring my endless storms of emails as I struggled to find the right perspective, title, and cover design for the book. You and I both know that without your dogged persistence and encouragement throughout this entire process, this book would remain nothing more than a sheaf of papers on the corner of my desk. And not incidentally, without you in my life, I very literally would not be where I am am today. The value of your friendship is beyond measure.

Finally, a huge thanks to my Canadian cover designer Donna Dean. Not only are you marvelously talented, but I'm in awe of your toughness in being able to survive those minus-45-degree Canadian winters, off the grid.

And I thought *I* was the Pioneer Woman.

PART ONE

The beginning is always today.

~Mary Shelly

1

It began with an awkward tugging at her right arm. Turning her head, she was astonished to see a bright crimson splotch growing just below her shoulder blade. *Too red. Too much red.* An instant later, screaming, white-hot pain catapulted her into full awareness.

She heard a strangled cry, realized it was her own. Descending slowly into shock, she stared as the trees around her swayed in an eerie dance, snarled and tangled together like knotted coils of serpents.

And then a cannonball hit her solar plexus. At least, it felt like a cannonball in the scrambled web of her consciousness as she quietly and almost gracefully collapsed on the forest floor.

In those last few seconds of consciousness as she looked up and tried to focus, a dark shadow materialized, mutating into the shape of a man hovering above her. His face, its surface gaunt and crevassed with moon-like craters, appeared to be streaked with soot as he stared into Tess's eyes. His own eyes, as acute and black as obsidian, were utterly barren of emotion.

Contemplating the mortally wounded woman, now lying in a swelling pool of blood, his razor-thin lips curved into a tiny smirk of triumph.

"It is finished," he whispered. He held a semiautomatic Sig Sauer tactical rifle, a silencer twisted onto its 18-inch ashen barrel.

He raised it to Tess's head as she slipped into the blackness.

2

Earlier that morning, the fog hung low and thick as cotton batting in Monterey's Del Monte Forest. A handful of cars dotted the parking lot, although later in the day summer throngs of tourists would descend on the coastal woodland and clog the narrow trails like arterial plaque. At this time of day, though, the paths were nearly deserted.

The big golden retriever whined and snuffled in the seat behind her, his eager breath coating the side window with a ragged circle of haze. Tess opened the back door, clipped on Dancer's leash, and he bounded out of the car. Once they cleared the road and entered the woods, she freed the leash and started on a brisk walk to warm up, then picked up the pace into a lazy trot. She'd never considered herself a real runner, and didn't enjoy pushing herself that much; jogging was much more her style.

About thirty minutes into the run, the golden dog was still sprinting up and back along the trail, darting off after a delinquent squirrel or fluttering leaf, then loping back minutes later with a delighted grin on his face.

Tess slowed to a walk and absently bent down to pick up a small branch fallen from one of the overhead pines, tossing it off the trail. It was one of those eccentricities about which hiking companions never failed to tease her, how she constantly cleared errant sticks, rocks, and whatnot from the route to make it easier for fellow travelers.

Dancer was up ahead, nose to the ground in rapt concentration over the remnant scent of some wild creature or perhaps another long-passed dog, his tail aloft and swishing lightly back and forth like a bushy windsock. Despite her reputation as a hardnosed investigative reporter, Tess Alexander's greatest weakness was dogs, and Dancer was no exception. Her throat tightened with emotion as she watched this creature who came into her life all those years ago and literally turned it upside-down with his inelegant antics, bizarre fixations, and unqualified, steadfast adoration.

Shaking herself out of her reverie, she took a step and spotted a particularly nasty ankle-breaker of a rock right in the middle of the path. As she stooped to toss it out of the way, a puzzling *pffft!* came from the cluster of trees to her right, followed by the deep *whumpth* of something hitting a solid object a short distance in front of her.

She looked up to see Dancer stretched out across the ground several yards away. The thought raced through her mind that he'd lain down while waiting for her to catch up, but in that same split-second she knew something wasn't right. He wasn't perched on his haunches in anticipation for her to start moving again: no, he looked as if he'd crumpled right where he stood a moment before. And he wasn't moving.

Stumbling, she raced toward him. Something was wrong with his head. Something red blooming there, something that didn't belong. Even from several feet away, she could see his eyes were open, but the golden light that had always been there was suddenly gone.

"Dancer!" The scream leaped from her throat, tumbled through the dank woodland, then was swallowed in the maw of the mushrooming fog as if the sound never existed. Her panic rising, Tess stumbled again and fell to one knee, feeling the sharp pain of lacerated skin. In the same instant, another peculiar *pfft!* sounded from her right, closer this time, and something ruffled her hair just above her forehead. She frantically tried to sort out the baffling sounds and images, but nothing made any sense, as if she were Alice plunging down a fantastical rabbit-hole.

Staggering, half-running toward Dancer, she threw herself forward at the dog's side and heard for the third time that same dull popping noise, followed by the explosion beside her head of the drooping branch from a burgundy-skinned Pacific madrone.

Gunshots. In that half-conscious state where terror has just begun to take hold, a primeval impulse told her to run.

And she rose, and ran.

Her mind shifted into a mode of pure instinct, oblivious to any thought or sensation except the sound of her own racing feet slapping the pine-needled trail, leaving behind scrabbling footprints among the moist leaves.

Once again obeying that primal need to survive and suddenly realizing that she made a perfect target in her Day-Glo green jacket, she saw an opening in the trees and veered off the trail. For a few hundred yards, she managed to swerve and parry around the understory bushes; it wasn't long, however, before she was crashing through the ever denser and more tangled underbrush, any hope of making a silent escape ebbing away like the moon-lured tide.

Finally she had no choice but to stop, her way totally

blocked by an impenetrable copse of head-high cedars, Monterey pines, oaks and thick undergrowth. At the same time, the murky shade spawned by the forest canopy and the dense, swirling fog made it difficult to see what was more than a few yards ahead. Trying hard to slow the hammering of her heart, she listened carefully for any signal of pursuit.

Nothing.

Not even the distinctive *chip-chip* of the woodland bushtits broke the silence. And that felt wrong. Because the forest was home to so many winged and walking creatures, if you listened hard enough you could always catch some sort of chirping or clicking or rustling from something.

But right now, all she heard was her own labored breathing and the wild thudding of her heartbeat.

Then her world turned into a macabre funhouse mirror of insanity, and the darkness closed in.

The three mountain-bikers veered off the designated bike trail and rode deep into the forest. After all, it wasn't like the Bicycle Police were going to come along and arrest them for being on a hiking trail where bikes weren't allowed, especially so early on a weekday. They'd planned to make a morning of it, biking the famous 17-Mile Drive from Pacific Grove down through Pebble Beach, then north up Highway 68 back into the town.

Coming around a corner, the lead man saw something lying next to the trail. It was reddish-gold, and fairly large, and it...

"Shit!" He came to a sudden stop, his tires kicking up clods of dirt and pine needles. "Guys, it's a dog! And it looks like it's been shot!" His bike fell sideways as he ran to the stricken animal, then realized with horror that it was dead. "Crap, he's still warm. This just happened."

"Who the hell would do..." The second man's comment was interrupted by a kernel of popcorn popping. All three men looked around in puzzlement, then came a cacophony of snapping and cracking as something crashed through nearby bushes. A few seconds later came another popping noise, and a woman's scream.

Without hesitation, the two men dropped their bikes and all three ran toward the sound. On the far side of a huge madrone, a man in black bent over what appeared to be a woman's body crumpled on the ground. She was utterly motionless except for the erratic, almost imperceptible rise and fall of her chest. A gaping wound in her abdomen leaked a grisly tide of blood that stained the fallen leaves and pine needles around her body a deep crimson.

"What the fuck?" hissed one of the bikers, as he and his two buddies stared into the nightmare scene.

The man in black spun to face the intruders as if they'd materialized out of thin air, his face a dark mask of consternation and fury. He raised his gun and fired, but the shot went wild because he was launching himself into a run at the same moment he pulled the trigger. For an instant, the three bicyclists hesitated, unsure about whether to follow him or see if they could help the woman—then in unison, all three moved toward the auburn-haired body spread-eagled on the ground..

"Tony, you got cell service? Call 911!"

The second man pulled out his GPS locator, and as Tony spoke with the emergency dispatcher, his friend relayed their location coordinates. The third man ripped off his jacket and used it to constrain the blood gushing from the woman's midsection.

And then they waited. And waited. And watched the life slowly ebb out of the gravely wounded woman.

In the distance, then closer and strangely muffled by the wall of fog came a wail of sirens, followed by slamming doors and urgent voices calling out for the men's location.

Within seconds, the paramedics shifted into rescue mode, administering oxygen, opening the woman's airway, inserting an IV, and packing her belly and shoulder wounds with hemostatic gauze in an attempt to slow the frantic hemorrhaging. After moving the wilted body onto a stretcher, they rushed with their cargo back toward the trail and trailhead, yelling over their shoulders for the three bikers to wait for the police.

Then the sky filled with a thunderous roaring and slapping as the half-dozen pines scattered near the open clearing jerked and whipped from side to side as if battered by a hurricane. Barely waiting until it landed, the team passed the dying woman through the wide doors of the cobalt blue Life Flight helicopter, then watched as it lifted and then disappeared into the churning mist.

The white-sheeted table was saturated with blood. All around, medical staff barked commands, countering and responding, shifting rapidly from one task to another, watching and listening and working, tightly-disciplined and focused—yet at the same time there was a pulsing undercurrent of pressure that an unwitting observer might conclude could at any instant plunge the room into a state of chaos.

The woman remained utterly motionless and mute,

almost insignificant on the trauma table that was clearly designed to hold bodies much larger than hers. A tangle of auburn hair, just a few shades darker than Dancer's own burnished amber fur, puddled beneath her head. Protruding from her mouth was a large endotracheal tube, while smaller IV tubes hung from both arms. One infused her with blood from a bag hanging above the left side of the table, while another introduced fresh frozen plasma. The ugly, yawning wound on her abdomen still hemorrhaged.

"She's heading into stage three hypovolemic shock," one of the trauma team said, his voice tight and rising in volume. "BP's dropping. Hypotensive."

"She's crashing, folks."

To the right, a cardiac monitor keened a steady one-note warning.

"Defib! Now!" The machine was already there.

"Charging."

Someone pushed the paddles into the doctor's hands, and in a smoothly practiced move he slapped one on the right side of the woman's upper sternum and the other in the midaxillary line of her exposed chest.

"Clear!"

The patient's midsection spasmed upward in a violent arc as the current hit.

The monitor continued to wail.

"Again. Clear!"

Once more, she jerked upward.

Nothing except the high-pitched whine of the machine.

"Increase to 360." The nurse adjusted the charge, watching as a small drop of sweat from the doctor's forehead formed a pea-sized spot on the back of the paddle.

"Clear!" Everyone could hear the apprehension in his voice as they waited for the shock to hit.

Seconds later, the monitor's strident wail ended, replaced by a muted beeping, at first erratic and then steadying.

Relief flooded the room. "We've got her back. Okay, let's see if we can't get her up to surgery without the whole damn thing happening again. Hopefully, Martinello is ready to move once we get there."

Robert Martinello, one of the top vascular surgeons on the west coast, was in his office just two blocks away when the woman arrived at the hospital by air ambulance. Alerted by the ER team, he arrived with his customary fanfare and aura of superiority, acknowledging the attending trauma team with little more than a nod and barely glancing at the woman on the table before pushing back out through the door.

"*Buona fortuna.*" He tossed the words over his shoulder with a slightly patronizing wave.

One of the attendants half-whispered, "Too bad he's so damn brilliant at what he does, because he's got to be one of the most arrogant buttholes that ever walked the earth."

Amidst shared nods of assent, doctors and nurses returned to the grim task of saving their patient's quickly-ebbing life.

Now it would be Dr. Martinello's turn to have *buona fortuna.*

3

She was vaguely aware of a hand on her left arm. Firm, strong, yet gentle at the same time. Then a smell, one she couldn't identify. Vinegar? No, something else. Something less astringent, but still somehow medicinal. She didn't want to think about it. The effort made her head feel like it was spinning off her shoulders.

She heard muted sounds, but couldn't understand them any better than the smell. Tiny beeps, a low hum, some type of soft clicking noise behind her head. And her throat: it hurt like hell. In fact, her entire body hurt like hell. She tried to move, but a staggering knife-like pain suddenly shot through her midsection. Aware of moaning, she realized it came from her.

"Ms. Alexander? Can you hear me? Tess?"

She didn't recognize the voice.

"Can you open your eyes? Come on, *cher,* open your eyes for me."

Who the hell are you? Leave me alone. The thoughts were huge, puffy, cotton clouds drifting through her brain.

"Tess, I know you're in there. It's time to open your eyes and see what the world has been up to while you've been gone."

Gone? Where did I go?

Suddenly she saw a vision of Dancer, twirling and galloping on a trail in front of her. And words. Or not-quite-words. Feelings. Thoughts. *It is not time.* That's what she heard, or more accurately felt, him telling her. *It is not your time.* Then, only darkness until this moment.

She struggled to comprehend. "Dancer..." The word came out in a labored, raspy whisper.

She heard a small chuckle, then the woman's voice. "Welcome back, *mon cher*...but I think you're going to have to wait to go dancing. For now, you just need to open your eyes."

And she did. Slowly, painfully. As the room came into gauzy focus and she saw nothing familiar, she tried to speak again.

"Where...what...where...am..." Her throat felt like it had been scoured with a road grader.

"You're in the ICU at the Stanford Medical Center. Just a minute, *cher*, and I'll call the doctor. Be right back."

Medical Center? That made no sense. It made even less sense that she was at Stanford University. She couldn't remember traveling to Palo Alto, or why. And what was she doing in a hospital? The puffy clouds gathered again, her head strangely detached from the rest of her body. At the spot where the nice woman once stood appeared a shape-shifting helium balloon painted with a leering Cheshire-cat grin, tethered to a human neck. Tess closed her eyes to escape the disconcerting image.

"Okay, thanks so much, doctor. See you shortly." The woman came back into the room.

Tess carefully opened one eye to make sure the balloon cat was gone. All she saw was a strikingly beautiful, molasses-skinned woman in a bright blue outfit, with wild black hair that was barely contained by a large butterfly clip at the crown of her head.

"Who...?"

"I'm your nurse, Billie Tremayne," she said.

"Billie. Lady Day."

The nurse smiled broadly. "Goodness, *cher*! I'm surprised that you'd even know who Billie Holliday was, much less that they called her Lady Day." Her voice was rhythmic and sweet, more like music than speech.

Tess glanced at the ceiling. "Clouds." Drifting away again.

"How about some ice chips? I'd expect you're thirsty."

At the mention of ice, Tess suddenly became aware that her mouth felt like the Gobi Desert. "Uhh."

The nurse half-filled a plastic cup with crushed ice. Scooping a few of the chips onto a spoon, she chided, "Now, *cher*, you can't see this if you don't open your eyes."

Again, one eye opened a slit. Good: no cat. Just the singing nurse. Singing nurse…singing nun… *"Dominique -inique –inique…"* Tess was singing, albeit discordantly.

"You really are a curiosity, *cher*: first Billy Holliday, then the Singing Nun. I can only ponder what else your foggy brain will conjure." Shaking her head in amusement, she spooned the ice chips into Tess's mouth.

Just then, a tall man wearing a white hospital coat over an eye-popping chartreuse shirt and beautifully tailored black slacks walked into the room. He projected an air of confidence tempered by a slightly goofy, genial grin and a scattering of laugh lines at the corners of his eyes.

"Hey, Billie." He casually touched her arm in greeting, and the nurse responded with a wide, vibrant smile.

"Doctor Holland. It's good to see you again. Our girl here is doing her best to wake up."

Tess cracked one eye open, started to close it again, then muttered, "Hey," at the doctor.

"Hey, yourself. I'm Dr. Roger Holland. Now stay with me, okay?" The doctor moved to the side of the bed and pulled out a small penlight. "I'm going to look in your eyes with this light; I need to make sure everything's all right in that brain of yours. You were asleep for quite a while."

"Nnn-hmm."

"Good…equal and reactive. Now, can you follow my pen with just your eyes? Don't twist your head." He moved his penlight back and forth from one side of her face to the other, carefully watching the movement in her hazel eyes.

"Try squeezing my hand." He nodded at the pressure of her fingers. "Good. Now, how's about we play Twenty Questions…except I only have a couple of them. Fair?"

"Slure. Sure."

"Okay, here's my first question," Dr. Holland said. "Can you tell me your full name?"

"Tess Elise Alexander. Just Tess."

"OK, just Tess. What's your mother's name?"

"Dead."

"Uh, what *was* her name? When she was alive."

"Belinda."

"Father?"

"Dead too. Frank. Franklin."

"Can you tell me what month this is?"

"Uhh…still July?"

"Just barely, but yes, still July. Good job. Okay, one last question, and then we're done: can you tell me where you are?"

"She said Slamford. Stanford. Hospital. Don't know why, though. Oooo…head hurts." A nasty headache pounded behind her right eye.

"That's probably the morphine we're giving you, *cher*," said Billie. "Gives some people a world-class headache."

"Mmmm."

"I need to take a look at your shoulder and your belly," said the doctor, lifting up the sheet covering her. The swelling bulk of all the tubes and bandages made it hard to tell whether she was thin or heavy, although her distinctly feminine curves would normally deter anyone from thinking of her as sickly model-thin. Today, however, she looked emaciated against the starkly white hospital linens.

Tess groaned a little during the examination, but the generous morphine drip helped keep her discomfort in check.

Holland nodded in approval as he worked. "The edema is starting to abate—any fever?"

"She's holding at 99.8."

"Good, so no evidence of sepsis." He directed his comments to Billie, who listened carefully. "The shoulder looks good. I'll set up a CT scan for tomorrow afternoon so we can see how things look in her gut. With this kind of injury, I always worry about necrosis. But she appears to be doing remarkably well, considering what a mess she was when they brought her in. I really think she's close to being out of the woods, but I want Dr. Martinello to take a look at her, too, and be there when we do the CT. Can you reach him?"

"Certainly." Billie scowled momentarily when Roger said the surgeon's name.

"Yeah, I know. No one's crazy about him, but he's the best in the business. I'm not sure if this gal would've survived if not for him. She's lucky she was in Monterey when someone tried to kill her. And that Martinello wasn't off on one of his Caribbean jaunts."

Drifting in and out of the cloud lazing above her bed, Tess heard the word. She forced her eyes open, and tried to concentrate on the doctor's face. *Hmmm…quite handsome, too. No: FOCUS.*

"Kill?" The mumbled word bore an edge of fear mingled with disbelief.

As Billie quickly moved to the side of the bed, Holland took hold of Tess's hand, clearly flustered that his patient grasped his unfortunate choice of words. "Now, Tess, there's nothing for you to worry about. Everything's all right, and *you're* all right…you're completely safe. How about we talk more about this tomorrow when you're feeling better?"

Tess shook her head like she was trying to clear it. "I don't…re…mem…"

"*Cher*, you don't need to remember right now," Billie said. "You don't need to do anything except rest. Time and our righteously good medical people will take care of everything else. Are we agreed?"

Tess stared at the beautiful nurse beside her, who just grew a huge and luxurious set of glistening, golden wings. "Oh. Okay." She closed her eyes and went back to the cloud.

Roger mouthed an apology to Billie for his blunder in mentioning the attempted murder, then glanced up at the morphine drip. "Let's bring the dosage down to 10mg now, then start DC-ing it gradually over the next day or so and see how she tolerates it. I'll order a Fentanyl patch if she's in too much pain, but I want to get her up and walking as soon as possible. Right now, she couldn't even sit in a wheelchair without falling out."

The doctor patted his patient's arm, then saw she'd already slipped back to sleep. "I know the cops will want to talk with her sooner than later," he said softly, "but for now, let's keep it quiet that she's come out of the coma and we've extubated her. I'd like to give her a day or so before she has to relive whatever nightmare brought her here. If she holds her own for the next forty-eight hours, we can let them interview her."

Billie nodded in agreement, then stepped over to the plastic bag containing the morphine and carefully adjusted its drip rate. "Now that she's more or less awake, I need to call her sister Karen. She just left for her hotel a couple of hours ago to get some sleep. Much as I hate to disturb her, I'm sure she'd want to know her sister's out of the coma. Plus there's been a whole passel of folk phoning to see how our patient is, and Karen can bring them up to speed."

"Good. I'll be in the hospital for at least a couple more hours, so let me know if you need anything. Or if there's any change."

Dr. Holland gave the nurse's arm another pat as he was leaving the ICU.

"I'm really glad you're here, Billie. You've taken great care of her."

Besides his heart-stopping good looks, that was one more reason why almost every nurse on the floor liked Roger Holland. Unlike some doctors who truly believed they had every answer to every question in the known universe, Holland genuinely appreciated just how crucial the nursing staff was to a patient's care, and often, survival. Certainly, he had an ego—after all, he was the head of the Hospital Medicine division—but it was tempered with just enough humility to keep him from coming off like a total jackass.

Before she left, Billie looked down at Tess, smoothing the thin blanket over the woman's body. "*Mon cher,* I do wonder what got you into this fix," she whispered. "I do wonder indeed."

Tess was incredibly lucky to be alive. Everyone said so: the paramedic team, the nurses, the doctors, the aides, even her sister. Because of her prolonged coma, only Karen was permitted to see her at first. Terrified her sister would never wake up, she was only vaguely relieved by assurances from the medical staff that comas were often the body's way of healing itself.

When Tess finally opened her eyes, the first person she saw was her nurse, Billie Tremayne, followed in no short order by the malevolent, nodding and bobbing Cheshire cat's head, courtesy of the morphine's hallucinogenic effects.

She wouldn't have much memory of it later, but she also met her doctor, Roger Holland, who had stayed at her bedside almost continuously for the first two days after she emerged from surgery, her life dangling by a slender, fragile thread.

By the next day, the morphine was making her itch furiously, so Dr. Holland replaced it with the Fentanyl patch in the hopes it could control her pain without creating its own brand of odd or ominous illusory residents like the disembodied Cheshire cat. She was still too drug-addled to communicate much at all, but she knew that something very bad happened to her.

She kept asking Karen about Dancer—where was he? who was taking care of him?—until finally, Karen had to tell her sister that Dancer was gone. Tess let out an inhuman cry that reverberated through the ICU, then sobbed uncontrollably until a nurse rushed over with a shot to sedate her.

The third day brought with it much more clarity, and renewed grief at the loss of Dancer. She found some comfort in the peculiar dream or vision of seeing the golden dog standing before her, whole and unwounded, and of the words that seemed to drift through the air from him: *It is not your time*.

The CT scan taken the day before showed no signs of liver necrosis, one of the most serious consequences of penetrating abdominal trauma, and the organ itself appeared to have begun the healing process. Her shoulder wound was deep, but because the gunshot was through-and-through, that lessened the risk of infection a lodged bullet could present. Everyone agreed that all things considered, she was a very lucky woman.

Except, of course, for the fact that someone tried to kill her.

And that someone *did* kill her beloved Dancer.

The pain and fury at losing him was with her every hour, every day. Karen and her husband Dan arranged to have the dog's body cremated, and held onto the urn that held his remains until Tess was ready to take it home.

There were days when in the midst of sobs she felt an urge toward vengeance she'd never known before. In the wake of Dancer's meaningless slaughter she wanted retribution so badly she could taste its bitter venom.

Give it time, Karen would murmur, rocking her weeping sister in her arms. Give it time.

4

He stood at the foot of her bed, amber eyes fixed on her and gleaming fur gently fluttering like flaxen wheat being stirred by a soft breeze. *Dancer.* He remained silent, unmoving except to cock his head slightly, keeping his attention focused on her. The air was warm and smelled of spring-born grass. In the distance, a sparrow trilled, while evening frogs and crickets harmonized without regard to the daylight hours. Now the bed was a field of wheat encircled by towering sentinel pines, their branches a tangle of interlinked arms. The ghost-dog stood watchful at her feet, his breath forming tiny clouds in the chill air, where glittering flakes of snow cartwheeled through the sundrenched sky.

She lay quiet as drifts of snow covered her in the glare of the bloodshot sun. Improbable became probable, and it all made perfect sense, even as dozens of jagged steel daggers swirled and tumbled among the plummeting snowflakes, and the breath of the dog bore unspoken words of dire forewarning.

Her eyes flew open, adjusting to the dimness of the room. Then a sound: the soft *snick* of a door latch. An instant flicker of pale yellow light rushing through the opening, then gone. In the dimness, a shadow taking shape in front of the door, then noiselessly inching into the room, a death adder in pursuit of its prey.

Slowly, quietly, hoping that what she needed was there, she reached toward the small table and felt cold metal against her palm. Before she could even think it through, she twisted in the bed, let out an involuntary yelp of pain at the move, then hurled the stainless-steel water pitcher at the creature moving toward her. The carafe hit its mark with a satisfying thud, then clanged to the linoleum and bounced several times against the wall, cubes of ice scattering in its wake and adding to the din.

"Uggh!" The man's single exclamation was rough and guttural in its surprise and fury. Then came shoes slapping and slipping on the ice-covered floor, followed by another burst of light as the intruder raced out the door. Within seconds, a night nurse bolted into the room, startled out of her rounds by the salvo of clashing metal and Tess's scream.

A few inches inside, she slipped on a cube of ice and stumbled awkwardly, barely averting a fall. She flipped on the room light and her mouth opened in shock. Melting chunks of ice littered the floor from the entryway to the bed…rivulets of water trickled down the walls and interior doors…a steel pitcher, lid open in a yawn, rested on the floor…the small bedside table slanted crazily against the side wall…an IV stand was halfway across the room…and then the patient: hair disheveled, hazel eyes wild and unblinking, her face a vampiric white, half-sitting in the bed with a disconnected plastic tube dangling uselessly from one arm.

Tess's lips drew back in a snarl, her arms raised in a gesture of self-protection as the blue-coated woman approached.

"It's okay, Tess. It's just me: Emma, your nurse."

"Emma?" Tess repeated the name as if it were a word of incomprehensible Swahili.

The nurse pressed the emergency call button once she reached Tess's side, and seconds later, another nurse appeared. Warning her colleague about the ice-covered floor and asking for a bolus of Ativan, she tried to calm the terrified patient.

"Did you see this?" the other nurse asked, pointing to something lying on the floor.

Emma turned her head and spotted the small hypodermic syringe, abandoned about three-quarters of the way from the door to the bed. "Don't touch it," she ordered. "And get Security in here."

The next ten minutes was a circus of hive-like activity. Thanks to the sedative, Tess soon relaxed enough to mumble her story to a security guard, while both nurses carefully worked to disconnect lines and tubes while trying not to touch anything that could be evidence, in preparation for moving their patient to another room.

An orderly appeared and tiptoed across the floor, then wheeled the bed and its occupant around the fallen syringe and remaining ice cubes as best he could, and out into the hall. One security guard remained stationed outside the room, awaiting the arrival of police.

Another summer day would soon dawn, and with it, even more questions.

On the morning of the fourth day after Tess emerged from her coma, she remained in her Ativan-induced slumber. Before she surrendered to its effects, she recounted her story to local law enforcement, who cordoned off the room and called in the county's criminal investigative unit to process the scene and gather evidence. By the end of the day, they learned the syringe contained a lethal dose of potassium chloride, which causes the heart to spasm uncontrollably and simply stop beating. While an autopsy would have revealed elevated potassium levels in Tess's blood, the coroner would likely rule that she died of a massive heart attack, since potassium is naturally released into the bloodstream whenever muscle tissue is damaged. Even if foul play were suspected, the end result would be the same for her attacker: permanent elimination of a major problem, and a job well done.

That afternoon, while the crime lab explored the evidence for DNA, fingerprints, or anything else that could point to Tess's nocturnal assailant, Dr. Holland finally relented to the pressure from Monterey County law enforcement to interview their victim about the shooting in the Del Monte Forest. He insisted on a thirty-minute limit, however, to which the detective in charge reluctantly agreed, no doubt secretly planning to push that constraint as far as he could.

"Hello, Ms. Alexander. I'm Detective Josh McKittrick from the Monterey County Sheriff's Office." He was a slightly squat, balding man who appeared to be in his mid-fifties, with deep brown, liquid eyes that reminded Tess of the cows on her grandfather's farm. He was dressed in black twill slacks and a skillfully tailored shirt of forest green, its French cuffs fastened with tasteful, square rose gold cufflinks. His tie was a Jerry Garcia design in a vivid, swirling mix of green and amber tones. Spiffy dresser for a cop, thought Tess.

"I'd like to get some details from you about the

shooting. We don't have a whole lot to go on except for what the fellows who found you told us, and the more we know the better chance we have of apprehending the person who did this."

Last night's sedative worn off, Tess was alert. "I want to catch this bastard as much as you do. Probably more." The detective broke into a half-smile that crinkled his nose and created the effect of a very stylish leprechaun.

"Okay, good. Now, ma'am, let's start with what you remember about the incident."

"First of all, my name is Tess. 'Ma'am' is for women who are stodgy and decrepit, and I'm neither."

"Okay, Tess it is." He smiled his leprechaun smile again and nodded, then waited for her response.

While the Fentanyl helped alleviate some of her pain, it wasn't nearly as effective as the morphine was. On the plus side, she hadn't seen any leering, helium-headed Cheshire cats for the last 24 hours.

"Unfortunately, I don't have much memory at all of that day—at least, after Da...Dancer...and I started out." At the mention of the dog's name, her throat tightened and she was forced to swallow several times before she could go on. She closed her eyes to gather herself, then began recounting events to the detective.

After she was finished, McKittrick asked, "What about earlier in the day? Did you notice anyone watching you, paying special attention to you? Did you see anything that seemed unusual or not quite right?"

"Not really." Tess adjusted her position in the bed and closed her eyes, recalling that morning in her mind. "I remember feeling uncomfortable when I was at the coffee shop earlier that morning, feeling like someone was staring at me. But I only saw this man..." She suddenly sat up straight, then winced in pain and her face went several shades whiter.

"Are you okay?" The detective's voice was filled with concern, and he moved closer to her side of the bed. "Can I help you?"

Tess groaned, and shook her head. "No, I'm okay. I just keep forgetting that I can't move that fast."

After taking a few deep breaths, she was ready to continue. "As I was picking up my coffee, my neck started to crawl and I knew someone was watching, staring at me." She thought quickly, then made a slight tweak to her story so the detective didn't summon the men in the white coats to take her away in a straitjacket once she told him about her visions. "I turned around really quickly and bumped into the table where they keep the napkins and sweetener, and spilled part of my coffee on my shoes.

"Guess I must've said 'Shit!,' and the place went quiet—you know, how there's this weird stop-action when someone says something too loudly in a restaurant or drops a glass or something?—and when I caught myself I realized everyone was looking at me. I smiled and several people laughed. Then I saw this one man who was sitting in the corner, very inconspicuous, and he was looking at me, almost looking *through* me. It was only for a second or two, and then he went back to reading his newspaper."

"What was he wearing?"

"I didn't pay any attention. He was so unremarkable that he almost blended into the wall. After he turned away, I didn't take notice of him again."

"Um-hum. Okay, can you tell me why you were in Monterey County?"

"I was working on a story, following a lead that took me to San Francisco first, then I headed south to visit my sister Karen in Pacific Grove. I stayed at her place for a couple of days, and then was heading back home."

"What story were you working on?"

Tess hesitated and idly ran her fingers through her hair—*Good God, I really need a shower and shampoo*—while trying to decide what to tell the detective. The risk, of course, was that exposing the story, even to law enforcement, could bring the whole thing crashing down around her. She could lose her story, but worst of all, she could endanger lives. A story was one thing, but someone's life was entirely different.

McKittrick scowled at her indecision.

"Detective, I need to give this some thought. I just can't risk..."

Combat warrior Billie Tremayne strode into the room, her face anything but pleased. "Excuse me, Detective," she growled, "but as I recall you were told to restrict this 'visit' to 30 minutes. Did you lose track of time?"

"No, ma'am, I didn't. But I was just..."

"I don't much care what you were 'just.' My patient needs her rest if she's going to recover. And that *is* what you want, isn't it, Detective? For her to recover?"

"That goes without saying," McKittrick snorted. "But if we're gonna solve this crime, we need information, and she's the only one who can give it to us."

"Well, crime or no crime, Detective, if Ms. Alexander has a setback and something calamitous happens to her recovery, she'll end up being able to tell you about as much as a toad on a rock, if you'll forgive me saying so. And that's something yourself will have to live your days and nights with. Are you willing to take that chance?"

McKittrick flushed, obviously unaccustomed to having his mandates questioned.

The nurse continued, clearly on a roll. "Come back tomorrow morning if you need to, so long as my patient" – emphasizing the *my patient* as if to declare ownership – "is up to it. Call first. If you'll come with me, I'll give you the direct line to the nurse's station." She walked to the door and held it open for the detective, who reluctantly sidestepped his way through it.

Billie tossed a look of triumph over her shoulder at Tess and said, "Okay, missy: you just close those eyes and get some rest. I'm going to make sure no one disturbs you until lunchtime."

Tess tried scrunching the rock-hard hospital pillow into a more comfortable shape, realized it was hopeless, and began pondering her alternatives with McKittrick. *How much can I afford to say? How much can I afford* not *to say? What are the consequences, either way?* Her head swam, she ached all over, she desperately needed a shower, and the more she thought, the less clear it all became.

She needed to stop for a few minutes, or a few hours. Just let it all develop as it would, on its own course, and the right answer would come. It always did. Well, it usually did.

She instructed herself to let go. Just let her mind become a soft, rolling, soothing river.

A few minutes later, she floated into a silky, peaceful sleep.

Although still in pain, by the afternoon of day five Tess was fully aware and spent some time trying to figure out how to handle all the questions from McKittrick. She struck on a great solution.

"Detective," she said after he settled into the ugly

brown vinyl guest chair, "how's your relationship with law enforcement in Great Britain?"

The detective looked baffled. "Excuse me? Great Britain?"

"Yes, Great Britain. More specifically, London. You need to call Chief Superintendent Charles Marley at London's Stoke Newington Metropolitan Police Department. He can fill you in on all the details of what preceded these attempts on my life, and I suspect you can get even more from him than you could from me. You're both law enforcement and he won't have any qualms about giving you the case details."

His face scrunched into a look of puzzlement. "I don't understand what a London Police Superintendent has to do with why you were attacked in California."

"Just talk with Superintendent Marley and the picture will be much clearer."

McKittrick still looked dubious, but agreed to make the call. Tess gave him Marley's number, telling him to set aside at least an hour to hear the tale.

Soon after McKittrick finished that transatlantic call, a beautiful bouquet with a thoughtful note arrived from the London police superintendent, saying he was horrified to hear what happened. Later than afternoon, another flower arrangement appeared, and another. Tess's room was quickly becoming nearly impassable because of all the flowers and plants: from her sister Karen and her family, Tess's editor and colleagues at the Foundation, two former editors, her neighbors, a number of friends, and even the innkeeper at the London B&B where she stayed that winter.

A far less pleasant result of the conversation between the two law enforcement officers appeared in Tess's doorway the following day.

The stranger held in his hand an FBI identification. His name was Ridley Jephson, and he stood easily six-foot-seven. Wide-shouldered, slim-hipped, and heavily-muscled without an apparent ounce of fat on his frame and with smooth skin nearly as black as onyx, he cast an imposing figure as he stood near her bed.

"So, what's a special agent with the FBI doing in the hospital room of a lowly reporter?"

"Not so lowly, I'd say." His deep, baritone voice carried a hint of what Tess guessed was his native Virginia, and together with his megawatt smile that spun light into every corner of the room, the effect was to diminish the intimidating effect of his size and physique. "I'd like to talk with you about your…" he feigned a tiny cough, "umm, 'experiences' overseas this past winter."

Most of the public thought the FBI operated only within America's borders, but Tess knew the agency also functioned in dozens of foreign countries through both its International Operations Division and the International Organized Crime Intelligence and Operations Center, which brings law enforcement organizations together to combat international organized crime.

"I was wondering when I'd hear from the feds." Because this was now a transnational case, it was inevitable that the FBI would stick its nose under the tent sooner or later. Dealing with the rigid, hidebound governmental agency was not something Tess enjoyed.

"Basically, ma'am, I just need to take a statement from you, since the Eurasian and European sex trafficking ring you've been looking into has definite ties to the U.S. Then of course, there's the matter of the attempts on your life here, most likely perpetrated by a foreign national or the proxy of a foreign national. Do I understand there was also an attempt on your life in Crimea?"

"Yes, there was: obviously, unsuccessful." Tess planned to say as little as possible, just enough to give the impression of cooperation.

"Perhaps you could start at the beginning." He pulled a small recorder out of his pocket, and sat down in the side chair. "And I will be recording this interview, you understand."

"No problem." Tess proceeded to give Jephson a rough sketch of how she'd become involved in the story and what happened since then, pausing several times to address the agent's questions. It didn't take long for him to see she was glossing over a number of key details.

"Ms. Alexander, do I need to remind you that it's a federal offense to lie to the FBI?"

"Agent Jephson, let me be clear here: I'm well aware that you or your London legal attaché have been in contact with Interpol and by extension, Scotland Yard and Chief Superintendent Marley, and have received a full briefing from them. Chances are, Marley felt duty-bound to share with you what he knew of the people involved in the case, which means you already know virtually everything you keep asking me to provide. What you need to remember is that I'm duty-bound to withhold the names of certain people, as well as some details, in the interests of protecting my sources. Even if you've already obtained that information through official channels." Jephson was handsome as hell and smooth as silk, but that didn't mean she was going to allow herself to be bullied by him, however politely.

The agent stared at her for several seconds, then smiled thinly. "Let's put it this way, Ms. Alexander: your cooperation would be appreciated."

"I *am* cooperating," she said impatiently. "However, it's my credibility as a journalist that's on the line here, not to mention the pledge I gave to my sources to protect their identities. For all intents and purposes, you're asking me to act as an investigative arm of the federal government, which I am most assuredly not. Giving you that information also destroys any chance I have of future sources trusting me with anything. Not incidentally, it also exposes me to potential breach-of-promise lawsuits from my current sources, something that neither I nor my professional liability carrier would relish."

"So, are you saying you refuse to provide me with the names of those sources, or the pertinent details of your involvement?"

"I'm not 'refusing' anything, agent. I'm protecting the identities of certain sources, and anything that would indirectly lead to the disclosure of their identities. Period. Otherwise, I'm being completely transparent and above-board." She hesitated for a moment, then made direct eye contact with the agent, who was now standing over her as she lay propped up in the bed. It was the kind of submissive position she hated, but she couldn't do a thing about it. Her voice carried a hard edge. "And just for the record, as I said before, you already have what you need. You simply wanted me to substantiate it all. Which I have. There's nothing of substance I'm holding back." She sighed deeply and allowed her lids to flutter closed for effect. "If that's all, I believe we're done here: I'm very, very tired." Tess was nothing if not an excellent actress.

Jephson's voice carried a note of irritation. "We will be back in touch with you, Ms. Alexander, if we need further information—you can be assured of that."

"Yeah, I'm sure you will be, Agent Jephson."

That afternoon, an armed officer appeared and stationed himself at the door to Tess's hospital room.

Over the course of the next few days, Detective McKittrick made three more visits to Tess's room in an effort to fill the holes in her statement. While providing generalities, she declined to give specifics beyond what she'd already said, and beyond what Superintendent Marley explained to the detective. I realize you have an investigation to run, she said, but I won't risk giving you more details for the sake of protecting the lives of my sources and the integrity of my information.

All of it caused no end of consternation for the detective.

After they agreed to disagree, McKittrick told her that neither his department nor the FBI were any closer to finding the man who'd attempted to kill her. Tess guessed they never would. If the assassin hadn't slunk back into the sewer from where he came, he'd probably been permanently terminated for screwing up the assignment, not once, but twice. The latter option was the most likely.

Another irritation was the press. Word was out that a respected, Pulitzer-prize winning investigative reporter had been attacked and almost murdered, and the media was ravenous for details. The three bikers who discovered Tess were interviewed by CNN and every other major television network, plus reporters for a number of nation-wide metropolitan newspapers and the Associated Press.

However, because no one could provide a reason for the attack, speculation ran wild. Maybe it was a mob hit. A criminal motorcycle gang. A former victim of one of her exposés. A jealous lover. A jealous colleague. An alien. Nothing was too outrageous or absurd, especially for the tabloids and talk radio. This was what she hated about working as a journalist: being associated in the public's mind with the braying pack of hyenas that characterized too much of the press.

Tess refused every interview request, knowing the furor would die down once another catastrophe-of-the-week took hold. Which, of course, it soon did, pushing her story to the middle of the pile, then to the back, and finally off the desk and the screen entirely.

She met with her three bicycle heroes just before she was discharged, explaining that a thank-you felt small and empty in light of what they'd done. They may not have known it at the time, but they risked their lives to save hers, and she would be forever grateful for their courage.

PART TWO

Evil is unspectacular and always human,
And shares our bed and eats at our own table.

~ W.H. Auden

It was important, Dumbledore said, to fight,
and fight again, and keep fighting,
for only then could evil be kept at bay,
though never quite eradicated.

~ J.K. Rowling
Harry Potter and the Half-Blood Prince

5

November: Eight Months Earlier

Fall was well on its way into winter, and Tess was deeply frustrated. She'd just finished three months of mind-numbingly boring investigative research into a supposedly revolutionary HIV vaccine that in the end turned out to be little more than unrealized expectations. Twelve weeks with her nose buried in impenetrable pharmacology discourses and courting impossibly nerdy, disagreeable chemists and scientists who either couldn't or wouldn't provide any meaningful information, and it was all for nothing. There was simply no "there" there.

Thanks in large measure to her status as the recipient of a series of prestigious journalism awards including the Robert F. Kennedy Award for Excellence in Journalism and a Pulitzer Prize, her investigative pieces now commanded very comfortable fees. But more than once, usually after an episode like the fruitless HIV inquiry, Tess considered giving up her twenty-year career as an investigative journalist. It wasn't an issue of money: even if her whole world collapsed and she found herself earning next to nothing like so many freelance writers, she had more than enough funds to support any lifestyle within reason, thanks to her father's decades-long acquisition of hundreds of shares of stock in some of the best, brightest, and most successful companies and start-ups of the twentieth century. That legacy left both Tess and her sister financially independent after her father's death.

When all the lights dimmed at the end of the day, however, Tess simply couldn't imagine a life outside of journalism. The work was exhausting, convoluted, and often dangerous, but she relished slogging like Doña Quixote through the sludge and offal of wretched deeds committed by even more wretched people, simply because she felt a fundamental obligation to expose it all to the light of truth.

She sighed deeply and took another sip of the silky, boysenberry-scented Lynmar Estate Pinot Noir from Sonoma County's Russian River Valley. Let the French worship their Burgundies and Bordeaux reds: to Tess a good California Pinot or Syrah could beat every one of them to a pulp.

Shaking off her fatigue, she flicked on the television just as her phone rang. She was one of those dinosaurs who still maintained a landline, partly out of habit but mostly because the nation's cell providers apparently didn't think anyone more than five miles outside a major metropolitan area deserved decent cellular technology. The same was true for Internet providers.

A pox on all their houses, thought Tess, as she reached for the handset.

"Hey, Skeeter." It was her old college roommate and good friend Jody, who'd come up with the odd nickname during their first semester in the dorm, and still occasionally used it, usually when she wanted to ask a favor.

"Hey, Jody! How're things in the big city?" asked Tess with a smile. Now that her friend had moved from teaching at Florida State to a professorship at Sacramento's California State University, they connected more often.

"Oh, you know: good days and bad. At least no school shootings lately." Jody's tendency was to joke about things that weren't especially funny, like mass shootings carried out by crazed killers with AR-15 rifles. Tess let it go.

"Really, how are you? And what's up?"

"I'm good, Tess. Things are good. But I ran across something that I thought you might be interested in. Are you in the middle of anything right now?"

"You mean, in the middle of something right at this very instant, or professionally?"

"Professionally. Are you working on a story?"

"Nope. Mother Hubbard's cupboard is completely bare at the moment."

"Well, I think I have something for you. Do you have time to listen?"

"Sure. Fire away."

Deliberately, Jody unrolled the story of a student in her Art of the Autobiography writing class. Her name was Ekaterina Voitenko-Palmer, a native of Crimea, who'd been in the U.S. for just over a year. Jody described her as a shy, stunningly beautiful young woman with hair the color of autumn wheat, who apologized after the first day of class for her English, asking that Jody not extend her any special privileges, and saying she liked to be called Katia.

Jody went on to explain how an encounter with Katia just a month ago left her puzzled and a little shaken.

The student approached her in the hallway after class one day and asked if she could have a few minutes to talk.

"I said sure, how about if we grab a cup of coffee at the Roundhouse?" The college featured a large and routinely congested student union, but also several smaller gathering spots including a coffee-and-snack bar in the iconic brick-faced roundhouse where the atmosphere was less raucous and quieter conversations were more feasible.

"She said she'd rather have some tea, and once we settled at the table, she seemed to have a tough time mustering up the courage to say whatever was on her mind. So I started with small talk and asked if she was enjoying her classes. She said yes, and that everyone was very kind and understanding about her poor English skills, which weren't really poor at all.

"I told her as much, saying she didn't give herself nearly enough credit, especially considering she'd only been in the U.S. for a short time—wasn't it just over a year? I asked. 'Yes,' she said. 'I was brought here in summer last year.'

"*'Brought here'* seemed an odd phraseology, but I pushed it aside and asked how she got to the States and northern California. She didn't speak for quite a while, then said, 'It is a long story, one with much *toska.*' She asked if I knew the word, then explained it can't be translated well because it has so many shades of meaning. She quoted Vladimir Nabokov as saying that *toska* is 'a dull ache of the soul, a longing with nothing to long for.' "

"That's quite an unsettling quote."

"Which is how I reacted. Then out of the blue, she asked for my permission to do something for her final class project. I was a little thrown by the sudden shift in the conversation, but asked her to tell me more. She said, 'I wish to describe the odyssey of a young woman away from *toska* and into life.'

"I was a little baffled and explained that the final project—in fact, the point of the whole class—was to write an autobiography. She blushed ferociously, apologized for not explaining herself well, then said that her chronicling of this woman's life was personal, was her *own*, and that she symbolized many others like her whose stories also need to be told.

"I remember reaching across the table to touch her hand, but she jerked her arm away like I was a sting ray, then started to apologize again. I didn't want her to feel any more uncomfortable than she already did, even though I was pretty shocked at her reaction to the possibility of being touched. Then I said I thought her project would work wonderfully as a final paper."

Jody hesitated before she continued recounting the story to Tess.

"I'd like to read you some of what she wrote, if that's okay. Then I can explain more."

"Sure."

Pages rustled in the background, then Jody began reading.

> My name is not really Ekaterina. Once you read my story, I believe you will understand the reason for my duplication.

Tess smiled. Katia clearly meant "duplicity."

> I was kidnapped while walking to school when I was barely 8 years old, in my town of Koktebel in Ukraine. Never again was I to see my mother, father, or grandparents. Never again was I to see the town where I was

> born, my teachers, my playmates, or the tiny kitten named Lesya we adopted just two days before. My life would never be the same after that day.
>
> I later learned that I was not alone, that many children from many other towns and cities in Ukraine were stolen just as I had been. Some of these children I would meet, but most were faceless and nameless to the world, just as I.
>
> The man who took me said he had an important message from my father, and that I was to go in his car and he would take me to him. Once inside, he gave me a piece of candy, and I suddenly became very sleepy.
>
> When I awoke, my arms and legs were tied, and I was lying on a filthy mattress in a small room with no windows and an iron lock on the door. Somewhere between the time I was taken and my waking, I had wet myself, and I was deeply shamed. I did not know just how much deeper my shame could become over the next 15 years.

Tess realized she'd been holding her breath for the last several seconds, and that her heart was pounding. This wasn't some anonymous subject's story: it was the story of Katia's life. And Tess knew that it wasn't going to get any better beyond page one.

Jody stopped reading, but continued on with the young woman's story in a voice that was subdued and troubled. "So, what do you think?"

"Huh?" Tess was in another world, totally focused on the horrific tale. "Oh, sorry: it's an incredible story. Terrible on every level."

"And perfect for an investigative piece, right?"

"I'm not sure I'd use the word 'perfect,' but it's sure as hell something I'd like to explore. Would Katia sit down with me?"

"I talked with her about that on the last day of class. Didn't mention your name, of course."

Jody explained how on that final day of the semester, she slipped a hand-written note into the project folder she handed back to Ekaterina, asking if they could talk after class.

"Once I unlocked my office door and we walked inside, Katia started to unravel. She was standing in the middle of the room and her eyes kept zooming from one wall to another, then to the door and back again. She started clenching and unclenching her hands, and her breath came out in these really sharp, short gasps. I couldn't figure out what was going on until I realized my tiny office with no windows and only one way in and out must have reminded her of all those rooms where she was kept and where terrible things happened to her. So we went back outside—luckily, it wasn't as blustery as Sacramento can get in late fall—and took a walk.

"I told her what a terrific job she did with her paper, and that I really didn't have words to express my sorrow at what she'd been through. Then I asked if she might be willing to talk with a very good and trusted friend who's a journalist, and who might want to investigate what happened.

"She hesitated for so long that I wondered if she'd heard me, but then said she'd felt compelled to take my class ever since she read about it in the online catalog. She said there was something that told her she'd find answers, or that someone else would help her find them. Then she said, 'Now you tell me that that this vileness I have lived could do good in the world. So yes, I will speak with your friend about these things.' "

A surge of anticipation raced through Tess. This could turn into an intriguing, if highly unsettling, journey, and could potentially make a genuine difference in peoples' lives. Perhaps even Katia's.

"Can you set up an introductory meeting with her for me? Anytime, anywhere—she can name it."

Jody promised to contact Ekaterina that afternoon and get back to Tess right away.

An hour later the phone rang again: Katia could meet with Tess the following morning in Auburn, one of the many foothill towns that dotted California's Gold Country, just thirty miles northeast of Sacramento and about forty-five minutes from Tess's home in Deer Valley. No longer the whistle-stop it once was, Auburn had exploded in recent decades into an energetic semi-urban landscape of fast-food outlets and big box warehouses speedily encroaching on the land once populated by saddle shops and neighborhood cafés and old-fashioned pharmacies with soda fountains.

The Starbuck's on Highway 49 was a convenient and neutral meeting spot, and when Tess walked in she immediately spotted Katia. Thin and willowy, with a pale complexion and ice-blonde hair that spoke of her Slavic ancestry, she was wearing a dusky, full-length skirt and tailored jacket over a soft gray cowl-neck sweater. When Tess approached her, she offered a miniscule, reticent smile, although her eyes remained guarded and cool.

Tess ordered and picked up her coffee and brought another pot of hot water for Katia's tea.

Like Jody, Tess began with small talk about the weather, her drive down the hill, and her dog Dancer patiently waiting in her car.

"I appreciate you sitting down with me, Katia. As you know, I'm a professional journalist, and I do investigative articles for newspapers, magazines, and even television. Ever since Jody—Professor Ross—told me about your story, I've wanted to dig deeper into it, see if I can find out more about the trafficking ring that kidnapped you as a child, or the one that trapped you for so many years.

"I know the idea of telling your story might be frightening, but you know even better than I that there are hundreds of other women just like you who've been victimized, and that these people will go on to hurt hundreds more unless they're stopped. You can be a part of that."

Katia stared out the window at the busy parking lot, her eyes unfathomable. She pulled her jacket closer and wrapped her arms around herself as Tess allowed the protracted silence it to linger.

The woman's voice was butterfly-soft. "Professor Ross told me much about you, your strength and compassion. She said you have loved one another as sisters for many decades, and that she would trust you with her life." She turned her face toward Tess and looked directly into her eyes. "So, I too shall trust you with my life. With my story. I shall entrust you with my truth."

Tess was stunned that she agreed so quickly. Despite Jody's recounting of that day in the Roundhouse café when Katia reacted so intensely to being touched, and her panicked reaction to being confined in the small office, Tess realized the woman was much less delicate than she'd imagined.

"Now it's my turn to thank you, Ekaterina. I couldn't go forward without your help. I want to read your entire paper before we meet, but let's set up a time and place where you'll feel comfortable and we can talk."

Normally, Tess preferred to interview her subjects in a neutral spot, but in this case she realized it was essential that Katia feel safe.

"Would you...could you...come to my home? I would feel more...peaceful there. And my husband could meet you. I know that would rest his mind."

"Of course. That would work perfectly."

Back home, Tess found the transcript of Katia's paper waiting in her email inbox.

After a light dinner, Tess focused on the document before her. By the time she reached the last page, she badly needed a break from the dark brutality of Katia's story. Her golden retriever Dancer was fast asleep in front of the fireplace, and she dropped down and lay by his side. He lifted his head and gazed into her face, his deep ochre eyes focused on her own. As she stroked his warm, velvety fur, what started out as incoherent emotions began to coalesce into something approaching rational, if no less harrowing, thought.

What Katia went through, what she'd survived, was incomprehensible and beyond horrific. Abducted as just a child, she'd been raped and brutalized by her abductor and his cohorts, then once they were assured that every ounce of the child's spirit and will was broken, they sold her into a life of sex slavery, available to the highest bidder to do with as he pleased.

Until she was 11 years old, she was trafficked to an assortment of pedophiles and child pornographers for whom she was forced to perform every manner of unimaginably perverse act. Video cameras were always within reach, and with her silken blonde hair, translucent mother-of-pearl skin and huge cerulean eyes, it didn't take long for the girl to become a favorite in the netherworld of child pornography.

Once she entered puberty and for the next several years, Katia was shipped from one "owner" to another throughout the alphabet-soup of Eastern Europe: Armenia to Tajikistan, Albania to Uzbekistan, often completely unaware of where she was. The fact that she couldn't speak the language was of no consequence, because the men who used her had little need of conversation.

Katia's term paper told horrifying stories of being savagely beaten when she failed to obey an order—never enough to do permanent damage, because after all, one wouldn't want to spoil the merchandise—and of watching a fellow captive's torture and murder to assure her compliance and submission.

> I knew her as Taevy, but I was never sure if that was her real name. She said it meant "angel" in her native Cambodian language. She was from the Khmer region, where I have never been, but which she said is very beautiful, with exquisite waterfalls, forests, and beaches. There is also much poverty and corruption, she told me, which is what brought her to the place where we were kept. She was sold by her father for 100,000 riel, or about 25 U.S. dollars.
>
> At 14, she was taken to a brothel in Thailand, and then to Bulgaria, where we met when she was 16. She was dead two weeks later.
>
> Taevy's problem was that she just wasn't beautiful enough. She was very thin, her hair was short and spiky,

> and her teeth were very bad. She also often refused to eat. It was her only way of fighting back, I think, but it seriously angered our owner. He used to scream at her, throw food at her, because such a skinny woman couldn't command the prices that someone whose bones weren't showing could bring.
>
> One day, he brought us into a room with shuttered windows and a heavy metal door. He stripped Taevy naked and tied her to a chair, and me to another one across the room. By then I had learned some of his language, so when he said, "This is what happens to bad girls," I understood.
>
> The things he did to Taevy I will not relate here, for they are too terrible for words. He used piercing implements and knives and steel wires, and before he finally slit her throat, she was begging for death.
>
> "Do you understand?" he said after it was over, grabbing my face with his bloody hands. I nodded yes. The message was very clear.

On the floor next to Dancer, the dying flames from the fireplace reflecting off the dog's golden fur, Tess brooded over Katia's story, wondering how she survived all the torture, the abject cruelty and degradation, the seemingly endless parade of noxious sexually-transmitted diseases like syphilis, chlamydia, and gonorrhea, not to mention untreated pneumonias, viral hepatitis, and a hideous skin condition that left her arms and legs raw and bleeding.

She would have died, she said, if she wasn't traded, traded like a container of guns or a kilo of cocaine, for a prepubescent chocolate-skinned child whose name Katia never learned, to a prosperous businessman in Dubai.

From Katia's viewpoint, it happened suddenly, like most of those transactions: one day she was with one man in one place, and only hours later was somewhere else with a different owner. Often with only the clothes on her back.

This man was different from most of her other captors, not because he was kinder or less sadistic, but because he was enormously wealthy. And he had other plans for Katia than as merely a plaything. What likely saved her life was that he decided this still-beautiful young woman with the iridescent skin and golden hair would make an excellent addition to his roster of sex workers, and would undoubtedly bring top dollar in Dubai's café society. That was, after all, *how* he became so fabulously rich.

Those first weeks in Dubai, a team of doctors treated Katia for her persistent pneumonia, while a phalanx of estheticians and beauticians and stylists worked to alleviate, or at least hide, the worst of her scars and the toxic effects on her skin and hair and nails of her prolonged deprivation. It felt, she wrote, as if she'd been granted a ticket into heaven.

Yes, she was still required to perform sexual favors when her owner desired it, but most of the time he was so bloated from his customary six-course meals that he couldn't summon the energy to fulfill his ardor. Plus, there was ample food, beautiful clothes, and a real bed with clean sheets and a genuine down pillow on which to sleep, so if she had to let the man screw her once or twice a week, it was worth it.

Until it wasn't.

One day, Abdul Hakim Al-Dosari announced he was moving her into a hotel in downtown Dubai. There, she would be expected to lure men into having sex with her—although in Dubai, bought-and-paid-for sex is so accessible that there's very little "luring" required.

Tess remembered watching a documentary about how seemingly-prudent men from all over the Middle East come to that sybaritic emirate on vacation or business trips to forget their lives as devoted husbands and Muslims, as do scores of Europeans and American expats. It seemed so bizarre to learn that in Dubai, where kissing, cuddling, or holding hands in public can get you arrested and where having sex outside of marriage is an imprisonable offense, the sex industry flourishes like a hothouse orchid.

Ekaterina's story was certainly proof of that.

The first day, she had sex with ten men in an eight-hour period. The next day, and the next, and the next, were the same. As each day crawled into another, and days into weeks and weeks into months, Katia numbly accepted that from now on, this would be her life, until she could find a way to end it.

What she hadn't counted on was a man named Anthony.

6

The day, Katia wrote, was not unlike every other. Up at nine o'clock, shower, Turkish coffee and breakfast of masala dosa—a very typical South Indian dish, similar to a crepe but made from rice and urad dal, a lentil-like black bean, and often with spiced potato filling.

Her late morning also included a side trip to the Areej cosmetic store in Dubai's Mall of the Emirates for some new foundation, then the local fruit and vegetable souk for some Safawi dates and almonds. This was what passed for freedom in Katia's world: once a week, an hour alone (but always watched over by one or more of her owner's underlings) to buy some personal items and perhaps take a short walk before the stifling desert heat made being outdoors nothing less than torturous. Then back to the hotel to dress, fix her hair and makeup, and make preparations for servicing clients.

Late that afternoon, she took up her spot at the glitzy hotel bar. She was sipping a spring water when a blond-haired man of about thirty in jeans and a light blue shirt under a deep azure linen blazer approached her.

"Mind if I sit?" He was one of those people whose eyes smiled along with the smile on his lips, but Katia had long since stopped paying attention to what men looked like, how they spoke, or even how they smelled. They were, like her, simply a commodity.

She flipped the old familiar switch in her mind, becoming the kind of demure yet engaging seductress she knew was virtually irresistible to Western men, especially men like this one, whose accent pegged him as upper-crust British. She gave a welcoming smile and gestured to the stool next to her. "I would love it."

She swiveled her stool so she was facing him at an angle. "I am Elena." She never used her real name when meeting with clients. *(But then,* Tess mused, *Ekaterina wasn't her real name either.)*

"Anthony. Anthony Learmont-Campbell." His voice was elegant and smooth, but with an underlying intensity bordering on ferocity that belied his slight uneasiness.

For several minutes, she chatted amiably and quizzed him in her broken English about a host of trivialities: how he was enduring the heat, what did he think of the food, had he done any shopping at the Mall of the Emirates, if he'd yet been up to the observation deck in the Burj Khalifa, the world's tallest building.

"So, what business for you is in Dubai?"

He drew a deep breath, paused, and turned to look directly into her eyes. "As a matter of fact, it's you."

From here, the conversation took on a perplexing, unearthly quality.

Anthony said she didn't know him, but he knew her. He knew her name wasn't Elena, that she was sold into this life as a very young girl, and that she'd been imprisoned in it for many years. He went on to assure her that he wasn't some "daft British nut-case," as he termed it, or a murderous stalker, and said all he wanted was to talk with her. He suggested they go somewhere quiet, where they would be undisturbed and where he could explain.

Her first instinct was to ditch this strange man. The rules were clear: she was to make contact with a client, come to an agreement on fees, then go upstairs to a room. The notion of going somewhere to chat was not just outlandish, but could get Katia in serious trouble with her owner if he found out. And he *would* find out, because his watchers were in the hotel, keeping a close eye on every one of his "properties."

Anthony persisted, finally proposing they go upstairs as if he were a regular customer, and they could talk in the room. And, he added, he would pay the full rate for her time.

Finally, Katia gave in. She figured he couldn't be any worse, any more treacherous, than some of the men she'd encountered over the years. Despite the oddness of the conversation thus far, her experience-sharpened survival instincts weren't picking up anything that hinted at him being another Jeffrey Dahmer; in fact, she detected something earnest and authentic about him that was strangely reassuring. She was also intrigued. How could he possibly know all that about her, and what did he want? More importantly, who was he?

The next hour was a jumble of conflicting emotions for Katia, from disbelief to hope to dread to optimism, and back again. Anthony's explanation was almost unfathomable: he was with an international non-governmental organization called the Antares Endeavor that conducted investigations into sex slavery and human trafficking, and his operatives recently heard of a ring of traffickers that started operating in Eastern Europe in the late 1980s. They were, he said, most likely the ones responsible for kidnapping her so many years ago.

But the work of Antares went beyond just investigating. In concert with local law enforcement agencies and other NGOs as well as what he called private "contractors," Antares also undertook rescue operations for victims of the sex trafficking trade.

He was here, in Dubai, on just such a mission. And she was the object.

With those words, Katia leaped from her chair as if to flee from the room. A trapped animal, instinct took over. Even though she knew that Anthony posed no danger, and that in fact he was there to help her, every part of her body was screaming for her to run. Instead, the room began to spin, drifting in and out of focus, and Anthony's voice suddenly seemed very faint and far away. Then he was at her side, easing her gently onto the bed.

He handed her a glass of water and stood with a hand on her shoulder as he watched to make sure she was all right. "I know," he said gently. "It's a tremendous amount to absorb all at once. If there were any other way to tell you, to let you know a little more gradually, I would have, but we just don't have the luxury of that kind of time."

His next words came as even more of a shock. "I have with me a plane ticket to Canada, and you need to be on that flight in ninety minutes."

Katia was thunderstruck. Canada? In less than two hours? It was impossible. Plus, she could never escape, not with her owner's sinister minions lurking everywhere. She tried to explain all this to Anthony, but he stopped her protestations mid-point.

"It's all been taken care of. You have a legitimate

Ukrainian passport under the name of Ekaterina Voitenko, and everything you need will be waiting for you when you deplane in Toronto. From there, someone else will handle your arrangements and your eventual resettlement in the U.S., but I expect you'll be staying in Canada for a few months at least."

"But what about my…the man who owns me?" she asked, her voice still shaking violently. "He will never let me go…he has…men…."

"Abdul Hakim Al-Dosari is no longer your problem." Anthony's voice was hard and resolute. "And from now on, no one owns you."

7

Tess spent hours reading and re-reading the young woman's autobiography, rolling it over and over in her mind as she tried to assemble the skeleton of a strategy. She believed the story held the seeds of something much bigger and more imperative that could have repercussions on possibly hundreds of other women just like Katia ensnared in a half-life of bondage and servitude of the worst kind. Maybe there was a way, she thought, to peel back the layers of this obscene entity to find out who was at its core. And expose them.

Galina.

The name exploded in her consciousness like a rocket-propelled grenade. And then, a succession of hazy images of sawtoothed peaks jutting into an indigo ocean bay, a gently swaying sign with indecipherable Cyrillic letters above a bakery door, an inky river rolling past neighborhoods of simple, sunbleached houses.

This kind of experience wasn't new to Tess.

Sometimes it was a string of images, sometimes a word or name or just a feeling, but it was something she'd known since childhood: that she was one of those individuals who, once in a while and often in times of stress or danger, could harness an internal sixth sense. Tess knew to trust those feelings, because virtually every time she tried to ignore them, the outcome was negative if not downright disastrous.

The image faded, and Tess took a deep breath. There would come a day when it would all make sense.

Drained and exhausted, she knew sleep wouldn't come easily, if at all. She couldn't stop thinking about Katia's life, the torment she'd been through, her rescue at the hands of the Antares Endeavor and the twists of fate that brought the wounded survivor into her life.

She also knew that Katia's story was destined to become intertwined with her own. Katia told of her experiences, probably for the first time, in Jody's class, but it wasn't going to end there for Tess. A substantial postscript was yet to be written, and *she* would be the author. The thought electrified her.

She got up and walked into the kitchen, where she poured herself another glass of wine and swirled the crimson liquid gently in the crystal goblet. Staring into its depths, ragged memories of her own losses tumbled through her mind.

There was her mother, murdered at the hands of a demented intruder when Tess was a child, her death the initial catalyst for Tess's drive to bring a voice to the voiceless, even those who were goaded into violence and murder by their own internal tormentors. The man who took her mother's life was one of those perpetually lost souls.

After being caught and convicted, he ended up in prison rather than a mental hospital because the prosecutor, whose judicial philosophy lay somewhere to the right of Attila the Hun, convinced a jury that someone who believed he was the incarnation of the Archangel

Gabriel wasn't insane. Within a month of his imprisonment, a fellow inmate murdered him.

Some might call that justice, but to Tess it was nothing short of one tragedy resting on the shoulders of another. Purposeless death wasn't justice.

And then, years later, as a cub reporter in Los Angeles, black-robed Death swooped into her life once again. Her sister Kathleen, just a year older than Karen, was murdered at the hands of her husband Ray in the tony enclave of Corona Del Mar near southern California's Newport Beach. Their storybook marriage was, Tess later discovered, more like something out of *The Burning Bed*: Ray could be tender, attentive, and kind, but then he would inexplicably morph into a man consumed by fury and suspicion, verbally battering his wife with demeaning accusations and condemnations with no basis in reality.

Eventually, the emotional assaults escalated into physical ones that became more and more violent and sadistic. As happens for so many victims of domestic violence, Kat was sure, thanks in large part to Ray's pronouncements, that she was to blame for every one of her husband's attacks. Assailed by the twin demons of fear and her own all-consuming shame at what she believed was her own responsibility for the abuse, she never revealed that dark secret to anyone, not even her sisters.

And then came the call from the Orange County Sheriff's Office saying that Kat collapsed in a pool of blood on the polished travertine tiles of the Newport Coast Shopping Center, and died in the ambulance on the way to the hospital.

A few hours earlier, in the midst of another beating, Ray had kicked his wife in the side and ruptured her spleen. She was on her way to buy him a birthday gift when she crumpled to the floor.

After Ray was arrested and given a life sentence without possibility of parole, Tess found herself adrift. The notion of composing meaningless articles about celebrity weddings and city council meetings and neighborhood squabbles chafed at her and soon led her to pursue bigger game, searching out and exposing the cruelty and corruption that festered just under the surface of polite American society.

Eighteen months later, that initial foray into the world of investigative journalism resulted in her first publishing award, which over the years led to dozens more—and even more important to Tess, a sense that she might be making a difference in the world.

Every time she considered quitting, every time an editor or colleague cautioned her that a story was too challenging or too dangerous, a talismanic image of the bloody body of her sister arose in her mind. For Tess, turning away simply wasn't an option.

Back in the moment, she pushed open the wide French doors and stepped out onto her deck. The opalescent November moon was nearly full, its light so dazzling that she could see her breath hanging in the early winter air. She inhaled deeply the mingled scents of the evening: soft and slightly lemony cedar, citronella-like Douglas fir, pungent and resinous mountain misery, and the honeyed, warm smoke drifting from her fireplace chimney. Across the canyon came the soft, echoing cry of a Great Gray Owl.

She always loved these mountainous woods, even as a child living in California's massive Central Valley where the closest thing to a conifer forest was Al's corner Christmas tree lot. Summers in July meant a two-week stay at the high Sierra Camp Pahatsi with hundreds of other Girl Scouts, and a chance to escape the valley's sweltering heat. Ever since those early days, she found strength and solace in the quiet magnificence of those mountains, all the while feeling their relentless pull.

Once she had the means to escape the life-sucking urban atmosphere, she began searching for a home in the hills.

Two years later, she stood among a gaggle of friends under a sparkling quilt of stars, toasting that new home with a celebratory glass of champagne. There were still days she had to pinch herself to prove this wasn't all just some sort of wishful dream from which she'd wake to find herself back in that smog-cloaked Los Angeles high-rise apartment, enduring in a city devoid of seasonality or, increasingly, humanity.

There was no doubt that L.A. had been good to her. It was there, working for the city's largest metropolitan newspaper, that she won her Pulitzer for an audacious investigative series exposing corruption inside the child protective services system. Shortly after, the Foundation for Investigative Journalism began courting her to work as an independent investigative journalist for their award-wining magazine, *Panorama*.

The notion of not being tied to a corporate news organization appealed to Tess's formidable streak of individualism and self-reliance: with the Foundation, she would be free to tackle important issues without having to plead her cause before some constipated board of directors who didn't want to spend the money or rock the political boat or offend the status quo. Since her inheritance liberated her from the need for a six-figure salary, it didn't take long for Tess to fold up her tent in southern California and depart for the Foundation's promised land in Berkeley.

Not exactly the rural life she longed for, but at least it wasn't Los Angeles.

That change also brought her respect inside an industry where, thanks to the proliferation of smarmy paparazzi, unprincipled pseudo-journalists and if-it-bleeds-it-leads newsroom management, the word "reporter" had become a four-letter epithet. It didn't help that a whole swath of the population still harbored suspicions about "fake news," promoted by a fear- and conspiracy-mongering former president who contended that the press was the enemy of the people. Remembering those days gave her the willies.

Her irrepressible curiosity was the hallmark, and sometimes the bane, of Tess's existence.

Some of her earliest memories were of forays into forbidden places within the neighborhoods surrounding her downtown Sacramento home and school, where she hunted in vain for ghosts or more worldly inhabitants who could tell her stories of those who once lived or worked or died there. Tess clearly remembered leading small bands of eight- and ten-year-old kids into the dilapidated houses of Sacramento's then-seedy Alkali Flat, once even sneaking into the abandoned Globe Mills building that loomed over the city's 12th Street corridor.

Later, she and her best friend Alex spent hours exploring the crumbling redbrick vacant buildings in the city's former railyards, trying to outwit the portly, myopic security guards circling the site two or three times a day when they weren't busy chain-smoking Marlboros or wolfing down baloney sandwiches.

Always, the foremost question in her mind was, *What*

happened? Who was here, what did they do, and why did they leave?

More than once, her exasperated father got a call from the local police station or school principal's office to liberate his adventurous daughter and pledge to put an end to these unacceptable exploits – but before long, she'd be back on the trail again, rooting through crusty alleys and fetid basements and derelict pioneer-era storefronts in search of answers to her unanswerable questions.

Some years later, she relinquished these kinds of physical investigations, much to her beleaguered father's relief. That relief was short-lived, however, when he found that Tess had traded her earlier fascination with adventure for a preoccupation with ferreting out wrongs and righting them. Or at least trying to right them.

Franklin Alexander understood all too well that whatever danger his adventurous daughter met while poking around deserted houses was nothing compared to what she could face when exposing the unsavory deeds of others, especially those in power. He also suspected that this new direction for Tess could become a lifelong obsession, and that made him even more uneasy.

But as usual, his pleas for restraint fell on deaf ears.

8

Tess knew absolutely nothing about Ekaterina's husband, except that his last name was Palmer: she didn't know how they met, where they met, where he was from, what he did for a living. But based on the few things Jody said from her conversations with Katia, he sounded like he was good for her and gave her the shelter and stability she needed. Hopefully he wouldn't turn out to be a worm. Or worse.

Luckily, Elliott Palmer was decidedly *not* a worm. Not even close. Amiable, intelligent, and well-spoken, he grew up near Calgary in southern Alberta, Canada, and attended the University of British Columbia. With a Master's degree in architectural engineering, he quickly made a name for himself as a commercial architect focused on renewable, green building design.

He met Ekaterina at the opening of the state-of-the-art public garden conservatory he designed in Vancouver. Transplanted to Canada eight months before, Katia just happened to wander into the park on the evening of the opening. She was captivated by the stunning conservatory building, and made her way inside just as Elliott Palmer strode to the bar to refresh his glass of wine, where he very literally bumped into her and knocked her to the floor.

That not-so-auspicious beginning soon led to several casual meetings over coffee and tea, slowly progressing to a lunch date, then a myriad of outings to public places like the Capilano Suspension Bridge, Sunset Beach, and the Vanier Park Observatory, and finally a formal dinner-date two months later.

"He was very patient with me," smiled Katia, "not to even mention his patience with my terrible English!"

"It wasn't all that terrible," Elliott countered with a chuckle. "Except that you kept mixing up 'chicken' and 'kitchen' when ordering something in a restaurant. And I remember the time when we were in an Italian café and you couldn't remember the word 'cake,' so you used the French word *gateau*. Unfortunately, in Italian it comes out as *gatto*, which means 'cat.' The poor waiter was awfully horrified."

"Oh, yes, I had forgotten that!" giggled Katia. The sound startled Tess, who had barely seen the young woman smile, much less laugh.

They were seated at a small table in the breakfast nook of one of Auburn's big old turn-of-the-century homes which the couple bought the year before. Hundreds of iridescent Christmas lights glittered above the sidewalks, marking the height of the holiday season. Neighboring homes showcased a cornucopia of alternately gaudy and glamorous decorations in their yards and windows, many with strands of multicolored lights that meandered along each building's eaves and shimmered in nearby trees and bushes.

Although her clothes were more informal than what she wore the day they met, even in relaxed lounge pants and a simple turtleneck sweater in a shade of soft cream, Katia seemed to convey a quiet elegance that was at striking odds with the dark details of her past. The house too was filled with graceful, understated artwork and furnishings in muted tones of peach and eggshell. A fire flickered in the living room fireplace, its massive native stone edifice a perfect companion to the room's twelve-foot coffered ceiling of chamfered oak beams, stained a deep mahogany. Closed on the street side, the silken drapes were open to the ample back yard where the dull winter light revealed silhouettes of oaks and century-old cedars swaying confidently in the wind as if their invulnerability were safeguarding the home and their considerably more fragile human occupants.

Tess brought Dancer with her, trusting that his presence might ease some of Katia's fears at having to exhume the memories of her grim past. As usual, the beautiful golden did just what his benevolent disposition guided him to do, settling peacefully at Katia's side. When the group moved into the more comfortable living room, he again sat beside her, close enough for her to stroke his fur.

"He can come up beside me, if he'd like," offered Katia. She patted the empty spot on the sofa next to her.

"It's okay, Dancer," said Tess.

The big dog boosted himself onto the couch, turned in a half-circle, then gently lay down with his head toward the young woman and eyes focused on her.

"I think I'll leave you three alone," said Elliott. "Besides, I have a project I'm working on, and I could use the time." He bent down and gave his wife a tender, lingering kiss and whispered something in her ear. She looked up, nodded, and presented him with a faint smile.

He touched her cheek, and she reached up and put her hand on his for several seconds. "I'll be fine, I'm sure." She was trying to convince herself. "Besides, I have Dancer here to give me strength."

Elliott straightened and swiveled toward Tess. "I'm really hoping you won't press her too hard. Please respect that she knows how far she can go and how much she can handle." His gray eyes were filled with concern.

"Absolutely. She can trust me."

"I hope so." He turned toward the stairway, then looked back at Tess. "I really do." She heard his footfalls up the stairs, then the soft creak of floorboards above as he crossed into his office.

"May I get you anything?" asked Katia. "A cup of coffee, perhaps? Elliott made a fresh pot shortly ago."

"That would be nice."

"I shall bring it to you, along with tea for myself, I believe." She disappeared into the kitchen, and Tess heard the click of a light switch.

She sat quietly, collecting her thoughts, projecting an outward calm but inside felt the familiar, disquieting buzz of electrified nerve fibers. It was always like this with the first interview, a combination of expectation and something-wicked-this-way-comes apprehension. You simply never knew what might happen in circumstances like these.

Katia called from the kitchen. "Milk? Sugar?"

"No, nothing, thank you. I take it black."

A minute later, she reappeared with two steaming mugs. Tess saw that her hands were quivering slightly, and she thought back to that day in the college café.

"Why don't we just sit for a moment and enjoy the fire?" suggested Tess. She hoped the pause would help to calm and reassure Katia.

They sat silently for several minutes, Katia stroking

Dancer's fur that shimmered in the glittering firelight, and Tess simply waiting for the right moment. Finally, Katia shifted her gaze from Dancer and looked at Tess expectantly.

Tess knew she needed to open the doors into Katia's memory softly. "Let's begin at the beginning." She quietly turned on the digital recorder, and placed it on the coffee table that separated the two women. "In your paper, you said that Ekaterina wasn't your real name."

"My name was Galina. Galina Shevchenko."

Tess felt an inward start, recalling how the name Galina burst into her head a few days before. "So, what name do you prefer?"

"I have left that small child behind, and the woman she became. I am Ekaterina now."

"What can you tell me about your childhood in Ukraine?"

Her face softening and becoming almost dreamy, the young woman spoke of her early life with a mother who loved to sing Ukrainian folk lullabies and a tall, austere father who went to work every day at a bank, and came home every night bearing a solitary Polish Irys toffee candy for his little daughter. She spoke of her best friend Oksana with fiery red hair and a chipped front tooth, then of her aging *babusya* and *didus*, her mother's parents who lived with them, certainly long gone by now, and of her days spent playing on the pebbled Black Sea beaches only blocks from their modest home.

"The song my Mama loved the most was '*Oy Khodyt Son Kolo Vikon,*' which means 'The Dream Passes by the Windows.' I would think of it, sing it to myself, during the bad times when I had no hope, and it would bring me peace, at least for a moment or two. One day perhaps I will sing it to my...to another...child...." her voice trailed off, and a veil of sadness crossed her face.

"Can you sing it to me?" asked Tess.

"Oh, I do not sing so well, I think. My Mama's voice was sweet and soft, but mine is not so much that."

"Please, I would love to hear it."

"Perhaps if I played on the piano you would not hear the poorness of my voice," she offered.

"Do go ahead, Katia," Tess replied softly, not wanting to disrupt the tranquil mood that Katia's reminiscences set. Besides, time would come soon enough to turn the talk to those joyless days beyond.

Katia rose and Dancer lifted his head in momentary inquiry, then jumped down onto the exquisite Aubusson rug where he turned and settled, the rose and emerald medallion like a halo around his golden shoulders.

In the corner of the room sat a beautiful 1914 Steinway Hamburg grand piano, its Brazilian rosewood finish glowing burgundy in the reflected firelight. Katia sat at the bench and looked upward, then closed her eyes for several seconds. Her lips spoke a silent, private invocation, and then she began to play and sing.

Oy khodyt' son, kolo vikon.
A drimota kolo plota.
Pytayetsya son drimoty:
De zh my budem nochuvaty?
De khaton'ka teplesen'ka,
De dytynka malesen'ka,
Tudy pidem nochuvaty
I dytynku kolysaty.
Tam budem spochyvaty,
I dytynku prysypl'yaty:
Spaty, spaty, sokol'yatko,

Spaty, spaty, holubyatko.

Then she sang again, this time in English.

The Dream passes by the window,
And Sleep by the fence.
The Dream asks of Sleep:
Where shall we spend the night?
Where the cottage is warm,
Where the baby is tiny,
There we will go,
And rock the child to sleep.
There we will sleep
And rock the child...
Sleep, sleep, my dear
Sleep, sleep, my little dove.

The dream had indeed passed by the little girl's window, Tess thought, leaving only unspeakable nightmares in its wake.

"That was beautiful, Katia. Thank you."

The young woman flushed and dipped her head in shy acknowledgement, then gently closed the piano's fallboard. "Would you care for more coffee?" She rose and turned toward the kitchen.

"Sure."

"I shall have more tea as well." Tears glistened on Katia's cheeks as she passed beneath the elegant glass chandelier that hung from the center of the ceiling.

Disturbed by her exit, Dancer padded softly after his charge, staying by her side until she returned to the living room, then lay down again at her feet. Once Katia curled her legs under her and patted the adjacent cushion, Dancer resumed his place on the couch. The only sound other than the whispering wind was the delicate clink of Katia's spoon against her teacup.

"Have you spoken with your parents since you escaped?"

Katia sat silently as if she hadn't heard, then sighed deeply. "Do you know of the Pulkova Airlines flight that crashed on the way to St. Petersburg in 2006?"

"I don't think so."

"My mother and father had traveled to Anapa, another resort town on the Black Sea, to see old friends that August, and they were all going on holiday to St. Petersburg. The plane was in a severe thunderstorm, and the engines suddenly stopped and the plane crashed into a field near Donetsk. All were killed. One hundred and seventy of them."

"Oh, how awful. I'm very sorry, Katia." Yet another loss. "Did you ever get to tell your mother and father you were alive before they died?"

"No. They never knew. I did not know they were killed until many years later when I was in Canada. I wish...." Her voice dropped down to nothingness.

Tess let the moment drift quietly before she went on. "Can you tell me a little more about Koktebel? What school did you go to?"

"It was called *Koktebelskaya Shkola*—Koktebel School. It was on a little side street near the center of the town. I used to love school, especially reading and languages. School began the first day of September for everyone, and my mother would come with me on that day. As little girls we wore flowered ribbons in our hair and white stockings, and we would always bring flowers for the teacher." Katia smiled softly at the memory. "That is where I met Oksana, on the first day, and we were best friends from then on. I often wonder what happened to her, but then think it is better to just leave the past where it is."

"Do you remember much about the town?"

"Little bits and pieces, mostly. I remember Mama taking me up into the volcano hills above Beach Koktebel and seeing the dolphins playing and swimming in the ocean below. I also remember watching the scores of flyers...*deltaplany*...oh, dear: I cannot remember the English word. People who strap themselves to devices with wing-sails and jump off cliffs to fly..."

"Hang-gliders?"

"Oh, yes, that is it: hang-gliders! They would descend upon Koktebel in summer when winds were perfect for their sport, and I would watch them circle and soar for hours. Often at night in summer, we walked along the beach promenade and ate *shashlyks* and *pyrizhky*, and my father would buy me a *polunytsya svizha*—strawberry fresh—to drink, while we watched the street performers.

"On weekends, we sometimes went to the seaside to swim and play, although it was often very crowded during summer months because Koktebel was one of the most popular resorts on the Black Sea. I remember walking on the beach and looking at the lapis hills in the distance; in the Crimean Tatar language, Koktobel means 'Land of the Blue Hills.' There were also many, many trees and flowers on almost every street."

"It sounds very beautiful, very peaceful. Perhaps one day you will go back to visit."

"No, there is nothing for me there. The people who loved me are gone, and since the Russians came to Crimea, things are not the same. And my last memory of the town is...sorrowful. I do not have interest in going back."

The door to the young woman's past was now open, and Tess sensed she was ready to walk through it. "Can you tell me about the day you were captured? How did it happen?"

Katia breathed a jagged sigh, then closed her eyes. "It was a beautiful day, just before school would be completed, and I was looking forward with eagerness to summertime. Just as always, I was walking alone to school. You must remember, in those days Koktebel was a very safe town—most of Ukraine was safe, or so we thought—and my parents had no worry with me being outside or even walking to the market or school alone, even though I was only 8 years old. We knew everyone on our little street, Dachnyi Lane, and because my father was a banker, he knew most of the townspeople. I did not fear people in those days.

"I had a favorite sweets shop on Lenina Street, just two or three blocks from my school, so I decided to stop there for a *khrustyky*, a Ukrainian fried cookie with icing sugar—I believe it is called here powdered sugar?—on top. I was not really paying attention to anything except the warm cookie I had just eaten, when a dark car drove by and then stopped about three meters ahead. When I walked past, the car door opened and a man stepped out and said my name. I did not recognize him, but he did not seem threatening, so I said yes, that is who I am. He told me he carried a very important message from my father, and that I was to go with him to the bank.

"I could not imagine why my father would need to see me so early in the morning, and that brought me anxiety. But since I wanted to find out what could be so important that he would take me away from my last school day of the year, I agreed to go with the man. We were in the back seat, and there was a woman seated next to him who had a beautiful smile. She noticed that I had sugar icing on my nose from the *khrustyky*.

'I see you like sweets,' she said with a small laugh.

I felt my face becoming red, and I looked down at my lap. *'Sometimes,'* I said.

'Your father told us you do, and I have a very special candy that he asked me to give you.' She reached across the man and handed me a wrapped *Leshchina*, which is a Ukrainian chocolate-covered praline with hazelnuts.

'You must eat it,' said the man, *'so you can tell your father how much you enjoyed it.'*

"I really didn't want another sweet after having eaten the cookie, but I also didn't want to disappoint my father, so I ate the candy. Soon, I began wondering why we were taking such a strange route to get to the bank, and then I felt myself becoming very sleepy. I tried to ask the man why we were going toward Sudak on the P29 road, when the bank was in the opposite direction, but my lips would not move to make the words. I saw the sea on my left when it should have been on my right, and that was the last thing I remember."

"What can you tell me about the man and the woman? Do you remember what they looked like, or whether they spoke Ukrainian?"

"Yes, they both spoke Ukrainian, although the woman's accent was Russian. He was a big man, maybe over six feet, and heavily-built. Dark hair, with hairy arms, I remember. She never got out of the car, so I could not know how tall she was; she was slim, with light hair and very blue eyes. Long fingernails. I remember that, because I had never seen a woman with long fingernails in Crimea, unless they were tourists."

"I don't suppose they used names when they referred to each other."

"No. And I never saw them again."

"So let's move to the next thing you remember. In your paper, you mentioned that when you woke, you were tied up and lying on a dirty mattress, in a room with a heavy metal door. What do you remember about the room?"

"Nothing, really. It was small, just big enough for the mattress and a tiny stand next to it. There was a little square window, but it was so filthy I could not even see light through it, and the glass had a cage...wire...in front of it."

"Was it still daytime when you woke?"

"I do not know, except that I was very hungry. There was a bare lightbulb hanging from the ceiling, and I could see *pavuks*...spiders...crawling on the walls."

It may have been the night of the morning Ekaterina was kidnapped, Tess thought, but because she was drugged, there was no way to know whether they'd traveled by highway or back roads, or even if they'd continued by car. They could have switched to a boat or ferry, even a plane. This was probably a dead end.

"Could you hear anything? What about smells?"

"There was no sound at all, almost as if I were in a...a, uhh...vault? No, I mean basement. It was like a basement. Walls of stone or concrete, and a heavy iron door. It smelled wet, and old. Nothing else."

"How long were you kept there?"

"I am not sure. They kept me drugged much of the time: not so much that I would fall asleep, but my brain was very clouded. Even the food did not help me tell day or night, because it was always the same. Hard, stale bread and a kind of broth that tasted more like salted water. And sometimes I only got one meal over many, many hours. Of course, I could not tell the hours in certainty because there was no light, even from the window. I would say that I was kept in that room for several days. Perhaps a week."

"Were you mistreated, physically, while you were there?"

"Not right away. Except when I would cry for my Mama and Tato. Then they would speak to me harshly, and sometimes slap me."

"They?"

"There were two different men, and a woman. I don't really remember anything about them, because the only time I saw them was when they brought me food. No one spoke to me or told me where I was or why I was taken. It was very terrifying."

Unfortunately, the terror was just beginning.

9

For the next two hours, Katia recounted the brutality of her life, day after month after year, never changing yet always shifting with the languages, the ethnic characteristics, the sexual and social peculiarities and predilections of her captors. Some memories were elusive and shadowed by the passage of time, some sharp and acrid as quinine. Through it all, the impassive voice recorder captured every sigh, every shuddering response, every whispered sob and every disordered utterance.

During her years as a subject for child pornography, Katia explained that the purveyors knew all too well how extraordinarily valuable a delicately beautiful, blonde, blue-eyed child with skin the color of ivory was to the millions of kiddie-porn consumers around the world. While there were any number of producers and sellers of the final product, just two people coordinated everything. One was to be called "*Matuska*," which Katia recognized as meaning "Mother," the other called "*Uchitel*," which she soon learned meant "Teacher." *Matuska* was ostensibly Katia's benefactor and caregiver, the one who explained why she needed to behave, to comply, to be a good girl—but when she misbehaved or cried or complained, the woman became her oppressor, administering severe slaps and beatings. The woman spoke Russian, which Katia was learning in school but did not understand fully, but because of the similarity between the Russian and Ukrainian languages, she could grasp much of what the woman said.

Uchitel also spoke Russian, but in a rough and unschooled dialect that Katia often misunderstood. His "lessons," however, needed little language: he was the one who showed the eight-year-old how to pose for the camera, how to smile seductively, how and what to do to the other participants and allow them to do to her, and how to act as if she were enjoying it all. Unless, of course, the premise of the film was that she was feeling anything but enjoyment. And fulfilling his role as "teacher," he was also the one who first raped the little girl.

Until she reached puberty, Katia stayed in one country, which she knew was Russia from the letters on street signs and billboards and the television programs her captors sometimes allowed her to watch. But after she became an adolescent and no longer valued as a commodity for child pornography, everything changed. Both *Matuska* and *Uchitel* disappeared from her life, and her long migration began.

"I sometimes speak to myself that I am an international traveler," Katia said with a joyless smile. "I have lived in such places as Ukraine, Russia, Turkey, Greece, Uzbekistan, Yugoslavia, Croatia, Germany, England, Dubai, and finally Canada and America."

"How did they get you through border crossings and past customs?"

"Oh, they gave me passports or visas. Passports that showed I was a dweller in that country, or that I was a student, or just on holiday. Of course, the documents were all imitation...false, but they were so professional that no one ever questioned them."

As Katia spoke about her later years, Tess began to sense a pattern. The girl was held for anywhere between eight months and a year in one country, then transported to a nearby region to spend another similar period there. Most of the time, the "keepers" changed but the main organizers remained the same, something Katia realized when she heard certain names being mentioned time and again over the years: Dragos, Ulrich, Radic, Ludmila. Clearly, these were part of, if not the heads of, the trafficking ring. Katia said she only knew their names from overhearing conversations between the people who held her.

After some years, she ended up in Europe, which by then was a flourishing avenue for the sex trade. Particularly valuable were women from the former Soviet bloc, like Katia, who could command top dollar from clients.

"A good thing, I suppose, is that I was not put on the street," said Katia at one point. "Because I was still young and not outwardly scarred or disfigured, I could bring a higher price than the street women, so I could be—I believe the word is "marketed"—on the Internet as a *buty kompan'yonom,* a companion. Men would come to a hotel and I would meet them there, although sometimes I was taken somewhere to meet them. It was all very civilized."

It was in Europe that Katia learned to speak English and French. It was also there that some of her worst and most violent abuse occurred.

"I could not understand that. The people of Western and Central Europe were always said to be so respectable, so cultured, especially when compared to the Balkans and Eastern European countries, where men are thought to be crude and brutal and uneducated. But I learned how all that careful refinement falls away when these men step into the bedroom, and their true selves come out. They can be cruel and unpitying, and often took great pleasure in the humiliation of me."

At first, Tess recoiled at this pronouncement: as much as she tried to avoid the tunnel vision of her occidental-world mindset, she was forced to admit that in the deepest recesses of her consciousness there lurked a fragment of xenophobia that presumed westerners were somehow more *virtuous* than people from Eastern Europe and the Middle East. That she could possibly harbor such bigotry was both a revelation and a repulsion. It just didn't square with the egalitarian image she had of herself.

Suddenly Dancer awoke from a sound sleep and raised his head, fully alert to something neither woman could hear. Then a door upstairs opened quietly, and Elliott stepped onto the upper landing.

Katia's entire bearing changed when she saw him, as if she'd been transported from an Edgar Allen Poe chamber of horrors to an emerald field lush with wildflowers. Her face, an ashen pallor as she revealed more and more about the life she'd led, brightened perceptibly and her lips curved in an open smile.

"Hello there," she called up to him.

"Hello yourself." His voice was warm and soothing. "How's everything going?"

"Fine, I guess." Katia looked quizzically at Tess for some confirmation.

"Yes, Katia's been a terrific help."

Katia's shoulders relaxed, and she smiled again in

Tess's direction. "That is good to hear. I really did not know if what I had to say would be helping. Helpful."

"It's extremely helpful, Katia."

Elliott looked down at the large grandfather clock that stood in the entryway. "Do you have a lot more to cover? I'm fine with it either way, but I just figured that if you needed more time, I might take a head'r to bed. I have a meeting early tomorrow morning."

"Are you okay with continuing on, Katia? Maybe another hour or so should do it. Or," Tess added without much enthusiasm, "we could finish up sometime later."

"I would rather complete tonight, if that is agreeable with you, Miss Alexan…I mean, Tess." Her cheeks colored again in awkward response to using Tess's given name, something Tess had been encouraging all evening.

"That's perfect with me. And it's clear that Dancer doesn't mind one bit." The dog's head rested on Katia's lap and he was once again snoring softly, assured that the person who opened the upstairs door was benign.

"Okay," said Elliot. "I'll leave you alone then, eh? Wake me when you come to bed, darling."

"I will. And thank you for…for being there." Katia put her hand over her heart, then gave a tiny wave to her husband.

"Elliott, it was great…."

"Tess, I'm so glad we…"

The two started speaking at the same moment, and then laughed as their words collided.

"Okay, I'll go first since you've been so gracious to allow me into your home," said Tess. "I can't say how much I appreciate your courtesy and hospitality. It was wonderful meeting you."

"I too am glad we met," responded Elliot with a smile,

"even under these circumstances. Good night, and drive safely going home," he said over his shoulder as he turned down the hallway.

"Good night." Both women spoke in unison, sparking more laughter.

"Some more coffee?" asked Katia.

"No thanks—I may be up all night as it is! I'm not accustomed to drinking coffee in the evening."

"Well, I must make a confession: it was un-caffeinated. Elliott loves coffee, but cannot drink regular after about three o'clock in the afternoon, or he too will spend the night in wakefulness. And I drink only herbal tea in evenings, because of the caffeine."

"I wondered why I wasn't feeling jangly," laughed Tess.

Katia returned to stroking Dancer's fur as the dog gave a deep, blissful sigh.

And so the saga continued, with the young woman revealing as much as she knew or could remember about where she lived and for how long, who were her keepers, and any other women she met who were also enslaved. Women's names were sometimes patently false, and for the keepers and organizational lynchpins, regrettably few. Except for the ones Tess began to think of as the Four Horsemen (even though one was a woman): Dragos, Ulrich, Radic, and Ludmila. These four were woven like a malignant thread throughout Katia's adult existence.

"So, you're positive you never met any of these four?" asked Tess.

"No, I am sure." A moment after she said those words, an expression of first puzzlement, then uneasiness, crossed Katia's face.

"What is it, Katia?"

"I...I am not certain. I seem to see something in my...memory...that is not clear...."

"Okay, just relax for a moment and close your eyes. Take a deep breath or two, and let the thoughts and pictures come to you. Don't try to force them, just allow them to surface." Tess let the silence linger as she watched Katia, alert for any sign that the woman might be entering psychic waters too deep or dangerous.

Katia pressed the fingers of one hand to her temple as if she could physically force the memories to emerge from the dark recesses of her mind, and her brows pinched together in concentration. The other hand anxiously clutched a clump of Dancer's fur. The dog awakened when he first heard the uneasiness in Katia's voice, but remained still and calm even as the woman fervently kneaded the fur on his back.

Although she was clearly struggling, she didn't seem anywhere near panic—and as much as Tess wanted to tell her to relax, she decided instead to let things play out and see what Katia could unearth.

No one moved, not even Dancer, for what felt to Tess like hours but was likely only minutes, as Katia tunneled deeper and deeper into the vortex of her memories.

Suddenly her eyes opened wide, and with a start she said, "London!"

"London? What about London?"

It was when she was in London, Katia explained, about two years before she was rescued. Six women lived together in a house in London's East End, once home to some of the city's most wretched slums where Jack the Ripper prowled and slaughtered. By then, however, while many East End boroughs remained mired in poverty and crime, some areas were far less menacing, and in the process of being gentrified. It was in one of those neighborhoods, near Victoria Park, that Katia lived.

Her memories of that morning returned with striking vividness. It was late autumn, she recalled, and almost all the dried leaves on the huge spreading chestnut tree in the front yard had fallen. All the women were ordered downstairs, and Katia was the last to arrive. Outside the tall sash staircase window, the lawn and walkway were completely carpeted in yellow leaves.

The other women gathered in a little knot downstairs, whispering anxiously and repeatedly glancing toward the door into the parlor. Delia, one of Katia's housemates, murmured that three foreign men were conferring with their keeper, and she feared they were going to be bartered away. No one knew, said Delia, who these men were.

The parlor door opened, and three men stepped out, followed by the women's owner.

"One of them seemed to be the leader," said Katia, explaining that the others deferred to him in both manner and conversation. "He spoke with a slight British accent, but I somehow felt it was not his native tongue. I was surprised by how kind his voice sounded, but this was not the first time I found a kind voice concealing a monster."

Then the man's phone chimed, and he pulled it out of his pocket and turned away. Katia, however, caught his one-word answer: *"Flemming."* The name meant nothing to her.

He spoke for less than a minute, then turned back to the women and asked each one to walk across the room in front of him.

"For some reason I felt it was important to remember what he looked like, all the details I could. So as the other women walked, I watched him instead of looking down as we were taught, hoping he would not notice. But he was much more directed...focused...on the women walking past him to perceive that I was looking at him.

"He was small and somewhat heavy, with very dark eyes and dark hair greased back from his face, which had a slight beard, short hairs that were only partly shaved."

"Stubble?" offered Tess.

"Yes, I believe that is the word. His teeth were very white, and his hands and fingernails were well-groomed, not dirty or torn. He was dressed very well, in a dark gray coat and white shirt, and even wore an ascot, fashioned with a diamond tie pin."

When it was Delia's turn to parade past the man, she accidentally caught her heel on a frayed edge of the carpet and tripped, tumbling sideways into the man. He in turn lost his balance slightly and crashed into the sofa table.

"One of his companions rushed over and said, 'Are you okay, Ulrich?' And it was then I knew: This was one of the *vatazhko*—leaders—whose name I heard whispered for so many years. Ulrich. Ulrich Flemming."

Tess's voice rose with excitement. "Katia, I can't believe it: you remembered his name!" Dancer was suddenly awake, leaping off the couch and darting to Tess's side. "It's okay, boy," she whispered as she knelt beside the dog. "I'm sorry...I didn't mean to startle you."

"Oh, poor Dancer," said Katia. "He thought something was wrong with you, or that you were afraid?"

"Yes, I suspect so."

Katia smiled. "I too am excited at the...rebirth...of my memory of that day."

"It's extremely useful," replied Tess with a smile. Then an idea struck her. "I have a friend who is an excellent artist. In fact, she often helps police put together sketches of suspects or missing people so they can publicize their faces. Could you meet with her and try to develop a sketch of this Ulrich Flemming?"

"I could try," said Katia, a little hesitantly. Then she took a deep breath. "No," she said with more force, "I *will* do it."

"That would be a huge help, Katia. It could make all the difference."

The two women sat quietly, each lost in her own thoughts, as Dancer lay curled next to his mistress's feet, his amber fur an almost perfect match to the golden oak floor. An unexpected peace descended on the room, as if Katia's revelation miraculously discharged the previous hours of building tension.

After a few moments, Tess returned to her inquiry. "How long were you in London?"

"Over a year, perhaps eighteen months. Time does not have much meaning in circumstances such as ours."

"Was it after you met Flemming in London that you were taken to Dubai?"

"Yes, shortly after. I am not sure how long, but within weeks. As you recall, I was not well when I arrived there."

Tess thought back on Katia's striking description of how she arrived in Dubai anemic and emaciated, seriously ill with pneumonia, and displaying the remnants of a series of brutal beatings bestowed by her last keeper. Apparently she'd been too ill to perform her duties up to the man's standards, and he used his fists to demonstrate his displeasure at being deprived of her income.

Katia went on to describe how she was nursed back to health, how she was presented with an entirely new and fashionable wardrobe, and how her corpulent new owner treated her more kindly than anyone she had known since being kidnapped. Until the day, a few months later, that Abdul Hakim Al-Dosari installed her at Dubai's Lyndmar International Hotel on Sheikh Zayed Road.

Then the kindness ended.

For five months, Katia was among the estimated thirty thousand sex workers in Dubai. She herself was known as a "bar girl:" women who haunt hotel bars throughout the emirate, either approaching men or being approached by them for sex, all under the watchful eye of their pimps or in the case of Al-Dosari, his minions. Even restroom visits were observed or accompanied, to thwart any attempt by these valuable possessions to flee. Although, Tess thought, *where* a woman could flee was problematic at best, since prostitution was a serious crime in the UAE and she would certainly be jailed if she went to the authorities.

The night Anthony Learmont-Campbell entered her life, everything changed.

Tess really hoped that one day she'd be able to sit down with that "daft Brit," as Learmont-Campbell referred to himself, and not just because of the treasure-trove of information he could no doubt share about the foul underbelly of sex trafficking. She also wanted to know how Antares found Abdul Hakim Al-Dosari, where he was now—hopefully rotting in the bowels of some roach-infested English prison—and more importantly why, out of the thousands of sex trafficking victims in Dubai, they chose Katia to spirit away to a safe harbor.

Katia didn't know either. She said everything was pretty much a blur after Anthony ushered her out of the hotel that night and they scrambled into the back of a waiting BMW, headed for Dubai International Airport.

The extravagances of Dubai had become familiar to Katia during her time there. There was the spired, sail-shaped Burj Al Arab, set on its own island…the 160-story Burj Khalifa hotel, said to be the world's tallest building, with its entrance through the Mall of the Emirates, the largest mall in the world…the two artificial islands off the coast known as Palm Islands…and the extraordinary wealth of the emirate itself. But she wasn't prepared for the enormous, gleaming, ultra-modern Dubai Airport, also the largest in the world, host to more than ninety million international passengers every year.

In the past, she'd been spirited from one secluded airport to another, or been driven by bus from city to city or even country to country. Even the trip to Dubai from London was by private plane, landing at the more remote Al 'Ain International Airport, a long, low-slung, bland and nondescript complex seemingly plopped down on a naked desert plain near the UAE's southeastern border. From there, two men in white dishdashas and black trousers drove her to Dubai and Al-Dosari's stronghold.

"I was overwhelmed by the vastness of the place," Katia said about her first impression of Dubai's magnificent airport. "From the outside, the buildings looked like a gigantic silver cocoon, then inside was all polished steel and glass, with a towering roof that seemed to be curved in on itself, and huge numbers of people walking, running in every direction, dressed in every type of clothing and speaking every language you could imagine. I had never seen so many people gathered in one place, and it was a little frightening.

"But Anthony was so kind, and made sure I was safe from anxiety as much as he could. He guided me onto the airport train, which took us swiftly to a huge area he called a concourse. There was a beautiful spot in the center with growing trees and plants and flowers and waterfalls that took my breath away.

"Then we went into a large, quiet room with chairs and sofas covered in leather, and he said there was even a shower should I wish to take one. I learned later that this was one of the airport's many passenger resting places. It helped me ease somewhat, although until we boarded our flight I was looking all around for Al-Dosari's armed men, fearful they would find us."

Katia and her protector unwound as much as they could in Lufthansa's luxurious lounge, then boarded the plane for the twenty-hour flight to Vancouver, Canada. Katia was far too uneasy to sleep, and spent most of the flight thinking about what her life might be like once she was actually free. *Free,* she remembered thinking. *I don't even know what that means, except as I remember being a child.* But free as an adult woman? She had no idea what such a state would feel like or what it would hold for her, much less how she would survive.

During the flight, which was indiscriminately sprinkled with an array of people from the Middle East, China, Africa, and the West, Katia spotted a dark-skinned, unmistakably Middle Eastern man seated across the aisle and one row back who seemed to be staring at her every time she glanced in that direction. Her skin began to crawl, and she rapidly became convinced that he was one of Al-Dosari's henchmen. A short time later on her way to the plane's lavatory, she saw another man, also of Middle Eastern descent, who caught her attention because he was glaring at her. Could he also be one of Al-Dosari's accomplices?

Not wanting to disturb the sleeping Anthony with her

possibly irrational fears, she returned to her seat and remained there like a cement effigy, silent, blind to anything around her and barely breathing, for the next hour, certain she would soon be back in her captor's claws.

Once he awoke and saw Katia's face and demeanor, Anthony realized that something was very wrong.

"Katia, what is it?"

She made only a tiny *urrrr* sound in her throat.

"Has something happened? Are you all right?"

She shook her head almost imperceptibly.

"Okay, try to take a deep breath. Good, now another. Can you look at me?"

Sluggishly, Katia finally managed to turn her head toward Anthony. Her face was colorless chalk, her eyes wide and filled with terror.

"Speak to me, Katia," Anthony urged. "You must tell me what it is. Please."

Something deep within her stirred, faintly reassured by his gentleness and unmistakable concern. It took several tries before she was finally able to explain about the men.

"I saw…feel……I am fearful…that they are with my keep...with Al-Dosari. They are…going…to bring…to take…me…back." Her speech was as halting as if she'd suffered a stroke.

"Can you tell me where they are, precisely, without looking in their direction?"

Although it took several minutes to extract and articulate it, Katia ultimately succeeded in describing where the men were seated on the flight, what they looked like, and even the color of their shirts.

"That's good, Katia. Now, all you need to do is rest. I don't want you to be frightened, but I need to leave you for a few minutes while I go speak to the flight attendant. I promise: *you will be all right* while I'm gone." He emphasized the words calmly and carefully, but with force. "You must trust that you're safe, that I will not allow anything to happen to you. Do you understand?"

The woman nodded, although fear still clouded her eyes.

"All right: now sit back, and close your eyes. Take some more deep breaths, and picture something beautiful. Maybe the sunset over your lovely blue Koktebel hills, maybe the sea lapping at a peaceful pebbled beach, maybe a lovely bird floating on the gentle summer air. Allow yourself to sink into that feeling of peace, knowing that you are now, and will always be, safe and protected."

Anthony's voice made Katia feel as if she were resting on a blanket of warm, soft kitten fur—and she suddenly pictured the tiny, mewling gray-and-white kitten she'd adopted just before her world turned to black. *Lesya*, she mused, and smiled. *Sweet little Lesya. How I loved you. How I would love to see you again.* She drifted on that unclouded waking dream as Anthony moved away.

It took some doing, but Anthony finally convinced the head flight attendant to give him the passenger information on the two men Katia saw. The scowling one she passed on her way to the lavatory was in fact a member of the Royal Canadian Mounted Police, returning to Ottowa after losing his wife in a tragic boating accident in Dubai. After Anthony approached him, he explained that he'd been born in the emirate, but emigrated to Canada and joined the RCMP two decades ago. He apologized profusely for causing any distress to the young woman, explaining that he was still grieving deeply over the loss of his wife of fifteen years.

The man who had been staring at Katia so intently was

not Middle Eastern at all, but from India. He was a very well-regarded film producer there, and after Anthony finished speaking to him, he understood that the man was admiring Katia's luminous, pastel beauty, thinking how wonderful she would be in film. He too expressed deep regret for upsetting Katia, and hoped the young woman wasn't offended by his unreserved admiration.

Anthony made his way down the aisle and back to Katia, who was still enfolded in her sheltering daydream. She opened her eyes as he sat beside her, and he noticed that her former leadenness was gone.

He gently described what he discovered, making sure not to ridicule her earlier fears. It's absolutely understandable, he explained, considering what you've been through. No one would blame you for thinking they could be Al-Dosari's followers coming to abduct you and take you back.

"But what you need to understand, Katia, is that you will never have to worry about him again. Never. He and his men are out of your life forever. If it helps, think of them as dead. That part of your life, with them and with all the others who came before, is over. You have been—I hope you don't think of this as overly-dramatic—but you have been reborn. Reborn into a new life where you never have to be afraid again. Unless it's of something like a mongoose, or a false widow spider."

Katia smiled at his attempt at humor, then cocked her head quizzically. "I know the name mongoose, but what is this 'false widow spider'?"

"Ahh, it's a nasty spider indeed. In fact, it's the most poisonous spider in the U.K., although nowhere near as deadly as its American cousin, the black widow. What makes ours bad is that it tends to prefer the indoors, so people can find them not just in outbuildings and shops, but inside their homes."

"Oh, dear!" Katia recoiled at the idea of finding a venomous spider indoors. "I am happy to not encounter one when I was in London." After living in so many countries, Katia was familiar with a wide range of biting and stinging creatures, from scorpions and cobras in the Middle East to pit vipers and the karakurt spider in Russia. "I have seen enough of evil spiders and insects and snakes that live outside, without having to fear they are inside as well."

The plane had a four-hour layover in Frankfurt—Katia remembered that she once lived there, but couldn't remember where, or even for how long—then the huge silver bird zoomed eastward, journeying toward an enigmatic new land and an uncertain future.

PART THREE

You may choose to look the other way,
but you can never say again that you did not know.

~ William Wilberforce

The truth. It is a beautiful and terrible thing, and must therefore be treated with great caution.

~ J. K. Rowling
Harry Potter and the Sorcerer's Stone

10

No sane person would want to be in Ukraine these days. That's what her editor at the Foundation said when she proposed her series for *Panorama,* and what the State Department official in the San Francisco Field Office told Tess when she said she'd be traveling there. Yes, she said to both men, I understand that, but it's imperative. Her editor finally relented, recognizing that Tess could easily quit and then sell the story anywhere—and if things worked out, it would likely be a blockbuster of an exposé that he wanted credit for publishing.

The State Department official was even more adamant when she said she also needed to go to the Crimea region. "It's simply not safe there," he insisted, his puffy face contorting into a grimace. He reminded Tess of the photo she once saw in *Smithsonian* magazine of a fish called the Blob Sculpin, a globular, flesh-colored sea creature with bulbous eyes and huge flaccid lips curved downward in a perpetual expression of displeasure.

"I understand the risks."

They argued back and forth for several minutes, until the clerk realized she wasn't about to be dissuaded. He handed her the official State Department travel warning about Ukraine, along with handouts on everything from travel restrictions to bans on bringing illegal drugs into the country. She would need a visa, he told her, if she planned on entering Russia through Ukraine. At the same time, he lectured, her passport needed to be dated at least six months ahead of when she planned to enter the country. Before she left, he warned her once more about her travel plans. She smiled, thanked him, and walked out into the drizzly San Francisco fog.

Rounding the corner onto Bush Street toward Noah's Bagels, she thought about the enormous difference between Katia's childhood Ukraine and the Ukraine of today, especially in its southern Crimea which Russia "annexed" in early 2014. Since then, tens of thousands of had died in the vicious fighting between Russian-backed separatists and Ukrainian forces intent on keeping the country independent.

No one could predict what the future might hold, but considering Moscow's military dominance and nationalistic tenacity, chances were good that Russia would once again absorb the entire Ukraine. Shades of Catherine the Great, Tess mused.

February in Ukraine was not her idea of a fun way to spend a winter. That day, the temperature was hovering below zero, a wicked banshee wind howled across the parking lot, and to make matters worse, she'd been sitting in this stuffy car with a silent and sullen driver for thirty minutes, waiting for her contact to show up.

"How long?"

Startled by the fact that the man actually spoke, it took a moment for Tess to grasp what he was asking. "I don't know. He was supposed to have been here a half-hour ago."

"Maybe we leave."

"No, we wait. You'll be paid, don't worry."

"No worry. I make sure you pay."

Tess shook her head and rolled her eyes at the implication, and wondered how she got saddled with this churlish dickhead for a driver. The phone representative assured her all their drivers were courteous, knowledgeable, and spoke "excellent English." So far, this guy was batting one for three: at least he seemed to know his way around Kiev well enough to get her to the right location.

The darknet email she received said to meet in the small lot on the northeast corner of the Ocean Plaza Trade Center on Antonovycha Street. Although parking in Kiev is nightmarish on the best of days, because they were meeting before the center opened on a Sunday morning, her contact insisted that parking shouldn't be a problem—and despite the driver's indecipherable muttering when she told him they needed to park and wait, there were in fact very few cars in the lot.

As she waited, Tess thought about the man she would be meeting. Shortly after talking with Katia on that December evening, Tess contacted an old friend who now worked as an analyst with the BBC in London. Harley Winston spent some years as an Associated Press correspondent in Ukraine during and after the Russian incursion, developing a solid network of sources who could show him the way down any number of the country's literal or figurative seamy alleys in search of facts for a story. One of those contacts in Kiev had fairly intimate knowledge of what was known as the Ukrainian mafia and their involvement in human trafficking, and that was whom Tess was meeting.

Just then, a boxy, bottle-green Suzuki SUV fishtailed across the fresh snow into the lot, slid to a stop, and flashed its headlights twice, then once. That was the signal.

"Okay," said Tess as she struggled into her heavy coat and lined gloves. "I have no idea how long I'll be, so I'll call when I'm finished." She pulled out $40 for the driver and handed the money over the seat back.

The driver snatched the cash from her hand without a word, and Tess was tempted to whack him alongside his head in return.

Shoving open the car door, she raised the hood on her coat against the biting wind and snow, and watched as the vehicle lumbered down the street. She made her way over to the Suzuki and knocked on the driver's window. When he rolled it down an inch she passed him her business card and ID. Harley was explicit about the need to present a photo identification, preferably something like a passport, to assure his contact that she wasn't an imposter.

Despite her down coat, Tess shivered uncontrollably in the brutal wind as crystals of snow collected on her lashes. The driver, his face concealed by a black balaclava, rolled down the window halfway and scrutinized her passport and face, back and forth and back and forth, before he satisfied himself that she was who she claimed to be. He opened the door as a gust of wind sent an explosion of snow into the car, at the same time catching Tess's hood and flinging it off her head.

"Let us go inside," the man said, raising his voice against the raging wind.

Nowhere near diminutive at five-foot-seven, Tess nevertheless struggled to keep up with his huge strides: he had to be at least six and a half feet tall, and even under his heavy parka she could tell he was built like a football linebacker.

Thankfully, the main door to the center was unlocked, even though most of the stores were still shuttered.

Wordlessly, he led them into the Kredens Café, where Tess noticed that the sign was in English although the wall menu and descriptive tags in front of the bakery items were in Cyrillic. They settled into one of the U-shaped leatherette booths at the rear of the restaurant, out of the staff's earshot. The smell of fresh-brewed coffee and baked pastries filled the air.

"I am Anton," the man said, pulling off his balaclava. He didn't volunteer his last name, but Harley said it was Kolesnyk.

"Tess. I appreciate you coming, especially in this awful weather."

Anton shrugged. "It is Kiev in the winter." His voice was deep and gravely, and heavily accented. "Would you like a coffee?"

"Yes, that would be wonderful. I'm frozen to the bone."

"Regular, or something else? Espresso?"

"I'd prefer a cappuccino. Large, if they have it."

Anton got up and strode to the counter, where he ordered their drinks. He came back carrying a plate with a trio of baked goods: a vanilla-colored muffin with what looked like raisins, a sugar-dusted flaky cookie, and a thin layered cake with fruit filling.

"I asked these to be cut in half so you may try some of them all," Anton said. "The one is called *yabluchnyk*, a Ukrainian layered apple cake. The muffin is *syrniki*, made with curd cheese—I believe it is called cottage cheese in your country—and banana and raisins. And the last is a specialty of Ukraine, a fried cookie with sugar icing called *khrustyky*. You must try each."

Tess was momentarily speechless, remembering that Katia was eating a *khrustyky* when she was abducted. She finally managed to choke out a few words. "They look delicious. Thank you."

"Not to mind," he rumbled quietly. "Anyone who is a friend to Harley Winston deserves my kindness."

Tess followed his lead and lowered her voice. Thus far they were alone in the café except for the waitstaff, but it was always best to be cautious. "Harley is a remarkable man, that's for sure. Did you meet him when he first came to Ukraine?"

"No, he was here for some months before we crossed our paths. Excuse me: before our paths crossed. It has been a while since I have spoken English, and I'm afraid I have become…er…rusty."

"No, your English is excellent."

The attendant called out something in Ukrainian, and Anton went to the counter and returned with their steaming coffees.

Tess warmed her hands around the generous, earth-colored mug.

"You must have one of these," said Anton, pushing the plate toward her across the table.

Tess reached for the sugar-coated pastry, and stared at it in her hands.

"Is something wrong?" Anton asked, frowning in concern.

Tess smiled thinly, and explained the significance of the little cookie. "It seems so extraordinary that you would have chosen this particular pastry. Maybe a good omen."

"Perhaps so."

They ate and drank in silence for a few moments, and then with a quick glance around the still-empty coffee shop, Anton spoke up. "So, how can I help you? Harley explained partly, but perhaps you could enlarge."

Tess spent the next hour giving Anton details of Katia's kidnapping, and a rough sketch of her later years. She also repeated the four names she had—Radic, Ludmila, Dragos, and Ulrich Flemming—although she doubted that they were involved in Katia's original capture. Through it all, Anton's expression was unchanged, and except for a few brief questions, he remained wordless, never taking his eyes off the woman seated across from him.

"I know it's a long shot," Tess concluded, "but I'm starting here in Ukraine because I want to hope the first link in this filthy chain: the people who abducted Katia. And for her sake, maybe see if she has any relatives left in Crimea, although I doubt it. Her parents are both dead, and by now grandparents are as well, I'm sure. Katia never mentioned any cousins, and she was an only child when she was taken, so unless her parents had other children later...."

"Yes, you are right that it is a 'long shot,' but worth a try. I have certain...connections, shall we say, with people who are involved in such crimes, or know of those who are—and sadly, there are many. You may know that Ukraine has long been a center for human smuggling of all sorts: forced labor, organ seizure, and sexual trafficking of women and children. Hundreds of thousands of innocents have been exploited by these practices in Ukraine in the last many years, even before Russia's invasion." Anton nibbled the last few crumbs of his *yabluchnyk*. "Where are you staying? And how may I reach you?"

"Here in Kiev, I'm at the Alfavito on…okay, here goes: Predlavnytsky Street."

"Very close. It is *Predslavynskaya*." His tone was mildly teasing. "But as long as you know how to say the name of the hotel, you will be fine."

"I won't have to worry about my pronunciation of the street name much longer, because I plan to head to Crimea tomorrow."

"How will you travel?"

"I don't have much choice, thanks to Russia's prohibition against direct flights from Ukraine to Crimea. Forcing people to fly from Kiev north into Russia, then from Russia south into Crimea and Sevastopol is absurd. That eats up an entire day, but I guess it's better than a miserable sixteen-hour train ride from Kiev to Sevastopol. Either way, it's still a long drive from Sevastopol to Koktebel."

"Yes, it has become very difficult to journey in this region. Do you have a registration in Koktebel? And will you have a car?"

"I'm staying at the Plan'orka Hotel off Lenina Street, near the Water Park. I think the town is small enough that I can walk if the weather is decent, or take a taxi."

"Be careful: you know that Koktebel is a travel…uhh, tourist town, although not so much in winter as summer, and often the private taxi drivers are not suitably honest with foreigners. Especially women."

Smiling inwardly, Tess thought about the potential aggressors she'd sidelined during her travels with a few well-chosen words, or in one or two cases a swift kick to the knee or southern extremities. "I have a good intuition for who's a bad guy and who's not, but I'm always cautious. With this particular story, I'm being *more* than cautious."

Anton arranged to call Tess on her disposable cell that evening, just to check in. They agreed, however, that if anything of substance needed to be discussed, they would use their respective darknet email addresses to ensure secrecy.

"May I drop you somewhere?" Anton asked. "Perhaps your hotel?" By now, a few customers were meandering into the little café, stomping snow off their boots and slapping their gloved hands together in an effort to warm them.

"I'd appreciate that," Tess replied. "The chance that I might get that ill-tempered asshole of a driver again is enough to make me want to walk back to the hotel, even in this blizzard."

As they left, Tess turned and called out, "*Dyakuyu!*"

The counter-man replied *dyakuyu* as Anton looked at her quizzically.

"I always try to learn a few polite words in the language of the country I'm visiting," Tess explained, then chuckled. " 'Thank you' and 'please' are about my limit in Ukrainian. My Russian isn't much better. And my Chinese and Japanese are even worse."

"Those are difficult languages for most westerners," Anton joked good-naturedly. "They require you to make sounds that you have never made before."

Pulling on his balaclava, he opened the shopping center's outer door, and both were instantly slapped with icy needles of snow propelled sideways by the fierce storm. Wind-battered, they shuffled carefully across the parking lot to his car. A minute later it crawled down the street and disappeared into the wildly spinning snow.

Anton called that night to report in. "I have had some luck in my shopping excursion."

Tess knew what he was referring to. "That's good news. When will I be able to see what you found?"

"Perhaps I could email you a photo?"

"Good. I'll be waiting for it."

She opened her tablet and logged into her anonymous Tor browser and ProtonMail.

Tess remembered trying to describe Tor and the darknet to one of her less-than-computer-literate friends.

"There are really three levels to the Internet," she explained. "There's what's called the surface web, where you can find information by using search engines like Google. One layer down is the deep web, with information that you *can't* access directly. For instance, you can't purchase tickets to an NFL game through Google itself: instead, Google points you to websites where you choose your seats and make your purchase. Technically, that seating and price information is on the deep web. There's nothing scary about it at all.

"Then there's the dark web, or the darknet. Think of it like the Internet's subterranean basement, one that has some really treacherous, hidden corners where all kinds of nasty things live. It also has a massive, impenetrable door with a huge bolt that can only be opened using a specific key. The door is a network called an onion network, and the key is a special browser called Tor.

"In an onion network, you get where you want to go by using the Tor browser, just like you would use Google on the regular web. Except with Tor, your data gets scrambled and bounced around to any number of places before you reach your destination. These 'onion layers' allow you to stay completely anonymous, and at the same time allow you to reach darknet websites. There are also darknet email systems with secure darknet email service providers, a little like Gmail for the dark web.

"All this is perfect for criminals and terrorists, of course, because they can do their dirty business secretly. But it's also great for people like whistleblowers and dissidents and investigative journalists like me, because when we're communicating with sources or people who would be in danger if their identities were known, we can protect them. We can also protect ourselves."

Her musing was interrupted by a blinking light on her tablet, signaling the arrival of a darknet email.

In it, Anton explained what he discovered in just the few hours since they'd met in the café.

> Reached a man with knowledge of Russian groups trafficking drugs & other commodities in Ukraine. He knew the name Ulrich Flemming, said he was known in those circles. He will look further & see if he can find out about others. He also said for you to be very, very careful.

Tess thought for a minute, excited by the possibility that Anton might be able to find a way to locate Flemming.

> *That's good news. Hope he can find out more about Flemming. Did he say if he thought the man could have been involved in the kidnapping in Koktebel?*

> No. He will try to find out. I have another person in Crimea who may be able to help. I am waiting to hear back from him. I will email you tomorrow with

more details.

With that, the connection broke off.

Climbing into bed, Tess was left to wonder if all of this would actually turn into useful information, or if it would become just another dead end like she'd encountered so many times in her journalistic career.

Sometimes you're the dog, she thought, and sometimes you're the hydrant.

The planes that took her from Kiev to Moscow and from there to Sevastopol weren't the best she'd ever been on, but they beat by a mile those bumbling, rickety Aeroflot aircraft she'd flown when she traveled to Russia as a young reporter. She once heard a story about a rather large traveler who sat down aboard an Aeroflot plane, and the entire seat structure collapsed under him. Tess remembered being white-knuckled any time she needed to fly that airline.

Although exhausted by the time she got to Sevastopol, Tess wanted to press onward to Koktebel since there was still daylight left, and she was anxious to see the renowned Black Sea coast. She stumbled across a driver who spoke fractured English, so all along the three-hour journey he pointed out sights and attractions that Tess otherwise might have overlooked. Luckily, she picked up a road map before she left Kiev and made sure to slap on a scopolamine patch to prevent what was a lifelong battle with motion sickness.

From Sevastopol they headed south through lowlands of winter-fallow farmlands, pastures, and bleached fields of winter wheat. Soon the road grew narrower and more winding as the landscape evolved into folded foothills and valleys along the southern tip of the Crimean Mountains until they reached the Yalia, the highest of the parallel ranges in the Crimean.

As the taxi rumbled along the Sevastopolska and Pivdennoberezhne highways, the driver pointed out landmarks and geographic features. First there was Yalta, where leaders of the Soviet Union, the U.S. and the U.K. came together in 1945 to plan the defeat of Nazi Germany. Then came the stunning Laspi Pass, the French-inspired Massandra Palace, summer home of Czar Alexander III, then Czar Nicholas' and his beloved Alexandra's summer Livadia Palace. Along the way they passed the neo-Gothic Swallow's Nest castle perched above Cape Aya, and below it, the incredible sail-shaped Parus Rock, formed when dinosaurs still ruled the earth.

Along the coastline, hook-billed cormorants with their huge three-and-a-half-foot wingspans swooped and whirled above the rugged seacoast ledges, while inland lay mile after mile of barren vineyards, their lifeless, winter-dormant vines pruned into twiggy stubs. The driver told Tess that wine was always an elemental part of Crimea, going back three thousand years. In fact, he said, the Massandra Winery once boasted almost 4500 hectares—more than ten thousand acres—of vines along the coast.

As the little car bobbed and weaved westward against the continued thrusts of the powerful coastal wind, a pair of Great Crested Grebes sporting wild, spiky tufts on their heads and with necks swathed in carrot-red feathers that looked like whimsical, Dr. Seuss-inspired Elizabethan collars, waddled nonchalantly along the gravel shoulder of the road.

The driver babbled on in his broken English about

Crimean wines, while Tess thought about all that had happened in that region since Vladimir Putin's takeover. One of the first things Russia did was nationalize and expropriate some four thousand former Ukrainian businesses in Crimea, including its lucrative wineries, many of which it sold off wholly or in part. The enormous Massandra vineyards were among the victims; other targets were the multitude of Crimean environmental conservancies and historic sites. One former Crimean official said the Russians plundered the peninsula like a war trophy.

Thanks to decades of a steadily languishing economy and a corrupt and unresponsive government in Ukraine, by all accounts a majority of Crimeans favored returning to the Russian fold after the annexation. But all Tess could see was a future where the very soul of Crimea was evaporating. *Like every invader, Russia wants to leave its own mark of conquest on the vanquished, and that often means destroying the best parts of what they've captured. Not so different from the people I'm hunting.*

Suddenly the driver cheerily called out, "You here! Koktebel!"

Tess looked out the window at a collection of boxy, whitewashed houses and buildings, many clad in ruddy red tile roofs, marching down a shallow hill to the mouth of the crescent-shaped Koktebel Bay. Its pale aqua waters were calm, but beyond, the sea was roiling and gray from winter storms. A few three- and four-story buildings dotted the streets in this village of barely three thousand people, hotels that used to cater to the masses of tourists who once clogged Koktebel in summer.

The cab crept slowly along the highway that slashed through the heart of the town before resuming its journey along the Crimean coast. Here, trees lined almost every side street and many back yards were speckled with laundry fluttering madly on rusty clotheslines. Through her slightly open window, Tess caught the astringent scent of salt on the chilly air.

Above the town, gray clouds shuffled across the top of the jagged, volcanic Karadag peaks, which thrust up through the surrounding forested hills like a dun-colored, spiked backbone of some colossal stegosaurus. Recognizing her surroundings from the vision that came when she first read Katia's term paper, Tess was awestruck by the land's untamed wildness and beauty, and charmed by the seaside village that nestled within it.

The Plan'orka Hotel overlooked its namesake river that meandered for less than two miles from its source in the hills above Koktebel and down through the town until it emptied into Koktebel Bay. A neat, simple two-story rectangle, the building was painted a soft shade of pink with white iron railings and balusters lining the second-floor room balconies and large front entry porch. There appeared to be fewer than twelve rooms in the hotel, which suited Tess perfectly.

Clambering out of the cab, she pulled out her phone and clicked on the translation app. This was going to be tough sledding, she thought, if she had to use this damn thing all the way through Crimea. Hopefully some of the people she needed to talk to spoke English, although according to her research, she shouldn't hold her breath on that one.

Approaching the front desk, she said, "*Vy govorite po-angliyski?*"

She'd decided it would be more politic to speak Russian than Ukrainian in Crimea, and was glad that 'do you speak English?' was one of those phrases she'd learned in almost every language.

The pimple-faced young man behind the counter smiled and scratched the side of his neck absently. "*Nyet.*" Then he looked down at the ground and mumbled, "*Prosti.*"

"He said no, and that he's sorry."

Jumping at the sudden and unexpected intrusion, she whirled around and saw a bearded refrigerator of a man standing behind her. "Excuse me? You speak English?" She was more than a little concerned that less than thirty seconds after she'd stumbled out of the taxi, someone who spoke English miraculously appeared inside the hotel.

"Yes. Good almost as Anton." His broad smile revealed two gold teeth on either side of his top incisors, and Tess noticed he was carrying her luggage. The fact that he'd mentioned Anton eased her mind slightly, but she was still seriously irritated. She didn't like surprises.

"First, I know what *nyet* means," she snapped. "But who, exactly, are you, and what are you doing with my luggage?" She glanced out the front window to the empty road, then glared back at the stranger. "And what happened to my taxi?"

"Vitaly. We will speak more outside." With that, he turned to the now wide-eyed teenager and shot off what appeared to be a series of orders in rapid-fire Russian. She heard her name mentioned, but that was the extent of her understanding. By now she was fuming.

"What *are* you doing?" she demanded.

No response, except for a quick hand motion that Tess took to mean she should be patient.

She gripped his forearm and squeezed it hard. "Hold on. What the hell is going on? I have no idea of who you are: you show up like some commanding general and expect me to just stand here like a good soldier."

Vitaly turned and calmly watched while Tess railed at him.

"You need to know I'm *not* a good soldier, I don't like being pushed around, and I'm not going to put up with…"

"Please, Miss Alexander," he said, interrupting her mini-tirade. "I am not 'pushing you around,' and I will explain all in just one moment to your satisfaction. Just one moment, please? Please."

Tess almost barked back at him, then thought better of it. Instead, she took a deep breath and tried to relax. *But I'm going to watch you like a hawk, Vitaly-whoever-you-are, until you convince me that I should trust you. Knowing Anton's name, and mine, is a step in the right direction, but I need to know* how *you know them. And what else you know. And why you're here in this tiny backwater town just eighty miles from the Russian border.* Every fiber of her being was on red alert.

Vitaly finished his conversation with the clerk, then turned to Tess. "He needs your charge card for the room."

"Yeah, all right. Here you go." She handed the card to the boy, who bashfully refused to look up and meet her eyes.

"*Spasibo,*" he mumbled.

"*Pozhaluysta,*" Tess replied, glad she could also say 'you're welcome.' The boy's neck and face were now the color of a ripe strawberry. He ran the card, then wordlessly handed it back to her with her room key, still sidestepping any eye contact. Tess forgot how shy a teenaged boy could be around women, unless she was his *babushka*.

"Okay, mister Vitaly: let me have my luggage so I can take it to my room."

"They will keep it here safely, as you and I need to

speak together first."

Tess glared at the big man with gold teeth and almost told him to go straight to hell, but something told her to hit the pause button and listen to what he had to say. For a few minutes.

"All right," she snipped, still annoyed. "But unless you can explain yourself in two minutes—*two minutes*—I'm walking off. Is that clear?"

Vitaly smiled again, this time a little condescendingly. "Yes, ma'm, it is clear. I shall..."

Tess interrupted, furious once again. "Don't you *dare* patronize me! You might not be accustomed to women who know their own mind, but if we're going to have any kind of meaningful conversation, you'd better get used to it and deal with me as an equal."

Clearly shocked by her outburst, Vitality took a step backwards and held out both hands pleadingly. "I am truly sorry, Miss Alexander, if I caused offense to you. It was not...in...uhh...intentioned, I assure. Please forgive my idiotness." This time, there wasn't so much as a hint of disdain in his voice.

Tess stood silently, willing her anger to recede. This guy was obviously a boor who'd spent too much time around ignorant misogynists, she thought to herself—but then, he lived in a region where many people still held onto outdated stereotypes about the social roles of women and men. *Maybe one reason why there continues to be such an epidemic of human trafficking here.*

"Okay, if you want to talk, let's go outside. But remember: two minutes."

"Yes. Two minutes."

Vitaly handed the bag to the dumbfounded clerk with a stern order. "*Prismotrite za bagazhom, my skoro vernemsya.*"

"*Da.*" Now the boy wouldn't even look directly at Vitaly, obviously intimidated.

He opened the entry door for Tess, and they walked outside into the wintry air. A sudden gust of icy wind blew a tangle of hair across her face as Tess pulled on her coat and wrapped her arms around herself. The temperature was near freezing on this late afternoon, and would dip further once the sun disappeared behind the wedge of the Karadag hills that jutted into the bay.

"What did you say to the young man? At the end."

"I said for him to watch your bag, and that we would be back. Again, Miss Alexander, I am sorry for my words to you. I am afraid that I have little accustom... experience...with fierce women."

Tess couldn't help but smile at his description of her as fierce.

"I know the air is cold, but may we please walk to be sure our conversation is not heard?"

"Of course." Tess began walking down Prymors'ka Street beside the hotel, and Vitaly quickly followed.

"Introductions first. I am Vitaly Dudnyk. Anton and I fought in the Patriotic War of 2014 against the Russian invaders, but we knew each other for many years before. He is now a confidential...*istochnik*...umm, I cannot find the English word...one who explores for information for other people, looking for truth."

"Perhaps you mean an investigator?"

"That is not quite the word, but it is fine. Oh, wait: informant. A confidential informant. He helps others, reporters such as you, and sometimes supporters for Ukraine independence, to get information they need to expose fact and truth, but he must stay *skrytyy*...hidden."

"And what about you? Are you also an *istochnik*?"

"Some. Sometimes. I also help people that Anton sends me, to interpret Ukrainian and Russian language to people who do not speak that. Anton speaks English much better. I was not true when I first said I speak almost as good as Anton, for you can tell I do not, but I do enough so others understand."

"Is that why Anton sent you to me? To help with translation?"

"Yes. To translate. And to make sure you…to help you, if you need…to be safe. I do not believe Koktebel is a dangerous village, but there are those in Crimea who would not like your investigator work. I do not know who they are, but they are probably near. So I am beside you. If you need." Vitaly spoke as if he knew he was treading on dangerous waters, trying hard not to make Tess feel as if she couldn't take care of herself yet at the same time wanting her to know that he would be there should trouble arise.

Tess stopped and turned directly toward Vitaly, all traces of her earlier irritation evaporated. "Thank you. Really. Having you help me with translation is going to make a huge difference. And having you there to help…well, I appreciate it. I'm sorry for coming down so hard on you before."

Vitaly cocked his head uncertainly. "I do not know this phrase, 'coming down so hard.' "

Tess grinned. "It means I was unpleasant to you. Unkind."

Now it was Vitaly's turn to smile. "Not unpleasant. Just forced. Forceful."

Tess resumed walking, even though the wind was cutting through her jeans like they were made of chiffon. *I should have thought ahead and worn something heavier. Like ski pants. I didn't expect it to be quite this cold, so far south.*

"So, how much do you charge for your 'services'?"

"It is taken care of," Vitaly replied. "I understand what you are looking for, and it is something that I care for. I hate these people who take children and women and do such things to them. They are monsters to me. I wish to see them all destroyed." His voice was hard and brittle, like steel being dragged across coarse concrete.

Again, Tess stopped walking to face Vitaly. "Why? Why do you care so much?"

Vitaly looked out toward the bay, now enflamed from the glow of the setting sun, and said nothing. Then he spoke softly, still staring out to sea. "My sister. She was taken from her school in northern Ukraine when she was just fifteen. We saw her not again, until six years later when a *bomzh*—scavenger—found her in a garbage bin in a back street of Moscow."

"Oh, Vitaly. I'm so sorry." The words came out tight and choked.

"It was very long ago," he said, turning back toward her. "But I will never forget. And that is why."

They walked on quietly until they reached the deserted amusement park near the seafront promenade. Ocean waves scraped idly at the rocky beach as Tess gazed out onto the bay and the sun just setting behind the volcanic hills. "It's beautiful, isn't it? Even in winter."

"Yes. I always loved Koktebel and Fedosia. Now, after Russia took it, however, I am not sure I love it so much. It is changed."

"Perhaps we should get back. It's getting colder and darker, and I'm getting hungrier. Do you know of a good restaurant?"

"Of course. Shall we go toge…do you wish me come

with you? If not, that is fine."

"I would appreciate you coming with me, Vitaly. I may want to talk to some people just to see if they remember anything about Galina and her family." She smiled roguishly. "Plus, it would give you a chance to practice your English."

"Ahhh, my English. It is very primitive."

"Nah, it's really quite good. I can understand everything. Well, *almost* everything," she added with a wink.

Vitaly grinned, his gold teeth glinting in the streetlight. "I believe that we shall do well together," he laughed. "Even though things did not begin so fortunately."

"Favorably," corrected Tess, slipping into her adopted role as English language instructor.

"Yes, favorably." They continued to banter as they walked quickly back to the hotel, eager to escape the dying day that was becoming colder with each passing minute.

11

The restaurant, which was really more like a café, with straight-backed wooden chairs and small round tables barren of tablecloths, was warm and cheerful, a welcome relief from the cold they endured while walking the half-block from Vitaly's car. The outside temperature was below freezing and the wind still whipped wickedly, making it feel even icier than it was.

"I am sorry for the weather," Vitaly apologized. "Winters can be very cold here, it is true, but this is colder than common. Wait: colder than *usual*. Is that correct?"

"Correct. Is it usually so windy, too?"

"Often, yes. But again, this seems not as normal."

The waitress delivered their menus, and Tess asked her companion for a few translations. He struggled here and there, but managed to explain most of the dishes. The smell of boiling cabbage, beets, and roasting chicken drifted out from the tiny backroom kitchen.

Tess settled on the boiled crawfish in white wine and tomato juice. Vitaly ordered a bowl of Borshch and *kremzlycks*, a garlic-flavored dish of pork and potatoes cooked in a clay pot and garnished with a massive blob of sour cream. An image of fat-clogged arteries whipped through Tess's mind.

The food was simple but delicious. Vitaly shared some of his soup with Tess, who'd always loved beets—next time, she vowed, that was what she would have. Just Borshch. Vitaly explained that in summer, it was served cold, but winter meant hot Borshch. And yes, that was how it was spelled in Russia and Ukraine, without the "t." Why, no one knew. It was one of those elements of the Slavic culture as enigmatic as who murdered the Romanovs.

Finishing her meal, she looked around at the other patrons inside the diner. Some were too young to be of help, but a scattering of older couples and singles might make for good information sources. She and Vitaly already discussed how he should approach people, explaining that Tess was an American distant relative of the Shevchenko family who wanted to find out if anyone could verify the story about little Galina being kidnapped. She was also looking for friends and relatives, he should say.

Tess suggested they begin with an elderly couple seated at a far table, so Vitaly took a last gulp of his coffee and got up. Tess was again struck with how huge the man was, not just in height but in bulk. Not fat by any means, but if he wasn't careful, all that muscle could easily turn to flab as he slipped into older age.

They approached the seated couple, who looked up curiously. Tess bobbed her head as Vitaly introduced her, and then he motioned to the two vacant chairs and obviously asked if they could sit. The man nodded, but the woman stayed still. People in Crimea were generally very friendly toward foreigners, but these two seemed to pick up on the fact that this wasn't an ordinary, bump-into-someone-at-the-market kind of encounter.

Vitaly started explaining the situation, his voice and face casual and open. Tess smiled from time to time, a bit inanely, she thought, because she had no idea what anyone was saying. Though this was something she'd experienced before whenever she didn't speak the language, it made her uncomfortable.

Vitaly and the couple—Ivan and Olga Kostiuk, Tess learned—spoke back and forth for several minutes, and then Vitaly turned to Tess.

"They remember hearing about Galina. Her father was a top banker in Fedosia, and knew most of Koktebel people, and everyone was very upset. She was, they said, a sweet child, very smart, very beautiful."

"Did anyone know exactly what happened to her? Were there any witnesses? Did her parents contact the police?"

Vitaly conveyed her questions to the couple as Tess sat patiently for another several minutes.

"Yes, police were called, but found nothing. No one saw anything. Or if they did, said nothing, as happens often with such incidents. Olga remembers Galina's mother was despairing and could not be comforted. It was very hard for her for many years. She always hoped one day Galina would be found and brought back."

"Did her parents have any children after that?"

Vitaly asked the question, then simply shook his head at Tess in answer.

"Any other relatives? Here, or in Ukraine or even Russia?"

Again, the answer came back negative. However, the Kostiuks admitted they weren't close friends, just acquaintances in the town.

"Can they suggest anyone in Koktebel I should talk to?" Tess hoped for a lead, any lead.

Olga and Ivan spoke back and forth, and then Olga

brightened and said something to Vitaly.

"She remembers well a woman who was friendly with Galina's family, and she remains in Koktebel. Her name is Lyudmyla Davidovich, and Olga says she lives on Klubnyi Lane."

"Thanks very much," Tess said to the couple. "*Spasibo.*" She reached out her hand, and both of them shook it warmly. "*Spasibo.*"

Tess glanced around and spotted two other couples and three single, middle-aged men she wanted to talk to. Vitaly approached each couple individually and gave his pitch for help and information. One couple just moved to Koktebel two years ago, and the other man and wife lived in Yalta and came down to Koktebel for the day. Neither pair knew anything.

They had better luck with the men. Kostyantyn Borisov was a native of Koktebel and seemed to know everyone. In fact, when he first walked in, almost everyone in the restaurant greeted him by name. He clearly remembered Galina's disappearance and the turmoil it caused among the town's residents. Everyone, Vitaly translated to Tess, was shocked that such a crime happened in their peaceful little village, to sweet little Galina. No, he said, no one had any idea who took her. Such evil people could certainly not be residents of Koktebel—but nevertheless, he would ask around and see if anyone knew anything that could be of help. Vitaly gave him the number to Tess's burner phone.

The second man, Pavlo, wouldn't give his last name. He was clearly uncomfortable with Vitaly's questions, avoiding eye contact and constantly knitting his fingers together. *Why is he so darned uneasy?* Tess played the part of the innocent American traveler, but watched his every move. *He looks like he's about to jump out of his skin.* The more he talked, the more perturbed Vitaly seemed to become with what Pavlo was saying. Tess couldn't be one hundred percent sure of that since she'd only known Vitaly for a few hours, but her powers of observation were keen as a razor and her instincts were seldom wrong. She might jump to a conclusion once in a while as she did when Vitaly first accosted her, but she always rectified her blunder quickly.

Toward the end of Vitaly's inquiry, another man Tess hadn't noticed before approached Pavlo and leaned over his shoulder, whispering something into his ear. Pavlo nodded, nodded again, then turned his attention toward Tess and spoke directly to her.

"Ne vvyazyvaysya v eto. A to doigrayeshsya."

"I don't underst... "

Vitaly interrupted her. "Wait. I shall tell you, just a moment." He spoke calmly and precisely, his dark eyes focused on Pavlo's like a laser. Whatever he was saying, it wasn't an invitation to afternoon tea.

Pavlo swallowed hard, then got up. The second man stared coldly at Vitaly for several seconds, then turned away and walked out the door after Pavlo.

"This is not good," whispered Vitaly to Tess. "Pavlo at first said he knew nothing, had never heard of the crime, did not know the Shevchenkos. Then he said something like, 'I have never heard of this 8-year-old girl,' yet I had not told him Galina's age. So I questioned more, about children kidnapped, and he became more nervous. 'I have nothing to do with such things,' he said, 'and you cannot say it. There is no proof.' Then he said there are people who will not wish for you to examine this matter. After second man came, Pavlo said he would no longer speak things, or speak to me."

"So, what did he say to *me*, at the end?"

"I do not wish to worry you, Tess." By now, he'd dropped the formal "Miss Alexander" in favor of her first name, as she'd asked several times for him to do.

"The only thing that worries me is that you're not telling me what he said. What were his words, Vitaly? No sugarcoating."

"I do not understand this 'sugarcoating.' "

"To make it seem more acceptable. Easier for me to hear. Just tell me his exact words."

Vitaly sighed and shook his head at the tenacity of this beautiful but stubborn American woman.

"All right. He said, 'Don't get involved in this. Or then you will finish badly.' "

"That was a very explicit threat." One of the most explicit she'd ever received.

"Yes, he was quite direct. And the other man as well, who I imagine is greater to him. Above him."

"Yes I agree: between the two of them, he seemed to be the one in control." Tess thought for a moment, then touched Vitaly's arm. "Listen, I'm sorry to have gotten you involved in this. You were only supposed to be my translator."

"No, I described before that I am also here for your safeness. "

"Safety," she corrected.

"Safety," he responded, and she caught a quick gleam from his gold teeth.

"Regardless, we need to see what that guy has to say." She motioned toward the bearded man seated nearby.

"Yes, let us go speak to the man in the blue *kurtka*. Jacket."

The man's name was Yaroslav Shadrova, and he too was a long-time citizen of Koktebel. As he listened to

Vitaly's story, he narrowed one eye and compressed his lips together in an arrow-straight line, his face hard and indifferent. If this guy knows anything, thought Tess, he's not about to say.

And he didn't. It was if he were both deaf and mute, except for the fact that his expression became more hostile and unreachable with every question. Once it was clear that Vitaly had nothing more to ask, Shadrova stood up, walked to the front counter, spoke in hushed tones to the man behind the counter, then disappeared out the door.

No one else remained in the café except the two of them and the first couple they'd spoken to, Olga and Ivan Kostiuk. The Kostiuks gathered their coats, said a few cheery words to Vitaly and Tess, and left, while Tess looked at the bill and tried to calculate what she owed for the dinner. She finally gave up and asked Vitaly.

As he took Tess's cash to the counter, a white-aproned man came out of the kitchen area. Tess had an idea, and quickly joined Vitaly. "Could you ask if he's the owner of the restaurant?"

"Yes," Vitaly translated.

"How long has he been here?"

"Twenty-five years," came the answer.

"Let's take one more chance in the hopes he might have some knowledge. Please explain what I'm looking for."

As Vitaly handed Tess her change, he listened intently to the owner's response to his queries. He said something else to the man, got an answer, then asked another few questions to which the man again answered. It seemed the owner did in fact know something.

But something was wrong. She watched as Vitaly leaned over the counter and spoke again to the owner in rasping, decidedly unfriendly tones. Then he whirled, took Tess by the arm, and propelled her toward and out the door. She didn't even have the chance to put on her coat, and was momentarily paralyzed by the freezing air.

"Hey!" she exploded. "Just a minute! Let me…

"We have no time. We must get to auto at once."

They half-ran across the street to his parked car, and Vitaly jumped in and started the engine without even waiting for Tess to open the passenger door.

"Wait, Vitaly! What the hell is wrong?"

"Put belt on," he ordered gruffly, and slammed down the accelerator. Thrown sideways as the car skidded onto the main road, Tess finally managed to buckle her seatbelt.

"Tell me what happened. What did he say that made you so…troubled?" She was going to say "afraid," but figured a man like Vitaly wouldn't appreciate having his courage called into question.

"Just quiet, please," he said. "I must think."

They drove in silence, until Tess realized they were headed in the opposite direction from the hotel. He pulled off at the entrance to the empty Karadag Nature Preserve, and stopped the car in a small turnout. He left the engine running to keep them both warm, then turned in his seat toward Tess. The car and its surroundings were dark, but she read alarm in Vitaly's bearing.

"I am fearful for you going back to the hotel," he began. "I cannot guarantee your protection, and I promised Anton…" He failed to finish his sentence. "What I have learned places you in danger. I believe you should leave Koktebel. Leave Crimea and Ukraine."

"I can't do that. But you need to tell me what happened with the owner of the café. Understand: I have taken risks before, and I'm sure I will again. Sometimes it ends up being dangerous, most of the time not. But I've made a commitment to find the truth. I try very hard to stay safe, because if I'm dead I'm no good to anyone. Let me do my job, and tell me what you found out."

He finally gave in to Tess's plea with a small shrug and a sigh. "Okay. Okay. It was all good at first, he was very agreeing. Agreeable. Then I say you look for people who might know something about Galina's kidnapping, and suddenly he was not happy. He said you should go back to America, leave it alone. He said the girl, Galina, was dead, and you should forget her. I asked how he knew she was dead, and he said he knew many things. What things? I asked, and he became very…mmm, I struggle for the right word…arro…arrog..."

"Arrogant?" offered Tess.

"Yes. Arrogant. He smiled saying he knew people in Koktebel, in Fedosia, in Yalta, in Simferopol, who knew other people with special occupations that might cause events like what happened to Galina. Then he laughed, and said it was 'a good business,' and I should stay out of it if I did not want to visit the graveyard on my back, and if I did not want to send you back to America in a wooden box.

"There is an old Ukrainian proverb that says, *Black souls wear white shirts.* This man began like a comrade, and then became not. He showed the truth of his soul, and it is very, very black. I know you do not wish to give up, Tess, but I wish for you not to be harmed."

"I don't wish for myself to be harmed, either. I'll be very careful, and tell you were I am going, who I am meeting with, as long as I am here in Crimea."

"No. You will rather allow me to go *with* you when you speak with people, even when you go to shops or see the country. I must do my job, and part of that is your…" He paused, then thought of the word he'd learned earlier. "Safety."

"All right," responded Tess reluctantly. "After all, I need a translator, and you're the only one I've got. Now, let's go back to the hotel. I've had a long day, and need my wits about me for tomorrow."

" 'Wits about me'? What means that?"

"It means I need to be able to pay attention. And that's hard to do when you need sleep."

"Oh. Another good Americanism I will have to remember. But really, I wish you would think again about returning to the hotel."

"Vitaly, I've paid for the room, my suitcase is there, and I'll be sure to lock my door and even put a chair in front of it if that'll make you feel better. Heck, I'll pull the whole dresser in front of the door."

" 'Dresser'?"

"Chest of drawers. We call it a dresser in the U.S."

"I shall be able to speak English like a native if you stay here much longer," Vitaly joked, then turned the car back toward Koktebel.

Tess spent a restless night, in spite of the chair wedged in front of the door, which she was sure she didn't really need. The bed was comfortable enough, but as usual, her mind wouldn't stop racing. What secrets did the men in the café really know, or were they just posturing like someone who knew someone who knew someone who knew someone who'd done something? Why did the owner insist that Galina was dead? What "good business" was he referring to? Tess's skin crawled, pretty sure he wasn't talking about selling cotton candy at the carnival.

But did he really know anything about trafficking? Anything about the people involved in it? What would this old friend of Katia's mother—she *had* to remember to refer to her as Galina, not Katia—have to say if they could find her? Where else might she be able to lead them?

The next morning, just a hint of pale winter sunlight illuminated the room as Tess opened her eyes and glanced at her phone on the nightstand. 6:01. She felt lethargic, almost drugged, but that was to be expected. She'd flown over sixty-five hundred miles in the last three days, ridden at least another hundred and thirty in a taxi with almost no springs, and her body was rebelling.

She pulled back the heavy duvet, sat up, and groaned. *Get up and get your ass into the shower,* she told herself. *That, and about a gallon of coffee, and you'll feel better.*

Tess wasn't one of those women who could step out of the shower looking like Julia Roberts—probably not even Julia Roberts could step out of the shower looking like Julia Roberts. Twenty minutes later, she'd finished the ritual of drying and fixing her hair and putting on makeup so she wouldn't look, in her words, like something out of a horror movie. The truth was, Tess was a beautiful woman even right out of the shower: slender, tall, with full, rounded breasts that hadn't yet surrendered to the inexorable force of gravity, high cheekbones and a classic upward-turned Irish nose, and thick auburn hair that fell lightly over her shoulders in deep curls. Attractive, she'd admit to, but that was it. Nothing to get all worked up about.

Downstairs, the hotel was hushed and empty. Outside the front window, the trees and bushes were motionless in the dim morning air, though they glistened with a light dusting of frost. She pulled on her coat and gloves and stepped onto the wide porch. The cold snapped her even further awake as she headed toward the small coffee shop she'd seen as she arrived. The only sound in the town was the soft, rhythmic *shoosch, schoosch* of waves lapping at the seawall. The sign above the coffee shop read "Kofe Alushta." Inside, bright lights offered a warm welcome.

"*Zdravstvuyte*," she greeted the gnarled counter woman in Russian, hoping she wasn't mangling the word too badly.

The woman replied with something Tess couldn't grasp, so she just smiled.

"*Kofe*?" the woman asked.

"Latté," Tess replied. It was one of those words like "okay" or "computer" that seemed to have universal meaning.

"*Kakoy?*" the woman asked, to which Tess just shook her head.

"I don't really speak Russian." She plumbed the depths of her memory for the right phrase, then tried what she could recall. "*Ya ne govoryu russki.*"

Now it was the old woman's turn to smile, showing a gap where a tooth once was. She gestured to the ceramic mugs lining the shelf to her left, and Tess nodded when she reached the largest one. "*Da.*"

The woman pointed to one of the little Formica-topped tables, and motioned for her to go and sit down.

"*Spasibo*," Tess replied, pulling out her small travel wallet.

"*Nyet, nyet*," the woman said, shaking her head and smiling even more broadly. Now Tess could see that two teeth were missing: one on top, one below. The woman reached across the counter and pushed Tess's wallet and money away. She said something unintelligible in Russian, laughed, and pointed again to the table by the window.

"Oh...I..." Tess fumbled for words, moved by the woman's generosity. "*Spasibo, spasibo.*"

"*Pozhaluysta.*" You're welcome. That much, Tess knew.

She sat down at the rickety table, in the center of which was a tattered and faded yellow silk rose in a hazy glass vase. A few minutes later, the woman set the steaming latté in front of Tess, along with a familiar sugar-dusted cookie on a chipped, washed-out white plate. Tess looked up at her with surprise.

"*Khrustyky!*" she said, stunned that once again she was offered the same pastry that little Galina bought on her way to school that day.

The woman's eyes widened, equally surprised that her foreign customer knew the name of this treasured Ukrainian cookie. "*Da!*" She laughed in delight, patting Tess's shoulder. "*Da! Khrustyky!*"

"*Spasibo.*" It was all Tess knew to say. "Thank you."

Tess sat at the table and gazed out at the steadily brightening, cloudless sky. It promised to be a beautiful winter day, hopefully without yesterday's punishing wind. As before, Koktebel Bay looked calm and serene, with only shallow waves kissing the shoreline. The beach and promenade were empty except for a few shore birds obsessively scuttling in and out across the pebbles, first escaping the surf and then dashing back to where the water was before. Tess wondered why southern Black Sea beaches are covered not in sand, but pebbles and small rocks. They reminded her of the beaches along so many of the magnificent rivers that raced through northern California, those too mostly pebbled. Nature was a mystery.

Thirty minutes later, she was downing the last of her coffee when she caught a movement on the sidewalk some distance up from the café. The streets, deserted since she arrived, showed the first sign of the town awakening. Tess turned again toward the sea and the brooding Karadag, but a minute later her attention ratcheted back to the far sidewalk. A tall, gaunt man in a long black overcoat was probably a couple hundred feet away, shuffling slowly up the walkway on the opposite side of the street. The image of a brain-eating zombie popped into her mind, and she shook her head at her overactive imagination. *Next thing you know I'll be seeing the headless horseman.*

Nevertheless, she kept glancing up as the man approached, and the closer he got, the more certain she was that he looked familiar. Where have I seen this guy? she thought—and suddenly, it hit her like an asteroid: the café last night. He's the owner. By now he'd crossed the street at the corner, just a few yards from the coffee shop's front door. Tess had the uneasy feeling that he was looking at her, and once he got to the window beside her table she had no doubt. The man stopped and turned directly toward Tess, fixing her with a menacing stare. Then a cold and emotionless smile broke across his face, and he slowly slid his index finger across his throat.

Tess's pulse surged into overdrive and she felt a sharp prickle down her spine, but years of confronting volatile people and situations had taught her to not only control her emotions, but conceal them, so she simply sat and returned the man's frozen glare. Seconds went by with neither one making a move, then the man abruptly turned and resumed his journey along the street.

Tess looked down at her hands, now clenched tightly in her lap. Beads of cold sweat dotted her forehead, and her fair-skinned face was drained of color. She glanced around the little café and saw she was still alone, making her feel even more vulnerable. *Okay, get hold of yourself. This guy is just a disgusting toad who wants to intimidate you. Take a step back, relax, and think.*

What she really wanted to do was run, but that wasn't going to happen. Not with Tess Alexander. As the minutes ticked by, she regained more of her composure, and even managed to smile at the gap-toothed counter woman, whom she realized was gazing at her with concern. *I probably should talk with Vitaly. Even though he'll just give me another lecture about getting out of Crimea.*

Just then, the door opened, and Vitaly strode in. One look at Tess's face, and he sat down beside her without ordering anything.

"What has happened?" His voice was thick with concern.

"What do you mean?" she asked. "Why are you asking?"

"There is a look on your face that tells me…it tells me you are anxious."

She was surprised at his perceptiveness. But then, like Anton, that astuteness was probably what saved his life over the years.

"I'm fine, Vitaly. But you need to know that just a few minutes ago, the owner of the café walked by, stared at me through the window, and then did this." She repeated the man's cut-your-throat motion.

Vitaly jumped up as if the chair were electrified. "When? Happen when this? Which way walk? Wearing what he?" He was so shaken that his imperfect English became even more jumbled.

"Don't worry. He's long gone by now. I just need to figure out what, if anything, to do about it."

"*You* will not do about it. I will."

"No, Vitaly, you won't. Remember what I said last night about keeping our wits about us? Well, that's what we need to do. This guy, and the other assholes in the café..." Vitaly smiled at Tess's use of the vulgar expression, "are just trying to intimidate me, and it's not going to work. I'm *not* easily intimidated. Didn't I say that to you yesterday? Yes, I think I did. Anyway, I won't be intimidated, I won't be terrorized, and I won't be bullied. I will go where I please, speak to whomever I please, and some brainless gorilla isn't going to stop me. Not today, not tomorrow, not ever."

Vitaly waited for a beat, then said, "You are finished?" He couldn't keep himself from smiling as he watched the woman's paroxysm of fury.

Tess took a breath, then said quietly, "Yes."

"All right. So what we are doing about this?"

"What we are doing about this," replied Tess as she stood up and headed toward the door, "is going to see Mrs. Shevchenko's old friend, and see what she can tell us."

"Wait!" called Vitaly. "I need a coffee!"

"I'll meet you back at the hotel," Tess shouted over her shoulder as she marched up the street toward the Plan'orka.

12

Lyudmyla Davidovich's home on Klubnyi Lane wasn't all that difficult to find. Like so many others, it was a small, whitewashed box of a house, except hers was highlighted with dazzling blue trim and an equally vivid blue metal roof. The yard was tidy and well cared for, even in winter. Two huge laurels dominated one side of the yard, and a five-foot holly overloaded with ripe red berries stood next to the porch steps. On both sides of the narrow limestone walkway stretched a winter-browned lawn, waiting for the first signs of spring to erupt into green again.

Mrs. Davidovich was the embodiment of Ukrainian hospitality. Her friend Olga called to say these two strangers might be stopping by, so she welcomed them as if they were long-lost family, offering steaming cups of strong Ukrainian coffee and fresh-out-of-the-oven layered apple cake.

Somewhere in her seventies by Tess's guess, Lyudmyla Davidovich's memory of her friend Iryna Shevchenko, her husband Sergiy, and their lovely daughter Galina was sharp and undimmed by the passage of decades. For well over two hours, she entertained her two visitors with stories about the Shevchenkos, the town, and the days when Crimea was fully Ukrainian, not a purloined Russian appendage.

Happy for the background details, Tess groaned inwardly at the thought of having to transcribe the plodding interview. Mrs. Davidovich spoke a curious amalgam of Russian and Ukrainian, Vitaly confided, which only added to the time-consuming process of translation and to Vitaly's concerns about its accuracy. Not to worry, Tess told him: we can always fill in the blanks later.

Finally, Tess took control with some direct and pointed questions about the day Galina disappeared, what the Shevchenkos said about it, and what kind of talk fluttered around the town afterward. From their earlier conversation, Tess gathered that Mrs. Davidovich was pretty much the titular queen of the local rumor mill, which meant she might be privy to information that not everyone else knew.

Another hour got consumed by the slow, question-translate-answer-translate process, but a few gems of information came tumbling out during the exchange. For instance, a teacher at the Koktebel School happened to be driving down Lenina Street just as a black BMW drove past the little girl. Recognizing her former student, she slowed down and kept glancing in her rear-view mirror to make sure nothing was amiss—even though, she said later, nothing bad *ever* happens in Koktebel.

The teacher saw a man get out of the car and speak to Galina. She described him as quite tall, at least six feet, and very stocky. He was wearing dark pants and a light blue shirt, and looked "very businesslike," according to the woman. His hair was dark and just below his ears, that much she could tell, and he appeared to have a moustache. When Galina got in the car willingly, the teacher's concern eased, and she continued on to the school.

One of the local hoteliers told police that a Russian-speaking man and woman were overnight guests in his establishment the night before Galina disappeared. He didn't recall much about them, he said, other than the fact that they kept completely to themselves, only speaking to him when they registered. That was the crux of what he told authorities, but later that week he elaborated with his old friend Mrs. Davidovich at a Tatar café in town where they were both having lunch. The innkeeper confirmed the teacher's description of the man, who registered as Alexandr Ivanov, the Russian equivalent of John Smith in the U.S. What no one else knew was that when he removed his gloves, the hotel owner saw a distinctive tattoo of a crowned ring on the man's forefinger.

Tess frowned and shuddered slightly. It was true, then: Galina's kidnappers were part of what is known as the Russian mafia. This particular tattoo symbolizes a *patsan*, someone of very high rank within Russian organized crime, a loose confederation of semi-autonomous groups and local cartels answering to a core leadership council. Tess pictured an octopus with tentacles that respond to a central brain, but that could be severed or injured without damaging the creature's main body.

Solntsevskaya Bratva was the wealthiest and most powerful of those tentacles, and Tess guessed this bogus "Alexandr Ivanov" was part of it. But finding him was out of the question: not only could there be lethal consequences to her and anyone else involved, but there were hundreds of *patsans* within the organization—and with only the vague description of a tall, dark, heavyset man to go on, the search could last forever.

Nevertheless, she'd snagged a critical clue that the

kidnappers were part of an organized crime syndicate, and not just isolated individuals who snatched children simply to sell them off and escape with the profit. That gave her at least a starting point.

The rest of the day Tess and Vitaly hopped from house to house, talking to some of the other town locals Mrs. Davidovich mentioned. Again, most people welcomed them warmly into their homes, although one or two simply looked stonily at the duo and slammed the door in their faces. *Just like cold-calling,* Tess thought, remembering her college days as a telephone marketer. *I really despised that job.*

They gathered tiny bits and pieces of information, but nothing especially worthwhile. That is, until their last interview of the day with another sixty-ish town gossip named Arina Federov Vasilchuk. With a cap of close-cropped silver hair and unusually straight, white teeth, she was born in Russia, she admitted soon after they walked in, grew up in Koktebel, married a man who worked at a pharmacy in Fedosia, and was not at all proud of what her birth country did to her *krasivyy Krym,* her beautiful Crimea. Paradoxically, she spoke to them in Russian.

She explained that she and her husband Fedir loved to explore when they were younger, in the days before Crimea was cut off from the rest of Ukraine.

"We would drive all over Ukraine: to Kerch, to Yevpatoria, to Simferopol, to Mikoliav, to Kiev, also to tiny villages no one knew," Vitaly translated, "and we would just make an expedition, seeing for interesting places or history sites. We would go into empty buildings and ruins and search, not to steal but just to look. We found many,

many interesting things in that time."

One day several years after the fall of the Soviet Union, they decided to drive to the abandoned underground nuclear submarine base in Balaklava, south of the port city of Sevastopol. Fedir Vasilchuk served in the Ukrainian navy as a young man and was always curious about the heavily guarded, restricted facility, but his duties never took him there. This was a perfect opportunity to see what was once the most top-secret military complex in the entire Soviet Union.

It was June, a beautiful day on the Black Sea coast, when they headed south on the Pivdennoberezhne Highway to go "expeditioning." It was only a week after little Galina Shevchenko was kidnapped, and both of the Vasilchuks felt like they needed to get away from the town's relentless grieving and speculating. She'd already heard rumors that the child was stolen by the Chinese, by the Americans, by Romanian gypsies, and by the Russian mafia, and it all made her sick to her stomach. Sweet, clever little Galina. She wondered if they would ever see her again.

The couple stopped for lunch in a small café just outside the village of Foros to enjoy the sweeping Black Sea views, then headed on to the abandoned shipyard.

There were no guards, no high-tech security, and no people. They walked through the unlocked chain-link gate and a partially open, massive iron door leading into the underground tunnels. Snapping on their heavy tactical flashlights, the pitch-black interior suddenly brightened enough to read the Cyrillic characters on a rusted sign fifty feet away.

The submarine base was actually a series of deep caverns stretching for almost two thousand feet before daylighting on the far side of Mount Tavros. They followed the entrance tunnel as it wound past a labyrinth of side tunnels and dozens of sealed doors, and from there, into a huge central tunnel framed by towering concrete arches over a water-filled canal. Two walkways bordered the canals on each side, so they followed them to the mouth of the tunnel, where blazing sunlight poured into the passageway.

"Fedir said we should return and search side tunnels," she explained through Vitaly, "so we went backward and took the first one, but it had a bolted bulkhead. We tried other tunnels, but each was blocked or flooded."

Not wanting to quit, Fedir tried forcing open first one, then another, iron door, but none of them budged. As he put his weight to the third door, it gave a painful screech and cracked open a few inches. More shoving yielded an opening large enough to squeeze through, but when they entered, it was nothing more than a small, nondescript, windowless room filled with cobwebs and the sour smell of rat droppings.

"We were disappointed and tried other doors, but all were bolted or rusted shut. We were almost to the main tunnel when Fedir tried one more door. The bolt was crooked, and to us the door looked lately used. He pushed hard, and it went open right away.

"When we walked in, there was an awful smell of urine and human waste. The ceiling had a hanging lightbulb, and a corner had a thin, soiled mattress. There was an empty metal food plate upside-down on the floor. On one wall we saw a small opening that looked as window, but no sunlight came. Spiderwebs wrapped the walls and corners, and the air felt wet."

As Tess listened to Vitaly's translation, she felt goosebumps rising on her arms. They looked at one another and nodded: this was where Galina was held on those first days. The Vasilchuks missed the girl and her captors by perhaps only hours, a day or two at most.

Of course, the trail was now long cold. By the time Tess heard the story, the abandoned base had been transformed into a naval museum where tourists could wander through the tunnels and gawk at displays of mortars, torpedoes, and grenades, remnants of a Cold War that most were too young to remember.

The skies were darkening with the sunset, so Tess and Vitaly said their goodbyes and headed back to the hotel. On the way, she checked her phone and saw a missed call. The voicemail message was from a woman who only identified herself as Anna; in broken English she said she had some important information about Galina Shevchenko, and could Tess meet her at 6:15 the next morning at the end of Ilyushyna Street?

"What was it?" asked Vitaly.

"Someone named Anna who says she knows something about Galina. She wants to meet early tomorrow morning on Ilyushyna Street." Tess was already punching in Anna's number.

"Wait!" commanded Vitaly. "You do not know who this 'Anna' is, and whether she wishes you harm. It is also not good to meet alone with someone you do not know."

But Tess was speaking into the phone and motioned for Vitaly to shush. She'd reached Anna's voicemail, so she just said she would meet her on the street the next morning.

Vitaly sighed in exasperation. "I shall go with you, of course."

"No, Vitaly: she appears to speak some English, and I can handle it myself. Besides, " she added with a smile, "by now, you must be getting sick of me: we've been together all day."

"Then another hour tomorrow morning will not make difference," smiled Vitaly. "We can go to Restaurant Papay after. It is near the Plan'orka, with beautiful view of Koktebel Bay."

Tess agreed, albeit reluctantly. She wasn't accustomed to having a babysitter and she resented giving up her independence, even if having a translator made the trip immeasurably easier. But she was silently grateful for the big man's presence.

The next morning, Tess dressed in black pants, ankle boots, and her favorite teal alpaca sweater, adding a scarf around her neck for warmth and topping it with her heavy parka. Then it was off to Ilyushyna Street, wherever that was. Vitaly double-checked the Google map to be sure, and drove north.

They arrived at the dark, dead-end street just before six o'clock. Tess demanded that Vitaly park several hundred feet back from her meeting spot with Anna, closer to the intersection with Vynohrada Street. From the woman's voice on the phone, she sounded pretty jittery, and Tess didn't want to take the chance of spooking her if she knew Tess brought someone else along. Even on the most innocuous of stories, sources could be paranoid.

She started walking down the unlighted Ilyushyna Street, where formless shadows seemed to pirouette from every side alley and every weathered doorframe. About twenty yards before the street's dead-end, she stopped for a moment because neither she nor Google Maps knew what was on the other side. She didn't want to box herself in just in case everything went sideways. She didn't think it would, but you never knew.

Then Tess got one of her feelings.

First came the telltale shiver along the back of her neck, and a slight lightness in her chest, as if a wire attached to her breastbone was being gently pulled by some unseen puppeteer gliding above her. The street scene disappeared, replaced by a an opaque curtain of pure awareness.

A man. Silent. Dark clothes. One hand obscuring something that shone weakly. Appearing from behind her…no, to the right of her…or both. Beyond, a bottomless river.

Then the intuition vanished.

Her heart thudded from the vision's intensity as she peered into the darkness ahead. A vague form emerged from the far side, and Tess stiffened, then relaxed slightly. She couldn't fathom where the person came from, but presumed it was Anna, as it was obvious the figure was wearing a skirt.

Tess called out and identified herself. "Anna? I'm Tess, the woman you called." No response. Cautiously, Tess began to walk toward the woman, who hadn't moved since she first stepped out of the shadows. *This is odd. Why isn't she walking toward me?*

Then as suddenly as she'd emerged, the woman was gone. Alone on the street and with her senses suddenly needle-sharp, Tess stopped, then realized she *wasn't* alone.

The skies had not yet begun to lighten, and although a pale quarter-moon floated above the street, it offered little by way of illumination. The air was ripe with the smell of dank and decaying shoreline vegetation from the Plan'orka River just a few hundred feet away, and Tess also caught the acrid scent of her own sweat, triggered by fear. Then she saw him: a man, dressed in solid black, who'd stepped onto the street from what Tess realized was an intersecting trail, probably from the river. He was slightly stooped in a combat stance and moved quickly toward her, carrying something that glinted in the insipid moonlight.

And then everything *did* go sideways. Considering the difference between her size and that of her hulking attacker, Tess knew there was little option but to take the latter option from the instinctive fight-or-flight response. She darted swiftly to the right, then switched direction back toward where the man materialized, hoping to confuse him by heading in the opposite direction than what he would have predicted. She heard a muttered *der'mo!,* which could be roughly translated as either shit, crap, or bitch, and the man reversed his course to follow her.

There were no buildings on this part of the street, nowhere to hide from her pursuer. He was big, but extremely quick for his size, and was gaining on her. Glad she chose the sturdy boots, Tess continued running in a zig-zag pattern, up and back, side to side, away from the river then toward it, figuring she could always jump in and swim if worse came to worse. *If I make it that far.* Weeds and grasses whipped at her pants legs as she ran, and more than once she swerved to evade a tree or large bush that suddenly materialized in her path. The man was only feet behind her, and she smelled the stench of his body odor mingled with his rancid breath. She knew he would reach her before she reached the river.

Something caught on the back of her coat, then yanked her backward. Powerful hands grabbed her waist, but she managed to turn sideways and kick, connecting with what felt like a knee. His grip loosened only slightly, then reasserted itself, this time at her neck. He was incredibly strong, and she felt the breath being squeezed out of her. She tried to call out for Vitaly, but managed only a strangled, birdlike squeak. Pinpricks of light swirled before her eyes, even as she continued thrashing and squirming, but the world around her was dimming rapidly. *This is what it feels like to be dying.*

She reached up behind her, hoping to shove her thumb into an eye, but only managed to grab a handful of her attacker's hair. It was enough, however, to get him to loosen his grasp slightly, and she raised her head with as much force and speed as she could muster, the back of it connecting with the man's face. She felt a dull and sudden concussion from her head-butt, and the pressure on her windpipe slackened. Inexplicably, her attacker went down with a loud *Oooph,* taking her with him. She tried rolling out from under his bulk, but was pinned to the clammy ground. It felt to Tess like the man was in the midst of a wrestling match with someone other than herself, which made no sense. A jumble of Russian-sounding words flew—now there were there two *different* voices—along with a swarm of somehow disembodied legs and arms smashing into one another and her. One of them slammed into her right eye, and for a moment all she saw were blazing, piercing stars.

Then she remembered the knife, or what she assumed was a knife, in her attacker's hand, and despite her spinning head, she redoubled her efforts to extricate herself, twisting and bucking and clawing at the reedy grasses to get a handhold. Suddenly everything went silent and still. She felt the man's leaden body atop her midsection and legs, no longer moving.

She also heard heavy breathing, and it wasn't her own.

A hand gripped her arm. "Tess? Tess? Are you alive?"

It was Vitaly: wonderful, conscientious, flawless Vitaly.

Her words emerged hoarse and strangled. "Vitaly...thank God! How did you…where did…where are you?"

"I am right here."

"What happened to… "

"I'm sure he's dead. Are you damaged?"

"I don't think so. But I can't move, and I feel like I'm going to throw up. You need to get this…this…body…off me."

The weight vanished, and Tess turned her head to the side and retched, choking on the man's reeking body odor that seemed to have infused her clothes. Vitaly put his arms under her and lifted her onto her feet. "Are you sure you have not been harmed?"

"My head is screaming and I know I'll have an awful black eye, but other than that and a few bruises, I'm okay. Thanks to you. How did you know someone attacked me?"

"I must be honest. I did not remain in the car as instructed: when you began walking, I got out and followed from behind, hiding in shadows in case you looked back. I saw a woman come from the side, and then saw the man about three meters away from you. I was too far to catch up with you as you ran at first. You confused him because you went to the side and back and side again—that was very good. Very smart.

"At last I reached him just after he captured you, and I jumped on him. Tackled him. We all went onto the ground. I fought to loose him from you, then saw the knife. We fought for it, then it fell out from his hand and finally I was able to grasp it and use it against him. And it was over."

Tess started shaking violently, and her knees buckled. Vitaly grabbed her before she collapsed, and just held her silently. In a few moments, she took a small step backwards.

"Thank you, Vitaly. That was way too close...." She left the comment floating unfinished on the cold winter air.

"I could not have allowed anything to happen to you." He hesitated, then chuckled dryly. "Probably Anton would have cut off my testi...uhh...he would have seen that I was to spend the rest of my days as a neuter in Siberia."

Tess coughed, then asked the obvious question. "What are we going to do with the bod...uhh, with him?" She looked down at the figure sprawled in the grass.

"No to worry. I shall take care for it. I want for you to go back to the car and wait, please." He handed her the keys. "It is cold, so engage motor and heat."

Tess nodded, not really wanting to know how Vitaly would "take care for it."

Back in the little Toyota and grateful for its efficient heater, her mind spun through the terror that just happened. Even with the heater blasting full-force she couldn't stop shivering as she recalled the life-or-death struggle with her nameless attacker. At the same time, she tried to wrap her brain around the grim reality that the man was now dead. Killed by Vitaly. She wondered if they'd ever know who he was.

Once Vitaly got back to the car, Tess demanded he tell her what he'd done with the body. "I want to know, Vitaly. Otherwise I'll end up agonizing over it forever." For Tess, it would be like a mystery that could never be solved, and that had always been her Achilles heel. She simply must see how the story ended, no matter how vile or disturbing.

The body was in the Plan'orka River. Vitaly dragged it to the edge, rolled it into the inky waters, watched it float on the sluggish current, then slowly sink and disappear. It would never be found, he said—or if it were, no one would bother to investigate. "That is simply the way things are in Russia."

Back at the hotel, a cup of tea—courtesy of the stunned innkeeper who was at the front desk when the mud-spattered woman with a huge purple bruise on her right eye arrived—and a soapy shower to remove the lingering acrid scent of her attacker's body, helped revive Tess. She joined Vitaly for breakfast at the oddly Polynesian-themed Papay Restaurant before heading to Simferopol to catch her flight. They snagged a table in front of the large second-floor deck with its fantastically-carved columns overlooking the bay and the nearby blue hills. Artisan flatbread baked in the restaurant's tandoor oven as a scattering of other diners enjoyed their omelets and oatmeal.

Vitaly inhaled sharply when she removed her dark glasses and he saw her eye, badly swollen and an ugly shade of purple-black from her cheekbone to her eyelid. He knew better than to ask if it hurt: he'd suffered enough black eyes in his lifetime to know that it did. A lot.

They made small talk throughout the meal, which for Vitaly was a mountainous plate of Ukrainian breakfast hash with paprika fried potatoes. Tess, who hadn't eaten since lunch the day before and was famished, opted for apple pancakes topped with berries and a light dusting of powdered sugar. They didn't speak at all of what happened the previous night.

She hated goodbyes. Especially in this case, when Vitaly had been practically glued to her side for three days. Before she hopped into the taxi for the ninety-minute ride to Simferopol, she gave him her home phone number in Deer Valley. She wouldn't normally do that with a source, but Vitaly literally saved her life—plus, she'd come to regard him as a friend.

As the cab pulled away from the restaurant, she turned around to see a grinning, bearded Vitaly waving enthusiastically, his golden teeth glinting in the morning sun.

13

The two four-hour flights from Simferopol to Moscow and Moscow to London were tedious and unremarkable, except for the assortment of stares her black eye drew. The swelling was nasty, and everyone looked at her as if she were a battered wife.

During the flight, she reviewed her notes and composed a text to her editor to let him know she was making headway on the investigation.

She had connected with Anthony Learmont-Campbell before she left the States, emailing him from the Plan'orka to meet her at Heathrow when she arrived at 6:40 that evening. Walking off the plane and into the massive Terminal 5 with its elegantly curved roof and huge pieces of angled glass floating above a steel bowstring arch looming five stories above the concourse, Tess felt an unexpected wave of dizziness. After the rustic atmosphere of tiny Koktebel, she was momentarily dazed by the huge futuristic structure and the hundreds of passengers swarming in every direction like a schizophrenic colony of ants.

A melodious female voice calling her name through the public address system snapped Tess out of her culture shock. The attendant on the courtesy phone said her party would be waiting at Caffé Nero on Level 3, near the British Airways counters.

She stopped for a moment at the entrance to the coffee shop, scanning the array of people for a lone man who looked British. As she wondered to herself what "British" looked like, a wiry, fair-haired man in jeans and a tweed blazer approached her.

"Ms. Alexander?" He had a refined, northern English accent which might have pegged him as a native of the area around Chelsea.

"Yes. Mr. Learmont-Campbell?"

"Anthony would be much easier, I should say."

"Good: Anthony. I'm Tess." She held out her hand, and he shook it warmly.

"Would you care for a coffee or tea?"

"I haven't eaten since an early breakfast: is there somewhere we could go for dinner? My treat."

"That's not at all necessary—please, allow me to host you. The Pheasant Inn restaurant is close by, although it's not terribly fancy. More like a pub, but they have both a restaurant and bar where you can dine. The food is excellent, especially for an establishment so close to Heathrow, and the menu is extensive."

When they reached the visitor parking garage, Anthony pointed his key fob to start the engine of a midnight blue Audi sedan, and the car doors opened with a soft beep. Tess sunk into the luxurious black leather seat as Anthony stored her luggage in the trunk—or, as they say in the U.K., the boot. After more hours than she'd care to count in a taxi that felt like its springs gave up a decade ago and then the uncomfortable, miserly seats on two airplanes, Tess felt a rush of pure bliss. If she weren't so hungry, she'd have asked Anthony if she could just sleep there.

Stepping into the Pheasant Inn, she was revived by the delectable smell of homemade soups, baking bread, and roasted meats. Although they arrived at the height of the dinner hours, because this was a weekday there was no queue and the pair were seated immediately in a slightly quieter back corner.

"Would you like a glass of wine, perhaps? Or a beer?"

"I'd love something, but I'm tired enough right now that if I drank any alcohol, I'd probably end up spilling all my darkest secrets."

"Oh, that would never do!" Anthony laughed at the idea of someone he barely knew, much less a journalist, revealing her family skeletons. "So, what about a sparkling water? Or tea?"

"Tea, I think. "

They ordered and chatted casually until the food arrived. Tess dug into her meal, a mouthwatering honey-glazed Norfolk duck breast with a wreath of cinnamon roasted vegetables. It was every bit as good as it looked. *Who says all British food is bland and uninteresting?*

By the time they were finished, it was close to eight o'clock. As weary as she was from traveling, Tess urgently needed to talk with Anthony about Galina. Katia. She surveyed the restaurant, which was slowly emptying out. They were secluded enough, she noted, to have a quiet conversation without being overheard. And there was plenty of time: the menu said the restaurant took the last order at 9:45.

Sipping her tea, Tess opened the dialogue. "As you know, an old friend of mine had Galina—uhh, Katia—as a student in her class last semester, and this past December I spent several hours interviewing her about her experiences. Obviously, you figured quite prominently in the story of her rescue. I'd like to ask you some questions about that."

"Well, as I explained when we spoke, it isn't customary for those of us who work for Antares to disclose details since it could expose victims to significant danger should their identities become compromised. But these are singular circumstances, especially since you know Katia and have all the details of what she's been through. So yes, of course you may ask me." She pulled out a small voice recorder and placed it on the table between them.

"So, first things first: how did you find Katia? How did you choose her, out of all the thousands of other trafficking victims in Dubai?"

"It's a bit of a convoluted story, but let me touch the high spots for you. As you can imagine, Antares has a worldwide cadre of sources we've cultivated over the years, many whom we only know through the dark web. They may or may not be actively involved in trafficking—as long as they can supply us with credible, accurate information, it doesn't much matter. They're usually the smaller fish in the organization anyway, and we're after the big sharks. And the victims they feed on.

"Regardless, some of these people channel information to us from time to time, information such as a key player who may be making a move to acquire new...uhh... 'merchandise,' or a new territory the traffickers are moving into. We don't ask where the information came from, and they don't ask what we plan to do with it.

"It was just that kind of information we received on a large trafficking ring in Saudi Arabia. We ultimately worked with international authorities to take down some of the kingpins. We'd hoped to eviscerate the entire organization, but these groups are so loosely organized that unless you can truss them all up at the same time, the ones you didn't get simply disappear back into the slime from whence they came. You have to be satisfied with getting the ones you can.

"At any rate, we apprehended some of the members of this ring, but not before one of the subordinates told our undercover proxy that the group was exchanging women with another major trafficker in Dubai. When the authorities captured the head of the Saudi ring, he gave up Al-Dosari in exchange for a twenty-year reduction in his eighty-year sentence. He provided us the location of Al-Dosari's headquarters, and which hotels and bars his women worked. Even better, he was able to give us the names of four of these women. I presume it was because he'd used their…services."

"And 'Elena' was among the names he gave you, I presume."

"Yes. We were fortunate that one of the victims from that ring was with Al-Dosari in Dubai, and remembered Katia because she was in such horrible shape when she arrived, and because during her convalescence the two of them became somewhat close. She gave us a good physical description, told us that the woman's real name was Galina, and she was from coastal Crimea. From there, we set our researchers to work, and it didn't take long before we discovered her identity."

"I have to ask: what happened to Al-Dosari? And his henchmen? You told Katia she would never have to worry about them again."

"And she won't," replied Anthony forcefully. "We managed to transport Al-Dosari to the U.K. and prosecute him because of his ties to one of the major trafficking rings here. He was sentenced to a life term at Wakefield Prison in West Yorkshire, which just happens to be one of the most notorious in Britain. We rounded up a half-dozen of his underlings, and as usually happens with these second-rate criminals, one of them ratted out most of the others in Al-Dosari's organization. It wasn't a gigantic ring by trafficking standards, but we got about ten of them off the street for several decades."

"Were you able to talk with Katia about her former captors?"

"Yes, we interviewed her after she settled in Canada and began to mend somewhat. Apart from scattered memories of the places she lived and some of the women she'd lived with, the biggest lead we got revolved around four names..."

He and Tess spoke at the same time. "Dragos, Ulrich, Radic, and Ludmila."

"Well, I guess it's time I gave *you* some information," she said. "While talking with Katia, she resurrected a memory from when she was in London, just before she got swooped up and taken to Dubai. The condensed version is that she came downstairs for a meeting in the house, which was in the East End near Victoria Park, and her keeper was with a man she'd never seen before. Through a series of events, he answered his phone with the name 'Flemming,' then later one of the other men with him called him by name—Ulrich—and suddenly there was a face to go with the name."

Tess opened her briefcase, pulled out a large envelope and handed it to Anthony. "This is Ulrich Flemming."

Anthony opened the envelope and only partially pulled out the portrait. His voice dropped to a whisper.

"How did you get this?"

"As I said, Katia was able to unearth memories of that day, with a very clear recollection of what Flemming looked like. I have a police artist friend who met with her and they came up with this drawing. Katia says it's an extremely good likeness of the man."

Anthony sat back, then looked at Tess with admiration. "Well, you're a veritable wellspring of intelligence, Ms. Alexander." He was smiling broadly. "This will be incredibly helpful for us." He tucked the picture back into the envelope and started to hand it back to Tess.

"That's your copy. I figured you would need it. Now, I need you to do something for me: keep me informed on your progress. I hope to find the house where Katia was kept, and see what else I can discover while I'm here."

Anthony was shaking his head, a troubled expression on his face. "No, Tess, you don't want to do that. These men, these people, are incredibly dangerous, and wouldn't hesitate for an instant to slice you open with a Zombie Killer."

Tess was puzzled. "Zombie killer?"

"It's a particularly lethal type of street knife with deep serrated edges made popular in horror films."

"Yes, quite lethal, I'd imagine. Regardless, I'm well aware of the danger. You haven't mentioned my black eye."

"I…uhh…it didn't seem quite…proper. To pry," he stammered, baffled by the non sequitur.

"Oh, you British and your famous concern with propriety," Tess laughed. "It's not prying, and I'll explain. A man in Koktebel tried to kill me two days ago. Fortunately, my translator-protector, provided by my Ukrainian source, was there and managed to…neutralize the attacker. But during the course of the battle, I was slightly injured.

"I'm telling you this so you'll understand that I fully understand the danger. I understood it the day I read Katia's paper that recounted her life, the day I met with her and heard the whole ugly story, and the day I made the commitment to expose the people responsible for her imprisonment. I've been down perilous roads before in my career, which you already know, since I'm sure you vetted me thoroughly before agreeing to this meeting. However, I admit that this may be one of the riskier I've traveled. But I'm not some brainless Janie Journalist who's out for an exciting lark: I'm experienced and tough enough to know how to keep my guard up and protect myself. I'm no good to anyone if I'm dead."

Anthony sat quietly, absorbing Tess's story and words. Finally, he sighed and said, "I still don't like it."

Tess started to protest, but Anthony motioned for her to stop. "I don't like it, but upon reflection, I have no right to object. You have, after all, laid bare some evidence that we might never have found otherwise, you've brought us an excellent portrait of one of the four main traffickers, and you survived a deadly trial by fire two days ago in Ukraine. All of that counts for something. But: I. Still. Don't. Like. It." he added, tapping his hand on the table between words for emphasis.

"Good then," Tess said. "We've come to an agreement." When she saw Anthony's scowl, she laughed lightly. "A compromise, then."

His response was a good-natured grumble.

Tess glanced at her watch and groaned. "It's almost 10:30, and I need to check into my lodging and get some sleep. Can we talk more tomorrow? Decide on logistics?"

"Of course. Where are you staying?"

"I'm at Elsinore House off Northiam Street. It's supposed to be quiet, small, and hospitable—plus, it's near King Edward's Road and Victoria Park, the area where Katia's house was. If I need to go somewhere, there's the Mare Street bus line within a block, and it's close to Bethnal Green Station."

"I'll drop you off, then: traffic at this hour shouldn't be a problem, and I live in Stratford, maybe 4 kilometers from your lodging."

Forty minutes later Tess rang the bell at the B&B's front entrance, and was greeted by a smiling Night Duty Manager. Tess turned and waved at Anthony, and he pulled away from the curb.

"Good evening, ma'am. Please allow me to assist you with your luggage. Just follow me, and I will get you checked in and to your room."

Tess gladly complied, and ten minutes later was turning down the crisp white bedsheets. She was glad a second-floor room with a view of the garden was available when she made her reservations: even though the B&B was on a quiet side street, she liked the idea of having a garden outside her window, even in winter. A massive London Plane tree stood in the center of the yard, and in the soft garden lighting she spotted a winter daphne in full bloom and scattered hellebores in shades of cream to rose pink to deep purple. *First thing in the morning, I'm taking a garden tour.* She thought about her home back in California, and the landscaping she'd created over the years with the help of a local crew.

Even in the depths of winter, being among all the living, growing things fed her soul and brought her a kind of peace that few other things could.

The next morning she was greeted at her door by a gorgeous, large white dog that Tess recognized instantly as being a variation of the golden retriever called an English Cream. His tag read "Harvey," and he led her to the wood-paneled dining room for coffee, sat patiently by her side waiting for stray crumbs as she nibbled a fresh-baked scone, and accompanied her on her expedition through the delightful garden. She joked with the owner of the B&B, the aptly-named Olivia Kitchen, that she intended to dognap him and take him back to America.

With Harvey curled at her feet, Tess called Anthony to let him know she'd be doing some reconnaissance for the next few hours. Nothing that could get me eviscerated: just a curious American tourist going for a walk around Victoria Park and the surrounding neighborhoods. Maybe someone thinking about moving to London—so of course, they'd want to investigate the district.

Before he could oppose her, she said she would call him later, and ended the conversation.

Stuffing the phone in her purse, she made a mental note to buy a couple more burner phones while in the city, just to be on the safe side. *Glad I found the chance to toss the last one into the Plan'orka before I had breakfast with Vitaly. Way too many chancy conversations with it.*

Giving Harvey one last belly-rub, she stepped outside. The morning was decidedly chilly, but almost tropical compared to Kiev or even Koktebel. Around 40 degrees, and set to warm into the 50s as the day progressed. Luckily, the skies featured only scattered clouds, but Tess brought her compact umbrella anyway. Make her look more like a local. Or at least someone who "got" London weather.

She wasn't sure where she should begin her search, or even what she was looking for. King Edward's Road was about a third of a mile long, with dozens of side streets and maze-like alleys, any one of which could be the site of Katia's London quarters. The only thing to go on was a vague description of a detached, Victorian-style house painted light green, and a very large chestnut tree in the front yard. There could be hundreds if not thousands of chestnut trees in London, Tess mused, and probably half of those were in the East End.

She started off toward Victoria Park Road, the main thoroughfare into Victoria Park. It was no use to think of how far she needed to travel in blocks, thanks to London's notoriously muddled street layout where streets begin and end with little rhyme or reason and with no linear relation to one another. Her best plan was to follow Victoria Park Road east to its intersection with Skipworth Road, head north to the eastern end of King Edward's Road, then walk west the length of it. The entire route was just over a half-mile.

Of course, just because Katia said the house was "near" King Edward's Road and Victoria Park, didn't mean it was *on* King Edward's Road, or *alongside* Victoria Park. Depending upon where the north-south and east-west lines were drawn, the area could be almost three-quarters of a square mile. There was nothing Tess could do but rely on her gut instinct and hope for a miracle of discovery.

It really was a lovely winter day, especially for perpetually-gray London. People rushed by in heavy overcoats, woolen scarves and thick gloves, but after several days in the deep-freeze of Ukraine and Crimea, Tess felt perfectly comfortable in her fleece-lined stadium jacket. Her boot heels clicked rhythmically on the concrete and cobblestones as she made her way to her starting point at King Edward's Road. She would travel its length first, then make forays down the numerous side streets and lanes, taking in the neighborhoods and looking for the green Victorian boasting a sweeping old chestnut in its front yard. Yeah, good luck, she thought. They've probably repainted the house and cut down the tree.

Much of King Edward's Road was lined with apartment complexes and rowhouses—what the British call "terraced houses"—with just one or two lone residences standing testament to the region's pre-Victorian history. Disappointed, Tess began exploring side streets and cul-de-sacs, wandering up and down tree-lined avenues and into and out of single-block lanes, finding nothing but more terraced houses in a seemingly infinite number of architectural styles from storybook Queen Anne with their ornamental turrets and towers to classical Victorians to the resolutely tall and narrow Georgians. It was only when she reached backstreets like Sharon Gardens that she began to see semi-detached residences and a sprinkling of free-standing houses, but none were green Victorians with prominent chestnut trees in their front courtyards.

Tess began to expand her search territory to the neighborhoods north of Victoria Park and around Well Street Common, what Americans would call a public park, with its remarkable massing of London Plane trees and coincidentally, chestnuts. Again, up one street and down another, sometimes doubling back because she'd hit a dead-end. No single Victorians, no monster chestnut trees.

It was nearing one o'clock, and Tess badly needed lunch and coffee. That morning, her B&B host suggested a restaurant just south of Victoria Park called The Chambers, which was now just a street or two away. May as well see if getting some food will improve my luck, she thought.

The restaurant was still busy from the noon lunch hour, and as is customary in Europe, the hostess asked Tess if she would mind sharing a table. No problem at all, she replied.

The hostess showed Tess to one of the two-person tables alongside a brick wall where a woman with blonde-streaked red hair sat, reviewing the menu.

"Hello," said Tess. "I hope I'm not disturbing you."

"Hiya...and nah, no bother at all," replied the woman, who introduced herself as Amy. "Just plain A-m-y," she said with a laugh and a heavy Cockney accent. "None of this swanky 'Aimee' or 'Amie' or whatever."

They made light small talk after ordering their lunches, sharing a few innocuous tidbits with one another. Just-plain-Amy was an enthusiastic conversationalist, animated and genuine.

"So," she asked, "what do you do? You're obviously a Yank—oh, 'scuse me—an American. What are you doing here in our down-and-dirty East End?"

Tess laughed. She already liked this fun and funny woman. "Not so down-and-dirty at all these days. From my walkabout, it looks like there's been a lot of redevelopment and renewal in these neighborhoods.

"As for what I'm doing here, it all boils down to me searching for some answers. I'm a freelance writer, working on a story about an immigrant from Russia whose parents died when she was a child, and she ended up being taken in by a series of foster parents who shuffled her to a whole number of countries. Apparently her last foster mother was a prostitute, and they ended up living in a brothel in East London. I'm just trying to get to help the woman connect with her heritage." Tess rehearsed her cover story until it sounded authentic.

"Bloody hell, what an awful story," said Amy. "Does she live here now?"

"No, she's in Australia."

"How did you find out about her?"

"It was through a friend of mine who lives in Sydney now." Tess hoped she wouldn't ask any more questions.

Fortunately, just at that moment the waitress arrived with their food, and the talk turned to fries versus chips in American and British English.

As they finished their meal, Amy began peppering Tess with more questions about her life, background, and the story. Much as she enjoyed Amy's vibrancy, Tess couldn't help wishing she'd been seated with a prototype of the reticent Englishwoman. What she hoped would be a relaxing meal where she could deliberate her next moves turned into something more akin to an interrogation, albeit a friendly one.

Then Amy's eyes widened, and she sputtered excitedly. "Wait! I must be daft as a brush! My brother Paulie is a Detective Chief Inspector at the Stoke Newington Met, the Metro Police Station. I know he could help you!"

"Well, I apprecia…"

Amy cut her off in mid-sentence. "No, he's really the dog's bollocks, not at all like your usual knob head copper!"

Tess couldn't help herself, and burst out laughing. "What on earth did you just say? 'Dog's bollocks'? 'Knob head'?"

"Oh, sorry, I forgot you're an American! 'Dog's bollocks' means really great, the best, and 'knob head' is someone who's daft. An idiot. Not that all coppers are idiots, but some of them sure act that way. Some act like a smile would kill 'em. But my brother's not that way at all. He's friendly and really cares about people and loves kids and animals and helps old ladies across the street and laughs a lot and is good-looking and I can ring him up. He sometimes bounces 'tween the Shacklewell station and Stoke Newington, so we can go to whichever station he's at—they're both only about three or four kilometers away from here and less than a kilometer apart—and I do so much overtime that my boss gives me the nod about things like long lunch breaks."

Even though Tess realized she would have to tell 'Paulie' something much closer to the truth than what she'd told chatterbox Amy, she also realized she may have unearthed a gold mine in the woman. More precisely, her brother. It was well worth a try.

"Okay, Amy, I guess you have a point. He could end up being a real help. By the way, what's his last name?"

"It's Collingwood. Mine too. After my divorce I took back my family name. Ain't gonna give it up again, ever," she added with a wink.

She punched a button on her phone, asked a quick question about where her brother was, then announced, "He's at Shacklewell. Parking's bloody awful, but the station is more friendly. My car's parked on Rutland, just a hop or two from here."

As they walked, Tess asked, "You drive a car to work? Don't most Londoners take transit?"

"Ya, but this is one of those days when I have two boxes full of tech equipment I need to deliver in Southwark and Hammersmith, so I need my car. Makes a bit of a shambles of my day."

They climbed into Amy's bright blue Citroën, and ten minutes later she snagged a parking spot only a few hundred yards away from the Shacklewell Metropolitan Police Station. "Wicked! That doesn't happen very often! I usually have to slog for blocks from where I parked."

"Maybe I've brought you good luck."

"Ya, and I get to see my Paulie, too!"

Amy identified herself at the wall-mounted loudspeaker, and held her driver's license up to the closed-circuit camera. Tess did the same with her passport. The door buzzed, and they walked inside. Immediately, Amy was warmly greeted by the duty officer, who ushered them through the lobby and into the inner office space.

"So, lassie, you here to see little Paulie?" The officer had a thick Scottish brogue, and his dense, wiry eyebrows danced as he spoke.

"Ya, Peter, that I am. Oh, by the way, this is my new American friend, Tess Alexander."

Tess held out her hand, which was enveloped in the man's warm grasp. "How do you do, Lieutenant. Or, should I say, 'leftenant?' "

His eyebrows wiggled again, and he smiled broadly. "Ahh, very good! Especially for someone from across the pond. Good to meet you, m'lady."

The two women took the elevator to the fourth floor, and Amy knocked softly on the glass door into one of the side offices. A handsome man wearing a white shirt and undone tie glanced up, then sprang from his chair in obvious delight.

"Amy! What a surprise!" He embraced her enthusiastically, and planted an affectionate kiss on her cheek. "What are you doing here on a workday? Don't tell me they sacked you?" he added with a wink.

"Nah, I'm still gainfully employed, like it or not. Paulie, I want you to meet someone: this is Tess Alexander from America—California, to be precise. Tess, this is my brother Paul."

"Good to meet you, Chief Inspector. I hope we're not interrupting you."

"How do you do, Ms. Alexander? And no, you're not interrupting at all—just doing some monumentally dull paperwork."

"Paulie, Tess could really use your help on something: she's come all the way here to find out what happened to a woman who got adopted as a child and then ended up with her foster mum in a house of prostitution over in Hackney. She can give you all the details, but she's looking to maybe find the house so she can help the woman find her real story. Oh, I'm sure I've messed that up," she looked at Tess apologetically, "but I think you get the point."

"Well, I'm certainly more than happy to speak with you and see what I can do." His eyes were direct and unguarded, and his voice carried a tone of honest sincerity. Tess felt her shoulders relax. He *seemed* decent enough, although she'd need more conversation with him to be sure. She still hadn't decided just how much she should say about her actual objective.

"Smashing! I knew you could help!"

"Whoa, little sis: I said I'd *see* if I could help. As you well know, I'm not some barrack-room lawyer who makes promises I can't deliver on."

"Yeah, yeah," Amy teased. "You're a man of your word, that's a sure thing." She looked down at her omnipresent phone and grimaced. "I need to get moving or my boss will have my arse! Now, you *will* make sure Tess finds her way back to where she's staying when you're done, right?"

"Right-o, Amy bird."

"Urrggg...you know I hate being called that!"

They both laughed and embraced, then Amy turned to Tess. "Maybe we'll see each other anon?"

"That would be nice, Amy. And again, thanks so much."

"Ta-ta!" she said with a grin as she bounced out the door.

They both took a breath in the aftermath of Amy's vibrant departure.

"She's quite a gal, isn't she?" laughed Tess.

"That's putting it mildly. She was even more of a tornado when she was younger, if you can believe." He motioned to a comfortable armchair angled at the side of his desk. "Please, Ms. Alexander, have a seat."

"Thank you for taking time out of your day to let me speak with you, Chief Inspector. One request, however: please call me Tess."

He smiled, and she noticed two small dimples appear. "Of course. Tess. And only tabloid reporters and barristers call me Chief Inspector. Paul is just fine."

"How is it that you end up having to deal with tabloid reporters? Doesn't the Metro Police have someone like a public information officer?" She was hoping he wouldn't take off on a rant about the press.

"Yes—here we call them media relations—but from time to time in major cases I'll be called on to make statements and answer questions from the media. I know some of my colleagues dread that part of the job, but I rather enjoy it. By and large, I find members of the press to be diligent and genuinely interested in helping. Of course, there are exceptions, but I tend to avoid those types."

Tess breathed a discreet sign of relief, then decided to jump in with both feet.

"I'm glad to hear that, Chie...uhh, Paul...because Amy wasn't quite accurate in her description of me, or what I'm doing here in London. Not her fault, as I wasn't completely accurate when I told her, either." She noted the tiniest of furrowing in Paul's brow, and pressed on. "My mission is a lot more complicated than what I shared with your sister, but I didn't want to risk putting her in a problematic position if she knew the actual story."

"Problematic?" There was skepticism in his tone.

"I think the word you British use is dodgy. Maybe even dangerous."

"Explain. If you please."

"It's a longer story than the one Amy told you. First, you need to know that I'm an investigative reporter." She waited for a negative response, but the officer's face was impassive. "I work for the Foundation for Investigative Journalism, but in the past I've been part of investigative teams on newspapers like the *San Francisco Chronicle* and the *L.A. Times*. I have a friend who's an instructor at a university in California, and that's how I found myself involved in this story."

For the next forty-five minutes, Tess painted in broad strokes Galina's—she made a conscious decision not to reveal the woman's new identity—victimization, what Galina discovered about the trafficking ring when she was in London, and how she was rescued by Antares. Tess went on to explain her own hunting expeditions in Koktebel two days ago, along with her thus-far-fruitless attempt to discover the East End brothel and whether or not it was still operating.

His intercom buzzed once during Tess's recitation, but

Paul asked that he not be disturbed. She also heard a soft ping from his cell phone, but he ignored it. Throughout the monologue, the inspector's eyes stayed riveted to hers; occasionally he dropped his head slightly in reaction to the recounting of Galina's worst horrors. Once Tess finished, the room was silent. *This is just how it was when I told Anton, back in Kiev. There are simply no words.*

Paul cleared his throat, started to speak, then cleared it again. "Thank you for trusting me with this information, Tess. This is a very grave situation, and I recognize as well the delicacy of needing to protect Galina and her new identity. There is in fact no need to give me that information, since we—you—are focused on her previous life, not the one she lives now.

"I may in fact be able to help in your effort to uncover the location of this house, but it will no doubt take a little time. We should also be able to ascertain if it's still being used to house victims of sex trafficking: in the past two years, the Home Office has worked closely with us and the other police municipalities in nearby boroughs to address the issue of sex trafficking in the East End. We know it's a problem the U.K. is not immune to.

"In fact, smuggling of women destined for the sex trade into the U.K. and the E.U. nets traffickers almost four billion dollars a year. A sizeable percentage of these women, like Galina, are from the former Soviet bloc, and most are not the typical streetwalker. Instead, they work out of saunas, massage parlors, hotels, and—also like Galina—private flats. " He paused and offered a wan smile. "But I'm probably not telling you anything you didn't already know, am I?"

"No, you're not. For the past few months most of my time has been taken up with research into human trafficking. I thought I had a pretty good understanding of its components even before all this began simply because of my job as a journalist, but I learned that I really knew almost nothing. The prevalence of this crime around the world is staggering."

Tess found it easy to talk with the inspector, whom she finally realized was quite attractive in spite of a seriously receding hairline. His eyes were a curious shade of grayish-green reminiscent of Chinese celadon, and along with his charming dimples, his smile had an impish quality that seemed at odds with his solemn position as a police investigator. That affable impression was reinforced by the fact that he hadn't bothered to fix his slightly-askew tie or fasten the top button of his shirt. *Self-assured, but not self-important.*

"Before we go on, may I ask you something that's somewhat off-center? Off-topic?"

"You want to know how I got this remarkable shiner."

He sat back in his chair, laced his hands behind his head, and grinned. "How did you reason that out, may I ask?"

"I saw you glance very, very quickly at it—if I hadn't been paying attention, I'd have missed it, even though you've been making direct eye contact with me this whole time. But I figured sooner or later you'd ask, so here's the story." Again, Tess launched into a monologue, explaining the violent encounter with her unnamed assailant on the dark streets of Koktebel. She left out the part where Vitaly stabbed the man and dumped his body in the Plan'orka River.

Some things were better left unsaid.

14

Paul stared at her across the desk, his smile evaporated and green eyes clouded. "I believe I said something before about this being a 'grave' situation, but this shows it's even graver than I thought. The fact that someone attempted to murder you indicates you're treading on some extremely unsafe—lethal, even—ground by looking into these matters. It's obvious you've managed to rattle the cages of some ruthless characters, and I don't doubt that you're still in their sights. I would strongly suggest that the better part of valor would be for you to get yourself on the nearest flight back to the States. And once there, perhaps get yourself a guard dog. Or a bodyguard."

Tess could tell he wasn't joking, so decided against making a smart-assed crack about preverbal Neanderthal security guards. "Paul, I've said it to others, and now I'll say it to you: I understand the dangers, and know I'm putting myself in a certain amount of peril by investigating this. But that's why I'm not hesitant about utilizing my men in Ukraine and Crimea who have certain talents that I lack. The fact is, I really don't have a choice."

Paul started to speak, but Tess squelched his response. "Okay, I *do* have a choice. But this thing dropped in my lap like some deviant gift from the gods, and I have an obligation to follow through and do what I can to expose even one tiny cog in this reprehensible machine. As trite and corny as it may sound, I believe I can make a difference."

Paul sighed, turned his chair around and glanced out the window behind him. Clouds were scurrying in, and the afternoon light began taking on an uninviting gray pallor. What remained of the sun glinted feebly off the golden dome perched atop the redbrick Ramandan Mosque just next door.

"Did you know," the inspector mused quietly, "that the Ramandan Mosque was the first Turkish Cypriot mosque in the U.K., and that the building was originally a Jewish synagogue? How ironic is that? What's even more fascinating is that it's become a mecca, if you'll forgive the pun, for the celebration of social and religious diversity. They've hosted meetings for supporters of the Black Lives Matter movement, for instance, and I remember an event they held to show solidarity with Native Americans at Standing Rock. It absolutely blasts to pieces the stereotype of the rigid, insular Islamic faith that so many have. People always manage to surprise, don't they?"

He turned back toward Tess and leaned forward. "I understand and respect your commitment, Tess, and it's not my place to tell you what to do." He smiled and added, "Besides, I have a feeling that even if I tried, you'd still go forward and do whatever you think is right. I just have concerns for your safety, given the dangerousness of the people you're going after: I know from my own experience that these sorts of men would have little compunction about slashing your throat if they thought you were a threat. And clearly, someone *does* think you're a threat."

Tess nodded soberly. "You know, Inspector, Amy was right about you not being the typical ramrod-straight police officer. In fact, her exact words were that you 'really care about people and help little old ladies across the street.' I can almost visualize it: you hobbling across a boulevard with some frail, silver-haired grandmother, making sure she doesn't get knackered by some wayward double-decker bus."

Paul burst into laughter. "How does an American know the term 'knackered'?"

"Ahh, a journalist never divulges her sources," Tess answered with mock solemnity.

In the comfortable silence that followed, she became aware of the soft ticking of a pendulum clock, and turned toward the sound. It was an elegant Vienna wall clock, obviously antique, with an enamel dial and polished, swept-top burl walnut case. Surprised, she saw that she'd been with the inspector for almost two hours, and that it was nearly five o'clock.

She stood and gathered her handbag. "But I've taken up way too much of your time. Truly, I appreciate your offer to help."

"It's no trouble at all, Tess. First thing tomorrow I'll see if Scotland Yard has any record at all of this chap Ulrich Flemming and any of his cohorts. We can do a deep dive into the dark web as well and see what crawls out from under."

"I've done a fair amount of sleuthing there myself, but I'm guessing you have a number of back doors and secret alleys that we mere mortals don't know about."

"Yes," Paul chuckled, "we of the Metropolitan Police are pretty god-like indeed."

Tess smiled and offered her hand. "I believe I gave you

my cell phone and contact information?"

"Yes, I do have it. It's been a real pleasure, Tess." He took her offered hand and put his other hand atop it as they shook.

He interrupted her just before she reached the door. "Wait a moment, Tess. This may feel entirely out of bounds, and if so, I apologize. It's nearly time for me to pack it in for the day, so may I interest you in going somewhere for a beer? Perhaps you'd even allow me to take you to dinner afterward. We can chat further about the case, or you could use your finely-honed investigative skills to persuade me to unearth my most fearsome family skeletons."

Tess was delighted at the invitation. Spending more time with this good-looking, witty, and utterly charming man would be about as far from a sacrifice as she could get. "It's a great offer, Paul, but you should know upfront that I really hate beer."

"Ahh, that's a real deal-breaker, I'm afraid," he teased. "Just so you know, we *do* have other liquid refreshments in Britain besides beer. Wine, for instance. Even—and I know this is bordering on heresy to a Californian—*French* wine."

Tess harrumphed melodramatically. "If forced, I suppose I could down a glass of that primitive swill."

Laughing, Paul buzzed the duty clerk and announced he was leaving for the day, but would be reachable by phone. He slung his navy police jacket over his shoulder and ceremoniously held the door open for Tess, who bowed in mock deference, and they both took the elevator to the first floor.

"There's a great restaurant called the Four Sisters just down Kingsland Road," he said as they walked down Shacklewell Lane in the dusky sunset. "If you don't mind the bus, we're almost at the stop right now, and it will take us right there in about six minutes. Ahh, maybe seven because of what passes for rush hour in this locality."

Tess pictured rush hour back in the States with peoples' mania for private cars, and how the highways around many cities like San Francisco and Los Angeles are so clogged it's like a perpetual parking lot. Even Sacramento, which used to be referred to as a "cow town," was virtually impassible during the daily push to and from work.

They chatted about nothing in particular on the short ride to the restaurant, its vivid cobalt blue exterior standing in sharp contrast to the alternately redbrick and white-washed buildings of the neighborhood. Inside, the atmosphere was a quirky mix of refinement and relaxed lightheartedness: the soft pendant lights and elegant inset beaded mahogany wall panels contrasting with the black-and-white George Booth and Gary Larson framed wall art cartoons, and here-and-there photos of cats and dogs in weird and comical poses. Somber, deep maroon leather banquettes lined the walls, adorned with linen tablecloths and napkins folded in the shape of rabbits, turtles, and elf hats.

Tess couldn't help but smile. "I'd love to meet these four sisters. Their sense of style is certainly eclectic."

"The thing is, there *are* no four sisters. Not human ones, at least. The restaurant was started by a couple of lifelong friends and their husbands who grew up in east London back when it was pretty much just a slum, made a killing in the tech industry, then decided to take their capital and do something fun and worthwhile with it. One couple started this restaurant, which gives all its profits to The Mayhew Animal Home, and the other opened a community center for homeless street kids. They all work in and contribute to one another's businesses."

"So, where did the 'Four Sisters' come from?"

"It was an improbable coincidence: Adelaide and Jeff, the couple who own the restaurant, adopted a pair of female dogs that were rescued from the Taiwanese dog meat trade, and unbeknownst to them, their friends Marceline and Richard, who run the kid's shelter, were adopting another two pups from the same rescue group at the same time. Come to find out the dogs were all litter-mates, sisters, and thus the name of the restaurant."

Tess shook her head and laughed. "You're right about it being an improbable coincidence. They sound like terrific people, with great hearts."

By now, the host seated them at a table and they were intently studying the menu. Tess ordered the hake with hothouse tomatoes and garlic aioli, and Paul had the grilled Aylesbury duck and lemon new potatoes. He opted for a Newcastle Brown Ale, while Tess semi-reluctantly agreed to a glass of French Rieflé Steinert Grand Cru Pinot Gris. It was, she admitted, delicious.

The conversation didn't turn serious until they were sipping Irish coffees almost two hours later.

"Tell me, Tess: what happened to the fellow who tried to knife you in Crimea?"

She was afraid the question might arise, yet she still wasn't sure how to answer. Bald-faced lie? Half-truth? Complete honesty? It wasn't so much concern for herself or Vitaly that made her hesitate, as much as it was the compromising position she'd be putting Paul in if he knew the man was dead, and that neither the attack nor the killing was reported. Not to mention the fact that the body was likely in the Black Sea by now.

"I'd rather not say."

"You know, of course, that even though Crimea has been claimed by Russia, I could probably find out fairly easily if I wanted to."

She let that lighthearted comment skitter through her consciousness, considered it, and then decided he was right. But would he want to? To what end?

"Yes, I suppose you could," she replied. "But let's just say that I'm just not comfortable explaining it right now. Later, perhaps."

Paul held her gaze across the table for several seconds, then sat back on the plush leather. "Right-o, I can live with that. After all, it's not my business, except for the fact that I'm helping you ferret out your prey."

It was true: he'd gone out on a limb to help her without question, without opening a case or reporting it to his superiors, and she could imagine they'd be none too happy to find out he was conducting unofficial, not to mention unsanctioned, business on the department's ten pence.

"Is there anything more you *can* tell me that you haven't already? Anything that might help me find the needle in this haystack?"

Just then, Tess's phone buzzed. Odd, she thought: hardly anyone knew this number, since it was a brand new prepaid phone. She apologized to Paul, then and glanced at the number and ID. It was Anton.

"Paul, I'm sorry, but it's my connection in Kiev. He wouldn't be calling me unless it was urgent."

"Go ahead, Tess."

She spoke quietly into the phone. "Is everything okay?"

"I have information that does not bode well for you, and about which we must communicate."

"I can be online in a mome..." She heard a click, and the connection ended. Anton was nothing if not succinct.

"I apologize, Paul, but I need to handle this. Sounds like it's serious." She pulled out her tablet, logged onto her darknet email, and almost immediately the amber light flashed to announce the arrival of a message.

Tess sucked in her breath, waiting for whatever bad news Anton was bearing.

> Vitaly discovered the identity of man who attacked you. He was part of main trafficking ring, an enforcer who carries out dirty work such as bribes, blackmail, intimidation. And murder. He was Ukrainian, and his name was Volodymyr Popov. He went by nickname of Babay, or Bogeyman.

Tess thought for a moment, then typed.

> *Popov. Isn't that Russian?*

> Yes. His ancestry was Russian, and that was his loyalty. He knew your identity even before you arrived in Crimea. You are lucky to have lived.

> *I was lucky because Vitaly was there, and he was there because of you. I owe both of you my life. How did they knew what I look like?*

> Vitaly questioned one of Popov's men, who said your photo was in newspaper and Internet. It seems you are quite prominent, quite recognizable even outside the west. The man said they know much more: your home, even your automobile.

She considered the dire ramifications of this news.

Thanks for telling me, Anton.

I shall let you know if Vitaly or I learn more. Be careful. Take no chances.

Tess logged off, broke the connection, and looked at Paul. "You won't like this, I guarantee. But here's the gist of the conversation: my contact unearthed the name of the man who attacked me in Koktebel. It's Volodymyr Popov, a Russian loyalist even though he's a native Ukrainian. I'm sure you know that's not unusual, since many Ukrainians think of themselves as Russians first, and were ecstatic when Russia snatched Crimea. Anyway, the guy was an enforcer for the main trafficking ring responsible for Galina's imprisonment. I'd just like to know how the hell they got onto me, how they figured out my identity, and how they knew I was in Crimea." She left out the part about them knowing where she lived and the car she drove.

"Well, it probably wasn't too hard to figure out, once they realized you were a well-respected investigative journalist who specializes in exposing rotten deeds and thugs like these traffickers who prey on the weak and vulnerable."

"Wait: excuse me? How do you know about my reputation and what kinds of issues I spotlight?" Tess's voice carried an edge of irritation. Evidently, the good chief inspector knew more about her than he let on.

"I'm sorry, Tess: I didn't mean to mislead you, not at all. But the minute you walked into my office, I recognized you. I just couldn't figure out why at first. Then when we got to talking and you told me you were a journalist, it hit me. Even though you're in the States, a lot of your investigative pieces got reprinted in papers like *The*

Guardian and the *Evening Standard,* and were covered on the BBC. And of course, there was the Pulitzer."

"Why the hell didn't you say something before?" she hissed, keeping her voice low so as not to disturb other diners. Her voice fell further to a heated whisper. "I don't like being misled, Paul, and that's what this feels like."

"I concede that, and I apologize. I didn't intend to keep you in the dark about knowing who you were, but it was just never the right time to mention it. Perhaps I should put it down to my police training, keeping things close to the vest. Regardless, it was wrong of me to be economical with the truth, and I'm sorry."

His genuine remorse blunted Tess's anger. After all, it wasn't as if the man actually *lied* to her. He just withheld information. As she did with him.

"All right, Inspector Collingwood, I forgive you. This once." She smiled and extended her hand across the table.

He took her hand and held it for a moment longer than necessary. "I pledge on my honor, Ms. Alexander." His eyes—*such gorgeous eyes!*—remained focused on hers. If this wasn't flirtation, Tess thought, she'd been living in a cave for the last few decades.

"I should be heading back," Tess said. "I'm supposed to meet my man from Antares at 8 a.m. to see what he was able to dig up today. And you probably have an early morning as well, especially since you have all that extra investigating to do, thanks to me."

Paul signaled for the check, and the two went back and forth for a minute about whether he should pay, she should pay, or they should split the bill. Eventually Paul won, and with a cheery wink, handed the waiter his credit card.

"I never asked where you're staying," said Paul as they were leaving the restaurant.

"It's a small B&B called Elsinore House off Northiam Street. It has an exquisite garden just below my room, along with a huge English Cream golden retriever named Harvey who attached himself to me the moment I stepped outside my door and dutifully accompanied me on my tour of the garden. Made me miss my own place in Deer Valley, and my own golden."

"Deer Valley. That's a beautiful name. Do you actually have deer there?"

"Yes, Inspector, we actually have deer. And foxes and coyotes and mountain lions and bears as well."

"Bears?" Paul seemed alarmed. "Truly? Bears?"

"Truly, bears. California black bears, to be exact, except most of them aren't black, they're brown. Don't ask."

"And you honestly have mountain lions? Pumas?"

"Yes, but it's very rare to see one. They're nocturnal and extremely secretive, so even people who've lived in the mountains for decades have never seen one."

Paul shook his head in wonder. "Guess I'm just too much of city kid. I should think I'd be terrified all the time." They stood outside the building under a stately Victorian streetlight, the sounds of the city echoing around them. In the distance, the peculiarly British *wah-wah-wah* of a siren cut through the air.

"Uhh, you said you're at Elsinore House. That's about twenty minutes on the 236 bus, and I'd like to come along, if you don't mind. Then I can just hop on the overground to my place up near Springfield Park in Walthamstow."

"Not necessary. I have no issues with taking public transport alone here in London."

"I don't doubt you can take care of yourself, Tess, but it's actually on my way, and it would be nice to chat a little more about your mountain wildlife. Or wild life."

"Not such a wild life," Tess laughed. "When I'm home, I'm afraid my life is quite boring."

"Nevertheless, I'd like spend a little more time with you."

Tess didn't plan on objecting. Another half-hour with Paul wouldn't be exactly torture.

They climbed onto the bus, followed by one more couple. Only a half-dozen other passengers were on board, so they took two adjacent seats near the back.

"You said you have a golden: male or female?" Paul asked.

"Male. A big boy named Dancer."

"How did he come to have that name?"

"He was a purebred, though he ended up being relinquished by the breeder. When he was about four weeks old the breeder's daughter saw him out playing in their field, and apparently she said something like, 'Daddy, look: he's dancing in the sunshine!' So they decided to name him Dancer's Sunshine Child."

"Great name. But, you said he was relinquished by the breeder. Why?"

"When he was still a puppy, the breeder noticed that one of his rear legs was a little bowed, and a millimeter shorter than the others. That put him out of contention as a show dog, and the breeder was concerned that it might be a genetic defect, which would also make him unsuitable as a stud. So he surrendered Dancer to Homeward Bound Golden Retriever Rescue, and that's where I got him."

For the rest of the trip they chatted about pets and their childhood homes, and then the busman announced, "Mare Street Victoria Park Road!"

"Let me walk you to your lodging," Paul insisted, and Tess knew it had nothing to do with him fearing she'd be accosted by some hoary hobgoblin on her way there. She guessed he was a good ten years younger than she, so it was a nice ego boost to know she was still attractive, even to a younger man.

When they arrived, Harvey was there to greet them, happily bounding from one to the other as if they were long-lost pals.

"Harvey!" Mrs. Kitchen laughed at her dog's antics, clapping her hands to get his attention. "You need to leave these fine people alone now. It's time for your bed." At the word "bed," the big dog turned and happily galumphed down the hall, his feathery white tail waving a cheerful goodnight.

Once they stopped laughing, Paul and Tess turned toward each other. A charcoaled, half-devoured log smoldered in the corner fireplace, while outside the window the famous London fog swirled and spun along the sidewalks and through the trees as if it were being stirred by some ethereal being hovering above the city. The innkeeper disappeared after the dog, and the only sound in the room was an occasional snap from the dying fire and the creak of ancient floorboards above their heads.

"I hope you don't mind that I intend to kiss you goodnight, Ms. Alexander."

"Not at all, Inspector. In fact…" The rest of her words were lost against his mouth. As they kissed, he gently cradled her face with his hands, then moved them to the back of her neck and through the dense waves of her hair. Tess felt a shiver run down her spine, but this time it had nothing whatsoever to do with dread. His face had the slightest hint of stubble that nipped at her skin, but all she felt was his mouth on hers, all she tasted was the sweet tartness of the mint he'd taken from the bowl on the restaurant counter.

They pulled apart, and he hovered barely an inch from her face. "I've been waiting all night to do that."

"Would I be considered...uhh, cheeky...if I said I was too?"

Paul chuckled at her use of the British colloquialism, then turned her chin upward and kissed her again, softly and sweetly. "Nope, not cheeky at all."

She put her arm around his waist as they walked to the front door. "I'll ring you once I have anything on your quest for the house where Galina and the others were kept. With any luck, I'll be able to hit upon it fairly quickly. And one more thing: can I take you to dinner tomorrow evening?"

Tess couldn't help but laugh at Paul's straightforwardness. "I'd love to go to dinner with you, Paul, but I just don't know what the day will bring. I need to see what my connection from Antares has come up with first, whether it leads us anywhere, and for how long."

"Okay, I'll try not to take offense," he responded with a grin. "I realize you didn't come to London just to be entertained by a captivating, spellbinding British bobby."

Tess reached up and lightly kissed him on the cheek as she opened the front door. "Now, you're sure you're not afraid of getting lost or ambushed by some dastardly denizen of the night on your way back to the bus stop?"

"Ahh, m'lady, there's not a soul in the whole of London would dare to accost this pillar of English law enforcement." He kissed her on the forehead and stepped out the door, then turned around and saluted.

Tess burst into laughter, and watched him march down the sidewalk.

In a few moments, he vanished into the heavy fog.

15

"We may have pinpointed Flemming."

Tess was chatting with one of the other guests, a delightful 80-year-old woman from Scotland, and munching another of the innkeeper's delectable scones slathered with clotted cream when the morning call from Anthony came in. She excused herself and moved into the empty parlor.

"Where is he?"

"Well, it's not quite as simple as that: we've actually located two of his residences, one just outside of Weybridge in Surrey, the other in Knightsbridge. Both homes have house staff, but Flemming doesn't appear to be in residence at either location at the moment. He may just be away at one of his 'commercial' properties, although that remains to be seen. We've not yet been able to locate the house in east London that Galina told you about. Did you have any luck on your walkabout yesterday?"

"As a matter of fact, I did, but purely by coincidence. When I stopped for lunch I got seated next to a woman whose brother is a Chief Inspector with the Metropolitan Police. I ended up meeting him and spent the rest of the day interviewing him. He's going to look into finding the house, and seeing what else he can dig up."

"Are you sure that's wise?" There was a note of apprehension in Anthony's voice. "The authorities have an essential role, to be sure, but sometimes they can become a bit too high-handed when it comes to..."

Tess cut him off. "You don't have to convince me, Anthony: I've dealt with enough law enforcement to recognize the tendency of some of them to resort to bullying and intimidation. But I'm a good judge of people, and not prone to being taken in by someone who's trying to either browbeat or sweet-talk me."

"Well, I guess I should trust your judgement, and hope this chap turns out to be helpful and not a pain in our respective backsides."

A vision of last night's delicious kiss with "this chap" whizzed through Tess's brain. "I hope that as well."

"If you have nothing else planned for the day, how would you like to accompany me on an expedition to Surrey, to see if we can discern the whereabouts of the elusive Mr. Flemming? My thoughts are to present ourselves to the staff as potential buyers in the neighborhood, wanting to speak with some of the homeowners in the vicinity."

"Does that mean I can't dress in my normal frowzy wardrobe? I understand Surrey is quite upscale. "

"It is, indeed. But no need to go to extremes. I get the feeling that your apparel doesn't include much that would qualify as frowsy."

"Not unless I'm working outside in the garden. In that event, I'm a veritable vision of Charles Schulz's Pig-pen. Or, as my Scottish neighbor once misspoke, Pig-sty."

Anthony erupted in a loud, very un-British guffaw. Once they stopped laughing, he asked, "Do you have anything that might stand in for a wedding ring?"

"I do. I often wear my grandmother's wedding band next to one of my other rings. I take it you'd like me to wear it for our journey?"

"Yes, please. I'll explain on the way."

"Are we on a timetable? I'll need to make a couple of stops along the way that may take an hour or so."

"Of course. May I inquire as to the stops?"

Knowing what she was about to reveal would seriously disturb him, Tess took a deep breath and told Anthony about the call from Anton, and the fact that apparently the traffickers knew what she looked like.

"Ahh, that really does muck things up and makes things even more dodgy for you than before," he said without a small amount of dismay. "I should go alone to Surrey, just to be on the safe side."

"Absolutely not!" Tess retorted. "I believe you British have a saying: *In for a penny, in for a pound.* That's where I stand: whatever needs to be done, whatever strategy needs to be employed, I'm part of it. I won't do anything to unnecessarily risk life or limb, mine or anyone else's, but I'm not some delicate little flower who needs to be protected from the big, bad world. Besides, that's why I need to make two stops on the way to Surrey."

Anthony began to argue, but Tess was resolute. "This isn't open to debate, Anthony. Plus, it will be a lot less threatening to whomever we're going to see if there's a woman along. And you know that."

Back at the B&B, Tess emailed her editor through the darknet to let him know her progress on the story. An hour later, Anthony and his deep blue Audi pulled up in front of the inn and for the second time, Tess allowed herself to wallow in the sumptuous leather seat. He kept glancing over at her as he maneuvered through the streets, until finally his curiosity got the better of him.

"What happened to your black eye? And something… something looks different about you."

"The wonders of modern makeup. There's almost nothing that can't be covered up if you have the right product and know how to apply it. And what you're noticing is that my complexion is markedly lighter, my brows are blonder and my eyes are blue. When we finish with the stops we're making, the transformation will be complete."

She directed him to the Ray Marston wig studio just off Old Street on Charlotte Road. She'd spoken to the manager earlier that morning and explained what she needed. He was more than confident he could help.

When she emerged less than an hour later, she easily could have passed for a Norwegian: her hair, now styled in a chin-length wavy bob, was a pale champagne blonde streaked with subtle shades of butterscotch. It looked absolutely natural, despite the fact that it came from the studio's ready-made collection.

Anthony let out a faint gasp when he saw her. "You look like a completely different woman!"

"That's the idea. Now, we need to make a detour into SOHO. The store is right off Regent Street, on Kingly." Another of her calls earlier that morning was to a handful of fashion retailers, zeroing in on one that sold the type of clothing and accessories she needed.

He pulled into a parking garage between Kingly and Regent, and they walked the few steps to the shop. While one of the sales staff brought Anthony tea and directed him to a corner sofa, another saleswoman opened a dressing room and hung up several outfits in the style Tess suggested on the phone.

Forty-five minutes later she stepped out, dressed in a

sleek gray skirt that reached a few inches below her knees, black opaque stockings, lace-cut black silk blouse open at the throat, and a waist-length black leather jacket with ribbed panels and silver zippers at the cuffs and down the sides and front. On her feet were three-and-a-half-inch black stiletto heels with a curvy crisscross ankle strap and back zipper closure. Her ears sported silver hoop earrings and three narrow ear cuffs on her left ear, and at her throat was an inch-wide velvet choker with a black and ivory Victorian cameo at the front. The look was somehow edgy and sophisticated at the same time.

If she hadn't stepped out of the dressing room that he saw her walk into, Anthony simply would not have recognized her. His dazed expression told Tess her transformation was successful.

By now it was after noon, so they stopped at a small pub for a thoroughly unremarkable lunch. Before she left the car, Tess checked her phone and saw a voicemail message from Paul. He'd been doing some digging, and also talked with one of his informants to see if there was any word on the street about a sex trafficking ring operating out of an East London house. He hadn't yet heard back.

Then they headed southwest through Hackney and Shoreditch, while Anthony provided a running account of the history of the area. For a time, the A501 followed the route of Old Street, which Anthony explained could date back to the Roman era, some two thousand years ago. "It was already being called 'the old street' when Robin Hood was supposedly prowling about Sherwood Forest in the thirteenth century. There's no definitive proof that the street dates back to Roman times, but it's highly likely according to many historians, as its eastern end connects with Kingsland Road which was once a Roman road named Ermine Street."

Fascinated by history, Tess was awestruck at the antiquity of human constructions in virtually every nation of the world except the U.S., where "old" meant the 1600s. But to think they were traveling on a road that could have been built by the Romans in the first century, literally took her breath away.

They continued west past the British Library, Regent's Park and Hyde Park and a dozen other parks, alongside and then south across the looping Thames River and the perpetually-congested M3 motorway, then east again, eventually crossing the River Wey and into the ancient village of Weybridge.

"Did you ever read *The War of the Worlds* by H.G. Wells?" asked Anthony as they approached the town.

"It was one of my favorites. And then, of course, Orson Welles commandeered it for his radio show, and people in America seemed to forget that it was ever a novel."

"Ahh, yes: Welles on Wells. At any rate, you might recall that Weybridge was the spot where the Martian fighting machine was destroyed."

"That's why the name was so familiar to me!"

As they drove slowly along Weybridge Road, Anthony explained a little about the town and specifically, the very exclusive estate where they were headed.

"Relics of the Iron Age have been found in Weybridge, so this is even older than the Old Road." Turning onto Heath Road, Anthony gestured to his left and toward the soaring spire of the St. James Church. "In the medieval ages, St. Nicholas Church stood on this spot. That means a house of worship of one sort or another has been here for eight hundred years. Pretty remarkable."

"How is it you know so much about history, even tiny towns like Weybridge?"

"I've always been keen on history, and even was an undergraduate history major at university. I could often be found poking around musty old libraries and museums and the like. The main reason I know so much about Weybridge, however, is that I was born in Walton-on-Thames, which is only about six kilometers north of here, and inherited my parents' home there."

Ahh, that explains the upper-class British accent, the nearly-new Audi, and the air of sophistication. Also explains how he can afford to work for what's probably poverty wages with an organization like Antares.

"But you maintain a home in London?"

"A flat, yes. I try to come back to the country house on weekends, but my schedule doesn't always permit. I'd love to live there full-time, but with my work with Antares it just isn't practical. Hopefully I'll make the move before I'm too decrepit to enjoy it."

"So, where are we headed in Weybridge?"

"St. George's Hill, an exclusive estate divided into lots in the 1900s, and one of the U.K.'s first gated communities. It's been home to a slew of celebrities like John Lennon and Elton John, but today it's become home to a sizable number of Russian businessmen." His voice took on a decidedly sarcastic tone. "Just coincidental that our Ulrich Flemming lives there as well, I'm sure."

They crept through the narrow streets, Tess admiring the meticulously-maintained homes and gardens. "You say it's a gated community. How exactly do you propose we get in?"

"It's all been pre-arranged."

"Once we get inside the grounds, how do we explain

our presence to Flemming's house staff?"

"I have the name of an old family friend living there whom we will say allowed us entry, because they knew we were house-hunting. And by the way, our names are William and Katherine Wyse-Jones."

"No need for false IDs, I presume? Unless you took care of that as well."

"No, the staff will not ask for proof of identity. Such a request would be considered the height of impertinence."

She couldn't quite tell if he was serious or mocking, so decided to stay silent.

Anthony expertly vanquished the spiderweb of turns until they reached the security entrance. He held out his official ID, the guard briefly checked something on his computer screen, nodded, and waved them in.

It was an exquisite development, with wide, gently curving streets and meticulously landscaped public areas, even in winter. Immense homes ranged in style from classical Georgian to contemporary, many set well back from the street and hidden by head-high rhododendrons and the dense, spreading branches of Scots pines. Everywhere were forests of trees, some winter-naked and some evergreen: English oak, European beech and ash, sycamore, silver birch, cedar, Sitka and Norway spruce, and of course, the colossal horse chestnut. By their massive size, it was clear that many had been part of the land for decades or even centuries.

Anthony pulled out his phone and checked an address, made several turns in quick succession, and pulled up in front of an imposing arts and crafts mansion that Tess guessed was easily seven or eight thousand square feet. Its vast lake of emerald lawn was bordered by yards of boxwood hedges, parading toward two perfectly-matched fifty-foot-tall cypress trees. Barely visible around the corner of the house was the clear blue of a shell-shaped swimming pool, still sporting summer umbrellas and chaise lounges.

Tess wouldn't have been surprised to see the Queen emerge from the front door.

Really tough life.

Tess and Anthony walked up the steps to the ten-foot-tall double doors and rang the bell. Abbreviated Westminster chimes sounded from within the house, followed by muffled footsteps. A slightly overweight, stern-looking woman with a skullcap of hair the color of dull steel and rimless glasses perched on the edge of her nose opened the door and scrutinized the two interlopers.

"Yes? Is there something I can do for you?" She spoke in a thick Scottish brogue.

"I do beg your pardon, ma'am," said Anthony, a wide smile on his face. "My name is William Wyse-Jones, and this is my wife Katherine." He handed the woman a pale ivory embossed calling card, which bore his counterfeit name and what Tess presumed was a completely bogus address and telephone number.

"Yes?" The woman repeated, this time more snappishly. This was not an auspicious beginning.

Anthony, however, was undeterred. His smile never wavered, and his voice became even more genial. "I fear we are interrupting you, so please forgive us. But we have come seeking a bit of information and help, as potential future residents of St. George's Hill. I wonder: is Mr. Flemming available?"

"No, the owner is not in residence at the moment.

There is only minimal household staff and the estate manager. Wait here, I'll summon him." With that, she closed the door and left Tess and Anthony standing in the chilly morning air.

"Not terribly hospitable," murmured Tess.

"Perhaps she's had a bad day," Anthony whispered back.

It took nearly five minutes for the door to open again, this time held by a beefy, dark-haired man wearing a white shirt, black tie, and black trousers. He was slowly rolling Anthony's card from finger to finger in his hand.

"Mr. Wyse-Jones, is it? What might I be doing for you?" Like the housekeeper who'd greeted them, he also spoke with a strong Scottish accent, and his tone was guarded.

"I appreciate you seeing us," Anthony answered, and then explained they were prospective buyers, referred by the Thatchers, and trying to get information on what it was like to live in St. George's Hill. "We should really like to speak with Mr. Flemming, since he could provide an owner's perspective. Can you tell me where I might be able to reach him?"

Since opening the door, the manager had been ogling Tess, clearly taken by her striking good looks. He didn't appear to be similarly taken with Anthony.

"That would not be possible."

"Oh dear, that's very disappointing," Tess said, and Anthony's head jerked toward her when he heard her impeccable British accent and an unfamiliar lilt to her voice. "I was truly hoping we might be able to speak to Mr. Flemming, even have him join us for dinner at the Mulberry. I've already spoken with the manager there, and he's assured us of a table." The Mulberry was a Michelin-starred restaurant in the town's spectacular Oatlands Park Hotel.

The estate manager's entire demeanor changed and softened. Not only was this stunning blonde directly addressing him as a problem-solver, but she knew the restaurant manager well enough to procure his guarantee of a dinner table.

"I am sorry, Mrs. Wyse-Jones, but Mr. Flemming is out of town. Out of the country, in fact."

"Oh, please call me Katherine, Mr…ahh…"

"Duncan. Duncan Ceannaideach. But don't worry about the last name, as it's hard for any but the Scots to pronounce. Duncan is fine." In the space of less than a minute, Tess not only charmed the unyielding, grim-faced estate manager out of his name, but actually wrested a smile from him.

"Duncan it is, then. I feel terribly presumptuous in asking, and I completely understand if you're unable to accommodate this, but would there be any chance at all that you could tell us where Mr. Flemming is? Even a cell number would be enormously helpful." Then she shook her head and added, "No, I apologize, Duncan. That's asking far too much of you, and I shouldn't have put you in such an awkward position."

He seemed genuinely torn, which is exactly what Tess calculated. *Come on, fella—just roll over and give us his number.*

"I wish…it wouldn't be approp…I have strict…" The man was being twisted by two opposing motives, and the indecision tortured him. Even his voice wavered.

The final blow came when Tess touched his arm, and then let it slide down to his bare hand. "Duncan, I understand completely. You're a fine man."

"Thank you, ma'am...uhh, Katherine. But I see no reason why I can't at least give you Mr. Flemming's cell. I'm certain he would want to meet you when he returns."

"And when might that be?" she asked sweetly.

"A fortnight or more, the last we spoke. Although it could be sooner, if he finishes his business early."

"I forget—I'm sure my brain is composed of Swiss cheese!—but what exactly is Mr. Flemming's line of business?" She was playing the ditzy blonde stereotype to the hilt.

"Import-export," Duncan answered. Nice, convenient line of work that could easily account for frequent trips abroad to places like Ukraine and Russia, and explain his obvious affluence.

"Oh, yes, of course." Tess smiled, made direct eye contact with the man, and placed her hand on Duncan's arm once more.

"I can't say how much I appreciate your help, Duncan. I do wish Mr. Flemming were here so we could speak in person, but the telephone will have to do for now." She took the card he held out, bearing only a phone number. "Perhaps if my husband and I do decide to buy here at St. George's Hill, you and I will encounter one another again." The man was fairly squirming with anticipation of what such an "encounter" might mean.

She turned and took Anthony's hand as they walked to the car. Just before she got in, she turned and offered Duncan a tiny, three-fingered wave. "Cheerio!"

Anthony gave a muffled groan, started the car and drove down the driveway. When they were safely out of view, he started to laugh, tried to stop, and finally gave in, unable to contain himself.

"You, Ms. Tess, are a thoroughly remarkable woman!

How on earth did you know what to do to win him over? Swiss-cheese brain, indeed!" He started laughing again until tears were running down his cheeks, and finally pulled to the side of the street to compose himself.

Tess waited for Anthony's hoots to subside, smiling complacently. "I figured he was the kind of fool who'd be susceptible to being charmed, so I just poured it on. Didn't mean to steal your thunder."

"Not at all," Anthony replied with a grin. "It was a real pleasure—an honor, even—to watch a true virtuoso at work. You baited the hook, cast the line, and reeled him in like a fat sturgeon."

Now it was Tess's turn to laugh. "He does look a bit like a sturgeon, doesn't he?"

By now the sun was peering out blurrily from behind an afternoon fog bank. As before, the couple drove in comfortable silence until Tess broached the subject of when they should call Flemming, and on what pretense.

"I don't intend to call him at all," Anthony answered. "Antares works with some top-notch hackers, and they can easily triangulate his location from the phone, even if it's a burner. They can also track his calls, which is just a first step in finding out who Flemming's associates are and chasing them down." He looked over at Tess, suddenly suspicious. "And don't *you* try calling that number, either. The last thing we want to do is spook him, which is sure to happen if he were to get a call or text from an unknown number. He'd just toss the phone and get another, and we'd be back at square one."

"I get it. I wouldn't want to do anything to blow this operation. One thing, though: I desperately need to take these shoes off. As sexy as they are, they're killing my feet."

"Go right ahead. They really *are* sexy, however."

16

She was happy not to run into the affable Mrs. Kitchen when she got back to the B&B, knowing she'd have to explain the drastic change in her appearance. Harvey didn't seem to notice anything different at all, however, greeting her just as happily as before and then flopping on his back for the obligatory belly-rub.

Back in her room, she looked at her phone and noticed that Paul had left two messages she missed because she had her phone off in the event someone was trying to track her cell. The first call came just after noon. He said his snitch talked to a guy who talked to a guy who knew the house was on a dead-end street off a side street off B113. Unfortunately, there are a lot of side streets off B113, and a lot of dead-ends and cul-de-sacs transecting them, so the informant would try to find out something more specific.

Paul's second call, which came in barely twenty minutes before Tess arrived back at the B&B, said the informant left Paul a message with the duty officer that he had an address. However, he needed to see Paul in person to deliver the information: it was just too risky to give it over the phone. Paul was heading out to meet him at 6:30. He said he was still hoping they could go to dinner this evening. It was now 6:00, so she called him back, disappointed when all she got was his voicemail. She said she was thrilled with his news, but that she needed to bow out of the dinner date he'd offered, simply because she'd had an extremely demanding day. Not knowing if he'd called from his office or personal phone, she was careful not to reveal any details about the investigation or the results of her day's travels. She could tell him in person, later.

Around 2 a.m. her phone buzzed, waking her from a strange dream about picking her way down a dark, narrow alleyway where a swarm of hands snaked from the walls like malevolent octopus tentacles, bushing against her face and threatening to pull her into the black depths of the passage.

"Hello?" Her voice was raspy from sleep.

"Is this Tess Alexander?"

"Yes…who is this?" *And how did you get this number?*

"This is Chief Superintendent Charles Marley of the Stoke Newington Metropolitan Police Department."

Tess was jolted wide awake, and swung herself out of the bed. "Yes, Chief Superintendent. What can I do for you?"

"Did you place a call earlier this evening to Chief Inspector Paul Collingwood?"

"Yes, I did."

"May I ask what the purpose of that call was?"

"I was returning his call from earlier in the day, and declined his offer to take me to dinner because I was simply too exhausted. Why are you asking?" Tess didn't need to ask: from the boulder that just landed in the pit of her stomach, she knew the answer was bad. Very bad.

"I'm sorry to tell you this, Ms. Alexander, but Chief

Inspector Collingwood was killed early this evening."

Tess's knees buckled, and her voice dropped to a strained whisper. "Oh. Oh, my God. What happened?"

"I can't divulge any details yet, but it looks as if he was meeting a contact and was shot."

"Shot by whom?"

"I'm sorry, ma'am, that's all I can tell you. The investigation is still ongoing. May I ask how you knew Inspector Collingwood?"

Tess didn't feel comfortable revealing the story to the Superintendent. "Well, I had lunch with his sister, who introduced us. Just yesterday. Then we went out to dinner last night."

"I see. Well, I'm very sorry to have awakened you with such unfortunate news."

"Thank you, Superintendent. Has his sister—has Amy—been notified?"

"Yes, she has."

"If you speak with her again, be sure to deliver my deepest condolences."

"Of course. Again, sorry for waking you. I'll ring you if I have any more questions."

Tess sat silently on the edge of the bed and thought. What happened? Was this a random shooting, or did Paul get too close to something he shouldn't have? But random shootings are extremely rare in Great Britain because of the restrictive gun laws—besides, something told her it wasn't random. She knew he'd been targeted. The idea that the trafficking ring would murder a police investigator was inconceivable, but was it? They'd certainly tried to murder her. How far was it from that to assassinating a cop?

She picked up her phone and dialed Anthony. After she finished explaining about Paul's death, she waited for him to assure her it was just a tragic coincidence. Except he didn't. As she knew he wouldn't.

"Tess, this is getting far too dangerous for you to be involved in. If these people are capable of and willing to murder law enforcement, how hesitant do you think they'd be to do the same to you? Oh, wait: they already have."

"Do you expect me to just pick up my marbles and go home? That might have been an option before—although a doubtful one—but now, with Paul's murder, it's out of the question. This has made me even more determined to dig under every rock and search every filthy backwater until I find the truth." She choked back tears. "His death is on me: If I hadn't told him about the case, hadn't agreed to accept his help, he'd still be alive."

Anthony shot back. "No, Tess, you're *not* responsible. The man who shot him is responsible. The traffickers are responsible. Saying you're responsible for his death would be like me saying *I'm* responsible because if I hadn't helped rescue Galina, then none of this would have happened and he wouldn't have been meeting with the person who shot him. Paul was doing his job. The fact that he was helping you was purely incidental."

Tess tried to absorb his words, but they simply whirled away without making any impact. "Anthony, earlier you said that things were getting too dangerous for me to be involved any longer. The truth is, they're too dangerous for *you* to be involved. Paul's death has made that very clear. So, no, I'm not quitting, but you need to. I'll go it alone."

Anthony sighed. "Of course you'll not 'go it alone.' I'm invested in this, too, remember? I care just as much as you, which means I'm staying in the game. I'll do whatever I can, and will continue to share with you anything I discover. It's just that now I'm even more uneasy than I was before, despite your obvious skill at disguises and assuming another character, as witnessed by today's events."

The rest of the night Tess slept in fits and starts, finally giving up a little after six o'clock. She padded down to the kitchen in her robe and slippers, and caught Olivia Kitchen just fixing a pot of coffee.

"You're up awfully early, Tess. Anything wrong?"

Tess smiled and put on a brave face. "No, Mrs. Kitchen. I just didn't sleep well last night."

"Well, the coffee's on and should be ready in two shakes of a lamb's tail."

Harvey, who'd greeted her at the bedroom door, leaned heavily against Tess's leg and thrust his blocky head under her hand. "Harvey, you are an absolute glutton for attention," she said, squatting down and looking into his deep brown eyes. "You're a love, you know that?"

"Oh, he does indeed! But he certainly seems to have bonded with you, like nothing I've seen in all his years here. You have some very special dog magnetism, you do."

Tess ruffled the big dog's silky fur and stood up. "How about another walk in garden before coffee, Harvey?"

He gave a quiet rumble in his throat and grinned as his ruddy tongue lolled out the side of his mouth and his tail wagged furiously. "Guess that's a 'yes'!"

She replayed Paul's last messages to make sure she had all the details, then deleted them. At a loss as to what to do now, she decided to assume her rocker-chick persona and take a walk through the area where Paul's informant said the house was located.

After changing her complexion and donning the

blonde wig, she decided against the excruciating shoes from the day before, opting instead for her own knee-high leather boots with three-inch heels that were extraordinarily comfortable despite their edgy style. She pulled on a pair of charcoal jeans, added a soft gray knit top and topped it off with the leather jacket. Appraising herself in the mirror, she admitted she looked nothing like herself. Except for the fact that she wasn't anywhere near skinny enough, she could have just stepped off a SOHO fashion show runway.

Firmly instructing Harvey to stay, she crept softly down the back stairs of the B&B and out the rear door without being noticed. Now if her luck would only hold when she came back.

She walked the mile to Wick Road-Morning Lane, designated as B113, and turned left. It could have been right, but left felt somehow truer. The homes were mostly Victorians, painted in varying shades of blue, eggshell, pale yellow, and green, and for the most part very well maintained. Front yards ranged from miniscule to small—customary for London lots—and most featured a collection of bushes and large broadleaf and evergreen trees.

For nearly two hours, she prowled side streets and cul-dec-sacs, searching for anything that even vaguely resembled the green Victorian that Katia described. She was just about ready to quit in frustration, when she felt a pull toward a dead-end street about two hundred yards ahead.

And there it was: the grand and enormous horse chestnut, devoid of leaves, standing guard in front of a lovely, three-story Victorian painted light green with white trim. Nothing to suggest this was a house of torment and suffering where women were imprisoned as sex slaves for who knows how long. Nothing to suggest it except, as Tess walked slowly by the house averting her gaze, the sudden explosion of strangely paralyzing cold, the prickle along the back of her neck and the razors that skittled down her spine.

A raven-haired woman, very young. Just sixteen. Naked and bound to the spindled headboard of a metal bed.

Then came a name: *Dragos Yevtushenko.*

Tess felt bile rising in her throat, and quickened her pace to escape the malevolent lure of the house. The moment she passed by the edge of the yard, the image, the subzero chill, and the tingling vanished and she felt normal again. Whatever "normal" was.

Because it was a dead-end street, there was no way out except to go back the way she came. She veered to the opposite sidewalk and focused on the homes on that side. Just your typical London house-hunter, out for a midday survey of a prospective neighborhood.

What time was it? Nowhere near five, for sure, but Tess needed a drink. Well, I'm not about to slide into some sleazy bar in the middle of the morning, she thought. At that moment her phone buzzed. It was Anthony.

"Where are you?"

"I just found the house. Walked past it. On my way back now. Why?"

"Meet me for lunch at the White Owl Pub. It's right on the corner of Morning Lane and Well Street. I'm there now."

Less than five minutes later, they were sitting at a small table in the pub's dark oak-paneled dining area under a smoked glass pendant light that was barely bright enough to read the menu by. Anthony ordered a Guinness and Tess asked for a glass of the house red wine. She took an eager gulp the moment it arrived, draining a third of the glass.

"Are you all right?"

Tess sat back on the leather banquette and simply looked at Anthony. He would think she was as crazy as a peach-orchard boar. Oh, to hell with it.

She explained what she saw and felt when she passed by the house, then told him about her history of "seeing" things. Like her vision on Ilyushyna Street in Koktebel, foreshadowing the approach of the man who tried to kill her. And other incidents, going back to her childhood. She decided not to mention the name she'd heard in her head. Not yet.

"Well, Tess, you're nothing if not unique," Anthony said when she was finished.

"I'm not batty."

"No, you're not. I've seen too many things in these past years with Antares to doubt that there are far stronger forces at work in our world than we can comprehend. I guess you're one of those forces."

"No, I just have a peculiar...oh, call it an affinity...for picking up on things that may be out of reach for others. I'm neither exceptional nor remarkable, Anthony. It's just that sometimes my "sensors" are really close to the surface. And unfortunately once in a while, like today, the things I see make me question the essential goodness of humanity and make me wish this special 'gift' of mine could have landed on someone else's head."

"I can understand that. It must have been most... distressing."

"And there's that famous English penchant for understatement."

Their food came, and as they ate, Anthony explained what he'd discovered. Ulrich Flemming was currently en route to Moscow from London. They'd missed him by just a day at the Surrey house. But because Antares now had a name and a face to go with it, they'd been able to rattle some cages among their informants and contacts, and what dropped out were the locations of two more of the organization's prostitution houses: one in Moscow and one in Kiev. The cage-rattling also revealed an especially odious fact: this particular ring was not just involved in prostituting women, but also advertised on the darknet the sexual services of children.

"For years, Russia has been one of the worst thorns in our side," Anthony elaborated. "Even though it's continually censured for its inaction by not just the U.S. State Department and the U.K. National Crime Agency, but by the United Nations, the Russian government still turns pretty much of a blind eye to the problem of human trafficking. Adding insult to injury, Russian government officials often facilitate the sex trade by enabling victims to enter the country, and providing protection to traffickers."

Because of rampant government corruption and Putin's crackdown on civil society, Anthony went on, Russia remained totally impotent in the tracking and prosecution of human trafficking. That's why Antares already notified international authorities and set up covert surveillance at the Moscow residence to track Flemming.

"Finally some good news," said Tess. "Will it push London authorities to raid the house here?"

"That's an unknown. First, there's the matter of actually capturing Flemming, which could take days or weeks. Then, there's the negotiation over which country gets to prosecute him. Obviously, I'm hoping the U.K. will win that one, but you never know. Finally, there's the tiny matter of the authorities being completely unaware of the

London house or its location, thanks to Paul's murder. We can't very well just waltz into Metropolitan headquarters and announce it. They'd want proof and evidence, and we don't have it yet. Not unless Flemming talks, which I'd wager he won't."

"Maybe *you* can't waltz into the Met, but I can," said Tess after a few moment's deliberation. Anthony started to interrupt, but Tess raised her hand. "Hear me out. You and I both agree that I'm virtually unrecognizable in my disguise. In fact, you didn't even know it was me when I walked in here until I sat down at the table. Am I right?"

"Yes, yes, you're right. Go ahead."

"Okay: I'm going back to the neighborhood to talk with the neighbors on either side and one or two across the street, and ask if they've ever noticed any unusual comings and goings in the house. I could present myself as a...let's see: how about a freelancer with the *Daily Mail*? I can get business cards printed in about an hour so I'll seem legit, and because I'm a freelancer I won't have to show the paper's official email or phone."

"Seems like you've got it all planned out." He sounded resigned.

"No, not really. I'm plotting as I go along, figuring what makes sense and what might work. Later, I can stash myself somewhere unobtrusive where I can observe, maybe that little side pathway I spotted across the street from the house, and get some photos. Then, and this is where the whole plan could go south, I'd go in to see the Superintendent who called to tell me about Paul's death, and reveal the whole story: who I am, what I'm doing, Paul's involvement, and my discovery of the house based on the details that Paul left me coupled with what Katia said. I could present the neighbors' observations, and my photos as backup. They'd be forced to at least open an investigation, or tag it onto the probe of Paul's murder."

Anthony shook his head throughout Tess's soliloquy, but said nothing. She let him stew for a minute, and then said firmly, "Anthony, you know this will work. You know I'm right. And you know it's the only way to rescue those women. You said it yourself: it could take days or even weeks to grab Flemming and at least twice that long to extradite him, and by then the ring will have closed the house down and moved the women somewhere else. We just can't take that kind of chance with their lives."

Anthony sat and stared at Tess, clearly weighing her words. "I hate to say this, partly because I may be consigning you to great endangerment, but you may be right. I think your plan is solid, although extremely risky. Isn't there some way we can mitigate that risk? Say, could I be with you? I could wait in the car, and be ready in case you ran into trouble."

"Having a car parked on the street is going to attract a lot of attention; plus, two people means twice the chance of being seen. On the other hand..." She hesitated, then smiled. "Tell you what: I'll do the interviewing of neighbors alone, but you can come along on the surveillance. That also means I gain credibility by citing you as a witness when I talk to the Superintendent, since I'm sure he's familiar with the work of Antares."

"That doesn't ease my mind much, but I guess it's about the best I can hope for. You are, without a doubt, one of the most tenacious women I've ever met."

"People have said that." She reached over and touched his arm. "Anthony, we can do this. We can have a genuine impact. Isn't that what it's all about, when all is said and done?"

"Yes, it is. I just wish it didn't imperil you as much as it does. You didn't sign up for this, Tess."

"On the contrary: I *did* sign up for it. I knew, going in, that this was a dangerous undertaking, that I was risking a lot. It's been my choice from the very beginning."

17

Tess found a print shop nearby and after slipping the clerk a twenty-pound note, arranged for a rush order of business cards under the name of Poppy Remington, with a phony email address and telephone number. The shop wasn't busy, and the twenty-pounds-richer assistant agreed to get them done in fifteen minutes.

Anthony was already headed back to wherever he spent his days, but not before getting Tess's promise that she wouldn't do any surveillance until he joined her. In the meantime, he said, I'm just a phone call away if you need me.

Business cards in hand, Tess headed back for the neighborhood with the house of horrors. She purposely stayed on the opposite side until she passed it, then crossed the street and walked up to the neighboring house. A middle-aged man with a beer belly answered the bell, but claimed to know nothing about his neighbors to the south. Always quiet, he said, no problems. Tess asked if there was anyone else who might have seen or heard something, but he said no, he lived alone.

She had a little better luck with the house on the other side, occupied by a couple in their eighties who invited

Tess inside for tea. Tess accepted, knowing that often people were more forthcoming in a relaxed atmosphere.

"Oh, I don't really know the folks next door," the woman said, "but the girls who live there—I've only seen one or two, but I think there may be three of them—seem quite reserved. They're seldom outside, even in good weather—not like today, when our London fog makes everything bleak as an Emily Brontë novel—except to occasionally go to the store, but always in pairs, never alone. And then oftentimes gentlemen will come by but won't stay long. I think they must be the young women's brothers, as they're dressed very well, not at all like these modern English lads who walk about in torn jeans and shirts flapping in the wind." She prattled on about the lack of propriety among today's young people, and how they were always so glued to their phones and never offering so much as a fare-thee-well.

"Can you describe any of the men?"

"No dear, I don't get that good a look at them, as someone usually comes to the door right away when they ring. Except," she added thoughtfully, "the very tall gentleman who doesn't ring the bell at all, but uses his key to enter. I've seen him three, maybe four times: once when I was outside tending my roses and he drove up. He was quite pleasant, spoke to me nicely and asked how my flowers were doing. He spoke with an accent, but from where, I couldn't say. Maybe Russia?"

Tess asked for a more detailed description, and the woman did the best she could, but in the end he seemed to be the stereotype of a million other brown-haired, tall, slim English immigrants.

Finishing her tea, Tess thanked the woman—Ethel Fitzwilliams—and her silent, wizened husband, and walked down the steps from her porch.

"Oh wait, Poppy: I just remembered something!" Tess returned to the porch, and Ethel told her that the very agreeable Russian-sounding man who came to visit the residents once in a while had a prominent scar on his face, slicing from just under his left eye to the side of his mouth. It made his smile come out a little crooked, she said. Tess thanked her for the added information and waved a friendly goodbye.

The description of the scar could help immensely in identifying the man, whom Tess was positive was Dragos Yevtushenko.

Now she headed across the street to the house directly opposite the green Victorian. This one was a boxy, two-story redbrick Georgian with a hip roof and off-white shutters. The dirt path Tess spotted earlier ran toward the back of the lot about two feet off the side wall, and she hoped it would be a good spot for clandestine reconnaissance. There was no answer to the doorbell, and peering through the gauzy curtains, Tess saw furniture covered with white sheets. They've obviously gone on holiday, she thought. Probably somewhere warmer, without fog.

Just as she was making her way down the walkway, a woman appeared in the doorway of the house next door.

"Hello—are you looking for Jane and Tom?"

"Well, more or less," Tess said, and walked up on the woman's broadly curved front porch to introduce herself. The homeowner was Elizabeth Finney, and she lived there with her husband Philip. Their children were grown and living on their own, leaving the Finneys to rattle around alone in their three-story Victorian. Philip, trim, balding, and middle-aged with a thick Cockney accent, stepped outside and offered his hand. Tess explained her mission, produced the phony business card, and the couple invited her in, again for tea. She declined, fearing she'd need to find a bathroom if she drank anything more.

As they talked, the Finneys showed themselves to be just as gregarious as the elderly couple across the street, and even more observant. Yes, they both agreed, there seemed to be a fair amount of traffic to and from the house, almost all of it male. Once a very imposing woman came by, accompanied by a tall, well-dressed man with some sort of scar on the side of his face. "I could tell," Mrs. Finney said, "because I'd just come from visiting Ethel and Redmond next door when he and the woman walked up the sidewalk toward me. He and I said good day and he remarked on the lovely weather, the woman said nothing, and they went inside."

Confirmation of Yevtushenko's scar. Tess pressed her for more.

"You said there were quite a few men coming and going to the house. Was it just at a certain time of day, or all day?"

"Oh, all day," Mrs. Finney said. "I must say, I wondered a bit about it, wondered if perhaps there was something...well, something going on that shouldn't be, but there never seemed to be any problems or trouble, no fights or scenes outside and apparently quiet inside, so I wasn't disposed to report it. After all, what's to report? A house that has lots of visitors? That's certainly not illegal, is it?"

"Certainly not," agreed Tess, privately fuming at the impulse among some people to stay uninvolved.

"Did you ever see the people who lived there?"

"Only occasionally. The only ones I saw were

women—sisters, probably, or roommates, what with the astronomical price of rents in London these days. They didn't do anything like yard-work or even tending the flowers. The only time I would see them was when they walked to and from the corner market, and even that happened very rarely. I believe that some of the men who visited them were delivery men, bringing in food and such."

"Now Elizabeth," countered Mr. Finney, "how would you know they were delivery men? Did they have uniforms on?"

"Well, no, but then, if the deliveries came from the market, they would be dressed in street clothes, like the store clerks are. I just assumed that they were getting food delivered. After all, Philip, everyone has to eat!"

Mr. Finney furtively rolled his eyes and appeared to marvel at his wife's naïveté. *Whoa: I need to get Philip alone and see what he has to say. I have a hunch he doesn't think all these male visitors are there to play Scrabble.*

"Excuse me, Mrs. Finney: may I trouble you for that cup of tea after all? I got a bit of a chill earlier standing outside." Tess hoped the wife would stay in the kitchen while she talked with Mr. Finney.

"Of course, my dear, no trouble at all."

Once she was out of earshot, Tess turned to Mr. Finney. "I get the feeling that you don't think all the visitors to that house are all that innocent."

Mr. Finney squirmed in his chair, crossed and uncrossed his legs, then leaned forward. "No, I don't," he whispered. "They try to hide the men sometimes by bringing them in the side door, but it's still too many 'guests' for one household. In my opinion, I think the women are…uhh…entertaining…clients, if you get my drift. I mean, isn't that why you're doing all this poking around, talking to neighbors and such?"

"I must say, Mr. Finney, you're awfully sharp. Did you ever think about going into private investigating? I suspect you'd do exceedingly well."

The man puffed up his chest like an outsized opera singer at the compliment, which is precisely what Tess hoped for. "Well, I *am* quite good at reading other people," he said proudly. "It takes a lot to put one over on Philip Finney."

"I'm sure that's true, Mr. Finney. With your powers of observation, I would wager you saw other things over there that troubled you, or didn't seem right."

Finney recounted seeing bruises on one of the women's faces, and some "seedy" characters roughly leading other women out the side door and into a waiting car. Once he even saw a woman, quite young, maybe just a teenager, being bodily carried out, kicking and screaming until the man covered her mouth with what looked like duct tape. Like the others, she too vanished down the street in the car. A day or two later another woman would arrive, stumbling from the car as if drunk or drugged, and would be pulled into the house. None of this happened during the day, Mr. Finney said. It was almost always in the dead of night.

"How did you see all this in the dark?" Tess tried to hide her skepticism.

"Well, as Elizabeth can attest, I have trouble sleeping, and I often come down here to read or watch the telly. What Elizabeth doesn't know is that I have a pair of night-vision binoculars that I use to observe the creatures that come out at night—badgers, foxes, and the like—and one night I was gobsmacked to see a man dragging a woman out through that place's side door and literally throwing her into a large black sedan. So I decided to watch the house, and saw that kind of manky thing happening over and over."

Tess bit her tongue to keep from demanding why the hell he didn't call the police, and instead just nodded.

"I don't suppose you could tell the make of the car? Or its plate?"

"It was always a black Bentley, newer. The only thing I could make out on the plate was OT. Afraid that isn't much help."

"No, you've been *very* helpful, Mr. Fi…"

Just then, Mrs. Finney came back with the tea. From then on, the conversation was just inconsequential bits of flotsam and jetsam from Mrs. Finney's memory, with occasional input from her husband. No, she couldn't remember what the large woman looked like, except that she was dressed all in black, very severe. No, she couldn't be sure of the man's accent, but it sounded Slavic. He only said a few words, so it was hard to tell. No, none of the women from the house ever spoke to her. No, she didn't know how many there were, she guessed three or four.

Thanks to that last cup of tea, Tess knew she'd never make it back to the B&B, and apologetically asked to use the bathroom. She returned and thanked the couple for their hospitality and forthrightness. If you don't mind, she added, I might contact you again later, just to see if you remember anything else. Of course, they both chorused: come back anytime.

Tess's head itched crazily from wearing the wig, so the minute she got back to the Elsinore she yanked it off and tossed it on the bed. The blue contact lenses came next, and she heaved a sigh of relief. She'd been lucky to sneak in the back door without being seen, even by Harvey, who probably would have barked enthusiastically and given her away. She couldn't imagine how she would have explained her drastically changed appearance to her hostess.

After a hot shower to wash her matted hair and strip off the layers of makeup, Tess settled onto the bed to check her phone and email messages. Within minutes, she was asleep.

She heard the sound of her phone buzzing, but it refused to stop when she picked it up. Pressing the "answer" button did nothing, but she kept at it, becoming increasingly irritated at the sound. Opening her eyes, she realized that her phone actually *was* vibrating on the nightstand.

"Hello?"

"Glad you picked up: I've called twice and left messages. How did it go with all the neighbors this afternoon?" It was Anthony, the concern obvious in his voice.

"Sorry, Anthony. My phone was off, and when I got back to the inn I'm afraid I fell asleep before I could check my voicemail." She recounted her conversations with the two couples, including the tip about the man with the scar. "I also have his name: Dragos Yevtushenko."

"What?!" Anthony's voice went up in surprise by at least an octave. "How the he…how on earth did you find that out?"

Tess confessed that she'd "heard" it in her head when she first discovered the house. "Sorry I didn't tell you before. Guess I was waiting for some kind of corroboration that my senses were right. But hearing both neighbors mention the scar and the Russian or Slavic accent confirmed it for me."

"All right, I guess I understand your reticence. But now I can get to work finding out what I can about this Yevtushenko. Having Katia know only the first name of Dragos didn't get me very far, but this puts me on a much more attainable course."

"Great. Are you available to do some surreptitious snooping this evening? I'd like to have something concrete that I've seen with my own eyes before I go rattling on about all this to Superintendent Marley."

"Well, since I made the commitment to help, I suppose now is as good a time as any. Unfortunately, tonight won't work, but how about I pick you up around seven o'clock tomorrow evening? Wear something warm and dark. No blonde bombshell, all right?"

Tess laughed at the idea of anyone referring to her as a bombshell, and said she'd be ready the following night.

The next day, she took a bus into central London to do some sightseeing, picking up a couple of disposable phones in the process. She got back to the Elsinore around five in plenty of time to get ready for the evening's reconnaissance mission.

The day before, she'd walked past a great-smelling pizzeria about two blocks south on A107, and figured that would be a good spot for quick dinner before she and Anthony set out on their adventure. She freshened her makeup, arranged her hair into a casual updo and slipped into her darkest clothes. She brooded over what to wear over the camel-colored sweater that would be both warm and dark, until she remembered the black leather jacket that "Katherine" and "Poppy" wore. Black wasn't exactly Tess's best color unless she happened to be blonde, but she was glad to see that at least it didn't look hideous against her deep auburn hair. It would have to do.

Sporting a red rubber ball in his mouth, Harvey bounded halfway up the stairs to greet her on her way down, and she playfully raced him to the bottom and spent several minutes tossing the slobbery ball for him to retrieve.

"Oh, Harvey, if you met Dancer, you and he would be best buddies! I'm going to miss you like crazy when I leave." The dog dropped the ball at her feet and looked up expectantly, and she threw it one more time before heading out the door. "You stay here, Harvey, and keep your mama company!"

18

The pizza was as delicious as it smelled, even though the small version was more than double the amount Tess could ever eat. About halfway through she realized she should have invited Anthony to join her, and called him. No problem, he said, he'd dined earlier with a colleague. She asked him to pick her up at the pizza place instead of the B&B.

Anthony was dressed completely in black, even wearing a black chauffer's hat to hide his straw-colored hair. She suspected he'd been on this kind of stakeout before.

He parked several blocks away near a late-night pub, figuring passers-by would assume it was a patron's car. He and Tess walked casually along the route to the neighborhood as if they were locals, then turned into the cul-de-sac where the house was located.

"I'm just hoping night-vision Philip isn't on duty," she said, directing them toward Tom and Jane's empty home. Staying as close as possible to the wall of the big Georgian residence, they crept down the dirt pathway far enough to hope they were at least somewhat hidden from prying eyes, yet still able to see the subject house.

Reaching into his deep jacket pocket, Anthony pulled

out a set of small field binoculars. "Philip's not the only one with night vision around here," he whispered, handing them over to Tess so she could try them out.

"Whoa, this is *so* cool! I've never looked through night-vision binoculars before. It's like seeing a completely different world!"

"Sorry I only have one pair. We'll have to share."

"Hmmm," Tess countered, "don't they say possession is nine-tenths of the law?"

"I should have known you were nothing but a rat in sheep's clothing." The humor helped dissipate the tension they were both feeling.

Thirty minutes went by, then an hour, then two hours, and not so much as a mouse approached the house. Maybe this was going to be a bust, thought Tess. A whole lot of time and effort for nothing.

It was just past midnight when a pale square of light beamed through the side door window, then the door opened to reveal a male silhouette. The man craned his neck to look up the empty street as if waiting for someone, then closed the door. The light stayed on. Tess pulled out her phone and attached a small mobile tripod.

"Yeah, it's not as cool as your night-vision specs, but it really helps keep the camera steady, especially when you're using apps like mine that let you control the shutter speed so you can take flashless shots in low light. But," she said, looking over at Anthony, "this is probably something you already know."

"As a matter of fact, I *didn't* know about the app, and your mini-tripod is very clever indeed. I usually have my SLR camera with me, but thought it would be too bulky for tonight."

Just then, an ink-dark Bentley pulled onto the street

and drove slowly down to the narrow concrete corridor that ran alongside the green Victorian. It pulled into the driveway and waited, spewing noxious tangles of exhaust from its rear end like a gargantuan, sinister black beetle waiting for its prey.

Tess placed her tripod and camera on a small brick ledge protruding from the exterior wall of the vacant house and focused on the door. Since every window in the vehicle was deeply tinted she couldn't tell if the driver was watching in his rear-view mirror, but only hoped she and Anthony were concealed enough by the shadows to be indistinguishable if not invisible.

Now the driver-side door opened and a huge, hulking figure crawled out, profiled in the car's interior light. Tess started snapping pictures, hoping Anthony could see more facial details with his binoculars than she could. A flame jumped to life in front of his face, and he lit a cigarette. That momentary light revealed a face that was jagged and pock-marked, with a broad forehead and thick boxer's nose. Most disquieting, however, was the persistent, almost angelic smile on his lips. Tess felt her skin crawl.

Minutes inched by, and still there was no activity in the house. Tess turned to Anthony and silently shrugged her shoulders in puzzlement, and he returned the gesture. Fully twenty minutes and three cigarettes later, the side door to the house opened. The chain-smoking driver unlocked the rear-seat door as the first man emerged from the house carrying a limp object wrapped in a sheet or blanket.

As he approached the car, an arm slipped out from inside the bundle and dangled in the frigid air. Tess stifled a gasp, so shocked she almost forgot to take a photo of the grisly scene. She wondered to herself if the woman was dead or just drugged. Either way, she despised the fact that neither she nor Anthony could do anything to stop what was happening. She tasted pizza rising in her throat, and silently choked it back.

Once the Bentley drove off, Anthony motioned for Tess to move further down the path, away from the house they'd been watching.

He continued to speak in a whisper. "I saw the plate number, so we're in good shape there, and with the photos you took, assuming they pan out, I'm thinking we have enough for the Superintendent to go on. What do you think?"

Tess envisioned herself as pretty tough, but she'd been deeply disturbed by what she'd just seen and could only stare numbly, her eyes glazed.

"Tess. Tess!" Anthony hissed, and with a shudder, she came out of her stupor.

"I…I'm sorry, Anthony. All that hit me harder than I thought."

"That's perfectly understandable. It really was appalling."

"You said you got the license plate?"

"The vehicle registration plate, yes. And hopefully, you got some decent pictures that will help cement your story for Superintendent Marley. Regardless, we're both eye-witnesses to a despicable crime, and with our evidence, we've got these buggers bang to rights. Scotland Yard should have more than enough to shut down the house and arrest at least some of the operatives. But now, I think we both need a good night's sleep. If that's possible."

"Yeah, if that's possible," Tess replied leadenly.

The Elsinore was dark and the front entry was locked when Tess got back, but Mrs. Kitchen had given her a key to the rear door when she told the woman how late she could be. Dropping the key on the hall table, she dragged herself upstairs to her room, where she didn't even have the strength to undress before collapsing on the bed into a fitful, nightmare-drenched sleep.

She knew that sound. It was a dog, lightly pawing at the door. Tess opened her eyes to brilliant sunlight streaming across the bed, and the sound of Harvey begging for her to come out and play. If he'd have been a human being, she would have found him an insufferable pain in the neck, but as a dog, his obvious adoration for her was endearing. She dragged herself out of bed and opened the door to find the big white retriever perched there, grinning as innocently as a newborn baby.

"Okay, Harvey, come on in." The dog hesitated to make sure she really meant it, then dashed into the room and bounded onto the bed. Tess started laughing, then plopped up beside him. "I don't think your mother would approve of you being on a guest's bed," she whispered into his ear, at which Harvey rolled onto his back with his legs waving gaily in the air as if he couldn't care less.

Tess glanced at the clock over her shoulder, surprised to see it was already after eight o'clock. "So, my fine furry friend: do you think the good Superintendent Marley will be in by now? Think I should call him and set up an appointment?" Harvey waggled his tongue in response, and when she reached across him for her phone, he gave her a wet kiss on her cheek. "Oh, you cad!" she teased, giving him a belly rub with one hand while dialing with the other. "I'll bet you do that to *all* the girls."

"Superintendent Marley's office." The secretary was

all business, not even the hint of a smile in her voice.

"May I please speak to the superintendent? This is Tess Alexander calling."

"In regard to what?"

"Paul Collingwood's murder."

There was a lengthy pause, then a softer, "One moment, please."

"Ms. Alexander? How may I assist you?"

"It's how I can assist you, Superintendent Marley. I have important information that relates to the death of Paul Collingwood, and I'd like to come in and speak with you about it. Today would be ideal."

"What information, may I ask?"

"I'm sorry, sir, but it's not something I can discuss on the phone, although I can assure you that I won't be wasting your time and that the information may go a long way toward you solving Inspector Collingwood's murder. I'm available all day. Is there a time that would work best for you?" Over the years Tess had learned that directness tended get the best results when dealing with bureaucrats and officials.

The tapping of computer keys sounded in the background. "I could make time for you at eleven o'clock."

"That would be fine, Superintendent. I'll be there."

She ordered Harvey to stay, and quickly headed for the shower. When she finished, she found him waiting patiently right inside the bathroom door. "And now you're spying on naked ladies!" Tess cried in mock horror. "You should be ashamed of yourself!" Harvey only grinned.

He stayed in the room while she fixed her hair and makeup and got dressed, then padded behind her downstairs.

"I wondered where you'd been!" said Mrs. Kitchen to

the happy golden, and Harvey rushed to her side. "Thought maybe you'd been kidnapped by some stealthy visitor from across the pond."

"Oh, but have I ever been tempted," Tess replied, gratefully accepting a cup of the woman's rich dark coffee and a hot buttered scone. "Do you have any idea when the bus arrives at the Victoria Park Road stop, heading north up A107?"

"No, dear, but there should be a stack of schedules on the entryway table. The bus comes by quite frequently, perhaps one every ten minutes. Are you traveling far?"

"No, just up to Stoke Newington." The woman's scones were like culinary heaven.

"Ahh," she offered, drying a coffee cup on an old flour-sack dish towel, "that won't take you long, depending upon where your off-point is. Not much more than thirty minutes, is all." She hesitated, then turned to Tess with a serious look on her face. "May I ask something, dear?"

"Of course."

"The young man you were with the night you arrived—well, maybe not so young, but you all seem young to me these days—might he have been the officer who was killed on the streets night before last?"

Shocked, Tess swayed slightly. "How did you know about that?"

"The story was on the front of the *London Telegraph* yesterday, along with his picture, and it's absolutely all over the telly. I was sure I recognized him, then remembered he was the man who accompanied you back here. Did you know him well?"

"No, we just met that day, but he was a kind and decent man, and I liked him very much."

"I'm terribly sorry, Tess. I certainly do hope they catch

the scoundrel who killed him."

"As do I. Do you happen to still have that newspaper?"

She bustled over to a stack of newspapers beside the fireplace, and ruffled through them. "Yes, here it is. Right on the front page, as I said. You may keep it, dear."

"Thanks, Mrs. Kitchen." Tess was one of those rare souls who still wore a watch from time to time, and she looked down at it, then took her cup to the sink and rinsed it out. "Thank you again for the coffee and your wonderful scone—I'd love to have the recipe. Mine always turn out dry as the Sahara, and just about as tasteless."

"I'll be happy to share," Mrs. Kitchen beamed proudly. "Mr. Kitchen, God bless him, always said mine were the best scones in East London."

"I'm sure he was right. Well, I need to go back upstairs to get a little work done before I head out. Harvey's more than welcome to come with me, if you don't mind."

"Don't mind a bit, dear. Keeps him out from underfoot while I'm dusting."

Tess raced Harvey up the stairs to her room—of course, he won—where she sat on the edge of the bed and began swiping through the gallery of photos on her phone from the night before. Some were blurry, even with the tripod, and others were indistinct, but there were more than a dozen clear shots of the front of the house, the Bentley and its driver, and the man carrying the blanket-clad body with an arm hanging limp outside the covering. She deleted the useless ones, and transferred the others to their own file for easy access when she met with the police superintendent. She also synced them to her tablet, just in case something unexpected happened to her phone.

"Harvey, I'm afraid I have to take off for the day." The

dog looked up, then tried to scrunch under the bed as if he understood her words. Who knows, she thought, maybe he does. "It's okay, big guy: I'll be back this afternoon and we can play fetch out in the garden." His ears perked up at the word "fetch," and he happily tagged behind her down the stairs and to the front door. "You behave yourself, you rascal!" She rubbed the dog's head, gave his chin a quick scratch, and was rewarded by a passionately wagging tail.

Superintendent Marley was the personification of a British police official. Somber and imposing with carefully trimmed steel-gray hair and a thick silver walrus moustache, he wore the requisite blue-black jacket (more properly called a tunic in Great Britain) adorned with shoulder epaulettes and rank insignia, over a perfectly-pressed white shirt, black tie, and trousers. His shoes were polished to a blazing shine.

While he stood a good half-foot above Tess when he greeted her, he nevertheless clasped her hand warmly and held it for a second or two longer than if it were purely perfunctory. She was puzzled, considering his somewhat detached telephone persona.

"I'm pleased to make your acquaintance, Ms. Alexander," he said, his lilting accent betraying his Irish ancestry. "Following our conversation this morning, I made some inquiries and discovered that you're quite a celebrated investigator in your own right, with even a Pulitzer Prize to your credit. Quite impressive, I must say."

"Thank you, Superintendent Marley, that's kind of you to say. I appreciate you taking time to see me this morning. I was devastated by Inspector Collingwood's murder, and want to do all I can to help."

"Yes, we're all profoundly saddened by his tragic loss, especially in such a violent manner. Please, have a seat. May I offer you some tea or coffee?"

Tess accepted the offer of coffee, and Marley buzzed his secretary and asked that she bring in a cup for each of them.

Pleasantries done, Tess launched directly into her account: Galina's life as a trafficking victim, her own eventful trip to Crimea and the U.K., how she met Paul and his agreement to help track down the East London prostitution house and its overseers, her alliance with Antares, their discoveries about Ulrich Flemming and Dragos Yevtushenko, and concluding with the previous night's grim and disturbing events. Throughout the entire story, Marley sat stone-faced and silent, barely touching his coffee and apparently oblivious to the sporadic pulsing of his cell phone.

Once she finished, silence hung in the spacious office like a burial shroud, until finally the superintendent broke the stillness by pressing his intercom and requesting their now-cold coffees be swapped for hot ones.

After the secretary left, Marley took a sip of the steaming coffee and looked at Tess over the rim of the cup. "You've left me quite speechless, Ms. Alexander. That is quite a tale."

Tess felt her stomach start to clench at being discounted. "It's not a 'tale,' Superintendent. It's the absolute truth."

"Oh, please, Ms. Alexander: I didn't intend to imply that you were prevaricating or dramatizing, not at all. Forgive my use of the word 'tale'—I simply meant that it was an astonishing narrative. But I don't doubt the veracity of anything you've said. And clearly, Inspector

Collingwood didn't either."

Tess's guilt bubbled to the surface. "And unfortunately, he paid with his life."

"That is not your burden to bear, Ms. Alexander. Inspector Collingwood was attempting to right a wrong, as was his sworn duty as an officer of the Crown, and it had nothing whatsoever to do with you. The responsibility lies with the man who took his life, not with you."

"Regardless, I'll always feel in some way accountable." Then she remembered the pictures on her phone. "Oh, there's one other thing: I have some photographs of what we saw last night which I'm sure you'll want to review. They at least provide verification that what I told you actually happened."

"I appreciate that, Ms. Alexander, as they could prove very useful should the case come to trial. Under British law I'm afraid we'll need to seize your phone as part of the investigation, and send it to our Digital Forensic Unit to extract the pictures and the embedded EXIF data to verify when and where the photos were taken. I'm hoping that won't be a problem."

"No, I expected you would need the phone. Just be aware it's a disposable, and that I've deleted some of the poorer photos as well as my past conversations with Inspector Collingwood, not as a means of deception but simply because it's my practice as a journalist so I can keep both information and sources confidential in case the phone falls into the wrong hands. But you're welcome to it. In fact, there's no need to return it to me, as I have others."

The officer placed the phone in a plastic evidence bag, marked it, then looked at the clock and turned to Tess. "It's nearly 12:30, I see, yet I still have a basketful of questions.

Perhaps we could finish this conversation after lunch? Say, around two o'clock?"

"That's fine, Superintendent. I've cleared my calendar for the day, so I'm at your disposal."

When Tess stepped out of the police station, the sun was still shining brightly, a rare sight for London in the winter season. Relishing the sunshine, Tess spent the next hour exploring the neighborhood and nearby Hackney Downs, a century-old forty-acre public park lined on three sides with rows of iconic London Plane trees. She wandered through the grassy surroundings, reveling in the everyday sights of people walking their dogs or jogging or seated on picnic blankets in the warming sun, and the sounds of children playing on the carousel. Ancient oaks and maples were scattered throughout the southern portion of the park, and in the northwest corner was a charming community orchard. By the time she headed back toward the Met station the air was chilled and the sun was distinctly more insipid. The fog was asserting its dominance over the city once again.

Back in Marley's office, Tess faced a new barrage of questions. Did she have a name and contact information for her Antares source? Who was her contact in Kiev? Who was the man who'd helped her in Koktebel? Who attacked her in Koktebel, and how did he know who she was and what she was doing there? What happened to him? How did she learn Yevtushenko's name? Very little of what the superintendent asked could Tess answer. Like a reluctant witness on the stand repeatedly saying, *I refuse to answer on the grounds that it might incriminate me*, she simply couldn't reveal answers to much of what he asked in order to protect her sources. And in the case of Yevtushenko's name, to protect herself from the Superintendent deciding she was several bricks shy of a full load. She instinctively sensed who would be inclined to accept her uncanny intuitions and who wouldn't, and the restrained Metropolitan Police Superintendent Marley plainly fell into the latter category.

Finally realizing he'd gone about as far as he could with her, Marley stood up and once again offered Tess his hand. "I understand your reticence in light of your obligation to your sources, Ms. Alexander. It just makes my investigation a trifle more problematic. Nevertheless, your efforts have been extremely valuable in leading us in the right direction, and on behalf of the Metropolitan Police Department, I'd like to express my appreciation."

"You're welcome, Superintendent. What's your next move? I hope the raid will happen as soon as possible so the women can be rescued from their situation."

"I'm sure you appreciate that I'm not at liberty to say, as the investigation is ongoing." Tess had heard that line at least a thousand times, and even though at some level she understood, every time it chafed at her like heavy-duty sandpaper.

"Of course: however, I'd like to be informed."

"Well, I don't think that will be possi…"

"Superintendent," she interrupted quietly, "I believe you owe me that much. Had it not been for me, you'd still be stuck in quicksand in your investigation of Inspector Collingwood's murder, wouldn't have any idea about the East End house or Ulrich Flemming or Dragos Yevtushenko, and you'd still be in the dark that a sex trafficking ring was operating in your own back yard."

He cleared his throat, hesitated, then his shoulders dropped in resignation. "You have a point, Ms. Alexander. If you'll give me your current contact information, I'll do everything I can to keep you at least on the periphery of the loop, if not in it."

"Thank you, Superintendent. In return, please rest assured that I'll hold the fact of your cooperation totally confidential."

They shook hands again, and Tess walked out of the big glass-front building and into the afternoon's drizzling, gloomy fog.

"I'm not sure there's much more I can do here." Tess was perched on the bed with her phone, Harvey once again curled beside her, his tail thumping rhythmically on the thick down comforter. "It seems at this point, Anthony, it's in your hands and the hands of the Met police."

"Well, yes—however, I thought you might want to be on hand when we corner Flemming once he surfaces at his Surrey residence."

"But that could be a week or two from now. Plus, you don't even know he's coming directly back to Surrey."

"Except that it *won't* be a week or two," Anthony responded, "and we *do* know he's heading back to Surrey. We just got a tip that he's booked a flight back to Heathrow early tomorrow morning, and should be at the St. George's Hill house before noon."

Tess couldn't help but wonder why he'd cut his trip to Moscow so short, and it made her distinctly uneasy. "Any idea why he's coming back so soon? You don't think he got wind of something, do you?"

"I can't imagine what it would be. You just talked with Marley today, and while he's moving fast, there's no way word could have leaked outside Scotland Yard this soon, even if they called in Interpol. I'm certain that our visit to

Surrey didn't set off any alarms, and the probes that Antares initiated into Flemming's location are extremely discreet, too much so to be detected. Unless…" He seemed to be contemplating something, then began thinking out loud.

"Unless it's the turmoil that's ensued in the press and elsewhere over Paul's murder. Let's see: we have to assume it was ordered either by Flemming or someone higher than he in the food chain. But if it wasn't Flemming, and if this ring is like many others where everything is extremely compartmentalized, with one faction operating fairly independent of the others, then Flemming might not have been aware of the killing. The news might have spooked him."

"But in that case, why would he come back? Why wouldn't he just stay in Moscow until everything blows over?"

"Because he needs to make sure that his U.K. operations are secure, that any potential leaks are plugged, and any obstructions are eradicated. Which puts you right back in his cross-hairs. We're confident he knows about you, knew you were in Koktebel, and he probably knows you're now in London."

"Wait, what? You know for a fact he was aware of me in Koktebel? How is it you failed to inform me of that little detail?" The irritation was clear in her voice.

"I just received confirmation early this afternoon, Tess, while you were with Marley. We've had our assets on it since you told me Volodymyr Popov's name, and they just learned that he was likely one of Flemming's thugs."

Tess tamped down her annoyance. "So, what are the plans for Flemming's arrest? At least I presume there'll be an arrest."

"Yes, at the Weybridge house, directed and coordinated by Scotland Yard. They didn't want to do it at Heathrow in the event his security detail might relay a message to his house staff to destroy evidence. Which is why they're performing a simultaneous raid on the East End house.

"Oh, one more thing: when I spoke with Superintendent Marley this evening, we had a lengthy conversation about the case, after which he agreed, albeit reluctantly, to allow us both to be at the Met station when Flemming gets brought in and questioned. His thought was that our familiarity with the case and Galina might give police an edge in the process."

"Sounds like he believed me after all. Even after I wouldn't disclose my sources. Which reminds me: how did Marley get your number? I certainly never gave it to him, much less your name."

"He wouldn't say, but I presume he has contacts who know the workings of Antares, just as we have contacts who know the workings of the Met. It's no problem, though: he seems like a decent enough chap. A bit stuffy, but decent nevertheless."

"Did you happen to mention that Flemming knew about my visit to Crimea and the U.K.?"

"Of course I did. He was quite troubled by it, just as he is about your overall involvement in the case, not because he's mistrustful of you or your motives, but because he's genuinely apprehensive for your safety. All of us know that Flemming isn't a solo operator and that he's not reluctant to go after anyone who gets in his way. If he doesn't already know, he will soon, that you are very much getting in his way."

19

Late the next morning, Tess and Anthony met at the Stoke Newington Metropolitan Police station, waiting for news of Flemming's arrest.

Tess was more agitated than she expected to be, perhaps because she'd never been involved this closely with the takedown of such a dangerous criminal, not to mention one who may well have engineered her attempted murder. Her stomach was in knots and her head felt like it was in a vise.

Finally, Anthony's phone sounded. He listened for several moments, asked a brief question, then hung up.

"Flemming came through the estate's security entrance about five minutes ago, then just after his limo stopped in front of the house, a phalanx of police cars roared in, blocked his car, and specialty firearms officers surrounded it. Another group of officers headed to the front door of the mansion and moved inside. The driver, two security guards, and Flemming stepped out of the car with their hands in the air, and Flemming calmly put his hands behind his back to be cuffed. It's over, Tess."

She could hardly believe it. It took less than thirty seconds to take into custody one of the men responsible for holding Katia as a sex slave for most of her life. Of course, she knew all too well that arrest and imprisonment were two different things, but if the jailing of Al-Dosari was any indication, chances were good that Flemming would suffer the same fate.

"It'll take at least two hours before they get here," said Anthony, "and I for one don't fancy the thought of just sitting around here waiting. Let's go get some lunch if you're up for it."

"Oh, yeah, I'm really up for it: I was so edgy this morning that I couldn't even manage one of Mrs. Kitchen's incredible scones."

After their lunch at a noisy pub where the food was mediocre but the raucous atmosphere was a perfect antidote to the morning's mounting disquiet, they arrived back at the Met station just before the squad cars rolled in from Surrey. Superintendent Marley was already there, and directed Tess and Anthony to a small waiting area connected to a long hallway.

Never one to wait around for something to happen, after several minutes Tess decided to walk into the hall, at the end of which was a steel-doored elevator. Once she heard the clunk of the elevator's arrival, everything shifted into slow motion: she turned toward the sound, saw the elevator doors inch open and an officer step out, followed by a second officer escorting a short, heavyset man with ink-black eyes, pearlescent teeth, and dark hair ironed back from his forehead. He wore a short beard, new since Katia first described him, but Tess would have recognized him instantly from the police artist sketch. As before, his dress was subdued and elegant, featuring an ascot at his neck and the diamond tie pin Katia so perfectly detailed.

Their eyes met, and at first Flemming looked confused. His lips started to form a small "o," then his eyes narrowed into snake-like slits as the muscles on both sides of his jaws clenched furiously. For an instant, his face contorted in rage and Tess swore she heard him hiss. Then just as quickly he regained control, appearing almost nonchalant, an ordinary citizen coming into police headquarters to explain and rectify what was obviously a huge misunderstanding.

All the while, Tess simply stared at him, stone-faced. She refused to give him the satisfaction of knowing that she was deeply frightened. Just by her presence in the station, Flemming certainly realized that she was at least partly responsible for his capture, only adding to whatever fury he felt that this single-minded American woman—a *woman!*—who somehow survived the attack in Crimea, was now a clear and present danger to his livelihood. With his arrest, Flemming might have lost day-to-day control of his followers and disciples, but anyone who thought he couldn't still exert his evil influence, couldn't still transform threats into lethal reality, was a fool.

Superintendent Marley stepped out of the interview room as they were ushering Flemming inside, and saw Tess standing in the corridor. A look of consternation crossed his face as he strode toward her. "I specifically asked that you remain in the waiting area," he said sternly.

"Well, I guess I'm not very good at following instructions. Besides which, it doesn't make a difference that Flemming saw me, except that it obviously threw him off his game. He already knows what I look like, and sooner or later he'd have found out that I was in some way involved in his arrest. This just made it sooner."

Marley scowled, then stomped off.

"Don't think you've won any points with the Superintendent this afternoon," said Anthony from his vantage point in the doorway.

"No, I don't suppose I have."

Eventually, Superintendent Marley got over his fit of pique and sat down with the two civilians to bring them up to speed on the progress of the questioning. As expected, Flemming refused to admit anything, especially any ties to the just-raided East End house. He was nothing more than a successful import-export entrepreneur, he insisted, and certainly wouldn't be involved in anything so tawdry as sex trafficking. What about his reaction to the woman he'd seen in the hallway that afternoon? Never saw her before in my life, he said, brushing off any assertion that he recognized Tess.

What he didn't know was that the Met's Trafficking Unit, working with its Forensic Investigation Specialist Crime Directorate, was busy unraveling a cache of files from a hidden safe in Flemming's Weybridge house, thanks to a tip from of one of the house staff who knew its location and who was terrified he'd be implicated in Flemming's crimes. They also confiscated his computer, tablet, and cell phone, none of which he'd been able to wipe or destroy before he was caught, and were hopeful they could crack the passcodes for all three. At the same time, the hunt was on for Dragos Yevtushenko and the driver of the black Bentley, either or both of whom might be convinced to flip on Flemming in return for reduced sentences or entry into the U.K.'s witness protection program.

While four women were rescued from the East London house, they were refusing to talk, terrorized into silence by their experiences. It would take months of counseling, explained Anthony, for them to trust that they were actually free and no longer in danger from their captors.

Some victims were so damaged by their imprisonment, especially if it was lengthy, that they never fully recovered: some took their own lives or died of drug overdoses, some returned to prostitution as the only life they'd ever known. Then there were the few, like Ekaterina, who managed to claw their way out of the cesspool and actually begin rebuilding their lives and souls.

Marley explained that Flemming's interrogation would likely go on for some hours, and that he would fill them in by phone once it was over. It was obvious he wanted these two unofficial interlopers out of his station, the sooner the better. Tess pondered objecting out of sheer stubbornness more than anything else, but the idea of sitting all afternoon in a windowless room inside a barren and cheerless police station wasn't especially palatable.

Anthony dropped her at the Elsinore, and Tess spent the rest of the day playing with Harvey and trying to plan out her next moves. She very much wanted to get back home, but needed to be absolutely certain first that there was nothing further she could do in Great Britain. She was sorely tempted to detour to Moscow to see if she could find Flemming's hideaway there, and equally drawn to explore Dubai, but neither of these destinations would further her investigation, and neither would help her locate any other members of the trafficking operation or more specifically, the thus-far-unknown Radic or Ludmila. Who were they? Where did they fit into the filthy machinery of the ring? Were they just cogs, or among the major spokes? And how the hell could she ever hope to find them?

Her phone buzzed at a little after noon the next day. It was Superintendent Marley. Tess was surprised he chose to speak to her rather than letting Anthony relay the message, only because she'd sorely tested his patience these last few days. His voice, however, was cordial and gave no hint of exasperation.

"I wish I could tell you that we managed to break Flemming, but regrettably, that wasn't to be. He continued protesting his innocence all afternoon and into this morning, saying nothing at all meaningful or useful. Eventually we charged him with kidnapping, human trafficking, operating a house of prostitution, and money-laundering. We may add more charges later, but that will have to do for now to keep him in Pentonville Prison without bail."

"Have you made any progress in locating Yevtushenko or the driver? Or Paul's killer?"

"Not as yet. Our technical experts are still trying to decrypt Flemming's home computer, and the hope is we'll find something there that will lead us to one or all three. That said, you've been of great assistance thus far, to be sure. When were you planning on returning to the States?" Tess picked up a note of hopefulness in his voice at the thought of being rid of her.

"Certainly within the next day or two unless something unexpected happens to keep me here longer. Speaking of which, there's something I need to ask of you."

The silence was palpable, and then Marley reluctantly responded. "I cannot promise I'll be able to comply."

"I need to speak to the women you freed from the East London house. Are they under arrest? In protective custody?"

"They are being safeguarded at the moment at an undisclosed location. So you see, there is no way I can allow you access to them."

Tess suspected that would be his response, and she was prepared to make her case. "Superintendent, I understand your need to keep these women in safe hands. I also understand what they've gone through, owing to my time with Galina. But it's because of that, because of my connection with Galina, that I believe I can reach them." She took a deep breath, and decided to reveal her secret. "Plus, I know the name of one of them."

"What?! How is that?" His annoyance was obvious.

"Up until now there was no reason to tell you, Superintendent. The women hadn't yet been rescued, and I couldn't be certain I would have a name until I spoke with Galina, which I did yesterday."

"And what is this name?" he huffed.

"Before I reveal her name to you I need to approach this woman. She has doubtless been severely traumatized, and I think she'd be much more willing to open up to a woman and a civilian, not to mention someone who knows Galina, than someone from law enforcement. If she refuses to talk to me, I'll give you her name. But if I can get some valuable information from her, information that might help put these bastards behind bars for the rest of their lives, it's worth your while to let me communicate with her."

This time, Marley hesitated for so long that Tess wondered if they'd been cut off. Then she heard his distinctive sigh. "This is highly, highly irregular, you understand. Not to mention probably against every regulation in the book, something I am *not* accustomed to doing. But in this case, in this *one* case, I will allow you to speak with the women. But it will be on my terms. *My terms*, Ms. Alexander," he emphasized.

"Absolutely, Superintendent Marley." She just hoped

those terms wouldn't be too onerous.

It turned out, they weren't. He wanted to move the women from their current safe house to another location, then have one of his officers drive Tess there. He also required that she consent to a debriefing with Marley afterward. She could live with that.

Tess's police escort arrived at ten o'clock the next morning. As with the arrest of Flemming, she was surprised at how quickly the Met's institutional wheels could be set into motion when the occasion demanded it and when someone with authority worked to grease them. She was genuinely impressed with the superintendent's efforts throughout this melodrama, no matter how grudging they were.

The officer charged with transporting her to the new location was a young sergeant with mousy brown hair and matching moustache, who greeted her with a smile more suitable to a hotel concierge than a glorified livery driver. He told her his name was Hugh Beaumont, and that he'd been with the Met for five years. Started out at the Marine Policing Unit at Wapping, he said, patrolling the docks and the Thames, and then moved up to the Stoke Newington Station a year ago. Yes, he liked this assignment much better, as he wasn't crazy about working the waterways: he couldn't really swim all that well, and it made him nervous to be on the water.

The ten-mile drive north from the inn to the borough of Enfield took a little over thirty minutes: up past Stoke Newington, through Stamford Hill, beside Bruce Castle Park, then continuing along Great Cambridge Road and across the long but narrow Pymmes Brook, known in the twelfth century as the *Medeseye* from the Old English words for "meadow marsh-stream." The route then took them past the upscale Palace Gardens Shopping Center and finally into Enfield Town, where they wove through a jumble of streets until pulling into the short entry drive that ran beside a modest, two-story stucco home at the end of a short dead-end street.

Five minutes earlier, Sergeant Beaumont alerted the onsite protection unit; as they pulled up to the residence, he handed over his credentials and Tess's passport to verify their identities. Both were asked to provide their fingerprints on a digital screen, which flashed a green "Verified" banner a few seconds later. Before they could proceed, however, an officer thoroughly searched both Tess and the sergeant for weapons. If the women had been watching, which Tess was sure they weren't as they were likely concealed in an interior room for safety, they might have been comforted by the robust security measures. Of course, they were still prisoners, just of a more benevolent overlord.

Tess and Sergeant Beaumont walked into the entry, then Tess was ushered through wide French doors into an adjacent parlor containing a small couch and two upholstered Chippendale-style chairs. A log fire sizzled in the open-hearth brick fireplace, adding to the room's coziness. Divided-light windows looked out onto the small rear yard, desolate in the pale winter light.

One of the protective officers asked if she would care for coffee or tea, but she shook her head. "Not right now, thank you."

A minute later she heard footsteps and four women entered the room. They were all dressed casually, but in clothing that was obviously not their own: everything was oddly-matched and by turns too loose, too short or long, or simply ill-fitting. Not one of them made eye contact with

Tess, or even acknowledged her presence. Their lifeless faces were like so many others she'd seen, victims of abuse or torture or worse who long ago abandoned any semblance of hope. She wondered if she would be able to reach any of them.

"I'm Tess Alexander," she began softly, "and I'm from the United States. I've been working to hunt down the people who held you and made you work for them, and bring them to justice. I'd like you to talk to me about those people, about where they held you before you were at the house in London, and anything that would help me find them. I presume you know that at least one of them has been caught, but we know there are others."

"Why would we trust you...believe you?" A tiny, brown-skinned woman with an East Indian accent who looked like she was barely a teenager spoke up, her face a mask of resentment. "You have no idea of where…how… what we…have lived. Who we are. Leave us alone."

"And why are you here?" That from a striking blonde glaring directly at Tess with snapping, sapphire eyes. "You're police…"

"No," Tess answered, "I'm *not* the police. Not Immigration, not any kind of official." She decided to take a chance and jump in. "I'm the friend of a woman who was in the house where you were about three years ago. She told me everything about her life, what she'd been through—what you've all been through—and about the people who kept you. About Ulrich, Radic, Dragos, and Ludmila."

All four women flinched as if they'd been jolted by an electric current. She continued on. "You would have known her as Galina." With that, the blonde staggered unsteadily, and slid down onto the couch. Her already-pale complexion turned ashen, and she began to swallow convulsively. Tess leapt up, and spotting a wastebasket in the corner, rushed it over to the woman, who vomited violently into it.

"Officer, we need some water," called Tess loudly toward the closed door. None of the other former captives moved, indifferent to the woman's distress. They'd seen far worse than this and had likely learned to ignore one another's suffering. Several seconds later a guard hurried in with a bottle of water, which Tess exchanged for the soiled wastebasket. "Can you please take care of this, sergeant?"

Once he left and closed the door again, Tess sat down alongside the shaken woman. "I'm sorry to have spoken so directly, but there was really no other way." She lowered her voice so that only the woman beside her could hear. "You're Raisa, aren't you?"

"What? No, I…that is not…how…how do you…." And then she fell silent, looking down at her hands that lay like fallen birds in her lap. Her nails were ragged and bitten to the quick, with cuticles so raw that one or two bore remnants of dried blood. Through the folds of her thin cotton sweater, it was easy to see the frenzied beating of her heart.

Tess simply sat, waiting. Across the room, heads bowed in whispered conversation, stood the Indian girl and a stunning, almond-skinned woman with arrow-straight hair in a shade of pure ebony that reached nearly to her waist. The fourth woman, just as pale-skinned as Raisa but with short mushroom-colored hair that framed her round face with a wild halo of corkscrew curls, sat alone, thumbing through a dog-eared copy of *Vogue*.

Raisa finally lifted her head and focused on Tess, her

guarded eyes searching Tess's for…what? Truth? Answers? It was hard to tell. After that she looked, one by one, at her three fellow captives, then back at Tess. She let out a shallow, stuttering breath and gripped the edges of the sun-yellow couch cushion. "Yes, I…I am Raisa." Silence, then a few more whispered words. "Galina told of me?"

"Yes, she did. She said you were from Chechnya, a very small town called Mekenskaya."

Raisa's face softened at the name of her birthplace. "Yes. Mekenskaya. Can you tell me of Galina? Is she safe?"

"Galina is well and happy. She was taken to Dubai from here, and later rescued by an organization that helps to free women and children who are victims of trafficking. I've been working with that same organization here in London to discover where you were being kept, where Galina was kept, and to expose your captors."

Skepticism gave her voice a harsh edge. "Why? Why do you care?"

The same question I asked Vitaly. "I care because I believe in justice. Because what happens to women like you should never be allowed to happen. A very famous man once said that the only thing necessary for evil to prosper is for good people to do nothing. We can't afford to turn away, or we're no better than the people who do evil."

Raisa seemed puzzled. "But you are not police?"

"No, I'm an ordinary person, a writer." She briefly described the types of exposés she wrote, then explained that while she sometimes worked *with* law enforcement, she wasn't *part* of it.

"You write in newspapers? Books?"

"Mostly newspapers and magazines."

"And you wish to talk to us?"

"Yes, I want very much to talk with all of you. I have some questions I want to ask, things that will help me to find the people whose names I mentioned. Can you speak to them for me?"

"I will ask. Please to wait." Raisa stood up and motioned for the women to follow her, and they walked out of the room. A few minutes later, Sergeant Beaumont stuck his head through the half-open door and asked if she'd like something. Coffee would be great, she answered.

It was delivered in a hefty mug, which was almost empty by the time Raisa came back. She was alone.

"They do not wish to speak now. They feel difficult about talking of the people you told to us. They are afraid."

"And you are not?"

"I am. But because you are a friend with Galina, and she trusted you, then I shall also trust you. They do not know Galina, so it is not the same for them."

"I understand. Thank you for speaking with me. One very important thing: unless you give me permission I will not reveal your name to anyone. The police hope you'll all be willing to give them your names so they can do their investigation, but it's up to you."

Raisa nodded, and sat down on the other end of couch from Tess.

"Would you like some coffee or tea?"

"No. My stomach is still not right. Perhaps later."

Tess set out her digital recorder, explained to Raisa what it was and that she used it for accuracy more than anything else, and then looked at the notes she'd written after her last meeting with the superintendent. She knew that rapid-fire interrogation would likely alarm the woman so she took it slowly, starting with innocuous questions about her home and family in Chechnya.

Thirty minutes later, she was ready to delve into touchier issues like Raisa's life in the East London house and anything she knew about the Four Horsemen. Three horsemen and a woman.

Flemming came to the house several times in the five years she'd been there, Raisa said—in fact, she was standing next to Galina on the day his full name slipped out. From what she could tell, he seemed to be in charge, and he was almost always there when women were taken away and new ones were brought in.

"A few nights before you were rescued, a woman wrapped in a blanket was carried out of the house and driven off in a black car. Can you tell me anything about that? Was Flemming there?"

Raisa swallowed hard and began picking at her fingernails. "No, he did not come at night. But I am sure he knew: there was a telephone call to Grigory, the man who directed the house, an hour before. I heard him say 'yes, sir' many times, so I knew he must be speaking with Flemming. Then Grigory went upstairs and got Eva, but she was very disturbed and crying and yelling. I saw him put a needle into her arm and very soon she was to sleep. I think Grigory may have given her too much of the medicine, though, because her breath was very weak, but then they took her away, so I do not know." She stopped and turned to Tess. "Did the police take Grigory?"

"Yes, they did. He's been charged, and the hope is that he'll tell them about the other traffickers."

"He will not talk, I am sure. He is too faithful to Flemming." She spoke the next sentence with particular disgust. "Grigory regards him almost as a father."

Tess then brought up the scar-faced Dragos Yevtushenko, and Raisa nodded in recognition. Yes, she confirmed, he was often with Flemming, but didn't come to the house regularly. In the beginning, he would arrive on foot with a heavy, unsmiling, dark-haired woman.

After this, Raisa hesitated, her fingers knotting together while her mouth opened and closed as if she were trying to decide whether or not to say something. Tess wasn't about to push.

"We also…the house also had a…woman. Not part of us. Part of Flemming and the others like him." A light flush crept onto her cheeks, either in shame or anger. "At first it was one, then another came. The one who was with the tall man with the scar."

Tess waited for several seconds, then asked calmly, "What did these women do?"

"At first, they were as friends to us, but that was false. They would speak gently if we were hurt from something a customer did, and would comfort us and apply bandages or ice if that was needed. But if we did something wrong, if we refused to do something for a man, then afterward she would scream and use filthy names and beat us, sometimes with a wide strap that was split into many tails with large, silver, metal ends that would cause blood."

Tess suppressed a gasp as she pictured the brutal punishment device. No, not punishment. Torture.

Raisa took a deep breath, then continued. "The fat woman was the worst. She always smiled when she beat us, and laughed when we cried out. She used the strap more than the others. I knew her when I was held in Bucharest."

"You knew her before? You mean, she was at the place where you were kept in Bucharest?"

"Yes. She also was two times to the place where I was in Syria, but did not stay there. This was the one whose name you spoke. Ludmila."

So, the mysterious Ludmila was an intermittent rotating house-mother. House-monster.

"Was she Russian, or…?"

"She spoke Russian. Some English when she was here, in London."

Okay: we have Ulrich Flemming, naturalized Englishman from Germany; then Dragos Yevtushenko, probably from Ukraine; and now a Russian Ludmila something-or-other. Radic, you're the only remaining mystery, though from your name, I'm guessing you're from Croatia. Maybe Serbia.

Tess asked Raisa if she could describe Ludmila. It was too much to hope for that she'd be able to provide enough detail for a sketch, but anything was better than nothing. She closed her eyes, and described a grim-faced, heavyset woman about 170 centimeters tall —maybe five foot six—with dark, gray-streaked hair that she always wore in a tight, netted bun at the back of her head. She had beady black-brown eyes and prominent furrows between her dark, disheveled eyebrows, sallow skin that made her seem perpetually ill, jowls sagging heavily from her jaws, and fleshy hands with fingers so short and wide they seemed almost stunted. She seldom wore anything but black, making the overall effect one of cold, ugly maliciousness, a perfect mirror of the woman's character.

"All of you seem to know the names of four people: Ulrich, Radic, Dragos, and Ludmila. That probably means that Ludmila was one of the four people in charge. Did you get that impression? That she was one of the leaders?"

"Yes, that is so. When she was with Ulrich, they seemed equal. And she often gave orders to Grigory, and on the telephone to others."

"Did you ever hear her last name?"

"Never. But it began with a 'Z,' as she would sometimes leave a paper for Grigory and sign it 'Ludmila Z.' "

"What about Radic?"

"I never saw him, only heard his name."

"And Dragos? What can you tell me about him?"

"He was often cruel, worse than the others, even Ludmila. He was not there often; most of the time, the others would talk by phone to him. And when they said his name, there was…I cannot find the word…*bespokoynyy*. As if they were not settled."

"Frightened? Uneasy?" Tess tried.

"Yes, that is it. Uneasy."

If his partners in crime are 'uneasy' just saying his name, seems as if this guy's more dangerous than most.

"Can you can remember anyone else saying anything about Dragos? Anything that would give us a hint about who he is, where to find him?"

"I cannot think so."

"Can you ask the other women? Perhaps someone heard something."

Raisa shifted in her seat uncomfortably as if she were having an internal argument as to whether or not she should approach the others. They'd made it clear they didn't want to get involved, and probably would be even more reluctant if they thought that Dragos could be more of a threat than any of the others.

"Raisa, I know this is hard: but unless we can find and capture Dragos, he will go on to enslave many more women and children in the years ahead. Your friends can help rid the word of a monster."

Raisa thought for several moments, then stood up. "I shall try."

Ten minutes later she returned to the room, a barely-perceptible smile on her face. After much prodding, one of the women admitted she once overheard Ludmila in the middle of a heated telephone argument with Dragos, speaking a mix of Russian and Ukrainian. She knew it was Dragos because the woman used his name several times, and she knew the language was Ukrainian because she'd grown up in Kiev.

Then another of the former captives, emboldened by the first admission, made an even more startling statement: she heard Ulrich refer to Dragos as "that crazy Ukrainian" when he was talking with Ludmila in the kitchen one afternoon, and later heard him talking with someone on the phone when he said something about *Solntsevskaya Bratva*—the Solntsevskaya Brotherhood, one of Russia's most lethal and powerful criminal organizations—and a moment later said Dragos's name.

This is a huge lead, tying all this to Russian organized crime. Before now, there was nothing but this pot of disconnected spaghetti strings, but now we may have a way to link them together.

"This helps very much, Raisa. There's one more thing you can do for me, if you're willing: please ask the woman who told you about *Solntsevskaya Bratva* to speak with me. Explain she won't be endangered and I won't reveal her name, and that whatever she says I will *only* use to find Dragos. It's very, very important."

Raisa shook her head and said, "I do not think she will agree. She was very frightened just telling it to me."

"Yes, I understand that, but try. Tell her you trust me, that Galina trusts me."

Raisa turned and walked out of the room without saying anything. Tess wasn't at all encouraged, but if nothing else, she remained the personification of the "hope springs eternal" mantra. Someone once described her as having a lethal level of optimism.

The minutes ticked by: five, then ten, then fifteen. That optimism was dimming quickly, like the sun behind the writhing, impenetrable English fog.

Then the door clicked open, and Tess turned to see Raisa accompanied by the curly-haired woman who was sitting by herself when Tess first saw her.

"She does not wish to tell you her name, but will speak more of what she heard that day. Please to turn off the recorder."

Tess switched it off, and slid the machine into her small leather briefcase. Raisa nodded, and the two sat down on the upholstered side chairs. The second woman was barely perched on the edge of the seat, as if ready to take flight at the slightest provocation.

"May I ask you some questions?"

The woman nodded rapidly, a small, drab bird pecking at a trail of seeds.

"Was this the only time you heard Ulrich mention the *Solntsevskaya Bratva*?"

Another quick nod.

"Did you ever hear him speak about the Ukrainian Mafia?"

No response. She'd hit a nerve. "Perhaps you heard something related to human trafficking, prostitution, that kind of thing, in Ukraine?"

There was a long pause. "I heard him say the words *Torgovlya zhenshchinami*—women trafficking. He said 'Mikhailovich' while speaking of Dragos." Tess knew that Vyacheslav Mikhailovich was an especially brutal Ukrainian-born boss of several Russian organized crime syndicates, including those operating Ukraine. *So, it looks like Yevtushenko is indeed connected to the Ukrainian mafia.*

Tess tried a different tack. "This wasn't the only time you overheard Ulrich on the telephone. Am I right?" She kept her voice soft and reassuring.

After a beat or two, the woman nodded.

"Okay, think back: did his voice sound like he was *giving* orders or *getting* them?"

Almost instantly she answered, "Getting. He would even say, 'yes, sir' sometimes."

"Did he ever mention Ukraine?"

The woman looked down, then shook her head.

"Are you sure? Remember, he will never find out you said anything."

She kept her head lowered, and dropped her voice so much that Tess needed to lean forward to hear. "I heard him…he one time asked…if Dragos would be going to Odessa soon. He said another name I did not know, asked if that man would be delivering more 'merchandise' from Ukraine to London. I did not know the word 'merchandise,' and had to ask Raisa." She raised her eyes to Tess, then stood up. "That is all I know." Before Tess could even thank her, she walked out the door and shut it behind her.

Raisa stood to leave. "Is there anything else you wish to know from me? I am very tired, and do not know what more I can report."

"Is there anything I can tell Galina for you?"

Raisa smiled for the first time. "Yes. Say I think of her, and that one day I hope to be as content as you have said she is."

"I hope so, too, Raisa. You deserve that. Oh, by the way: what is your last name?"

"Navitski. I know you will need to give it to the police and I am settled with that."

"Thank you. You, and the other women, have been very helpful." She started to move toward her, then remembered how averse Ekaterina was to touch, and simply held out her hand. Raisa looked at it, then up at Tess's face, and finally extended her own hand and allowed Tess to clasp it.

When she got back to Elsinore House, Tess called Superintendent Marley to ask if she could come in the following day for the debriefing. Then she set about making flight reservations back to California the morning after. It was one of the longest ten days of her life, and she was more than ready to be home again, sleeping in her own bed.

She was lucky enough to snag a flight leaving at ten o'clock in the morning and arriving in Sacramento at around seven the same evening. The sixteen-and-a-half-hour flight included a two-hour stop in Dallas-Fort Worth, but that was better than saving an hour on the layover and taking a chance on delays thanks to the not-fit-for-humans winter weather in Minneapolis. Unless Sacramento was fogged in, in which case all bets were off and she'd end up in San Francisco. But if the gods were smiling, she should be clicking her garage door opener by nine that night.

The interview with Marley went off without a hitch. He was visibly delighted to have Raisa's name and the wealth of information on Flemming, Yevtushenko, and the no-last-name-yet Ludmila Z. Radic was still a mystery. The Superintendent tried but failed to hide his equal delight at the news Tess would be leaving the next morning. The man was neither accustomed to nor thrilled with having a civilian mucking about in an investigation.

The Investigations Division had developed a couple of leads on Paul's murder over the past two days, but Marley admitted it could be a very long and tough row to hoe. I suspect, he said, that we may find Ludmila or Dragos before we crack the case of Paul's assassination, simply because his killer was likely an extremely low-ranking underling who might already have been "expended."

As they shook hands, Marley promised to keep Tess apprised of any new developments, and she passed along her darknet email address just to be on the safe side. She also gave the Superintendent a small thank-you gift of a bag of fresh almond toffee, a jar of northern California strawberry preserves, another of local honey, and a bottle of 2013 Reserve Syrah from Naggiar Vineyards in Grass Valley, a small town a few miles from Deer Valley. She'd ordered it two days before from her good friend Phil, the owner of the Deer Creek Confectionary, and he shipped it FedEx overnight to the inn. Marley was dumbstruck at the gift, and Tess wondered if it would help to modify his opinion of her. Once again, she thought, hope springs eternal.

That night, she and Anthony enjoyed dinner at a lovely restaurant in Stratford, and as they shared dessert wine together, she presented him with package similar to the one she'd given the Superintendent.

"I can't thank you for everything you've done in these past days, not to mention tolerating my stubbornness!"

They both laughed as he said, "Yes, you really are quite persistent. But it's been a genuine pleasure, Tess, in spite of the horrific subject matter we've been dealing with. There's a part of me that wants to say I hope we'll be able to work together again, but a bigger part that hopes we won't, for your sake. But keep in mind: you've already made a huge difference and as time goes on and progress is made in the investigation, the difference will be even greater. You're a remarkable woman, and I'm honored to have met you."

"That goes both ways, Anthony. I have enormous respect for your work, and the work of Antares."

She took a cab for the short ride back to the B&B, where she was greeted at the front door by a wildly exultant Harvey. God, she missed her Dancer, but Harvey was a wonderful substitute. With the permission of Mrs. Kitchen, he spent the night in her room, starting out on the floor beside her bed. Somewhere in the middle of the night, he jumped up and quietly lay down alongside Tess like a soft, snowy pillow.

PART FOUR

We have a responsibility to stand watch
over one another –
we are watchers, all of us,
watchers guarding against the darkness.

~ Dean Koontz

Sometimes the winds of madness
simply erupt on humanity.

~ Elie Wiesel

20

Dancer was delirious at seeing Tess after so long. (Of course, who knows how dogs experience time? Does an hour feel like a day to them, a day like a year, or like a minute?) He glued himself to her side as she unpacked and drifted into the kitchen for a glass of her favorite flavored water, then roamed through the house room by room, reveling in being home. As she showered off what felt like layers of grittiness from the interminable plane flight, Dancer lay at the edge of the tiled enclosure, head on paws, a Great Protector watching over his charge.

When she finally fell into bed, he joined her. They passed the night and well into the morning that way, Tess snuggled under the frosted down comforter and Dancer atop it, his golden head resting on her shoulder.

The next day, jet lag brought with it a dense brain-fog to which Tess surrendered without hesitation, intermittently watching episodes of television shows she'd recorded over the last two weeks, napping, and nibbling on crackers, cheese, and fresh winter mandarins from the nearby Sierra foothills. Her longtime dog- and house-sitter Priscilla had set out a bounty of fresh fruit for Tess, opened a bottle of 2013 Rodney Strong Russian River Valley Pinot

Noir, and stocked the refrigerator with milk for her morning latté, paper-thin slices of prosciutto, roasted garlic hummus, salad makings, a luscious New York steak, and a bottle of aromatic Grgich Hills Estate Fumé Blanc. She also supplied the indoor log holder with plenty of firewood and kindling, and laid a fire ready to be lighted. It was wonderful to be home again.

Tess allowed herself some time to relax, contact her editor at *Panorama,* have a few dinners with friends and neighbors, take long walks in the backcountry with Dancer and her best friend Zoey and her three dogs, head up into the Sierra for some snowshoeing, and take care of a slew of tasks and errands before diving back into the case. During those weeks, she also sat down with the editor of the *Sacramento Bee* newspaper about his offer that she head up their investigative unit when the current chief of that team retired in late spring (*thanks so much, but I'm happy at the Foundation*), and her San Francisco-based contact from the Antares Endeavor who'd smoothed the way for her with their cohorts in Britain (*Anthony was an incredibly valuable partner – could never have accomplished as much without him).*

By the end of March, even as the last gasps of winter sporadically dusted Deer Valley with snow, Tess spotted a half-dozen pale green buds cautiously emerging on the weeping cherry outside her window. It would be more than a month before she could even think about doing much outside, but she was especially eager for spring to arrive this year. Maybe it was the glacial weather of Ukraine and Crimea or London's thick, unyielding fog, but she was more than ready for this winter season to slip into the annals of history.

The British and Interpol investigation into the trafficking ring had hit several snags. Superintendent

Marley told her that the Modern Slavery Human Trafficking Unit of the National Crime Agency tracked down Ludmila, now identified with the last name of Zhuravlyov. She'd not been at the East London house on the day it was raided, and alerted by other members of the trafficking ring, managed to escape Great Britain. As was hoped, the house "manager" Grigory started squealing almost immediately once he was in custody, and gave the authorities everything they needed to find the woman, who went into hiding in Flemming's Moscow human stockyard.

Of course, Russia was refusing to extradite her to the U.K. for prosecution, piously citing the clause in its constitution that prohibits deporting or extraditing any Russian citizen to another country. The only hope was that Russia might decide to arrest and prosecute her on its own, which would probably lead to Zhuravlyov scurrying like a rat back into the arms of U.K. prosecutors just to escape the horror of a Russian prison.

I don't suppose the Russian authorities closed down the Moscow house? asked Tess, and Marley almost laughed. He explained that a highly-placed government bureaucrat came to the absent owner's defense, insisting the establishment was a perfectly legal "women's hostel" and providing the official permit papers to prove it. In the meantime, a Russia-based operative was keeping an eye on Ludmila Zhuravlyov in case she decided to bolt. That was the best they could do for now.

"So what about Yevtushenko? Any leads there?"

"Yes, and I'm afraid the news isn't good. Your discovery of his name, coupled with the tips from the young women at the East London house, allowed Interpol to verify what was only a guess before: that Yevtushenko is not just part of, but he is one of the *principal* Ukrainian crime bosses in the Odessa region. He's very dangerous, he's very clever…"

"…and completely untouchable," inserted Tess.

"Yes. Unless, of course, he decides to enter the U.K., in which case we have him. But otherwise…." The superintendent sighed.

"Otherwise, you're out of luck."

The good news was that Ulrich Flemming, whose high-dollar attorney continued to insist that the man was guilty of nothing more than being a prosperous entrepreneur, was indicted for human trafficking, money laundering, and five other related charges. Plea deals were struck with Duncan Ceannaideach, the Weybridge estate manager, and the London brothel's house-man Grigory Chaykovsky, both of whom provided enough detailed testimony to ensure that Flemming would never see the light of day except through a prison cell window. To add icing to the cake, Raisa came forward and offered to testify. Superintendent Marley was confident that under the elephantine weight of all the statements and the huge cache of evidence they'd uncovered, Flemming would ultimately concede rather than face a jury where a guilty verdict was virtually assured.

As pleased as Tess was at the news about Flemming, she wanted to continue digging to see what else might slither out from under the sludge and filth. She felt strongly that the story wasn't over yet, and wondered idly if there could be a U.S. connection. Maybe even a California one.

People had this mistaken idea that crimes like human trafficking only happened in the squalid back alleys of cities like New York or Detroit or Chicago, but in fact traffickers skulked just as effortlessly through the innocent streets of America's lesser towns and whistlestops. Children were abducted walking to school, teenagers were lured from parking lots at the local Seven-Eleven, women were entrapped at massage parlors or hotels. No place was invulnerable.

Over the next month, Tess and her research assistant at the Foundation buried themselves in documentary and digital exploration. This is something else that people are mistaken about: they think that reporting is just sneaking around interrogating people. In fact, reporting, especially investigative reporting, takes a tremendous amount of work beyond talking to people and playing Polly Private Eye. A journalist needs a solid grounding in facts about the subject or she comes off looking like a bozo. Which, sadly, some of them are. Tess, on the other hand, tended to be almost neurotic about getting the facts and getting them right, and the only way to assure that was through exhaustive research. For this woman whose strongest trait was curiosity, it was a part of the job that she loved.

Her editor contacted Tess to say he was anxious to see the story, although he wasn't trying to pressure her. Would it be possible for him to see a draft of what she had so far? He knew very well what her answer would be, but regardless, each and every time she did a piece for them, he cajoled her for an in-progress draft. And each and every time, Tess declined, citing the sensitivity of the subject and her need to do a final fact-check before anyone saw the story. This time, Tess was also concerned about divulging information to anyone that could expose them to danger, although she didn't say as much to the editor.

It was late May when she reconnected with a source

she cultivated a few years earlier in the Sacramento District Attorney's office, just to see whether he knew anything about Ukrainian-based sex trafficking operations in the state's Central Valley. He agreed to meet her for lunch at the Fox and Goose Public House in downtown Sacramento.

The weather was perfect, a soft sunniness that epitomized the idea of Spring Fever. She drove the entire seventy-five miles with the sunroof and the driver's window wide open, and to hell with what it did to her hair.

Inside the distinctive redbrick building, the atmosphere was cool and inviting. Originally home to the Fuller Paint and Glass Company, nearly every wall was segmented by huge squares of frosted glass, some glistening in shades of gold, green, and blue. The battered wood floor, likely a relic dating back to the building's birth in 1913, squeaked pleasantly as the hostess guided Tess to her table.

Rodney Sanders, bespeckled and balding, stood up and gave Tess a warm hug.

"Hey, girl, it's been way too long!"

"Yeah, it really has. But frankly, I can think of better things to do than spend half an hour battling Sacramento traffic and all the city's interminable one-way streets that always seem to be mutating. Can't the city planners make up their minds?"

Rodney laughed in acknowledgement, then the conversation turned to what each of them had been doing since they last saw one another. Once their food arrived, Tess told Rodney what she was looking for, and without disclosing any real details, a little bit about why.

"Ukrainian, eh? We've bumped into a few characters from that part of the world during prostitution stings, but as for actual human trafficking...." He seemed lost in thought for a few moments as he speared an errant chunk of beef from the hamburger he'd been devouring. "I just flashed on a woman, really not much more than a kid, that we snatched from a South Sacramento hotel for prostitution, who told us she'd been recruited in Ukraine. Hmmm, let me see…."

After burrowing through his mental file cabinets for another minute or so, he continued. "Yeah: she was from one of the larger towns in Ukraine—Kiev, maybe, or Odessa—and hooked up with this slimeball who convinced her he was a modeling agent with 'connections' in the U.S. Eventually he got her to Mexico, then snuck her across the border to San Diego, and somehow wound up here. We grabbed him about six months later in another hotel where he was pimping girls. He'd rabbited from the first one before we could get him, but this time he pretty much flipped on his bosses back in Ukraine."

"Can you get me the information, Rodney? It would be just too good to believe that he could be connected to the ring I'm trying to uncover, but maybe there's a link I can follow. Even though these rings work independently, they each have ties to a central group. Of course, that doesn't make it any easier to track since the leadership of the main cell is almost always obscured, even from the sub-cells, so it's not like you can go ask Genady or Igor who the head honcho is."

"I should be able to dig through the files and find something," he said. "I'll also talk to our investigator on the case and see what he can remember. Don't guess you have a name you can share with me?"

Tess wanted to be careful, since even mentioning Yevtushenko's name could have unknown repercussions. Besides, it was highly unlikely the name would mean anything at all to the D.A. "No, I don't have anything," she said. Half-truths were, unfortunately, part and parcel of her line of work, even though she was never comfortable with them unless she was dealing with a scumbag. In that case, all bets were off.

That next morning as Tess was refilling her coffee in the kitchen, Dancer froze and gave a low, throaty rumble, then raised his upper lip and growled. Tess was astonished: he never did this, never exhibited the most miniscule sign of aggression, even toward a squirrel.

"Hey, what's up?" she asked, walking to the front door and peering through its leaded glass to see what alerted him. Nothing. She turned the handle, but before she could get the door even halfway open, the dog burst through into the yard, growling and barking ferociously.

"Dancer!" Tess was almost speechless at his actions. "What the..." And then she felt it: the softening at the edges of her consciousness. *Someone was watching now, and coming. Not right away, but they were coming.* Suddenly everything was blackness, as if she'd been enveloped in a gelatinous, impenetrable shadow. There was no seeing, no hearing, no sensation other than abject terror, trapped in that dark mass with no escape. And then she felt Dancer's cold nose against her hand, and the revelation, or whatever it was, vanished.

Rocked by vertigo, Tess tried to steady herself on the wall of the house, then felt her legs give out and she dropped to the porch floor, cracking one knee as she fell. The pain obliterated her dizziness and she sat, gripping her knee and moaning. Dancer, back to his normal tranquility, stood beside her, confusion in his eyes.

"It's okay," she said reassuringly. "But what did you see or hear?" Dancer merely cocked his head and kept looking at her. *This is one of those times I wish dogs could talk.* She stood up, wincing from the pain, and took a few steps. No permanent damage done, but it hurt like hell and there'd sure be one big-ass bruise. She shook off the remnants of her frightening vision, unsure about what it meant. Like most of the events she thought of as waking dreams, the meaning would become clear in time.

It took a few weeks for Sanders to get back to her, apologizing for the delay but explaining he'd been totally occupied with a home invasion killing since they last spoke. He'd found a few files, but said he'd keep digging through the digital archives for the rest.

It was well into June before he connected with her again, saying he uploaded some files from the prostitution bust and the arrest of the Ukrainian pimp into his Dropbox account. The cases were three years old, Sanders reminded her, so some of the players and details could have changed. In the meantime, he spoke to the lead investigator on the case, who agreed to search out his personal files for other names and details.

Shortly after that, her home phone rang.

"Tess? It is Katia."

"Katia! How nice to hear from you. How were your holidays?" They hadn't spoken since before Christmas.

"They were very calm and relaxed, thank you. Elliott and I stayed home, had a small roast, and watched the Christmas lights. It was lovely here."

"It was beautiful up here as well. It isn't often we get a white Christmas, so having snow was a real treat."

"I wanted to inquire of your trip to Crimea and London."

Tess gave her a very brief outline, minus the more disturbing elements like the attempts on her life and Paul

Collingwood's murder. Not wanting to get the woman's hopes up until his imprisonment was a certainty, she also left out any mention of Flemming's arrest, and failed to say anything about Yevtushenko's disappearance or Ludmila Zhuravlyov's escape. It would have served no purpose to saddle Katia with the likelihood that neither Dragos nor Ludmilla would ever face justice. At least, not in this world.

"I remain so grateful to you for all you have done," said Katia. "You have raised a great burden off my shoulders."

"You deserve to have some peace."

"And that is a further reason for my call. I was not completely truthful with you about what I know. One of the women I met when I was first brought to Dubai, we became friends. She is the one who helped Anthony find me."

"Yes, he told me."

"Her name is Aminah. What Anthony did not tell you because I did not tell him was that Aminah escaped just after she spoke with him. Then the day before he found me, I received a letter from her through a post…ahh, a courier. She said she was safe, in Jordan, and that she was assured of passage to the United States.

"I knew I should not have done so for my own safety, but after I arrived in Canada I sent her a letter, saying where I was, what my new name was. We have been corresponding since. One other thing which I did not tell you or Anthony: when Aminah was in the hotel in Saudi Arabi, her keeper used to mention the names of Ulrich and Dragos."

Tess was thunderstruck. Another victim of Al-Dosari, one who could also have ties to Flemming or Yevtushenko, alive and well in the U.S. and in contact with Katia.

"Does Elliott know?"

"Yes, I told him a few months ago. I could not hide it from him longer. He became very understanding, as he is always, and said that as long as I felt safe trusting her, he would trust me. One more thing: she lives in California. Near Los Angeles, in a house on top of another. I cannot remember the word. Not apartment…"

"A flat?"

"Yes, that is it. A flat. She lives in a flat above a family from Riyadh, who took her in when she came here. An organization for refugees helped her, and then found her a place to live with this family. Now she lives by herself in the family flat, so she has safety among people who are also Saudi."

"And this house is in Los Angeles?"

"Outside of there, a place called Bakersfield. Not so much cost to live there, she says. She was in school at Bakersfield College, but now works in the college office. In our last speaking, she said she would like to meet with you, if you would agree."

Tess was elated. "Of course." Then she paused. "Are you sure Aminah is ready to talk about her experiences?"

"She told me she can speak of it without too much distress. She is very strong. Much stronger than I."

"I doubt that, Katia. You are an amazingly strong woman."

She could almost hear Katia blushing. "Shall I contact her on your behalf?"

"Yes, absolutely. The best idea would be for you to be our go-between—that is, you can relay her information to me, and then convey my information to her. That way, we've lessened the risk. And by the way: is she still going by the name of Aminah?"

"Yes, she kept her name. Aminah Maghribi."

"Can you call her?"

"I shall do so immediately."

"Find out what days and times she's free, then I'll handle finding a secure place to meet. I'll let you know where and when, and you can get that to Aminah."

"Thank you again, Miss Al…Tess. I hope she will be of help."

21

She hated Bakersfield. Perfect name for the city, though, because it sprouted like a clump of steel and concrete toadstools on the raw, barren fields of the furnace-like valley floor. During summer, the temperatures refused to fall below 100 degrees for days on end, and many times topped 110. In winter, it was fog. More precisely, tule fog: an impenetrably thick, static cloud layer endemic to the state's Central Valley in the winter months. At its worst, it could reduce daytime visibility to less than an eighth of a mile. Nighttime, forget it. You could run into a wooly mammoth before you even saw it.

Set in the southern interior of the San Joaquin Valley, Bakersfield was renowned for two things: being the home of country music legends Merle Haggard and Buck Owens, and having the second dirtiest air of any city in the nation. Country music and air pollution: they somehow deserved each other, Tess thought. *Having to live in this monotonously flat, parched, mouse-turd brown landscape would make me consider becoming the next wingless flight off the nearest bridge.* But at least she'd only be there for one day. And at least it wasn't in the middle of August.

But no matter the time of year, except maybe in the spring when the land was green instead of brown, the drive down Interstate 5 was mind-numbing. Mile after mile of desert-like expanses, interrupted by intermittent highway signs pointing toward a handful of forgettable towns—Vernalis, Jet, Stomar, Volta—and dusty roadside rest stops with their ubiquitous fast-food outlets. After cutting east to Highway 99, Tess was relieved when the low-slung skyline of Bakersfield came into view. The 350-mile drive from Deer Valley took almost six hours, but felt more like six days.

Earlier, she reserved a suite at the 1920s-era Padre Hotel where she once stayed when on an assignment in the region. The eclectic boutique inn did its best to make up for its setting in the middle of a generally unappealing, charmless city, with amenity-laden guest rooms, both a fine dining restaurant and a casual café, two separate lounges, and a top-notch staff. It was also pet-friendly, so she brought Dancer along, remembering how he'd soothed Katia during their interview.

The suite was perfect, with a separate living room where she and Aminah could talk in comfort and a huge Jacuzzi tub in the bathroom where she could relax tonight. Exhausted from the drive, Tess peeled off her clothes and slipped into the churning water with a glass of Viognier from the bottle that was waiting for her when she arrived. Rather than opting for the corner dog bed, Dancer lay beside the tub and slept while Tess allowed the powerful jets to work out the knots in her shoulders and back. Done, she wrapped herself in the hotel's fluffy white bathrobe, flipped on the television, fed Dancer, and ordered a large Caesar salad and crusty French bread. She also made sure room service was set to deliver coffee, tea, and a fruit bowl before her eight o'clock meeting with Aminah the following day.

The woman who stood at her door that next morning was stunning: tall, slim-hipped, with glowing chestnut hair falling in deep waves below her shoulders and a flawless complexion the color of soft cinnamon. Her arresting green-gray eyes, reminiscent of the Afghan girl immortalized on the cover of *National Geographic* magazine in the 1980s, were cautious and shy. Tess reached out her hand, and Aminah lightly clasped it.

"Come in, Aminah. Would you like some coffee or tea?"

"Tea would be nice. Thank you."

As Tess prepared the tea, she chatted informally about her drive south and that morning's clear blue skies.

Just then, Dancer walked into the room, stopping midway before he approached Aminah.

"Oh, what a beautiful dog!" she said with an ecstatic smile. She reached both hands out toward Dancer, and he happily trotted over and allowed himself to be engulfed in caresses. "What is the name?"

"His name is Dancer."

"I had dogs as a child, and my neighbors below me have a...oh, I cannot recall the type. Large, with short hair, which is much better for the heat here. I find dogs help me relax, and be happier."

Once the two women settled and Dancer stationed himself at Aminah's feet, Tess opened the conversation by asking about the woman's friendship with Katia. From there, she guided Aminah back to her experiences as a captive in Dubai, then focused on Saudi Arabia. She needed to find out what, if anything, Aminah knew about Flemming and Yevtushenko.

"There was once I met the man called Dragos," she said, her eyes lowered. "He was not a nice man." She began to interweave her fingers nervously, and kept her eyes down as she spoke. "He came to the hotel where I worked and needed to speak to me alone. But first he insisted I have a drink, which I do not like but had to do with him because he was above me. When I was with customers, the bar-man knew to give me just sparkled water, but this time it was liquor. Strong-tasting but also sweet.

"We went upstairs to his room which was very large, with much luxury, not like the rooms we used, and he said I should sit on the big sofa. I began to feel dizzy, and then he...he began to undress me. When I was naked he tied my hands with plastic cords and took off his belt, then beat me with it while he..." She tried to choke out the words, but failed. "Then he did other things to me which I do not want to say, and after many hours he allowed me to return to my room. I could barely walk because of the beating and the other things. He was very, very cruel."

"I'm so sorry for what you went through, Aminah," said Tess softly. During the woman's account, Dancer rose and rested his head in Aminah's lap. "I don't mean to make you dwell on this, but do you remember if he said anything during this time? Anything about his life, where he lived, anything like that?"

Aminah paused, one hand fondling Dancer's fur, trapped between trying to remember and wanting to forget. "He often said other names, comparing me to them in what I was...performing, and once when he stopped and was starting to sleep he said under his breath about needing to get back to Odessa. When he woke I wanted to have him talk, as I was trying to keep him from hurting me again and hoping his mind would be on that instead of me. I got him a drink from the room bar and asked him to tell me about Odessa, as I had never been there. He spoke long about the city, its beautiful women, and its old history, much of which I did not understand because he spoke Russian mixed with English. Then he said the city's beautiful streets are lined with many trees, and that his house was large and built in the Italian style on a street that has no cars and is made of round rocks, which I do not understand."

Ahh: a pedestrian street of cobblestone.

"Did he say anything else that might help us find him?"

Aminah continued talking about the things he said, most of which weren't terribly helpful in terms of searching him out. After three hours, Tess ran out of questions. At least she found out that Yevtushenko *did* live in Odessa, and with the description of the street, she was hopeful she could identify it. Whether that would make any difference in the grand scheme of things was questionable. It was, after all, Ukraine, which like Russia, forbade the extradition of its citizens.

But if he slithered back into the U.K.…well, there's that "hope springs eternal" thing again.

A few days later, Tess opened the files from Sanders, which included notes from the other D.A. investigator on the case of the Ukrainian pimp. Halfway through reading that investigator's handwritten notes, she was astonished to see the name "Yevtushenko." With the glut of sex traffickers in and around Ukraine it seemed almost impossible that the same man would be linked to both the D.A.'s old case and her current investigation, but there it was, scribbled in fading black ink.

So, Tess thought, Dragos had been in the business for

some years, which meant in that time he'd likely built up an extensive empire and accumulated boatloads of money, both of which made him an even more elusive quarry. But thinking about the money made Tess realize that he couldn't just spend or bank it: he needed to launder it first. She remembered how in 2016 Deutsch Bank was caught in a huge money laundering scheme that enabled some of its Russian clients to secretly move tens of billions of dollars out of Russia to the bank's locations in London and New York. Of course, Deutsch Bank's fall from grace didn't mean that other banks weren't playing the exact same game. In fact, these kinds of operations were so prolific that international anti-corruption units call it the "Russian laundromat." Could Interpol use that to capture the spider in his own web of filth?

Tess looked at the clock, did some quick calculations, and put in a call to Superintendent Marley. He took it right away.

She explained what she found out from Aminah about Yevtushenko's location in Odessa, and the information she gleaned about him from the Sacramento D.A.'s office.

"I spent some time on the Internet yesterday," Tess continued, "and discovered a pedestrian-only, cobblestone street in Odessa called Deribasovskaya Street. The homes along it are built in several European architectural designs including Italianate, which according to what he told Aminah is the style of Yevtushenko's home,. I'm guessing it's his private residence, because Deribasovskaya is in the heart of the city, very upscale, busy and famous for its nightlife. Perfect spot for a prostitution-ring baron to sit back and enjoy the spoils of his trade."

"Very interesting. Perhaps with the help of Interpol my digital force can poke around and see if they can find the specific property. Though honestly, I don't know it would do us much good, unless..."

"Unless we have someone watching it who can put out the alert if he decided to take another journey to the U.K.."

"Excuse me: 'we'?"

"I have an excellent contact in Kiev I can recruit to do some covert reconnaissance. I don't expect you have an operative in Ukraine?" She knew he didn't.

Tess was accustomed to the Superintendent's longsuffering sighs. "No, I don't expect we do, although I could certainly call upon Interpol. Is this 'contact' of yours reliable?"

"Extremely. Plus he's Ukrainian, so he knows the language and can blend in. He's also very tough. And he speaks excellent English, so he can communicate directly with you as well."

Next, Tess raised the question of how Yevtushenko was laundering his assets. Were there any ongoing operations in the U.K., she asked, that were investigating Ukrainian money-laundering schemes like the Russian one at Deutsch Bank? If they could locate Yevtushenko's domicile, they might be able to tie him to a bank account and nab him that way.

Marley seemed doubtful, but said he'd look into it and talk with his Interpol counterpart. They went on to discuss the pros and cons of someone surreptitiously stalking Yevtushenko, after which Marley opined that he couldn't very well stop someone in Ukraine from snooping on someone else in Ukraine. Fine, said Tess, I'll contact my fellow and keep you informed.

She sent a darknet email to Anton. It was around 7 p.m. in Kiev, and she didn't know if he'd be home or not. She grabbed Dancer for a walk, and when she got back there was a reply from Anton. He would try to find Yevtushenko's address, and see what he could do. His plan was to use a trusted "colleague" in Odessa as his backup since it would likely be at least a several-day-long stakeout. Tess messaged him back with a generous payment proposal, to be augmented if the job took more than a week. She didn't doubt he'd accept it.

Back with Sanders' digital files, she focused on the ones from the South Sacramento bust to see if there was anything worthwhile the victim shared, anything that might be tied even tangentially to Yevtushenko. She fixed another pot of coffee and wandered out with her laptop to the little gazebo, Dancer padding alongside her as always. The day was mild and sunny with a barely-perceptible breeze, typical for early summer in this part of the Sierra. The native dogwoods and madrones were in full leaf by now and ripe, emerald blades of grass carpeted the rocky hill that rolled down to meadow below.

She leaned back and closed her eyes, luxuriating in the moment and the warming sunshine.

Dancer gave a tiny whine, and Tess smiled at the dog's prodding that she get back to work. Or pet him. One or the other.

Before she could open the D.A.'s file, she was hit with a sudden feeling of uneasiness, and goosebumps danced up her arms. *Someone's watching me.* She looked around in every direction, but saw nothing. No suspicious movement in the trees, no colors or shapes that looked out of place. She got up and walked toward the front of the house, thinking that perhaps it was her neighbor Carla wandering down with a cup of coffee and her dog Roxie for a morning chat, but the driveway was empty. And then the feeling vanished. Laughing at herself, she put it down to the residue of all the craziness she'd been through overseas and returned to the gazebo and Dancer. He hadn't alerted her to anything, and that eased her mind.

Freshening her coffee, she began reading the file. It took two hours for her to finish wading through the volume of arrest records, charges, indictments, evidentiary records, information, subpoenas, witness depositions, motions, and the final plea agreement. There wasn't much in the defendant's files, since he was a lower-level pimp who ended up flipping on the boss above him and whose contact with Yevtushenko appeared to be limited to bringing him potential conscripts.

Rather, her focus was on Anichka Yevdokymenko, the young Ukrainian woman picked up in the raid, and her detailed statement, including the name of Yevtushenko, about the operation. The "modeling" job for which she was recruited involved meeting with an older man with a scar on his face, introduced as Mr. Yevtushenko. He asked her to undress down to her bra and panties because, he said, the job was to model swimsuits for a top-of-the-line catalog company in Hollywood. He was very respectful, Anichka said, and never even attempted to touch her. He asked her a question or two about her family—she was the only child of a struggling single mother from one of Odessa's poorer districts—and whether she was comfortable with the idea of going to America. America, the land of opportunity? Why would she *not* want to go there? And the fact that she'd be in Hollywood only made it that much better.

After that, she was told to gather a few essential articles from her home like a toothbrush, sanitary items, comb, and underwear, and return to the building where her interview took place. No need to bring clothes, they told her, as you'll be given all new ones once you get to California. And don't bother to leave a note for your mother: we'll contact her and let her know where you are, and provide a modeling contract for her to sign as your legal guardian. It sounded perfectly reasonable and above-board to a naïve fifteen-year-old who had never traveled outside a thirty-block radius in downtown Odessa.

Of course, none of it was true.

Vasyl, the man who recruited her and was to become her pimp, met her when she returned and took her to one of the better hotels in Odessa. She had her own room, a bathroom she didn't have to share, and wonderful food that was delivered right to her door by a man in a clean white jacket and perfectly-pressed black pants. That next day she spent the morning and afternoon watching movies on the forty-inch television, luxuriating in the deep soaking bathtub, and nibbling on more of the delicious food they brought her. She was beginning to miss her mother a little, but once she got to California, she could send for her and they would live together in a big house by the ocean where a newly-rich Anichka could take care of her.

That evening, Vasyl visited her again with Mr. Yevtushenko, who once more was kind and courteous. He explained that Anichka's mother was thrilled that her daughter was getting such a glorious opportunity, and that Anichka shouldn't worry about her at all. When the girl asked if she could please call her mother, the sympathetic Mr. Yevtushenko said she really shouldn't just yet, because it would be too hard on her mother to hear her voice and not have her there. Better to wait, he said, until you're settled in Hollywood. Vasyl simply stood to one side of the older man, smiling and nodding from time to time.

Anichka never even noticed that the room had no telephone.

Vasyl stayed behind after Yevtushenko left, and the two of them watched old American movies together on the wide, sumptuous bed. During the evening, Vasyl, whom Anichka described as having a charming smile, long-ish blonde hair and blue eyes the color of the ocean, began by cuddling and stroking her, especially when she began to cry at the thought of leaving her mother. He said all the right things, was kind and compassionate, and the shy teenager slowly began to relax. When he kissed her, she was thrilled that this good-looking older man—he was all of twenty-eight—found her desirable. When he slowly began undressing her she didn't object: it was exciting and romantic like in the movie they just watched and in the dozens she'd seen and fantasized about in her dismal, dreary apartment. She suddenly felt grown-up, a real woman, with this man who was going to take her to the country of her dreams. Sex, after all, was a part of love, and by his rapt attention it was obvious to the young virgin that he was falling in love with her.

They remained at the hotel for two days, making love and ordering room service with blood-rare steaks, champagne, Russian caviar, and decadent desserts Anichka had never even heard of. If this wasn't love, then nothing was. She couldn't have known that she was experiencing the classic "grooming" that sexual predators use to subjugate their victims and break down their autonomy.

On the third day things began to change. Vasyl was a bit more impatient with her occasional weepiness, snapping at her about how if she kept eating, she'd become like the "fat cows" on the streets of Ukraine. He was also pressuring her to perform sex acts that made her uncomfortable, and some were actually painful. That's when he would turn kind and benevolent again, soothing her with words of love and assurances that everything they were doing was "normal" for two people who cared about each other.

That evening there was a knock on the door and another man entered the room. He too was blonde and blue-eyed, but even better looking than Vasyl. His smile was wide and confident, his voice like honey, and Vasyl introduced him as Alexei. He handed Vasyl two yellow pills, which he insisted that Anichka swallow. It would help her to relax, he said, and then they would all have fun. Anichka had never taken drugs before except the tonics her mother gave her when she was sick with the flu, but she readily agreed. Again, Vasyl loved her, and would never ask her to do anything that would harm her.

After they all had champagne, Anichka said she felt very strange, as if she were in a dream. The room's walls and ceiling were wavy, and both men looked like they were in front of fun-house mirrors. Then Vasyl was pushing her down onto the bed, yanking off her clothes, roughly spreading her legs apart and forcing himself inside her. After he was finished, it was Alexei's turn. Anichka said she was unable to stop them: whatever drugs they gave her rendered her virtually helpless. The only thing she was fully aware of was the searing pain as the two men raped her throughout the night.

The next morning Alexei was gone, and Vasyl tenderly bathed Anichka and soothed her body with luxurious, perfumed lotion, then ordered a special breakfast of *blinchiki* with ripe strawberries and cream, fat kielbasa, roasted potatoes, and rich hot chocolate. He explained that sharing a woman the way he'd shared her with Alexei meant that he loved her, was proud of her, and wanted his friend to see what a beautiful, desirable woman she was.

However confusing it all was, however physically painful it was, everything Vasyl was saying made the young girl feel special, even extraordinary. Not only was one man in love with her, but *two* were. Perhaps he was right, that this was how men showed their love.

Anichka's lengthy and exhaustive statement of her next three years under Vasyl's control detailed how she was "shared" with other men in the Ukrainian hotel, how Vasyl never left her alone, and how he became increasingly harsh with her. The sumptuous meals declined in frequency then ended, replaced with simple, utilitarian food like borsch, goulash, cabbage rolls, and varenyky, a boiled potato dumpling. Many days she got just two meals, and even those became more meager as time went on.

When Vasyl announced they were leaving for the U.S., Anichka's hopes soared. They would finally be going to Hollywood where she could begin her modeling career and leave the last weeks behind forever. She was handed a new passport with a new name, Anna, and warned against speaking to anyone on the airplane. Once the long flight ended, she was confused at the language, which didn't sound at all like the English she'd been learning in school and from the old black-and-white American movies. And the people didn't look American, either: they were all olive-skinned with very dark brown hair and dark eyes. Before long, she sounded out the letters on a sign above their new hotel—a ramshackle pink stucco building on a filthy, rank-smelling alleyway in the center of the town—and realized they weren't in Hollywood, but Mexico.

Vasyl kept her there for another three weeks until he could sneak her across the border into the seedy East Village area of San Diego. There, "Anna's" life became an interminable succession of drugs, beatings, and sexual encounters with strangers, some brought to her by Vasyl and later, by way of her own efforts on the street. Three years later, Vasyl moved them northward, where the now-twenty-year-old was installed in a South Sacramento motel to ply her trade along with a band of other women. The following year, the police raided the motel-cum-brothel, and the group of prostitutes ensconced there were arrested.

Tess closed the screen, wondering if Anichka could be helpful in the effort to ensnare Yevtushenko or even some of his underlings. Trying to talk with her might be a waste of time, or it could be a Mother Lode. Tess wasn't willing to discard anything that could be a possibility, so she placed another call to Sanders in the D.A.'s office.

"I take it you read the files?" he asked.

"Yeah, they were quite…uhh, enlightening. Do you have any idea of what happened to Anichka, the woman who was picked up in the South Sac raid?"

"No, not really. But I can find out pretty easily, if you want."

"That would be a big help, Rodney. I owe you one on this."

"Yeah, right. Maybe next time I'll let you take me and my lovely bride out to dinner at The Firehouse." The Firehouse was one of Sacramento's premier fine dining spots, eminent enough that every governor starting with Ronald Reagan had held his inaugural dinner there.

"You've got yourself a deal." Tess laughed.

Once Sanders got back to her, he said that Anichka lived in San Francisco, supposedly clean and out of the sex business. He gave her a phone number and address in the outer Sunset district, which Tess knew housed a fair number of massage parlors that were little more than fronts for brothels, making her wonder just how "out of the business" the woman really was. Without a strong and sustained support system, most female sex workers, whether or not they were victims of trafficking, had a hard time renouncing that line of work simply because it was all they knew. Throw drug addiction into the mix, and the chances of quitting the sex trade were even slimmer.

After a month of no word from Anton, she sent him an email asking about the surveillance on Yevtushenko. He responded that the man seemed to be staying put in Odessa and hadn't initiated any travel plans. Tess didn't ask how Anton could possibly know that, but assumed he somehow managed to tap into Yevtushenko's communication system. Either that, or he had a man on the inside—which, with what she knew of Anton's connections, wouldn't have surprised her.

It was nearing the end of June before she reached Anichka, who didn't seem to understand who Tess was and why she was calling. Tess explained, then explained again, that she was writing an investigative piece about sex trafficking, and that Anichka's name came up in the course of her research into how women were lured from Ukraine. Would she be willing to meet to talk about her experiences? Tess didn't mention Yevtushenko, figuring the name alone could easily frighten the woman into silence.

Anichka was extremely reluctant, telling Tess she'd left that life behind after her arrest in Sacramento. But Tess pressed, saying she could meet wherever Anichka wanted and that the interview wouldn't take more than an hour. And, Tess assured her, I'll keep your identity completely confidential. Finally Anichka agreed, proposing they meet that Friday in a San Francisco coffee shop on Moraga Street near 25th Avenue.

The day before the interview Anichka cancelled. I have the summer flu, she said. How about the week after next? They agreed on a time, but two days before the meeting, Anichka once again cancelled. Something came up, and she wouldn't be able to get together until the following month. Tess suspected the woman would flake out yet again, but agreed on a date to meet her at the coffee shop.

Even if the interview turned out to be a bust, Tess reasoned, San Francisco would be a nice respite from July's summer heat.

PART FIVE

Evil walks among us, wearing a mask
which looks like all our faces.

~ Dean Koontz

There are black zones of shadow
close to our daily paths,
and now and then some evil soul breaks a passage through.

~ H.P. Lovecraft
The Thing on the Doorstep

22

Tess loved San Francisco, at least to visit. She lived there right out of college, but the endless soggy, gray days finally got the best of her and she headed for the sun as soon as she could. But the city possessed undeniable charm and a quirkiness that appealed to Tess's unconventional side, even though she couldn't keep the nagging idea of earthquakes from nibbling at her mind whenever she was there.

This time, she arranged to spend a couple of days with her sister Karen near Monterey after meeting with Anichka. It was another two-hour drive down the miserable 101 freeway—miserable, at least, until you finally inched your way out of San Jose—but it was worth it: the sisters hadn't seen each other since Christmas, and they were long past due for time together. Not to mention the fact that Karen's yellow lab Chloe and Dancer were best buddies, so silliness and laughter were pretty much guaranteed.

The day was destined to be a warm one, turning blazingly hot in the foothills and Sacramento Valley below. Tess got an early start and missed the worst of the heat. The traffic, however, was another story. As usual, there was a two-mile backup just before the Bay Bridge toll plaza, where the road resembled a parking lot rather than a major interstate freeway. The clog finally gave way on the bridge itself, then reasserted itself on the other side and onto Highway 101. She jogged west onto Highway 280 then north onto Highway 1 where things bogged down again. In this area, the "highway" was actually a city street, 19th Avenue, that shot north like an arrow through Golden Gate Park and the Presidio until meeting up with the western leg of 101 heading out of the city and toward Marin, San Raphael, Novato, and points beyond.

From 19th she turned left onto Noriega, then right on 25th Avenue to Moraga Street. Parking in this part of the city, or *any* part of the city for that matter, was problematic, and Tess figured she'd need to hike at least four or five blocks to the meeting spot at the Wooden Ship Café. It turned out to be closer to seven blocks. The walk felt good, though, after more than two hours of driving, and Dancer was entranced by all the wonderful new urban smells. It was one of those Chamber of Commerce mornings in the city with no fog, little wind, and temperatures hovering in the mid-60s.

That morning Tess called ahead to see if the coffee shop had outside seating, and the friendly staffer told her there was a heated, covered patio where dogs were welcome. She was sure there would be no problem finding an empty table at ten o'clock.

Tess tied Dancer's leash around the leg of a corner table and went inside. Anichka described herself as medium height, thin, with blue eyes and light brown hair cut in a short bob, and as Tess surveyed the handful of customers she spotted her.

"Anichka?" Tess approached the woman and held out her hand.

"I go by Anna." Her tone was vaguely belligerent and the expression on her face matched it. She refused Tess's handshake, keeping her eyes down at the mug of coffee in front of her.

This was going to be challenging. "Do you need a refill on your coffee? Something to eat?"

"No. I'm fine."

When Tess returned with her own mug of steaming coffee, she suggested they go outside where they could speak more privately. "You remember that I told you I'd be bringing my dog, Dancer?"

"Uhhhh…yeah, I guess."

Dancer lifted his head when Tess emerged, looked at Anichka, but made no move to go to the woman, who glanced at the dog then sat in the chair furthest away from him. She never once raised her eyes to Tess's face.

Tess didn't even try engaging her with small talk. "As I told you on the phone, I learned about you while I was doing research on sex trafficking. I know someone in the Sacramento District Attorney's office who told me about your arrest and how you were recruited in Odessa and then finally brought to Sacramento by Vasyl."

Anichka looked up when Tess mentioned Vasyl's name, but her eyes were blank and red-rimmed. *Oh, great: she's loaded. Or was last night.*

"In your statement to police you mentioned that Vasyl took you to meet a man with a scar, who told you about becoming a swimsuit model in Hollywood. You said his name was Mr. Yevtushenko. What can yo…"

"I know no one by that name."

"You gave his name to the police. You talked about how he came to the hotel the next day, told you that your mother gave permission for you to come to Ameri…"

"You are wrong." The young woman stuck out her chin and shook her head, concentrating on a spot near the corner of the ceiling.

Tess spoke in the firmest tone possible. "Anna, I am *not* wrong. I don't know why you're refusing to admit this man was involved with your abduction especially since you told the police about him before, but if you're worried he'll find y…"

Once again, Anichka cut Tess off in mid-sentence. "I do not worry about him. I have nothing to worry since I do not know him. He means nothing to me."

Tess sighed in frustration. Why did this woman agree to meet with her when all she was did was refuse to talk? "Okay, let's go in a different direction. While you were with Vasyl, did you ever hear him mention the name of anyone who might have been his boss?"

"Vasyl has no need of a boss. He is with himself. Independent."

Tess caught Anna's use of the present-tense to describe the man. "Well, I'm sure that eventually you realized you weren't the only woman he was selling. Did he ever talk about how he got the others to come with him? Or mention anyone else? Like an associate? Someone in the same business?"

"Vasyl does not speak of such things."

"What *does* he speak of?"

"I…he…." She said nothing more. Did she realize she'd made a mistake by implying that Vasyl was still in the business, and that by extension, she was as well? Tess figured there was nothing to lose by asking.

"Anna, are you still working? Here, in San Francisco? Remember: everything you tell me is confidential."

"Confidential," Anna snorted. "Confidential is a lie."

"No, it's not a lie. I'm not trying to get you or Vasyl in trouble. I'm not a cop and I'm not working for the cops. I'm just trying to find a way to expose this man, this Yevtushenko, before even more women end up hurt."

Anna slowly raised her head and looked directly at Tess for the first time that morning, speaking barely above a whisper. "I cannot help you. I must help...protect myself, or...." Her voice dropped even further, forcing Tess to strain just to hear her. "He is a monster, a monster who wears the clothes of a saint. He owns...he has power to..." Then she shook her head and stood up. "I say nothing more. Leave me alone." With that she charged through the gate that enclosed the little patio, knocking aside an elderly woman who was just stepping through it. Tess jumped up, not to follow Anichka but to make sure the old woman wasn't hurt. It was clear she wasn't, as she raised her long-handled umbrella and shook it ferociously at the departing woman.

"Ruffian!" she shouted. "Hooligan! Good-for-nothing!"

Tess offered her arm but the woman brushed it aside. "I don't need any help, young lady! I can perfectly well take care of myself!"

"Yes, ma'am," Tess replied, "I can see that. I hope you have a good morning."

"Good morning, eh? Fiddlesticks." The woman stomped through the door and up to the counter, and banged on it several times with her umbrella. "Where's my hot chocolate?"

As she and Dancer walked the long blocks back to the car, Tess fumed over having driven all the way to San Francisco just to be shut down. Not that it hadn't happened before, but it was still irritating as hell. Beyond her irritation she was puzzled over what just happened with Anichka. She was ninety-nine percent sure the woman was back on the streets and almost as sure that Vasyl returned to the fold, this time in the City by the Bay. But it was Anichka's reaction to Yevtushenko's name that intrigued her, as if the man's reach somehow extended all the way from Ukraine to San Francisco, to the point that Anichka was terrified to even speak of him.

A monster who wears the clothes of a saint. Despite the warm sun against her face, Tess gave an involuntary shiver.

Because it was a weekday, and only late morning, there wasn't much traffic to battle as Tess wove her way out of the city and south on 280. She had plenty of time before her sister was expecting her, so she decided to swing off onto Highway 1 at Daly City. It was a much longer drive than going via 101—three hours as opposed to two—but it had been years since she took the meandering Pacific Coast Highway, and she knew the long, picturesque drive would help recharge her internal batteries. Once the highway passed Pacifica, there were only two or three small towns scattered along the way. After that, until it reached the civilization of Santa Cruz, the road wound south for sixty-odd miles alongside the isolated, treacherous, spectacular north coast where for eons, the untamed ocean waged battle against the granite shoreline cliffs.

Tess reveled in every bend in the road, every snaking switchback, pulling off a half-dozen times just to take in the breathtaking ocean views. At Half Moon Bay she stopped to let Dancer gallop on the beach and nosedive into the waves. This was followed by lunch on the patio of the historic Miramar Beach Restaurant, where during Prohibition smugglers in small boats known "rum runners" would drop their illicit cargo at the oceanside restaurant.

She pulled up in front of her sister's single-story, turn-of-the-century Victorian at 4:30 that afternoon. The modest clapboard house featured two beautiful bay windows peering out onto the two-block-long Caledonia Park, just north of the town's main thoroughfare, Lighthouse Avenue. By then the region's ubiquitous fog had vanished, and the nearby bay waters glittered as if lit by a thousand holiday sparklers. Suddenly the air was filled with excited yelping, and a tank-sized yellow Labrador retriever bounded out of the house and through the yard, vaulting across a small table and knocking over a garden statue and empty flowerpot on his way.

"Chloe! Settle down! You're going to kill somebody!" Karen Smithfield came running up behind the dog, trying her best to sound formidable but unable to hide the grin on her face or the laughter in her voice. "Or I'm going to kill *you*," she added, grabbing the dog's collar to keep her from obliterating the white wooden fence in her eagerness.

"Hey, Chloe! Guess who I brought? As if she didn't know," Tess added with a laugh. Dancer was sprinting up and down the fence line, mirroring Chloe on the other side and stopping every few steps to stick his nose through the wide slats and gaining a welcoming slobber from Chloe in the process. "Come on, Dancer, let's use the gate."

The two women hugged lovingly as their dogs romped through the yard. "Wow, sis, I've really, really missed you!" Karen was two inches taller than her older sister, rail-thin, with platinum blonde hair in a short pixie cut hair that perfectly accented her heart-shaped face. At first glance, you would never take them as sisters, but a closer examination revealed that their hazel eyes were virtual carbon copies, their full lips formed the same smile with upturned corner dimples, and in the midst of a giggle-fit their unrestrained laughter carried the same inadvertent screwball snort that only served to make them laugh even harder.

"I've missed you too, kid. You look terrific, as always." Tess envied her sister's eternally-svelte frame that allowed her to wear anything from a ratty T-shirt to a Dior evening gown and have them both drape perfectly as if she were a Paris runway model. She could also eat anything she wanted without gaining so much as an ounce, a fact that Tess concluded was proof positive that the Universe was basically depraved.

"Come on in. Elia's at her best friend's doing homework and Dan's still at the office, so we have some time to ourselves." The house was warm and cozy, and a fire blazed happily in the gas fireplace. "I know it's not five o'clock yet, but how about a glass of wine to unwind?"

"Sounds perfect. My day started out pretty shitty, so I figure I deserve some liquid comfort. Let me just take my bag downstairs and get into something more comfortable." Tess walked down to the guest bedroom, which despite its designation as a basement room had wide French doors opening onto the expansive back yard and three-foot-tall casement windows on each side. She changed into black leggings and a teal green chenille tunic sweater, pulled on a pair of thick socks, and tramped back up the stairs to the living room.

Karen emerged from the kitchen with two glasses of sparkling Gloria Ferrer Blanc de Blancs. "Here's to sisters," she toasted once they both settled into the pale blue oversized sofa. The seats were so deep that Tess opted to curl up rather than stack pillows behind her. "Now, tell me what's been going on," Karen probed. "What's this project that's taken you to...where was it? Russia?"

Tess already decided to hold back on what she told her sister simply because she knew Karen would be both horrified at some of Tess's exploits and terrified for her safety. Better to let her read all the gory details in the *Panorama* article after it was all over.

She was interrupted midway through the story by Dan Smithfield's boisterous arrival and the two dogs sprinting through the door after him. Dan grabbed Tess in a huge bear hug and lifted her off the ground. "Where the hell have you been, Mighty Mouse?" he roared. "I hear you got stuck in some Romanian backwater province a few months ago!" Dan wasn't the greatest when it came to minor details like the names of countries, but that was about his only fault. He was genuine, kind, and good-humored, and Tess cherished him.

Bringing up the rear behind the two dogs was their daughter Elia, a gloriously beautiful child who was set to become a stunning woman. At 12 years old she still adored her Aunt Tess, having yet to metamorphose into the teenage porcupine that was bound to emerge one day soon. The girl, nearly as tall as Tess by now, threw her arms around her and cuddled against her sweater. "Oh, Auntie Tess, I've missed you *soooooo* much! And Dancer, too!" Hearing his name, the dog trotted over and happily pressed his muzzle in between the two of them.

"I've missed you too, pumpkin. And I brought you something from the other side of the world. I've been waiting to give it to you for months." Tess picked up a beautifully wrapped, small square box and presented to the young girl.

"Oh! What is it?"

"Open it up, silly, and you'll see."

Elia tore into the wrapping, opened the lid of the box, and gasped. She pulled out an exquisite glass globe with blue, green, and gold bubbles and swirls. On its base was an engraved artist's signature and the notation, "Romania."

"Oh, Aunt Tess, it's beautiful." Tears filled the girl's eyes. "You brought it all the way back for *me*?"

"Yes, sweetheart. You'll see that the artist was from Romania. I wasn't there, but very nearby, in the country of Ukraine. I found this in a shop next to the inn where I stayed." Late on that second afternoon after she and Vitaly finished their interviews, Tess saw the shop was still open and wandered in to kill some time before they went out again. She saw the glass globe, and knew it was perfect for her niece.

"Thank you, thank you!" Elia said. "I'm gonna go put it in my room!"

As the girl ran down the hall, Karen hugged her sister. "That's so incredibly sweet, Tess. I'll make sure she takes very good care of it."

"Well," laughed Dan, "Romanian, Ukrainian…at least I was close!"

They all headed into the kitchen to start fixing dinner. Dan was one of those equal-opportunity husbands who did household chores, including cooking, alongside his wife as if it were the most natural thing in the world. The three of them bantered happily as they worked, then throughout the meal of grilled salmon, artichokes, salad, and warm French bread. Elia regaled them with stories of her day at school, and a younger boy in the after-school program who accidentally tripped the teacher's aide and gave her a bloody nose. It was an awful mess, she said, but everyone, including the aide, laughed about it later.

That evening after Elia went to bed, Tess finished giving Karen and Dan a few highlights of the story she was working on. Karen, as usual, was frustrated by Tess's reluctance to provide blow-by-blow details, but was mollified by her sister's insistence that much of it remained unsubstantiated and highly confidential.

That next day Tess and Karen spent hours playing with the dogs on the beach, shopping, and simply catching up. While it wasn't all that easy for Tess to relax her focus on the story and push these last months to the back of her mind, she needed to get away from it from time to time. She'd known too many burned-out reporters who went on to second careers as alcoholics, addicts, and lonely, bitter misanthropes, and she refused to join their ranks.

The four of them spent that evening after an early dinner joking and laughing through *Indiana Jones and the Raiders of the Lost Ark*.

Tess was unusually restless that night, dreaming of dark, snake-filled waters and menacing creatures with steaming eyes that crawled through the muck on taloned feet. She awoke several times in a cold sweat, finally giving up a little after five o'clock and dragging herself out of bed and into the shower. She wanted to leave early so she could take advantage of the cool morning and go for a jog with Dancer in the Del Monte Forest, but hadn't planned on it being quite *this* early.

Shed said her goodbyes to Elia the night before, but hated to leave without saying something to Karen and Dan. Turning on the small TV in her room, she half-watched the morning news on KSBW as she was getting ready. By six-thirty the anchors were repeating their lead stories, so Tess switched it off, fed Dancer, shook the sand out of his bed and her shoes, and packed up the car. By then a beam of light shone under her sister's bedroom door, and she softly knocked. Both Karen and Dan were in light bathrobes and walked with Tess, Dancer, and Chloe to the front door.

Once again Dan engulfed Tess in a smothering hug and Karen joined him. "This was great, Tess. I just wish you could've stayed longer."

"Me, too. But you know what they say about time and tide waiting for no man. Or woman. I'll stay in touch and let you know when I wrap things up with the story. Shouldn't be too terribly long now. At least, that's my hope." She bent down and gave Chloe a kiss on the top of her head. "Next time, ask Mom and Dad to bring you up to the mountains for a visit." The big dog slapped her tail against Tess's leg, then gave Dancer a wet kiss.

"She's gonna miss him," said Karen. "And *I'm* gonna miss you. Let's not let it be so long next time, okay?"

Tess watched the two people and their yellow dog in her rearview mirror as she drove off, waving out the window and fighting back a lump in her throat.

Once on Forest Avenue, she started scanning for the neighborhood coffee shop where she liked to stop when she visited Karen. There it was: Monterey Bagels & Brew. She looked for a parking spot along the street, inadvertently missing the entrance into an adjacent lot. That side of the street was marked as either no-parking or loading zones, so she drove two blocks up, turned around, and found an empty slot about a block up from the coffee shop. She told Dancer she'd be back in a bit and he looked dejected, which he did every time she left him, whether for five minutes or five hours. She was sure it was all a ploy to guilt her into taking him along, and sometimes it worked. Not this morning, though, since the café didn't have outdoor seating.

Inside the small shop at least half the tables were occupied, even though it was just a few minutes before seven o'clock. The smell of coffee and bagels was enticing, and Tess got in line to order then stepped aside to wait.

"Tess?" came the call from the barista, and she reached for her waiting coffee and toasted blueberry bagel. Without warning, icy fingers crawled up her spine and neck and she began to feel as if her body was floating just an inch or two off the ground. The pastry-filled display case suddenly turned into the snake-infested waters from her dream, and she struggled to catch her breath. Then as quickly as it happened, everything returned to normal, with the bagels and coffee cakes and fruit-filled croissants inside the glass-front counter, but leaving Tess left with a palpable feeling of being watched.

She stepped back and turned around, drink and bagel in hand, then felt the floor start to give way underfoot.

"Oh, shit!" The feeling was so real that she let out a startled, involuntary cry. An older man standing a foot or so away reached out and grabbed her arm to steady her, as she realized the entire café had gone silent and everyone was looking in her direction. Most of them seemed quizzical or even concerned, so Tess responded with a laugh and a thank-you to the gentleman.

Amidst the chuckling patrons was an unsmiling, otherwise-unremarkable looking man who seemed to be staring a hole through her. His face was deeply creased and his eyes were dark as a midnight shadow. Then he went back to reading his newspaper and she put him out of her mind. She did wonder, however, what the ominous reptile-filled vision was about. Weird, she thought, because I'm not especially afraid of snakes. Maybe a remnant of the slithering asps in the *Raiders'* Well of Souls scene.

The strong coffee was the perfect morning potion, and the bagel, literally stuffed with ripe, fresh blueberries, was the best she'd ever tasted. *Maybe I'll stop by for a half-dozen on my way back from our walk, and put them in the freezer when I get home. Okay: and maybe snack on one while I'm driving.*

She wandered over to the news rack and picked up a copy of the free *Monterey County Weekly*, browsing through the stories as she sipped her drink. By the time she finished, she realized that every table in the little café was full and the line at the counter was two-deep.

Tess got up, gulped down the last drops of her coffee, and headed out the door for the mystical Del Monte Forest.

23

True to type, she dismissed the failed attempt to kill her on that foggy Monterey morning or the subsequent attack in the hospital, pushing forward with her recovery at a rate that surprised almost everyone. Crediting sheer stubbornness and an urgent desire to get back home, the truth was that Tess hated being ill, and even more, needing to be taken care of. But as the fetching Dr. Holland kept reminding her, she'd sustained a near-lethal injury, and he refused to consider the notion of her being alone in what he teasingly referred to as "the wilderness" right away.

"Tess, I know you're tough and independent and more than a little pig-headed..."

"Pig-headed?" Tess interrupted with a laugh. "I take deep offense to that characterization, Dr. Holland." During her time in the hospital, Tess and the doctor had developed a playful, bantering relationship that they both obviously enjoyed. Plus, Tess thought, the man was wonderfully good-looking and possessed a wicked sense of humor.

"No, I stand by my words," Holland replied with mock solemnity. "You *are* a little pig-headed. Regardless, you need to remember how badly you were injured, and it's going to take a while before you're back up to full speed.

Even half-speed. So what I want is to discharge you to a sub-acute rehab facility in the area where I can keep an eye on you."

"Excuse me? 'Sub-acute rehab facility'? What you're talking about is a convalescent hospital, and I'm *not* doing that. Not now, not ever. End of conversation."

"Tess, be reasonable. You simply can't go home where you'll be alone and with less-than-perfect medical care available. You don't have the physical strength yet to manage on your own, and that's a fact. You'll need help, 24/7."

"So I'll hire a home-health aide. Big deal."

"Yes, it *is* a big deal. A home-health aide doesn't have the competency to take care of you. You need skilled nursing and you need to be close enough that I can continue to monitor you."

Her jaw set in a hard line, and her eyes lost any trace of softness. "I absolutely won't go into one of those places where people are just waiting to die, even if it means shooting myself first or taking a handful of pills. I'm deadly serious, Roger."

"I appreciate what you're saying, but..."

"But nothing. Find another way." Tess had dug in her heels and wasn't budging.

The doctor breathed a defeated sigh, then said, "Okay, I'll see what I can figure out." He lightly touched her arm. "I can't promise anything, though."

"Find a way, Roger."

As it turned out, the doctor *was* able to find a way, thanks in part to a chance circumstance and in no small measure to the fact that Tess had financial resources. Her nurse-angel Billie Tremayne was retiring from the hospital, and Roger talked her into taking a temporary job as Tess's full-time nurse. Days only, he promised her—I'll find someone else to take the night shift.

"And it's only for two or three weeks," he pleaded, "a month at most. After that you can head back to your beloved New Orleans and spend your days sipping sweet tea under a banyan tree."

"I've never seen a banyan tree in New Orleans, doctor," Billie replied with a grin. "We have southern magnolias. And oak."

"Okay, then: sipping sweet tea under a magnolia. Sounds almost as poetic."

It didn't take long to convince her that this would be a comfortable way to ease out of nursing. Plus, she'd come to really like "Miss Tess," as she called her patient. That gal is certainly *douce*, but also *entêté*. Sweet, but stubborn.

A day later, Roger located a short-term rental just a mile from the hospital, arranged for a second nurse to cover the night shift, and scheduled Tess's discharge for the following morning.

The charming two-bedroom cottage that Roger Holland found was perfect. On a quiet side street, the shaded front and back gardens were filled with mature azaleas, rhododendrons, and lush ferns, plus a small pond complete with several resident frogs that sang Tess to sleep every night. By then she convinced Detective McKittrick to replace the 24/7 police guard with something less intrusive, so he just had officers drive by the house several times a day, insisting on staying in touch with Tess and her nurse by phone. The FBI was unusually silent.

Even as she resisted the help, Tess was inwardly glad for Billie Tremayne's cheerful, assured presence and wealth of medical knowledge, not to mention her talent at Louisiana cooking. At this rate, she thought as she scooped up a second serving of shrimp étouffée, it won't be long before I put on those twenty pounds I lost in the hospital.

The good doctor came by almost every day. After a while Tess began to wonder how much of it was out of medical necessity, how much was Billie's exceptional cooking (he often managed to arrive near dinnertime), and how much was their own growing friendship-slash-relationship. Undoubtedly, he was an excellent physician: Billie sang his praises to the heavens and said every nurse who'd worked with him concurred.

Unlike some doctors who started believing in their own infallibility and superiority somewhere around their second year of residency, Roger Holland was unpretentious and occasionally even close to humble. He'd been consistently supportive whenever Tess tumbled into a cycle of grief over losing Dancer, never once implying that she should "get over it," or that he'd been "just a dog." He respected his nurses, Billie said, trusting their opinions and observations, and was unfailingly courteous to patients and staff alike. In short, he was somewhat of a rare breed. If he'd been a surgeon, she laughed, he'd be a fully endangered species.

The doctor was careful not to cross any ethical boundaries with Tess, even though as the days wore on she began to wish he would. Having a fling with the doc might help alleviate her escalating boredom at being confined to the house, even though she'd finally gotten out for short walks with Billie. With the lure of home becoming stronger every day, she redoubled her efforts at rehabilitation, hoping that Roger would give her his blessing to leave sooner rather than later. Every time she brought up the subject, however, he pointed to her inability to do this or that, which she needed to be able to handle once she was home alone. She knew he was right, but bristled at the notion nevertheless.

After two weeks she felt strong enough emotionally to get back to work, and early one morning called Superintendent Marley in London.

"Well, Ms. Alexander," he said with an obvious smile in his voice, "I never thought I'd be saying this: but I'm awfully glad to hear your voice."

"Thank you, Superintendent. I'm glad to have a voice to speak with. And thank you for the beautiful flowers and your note."

"I was absolutely devastated to hear of the tragic death of your dog and the attempts on your life. Do you think...do they have any idea of who..."

"I think we both know who was behind it, even though we'll probably never be able to prove it. The authorities here have run into a brick wall as I knew they would, and I'm quite sure that the man who actually mounted the attacks has either gone to ground or is *in* the ground. I think for the moment I'm safe, but based on what I know about Yevtushenko I don't believe he's the type to give up. And speaking of Yevtushenko, is there any news about him?"

Not really, answered the superintendent, although Scotland Yard's digital forensic team was digging into ways of accessing his financial records. If they could get him on money-laundering, then other things might fall into place.

After securing the superintendent's promise that he would keep her in the loop, she opened her darknet email client and saw three different emails from Anton that had accumulated while she'd been in the hospital, the last one simply asking, *Where are you?* She shot off a quick response, apologizing and inventing another half-truth about how she'd been overwhelmed with interviews and research. No sense worrying the man.

It took several hours for Anton to respond.

> I am relieved to hear from you. There is nothing new with Y. I have system in place to alert me should he try to leave Ukraine, eliminating need for surveillance. Is that acceptable?

Tess replied that it was more than acceptable, and that she would wire a payment for his work thus far. She didn't ask what his "system" was for keeping on top of Yevtushenko's moves, but as she did with Marley, asked that he keep her informed.

That next week Tess once again broached with her doctor the idea of going home. Almost three weeks had passed, she argued, and he'd told her a month, so they were close. She was still restricted from lifting anything heavier than ten pounds, but couldn't think of anything that heavy she would need to hoist.

"Come on, Roger. I really need to get back home, if for no other reason than my own sanity. I appreciate all your efforts in setting me up here, but it's not *home*. I need to get back to my tall trees, my garden, all of it. I don't want to leave AMA, but I will."

"That's ridiculous, Tess."

"Look, I'll make you a deal," she retorted. "If you let me head back at, say, the beginning of next week, then you can come up every weekend to check on me for as long as your worried heart desires. I have a guest house with all the amenities, decent broadband access, even cell service if you stand in just the right spot on the property that we call 'the phone booth.' All the luxuries of a four-star hotel. In Botswana."

He laughed in spite of himself. "I have to admit, you've made a pretty convincing argument. I'm just not sure that I can trust you to..."

"Yes you can, Roger," she interrupted again. "I'll lay off the running, I won't lift, I won't work on my landscaping, I won't do any chainsawing. The *last* place I want to be is back in some damn hospital, so you can be certain I'm not going to do anything that might land me there."

"I can come up every week?"

"Every week. Twice a week if you want."

"Well, that might be a bit excessive," he chuckled, then paused for a few seconds and said lightly, "although the idea of seeing you more often isn't exactly excruciating."

Tess sensed heat rising on her face and felt like she was seven years old again when McCartney Smith (yeah, named after Sir Paul) said he wanted her to have his baby. Looking back, she didn't think either one of them had the foggiest idea of what that meant, but at the time it was enough to make her blush furiously and sock him in the arm.

She wasn't at all tempted, however, to sock Roger Holland in the arm.

"So," she managed to choke out, "do we have a deal? I know Billie wants to get back to New Orleans, too, so that's an extra incentive."

"All right. Tuesday of next week. Not a day sooner or I'll call the Highway Patrol and tell them you're driving under the influence." He was joking, Tess but figured he was just concerned enough to do it if he thought she was endangering her recovery.

She raised her right hand. "I swear on my sword that I will not leave Palo Alto before Tuesday. But," she asked, "why Tuesday, specifically? Why not Monday or Wednesday?"

"Because I'm off next Tuesday, and I can be here to make sure you haven't left before that."

Tess sighed and rolled her eyes. "Oh, ye of little faith."

When Tuesday came, Tess was impatient to get on the road. Up before six, she started the coffee, stripped her bed of its sheets, and grabbed her towels, tossing them all in the apartment-sized washing machine. Billie had left the previous afternoon, and Tess already washed and dried her towels and linens. She poked around the little house to make sure she hadn't missed anything that needed to go in the washer, then settled down with her coffee and one of Billie's luxurious muffins to watch *Morning Joe* on MSNBC.

By the time Roger Holland drove up a little before eight, Tess's car was packed and she was ready to get on the road. She handed him the house key and two bottles of Sierra foothill wine, a 2013 Estate Viognier and a 2014 Reserve Syrah. Once again the owner of the Deer Creek Confectionary came through for Tess, shipping the wine with only a few days' notice.

"Wine snobs are beginning to admit that the Sierra foothills are producing some pretty darned good wines," Tess explained. "There are a couple of great wineries in the area near me, so if you'd like, we can visit some tasting rooms while you're up there checking on me."

"I'd really like that," he replied. "And thanks for the wine, Tess. You really didn't have to, you know."

"It's not a question of 'have to,' Roger. I wanted to give you something from my part of the state in appreciation for what you've done for me, even though two bottles of wine are an awfully paltry thanks."

She reached up to give him a hug, and for a moment he held her out and just looked at her, his eyes softening. Then he bent down, encircled her in his arms, and very softly kissed her.

"I probably shouldn't have done that," he said. "Professional ethics and so forth."

"To hell with professional ethics, doctor," she smiled as she drew him down to her. "It's not like I'm going to rat on you to the Medical Board."

He kissed her again, long and smooth, and when he pulled away he touched the dimpled corners of her mouth with his fingertips. "I have a hunch you're going to be a heap of trouble for me, Miss Tess."

"Awww," she responded slyly as she slid into her car, "what's the fun of life if there isn't a bit of trouble to make it interesting?"

The house was stale and incredibly empty. Tess walked from room to room opening doors and windows to bring in some fresh air, even though the day was quite warm. Rounding the corner at the top of the stairs, she saw on her bedroom floor Dancer's overstuffed bed, his favorite ratty, chewed up penguin toy resting on top of it. With a moan of pain that had nothing to do with her injuries, Tess stumbled to the dog bed and lowered herself onto it. She lay there, curled up like a newborn puppy with her arms clasped around her knees, sobbing softly, until exhausted, she finally fell asleep.

The next morning she was awakened by a phone call from Will Dorsey, the Deer Valley Chief of Police whom she'd known for years, and who'd been alerted by Detective McKittrick. He didn't have the manpower to offer her round-the-clock protection, he explained, so he reached out to the county sheriff for help. Between the two of them, they would have an officer stop by her house a couple of times a day to make sure she hadn't seen anything suspicious. The timing would be irregular, Dorsey said, just in case any lurking bad guys tried to detect a schedule.

He also demanded that she install a home security system right away, something he'd been begging her to do for years simply because her line of work often brought her into contact with some pretty sketchy characters. I'm not taking no for an answer, he chided, adding that he already contacted the most reliable alarm company in the region; they would call her that day to set up an appointment.

"I'm just really sorry this happened, Tess," he said. "And I'm terribly sorry about Dancer, too. He was one hell of a fine dog."

Her eyes filling with tears, Tess agreed, then thanked the chief for his concern and sympathies. He gave Tess his private phone number, said he was available to her any day, any time. Just call, he added, and I'll be there in a heartbeat.

She shouldn't have been surprised to see FBI Agent Jephson standing at her door.

She invited him inside, offered him some iced tea, and they sat at opposite ends of the small dining table. Outside the window, several iridescent hummingbirds battled over space at the feeders, even though there were more than enough feeding ports for them all. Short man syndrome, thought Tess to herself.

"I'm glad to see you looking so well, Ms. Alexander," the agent said, his deep voice filling the room.

"Thank you, Agent. What can I do for you?"

"I was hoping you could fill me in on a few things." He caught Tess's frown and quickly added, "No, I won't push you for your sources. Just need to clear up a few details that remain a bit fuzzy."

"I'll do my best," Tess said.

"Can you give me any description of the man who attacked you in Crimea?"

"I wish I could. Unfortunately, it was dark, he was dressed in all black, and he came up from behind me. I never got a look at his face."

"What about afterward?"

"Afterward? You mean, after he attacked me?"

"Yes. What happened to him? That was never very clear in your statement."

No it wasn't, Tess thought. "Well, my translator managed to wrestle him to the ground, but he got away. I left Crimea that morning."

"Do you know anything about him?"

Tess decided it would do no harm to give the agent what little information she had. "His name was Volodymyr Popov, a Russian-Ukrainian whose nickname was Babay, or Bogeyman. Apparently he was one of the trafficking ring's main enforcers."

Jephson raised his eyebrows. "How did you come by that information?"

"Through my Ukrainian informant who located and questioned one of Popov's underlings. During the questioning, he also learned that the traffickers knew my identity, which was news to us all."

"And you have no idea of what happened to this Popov?"

"No, I have no clue as to where he is." Not a lie, since she didn't know where the Plan'orka deposited the body.

"How did the traffickers learn of your identity?"

"The man said they'd seen my name and photo in newspapers."

"Ahhh. That makes sense. How about the man who attacked you in Monterey? Know anything about him?"

"Nothing beyond what I've already shared with Detective McKittrick and you."

"How do you suppose he knew where you were, and where you were going that day?"

Tess thought about those two incidents at the house where she felt as if she were being watched. "I can only guess that he or someone else connected with the ring had been following me for some time, keeping track of my movements. He probably followed me to San Francisco where I met with a potential contact, then down to Pacific Grove. I believe the detective told you about the man I saw in the coffee shop that morning, and how he may have been the same man who tried to kill me?"

"Yes, but can you give any better description? What's in your statement is rather vague."

"That's because he simply didn't make that much of an impression on me at the time. I noticed him for a second or two, but honestly didn't pay much attention. If it *was* that same man in the forest, all I have is a hazy memory of a pock-marked face and dark, almost black, eyes. Frankly, Agent Jephson, I think that's a dead-end: my suspicion is that whomever hired him to take me out ended up taking *him* out because he didn't get the job done. He's probably fish-food in the bay by now."

The agent nodded solemnly. "Yes, I expect you're correct. The law of the jungle. Now, what about that contact in San Francisco?"

"It turned out to be a total bust, Agent. I drove all the way down there, and she refused to tell me anything."

"Can you give us her name?"

"No, but I *can* tell you that she was initially recruited by Dragos Yevtushenko in Odessa, ostensibly to be a swimsuit model in Hollywood. One of his men kept her imprisoned in a hotel room in Odessa and gradually turned her into a sex slave. After that, he got her into Mexico and across the border into San Diego. From there they ended up in Sacramento, where he was busted for pimping and she for prostitution. Some 'swimsuit modeling' job, eh?"

The agent sighed and shook his head. "It's almost always something like this that entices the younger girls: the dream of either modeling or acting. Then before they know it…."

"Yeah: they're a fly caught in a poisoned spiderweb. Reminds me of what someone wrote about Charles Manson: for young people searching for heaven on earth, Manson instead gave them something closer to hell—then he convinced them that this hell was everything they'd ever wanted."

They were both silent for several seconds, then the agent asked, "Don't suppose you could give me the pimp's name? It could be important if he's connected to Yevtushenko."

Tess thought for a moment, then realized Jephson could probably find out on his own with a bit of sleuthing.

She only hoped it wouldn't lead him to Anichka. "His name is Vasyl Hordiyenko. Fairly small-time pimp, probably one of dozens who recruited girls for Yevtushenko and Flemming. His trail goes cold after he was released from jail for pandering, but then I've never tried to track him, figuring he wouldn't be terribly useful."

"You're probably right about him being useless, but it won't hurt to try to find him. I understand you have someone who is 'monitoring' Yevtushenko in Ukraine."

Tess wondered how he knew, then remembered she'd told Marley. "Yes, but Yevtushenko hasn't made even the slightest move to leave Odessa, much less Ukraine. I was hoping he'd take a trip to Europe, maybe to check up on another of his charnel houses, where Interpol or Scotland Yard could nab him, but so far, no such luck."

"We've put him on the no-fly list and have border alerts in place in Europe and the U.S., though I expect he uses a private plane and has ways of circumventing customs and border patrols. Plus, we know that in the past he traveled freely between Ukraine and Russia, likely by paying off border guards. I see no reason why that would have changed. That being said, I'd really appreciate the name of the fellow who's watching him."

"I'm sure you would, Agent, but that's not going to happen. He's put his life very literally on the line for this and for me, and I need to protect him."

Jephson frowned and mumbled something under his breath, then stood to leave. "I hear you finally installed a security system here at your home. Glad to know it. You're aware you're still in danger."

"Yes, I'm aware of that."

"Take care of yourself, Ms. Alexander."

Roger Holland was utterly captivated. By the soaring evergreens, by the lush and blooming landscape, by the charming town of Deer Valley, and most of all, by his beautiful, headstrong, extraordinary patient.

The 180-mile jaunt from Palo Alto northeast into the Sierra mountains didn't appear to faze him in the least. In fact, he insisted that the drive offered him time to decompress from the frantic pace of the hospital and the demands of both patients and hospital management. As Stanford's Chief of Hospital Medicine, Dr. Holland and his staff of hospitalists juggled the requirements of providing inpatient care along with overseeing the medical residency program; Holland also had the unenviable task of acting as intermediary between the clinical needs of his medical staff and the political calculations of the hospital administrators. It was, he said, a tightrope act that was wearing ever more thin with each passing year.

"So," Tess asked him one morning as they were walking through the exquisite grounds of the Empire Mine State Park in nearby Grass Valley, "why not just call it quits? Hand over your Division Chief's hat and be done with all the political bullshit? Go back to being a regular doctor?"

"Don't think I haven't been tempted," he said thoughtfully. "The job pretty much doomed my marriage—or, more accurately, my obsession about the job doomed my marriage. I was younger and stupider then, and figured that our relationship could just take care of itself. She tried to be understanding and tolerant, but when your partner is gone ninety percent of the time and the few times he's home he's pretty much of an emotional zombie, tolerance and understanding can go only so far. Like I said, stupider."

Tess couldn't picture the man ambling along beside her as an emotional zombie. But then, that was ten years ago, and she knew better than most how much life, and how people, can change over time.

This was Roger's second weekend at Tess's home, and while she was making so much progress in healing physically that she seriously doubted the need for such close medical attention, she wasn't about to dissuade him from making those weekly house calls. The kiss they shared when she left the Palo Alto cottage and the multitude since then had re-colored their relationship, and Tess was eager to see where it would lead.

That evening they lay on matching chaise lounges on Tess's wide back deck under a bottomless charcoal sea of dancing stars while she pointed out the late summer constellations: Queen Cassiopeia, the Great and Little Bears Ursa Major and Minor, Sagittarius the centaur with the body of a horse and torso of a man atop it, and the beautiful winged horse Pegasus.

"It's exquisite, Tess, all of it," he sighed. "It's a wonder that you ever want to leave." His eyes now adjusted to the darkness, he popped a plump, yellow-green grape into his mouth from the basketful they'd picked earlier that day and that now rested on the table between them.

"Quite often, I don't. I'm lucky to have the kind of job where I can do a lot of my work from home." She reached across the table to seize a grape for herself, and he stopped her hand midway with his own then wound his fingers through hers as he stood and walked to the side of her chaise, then gently pulled her to her feet. "This setting isn't the only thing that's exquisite. As corny and clichéd as this may sound, the woman I'm looking at is equally so." He tipped up her chin and touched his mouth to hers. His lips were cool and warm at the same time, and sent a fiery shiver skittering down her spine. She could taste the grape's spicy-sweet juice on his tongue as her breath quickened, and in an instant the wheeling stars became the earth and the earth the sky until it was all one, and she was a part of it, spinning and gyrating to the symphony of the universe and her own desires.

An hour later they lay together on Tess's bed in mutual exhaustion, damp with sweat, their arms and legs intertwined like the roots of a tropical rainforest tree. As he finger-combed her tawny hair, arranging the thick, wavy strands into an Aphrodite halo around her face, Roger leaned over and kissed her gently.

"Are you okay? Uhh, your injuries: are they…are you…did I…I mean, I tried to be gentle…." Flustered, he gave up.

Tess opened her eyes and smiled. "I'm fine. It's all good. Better than good. If there were any doubts I'd have stopped things before they got started." Their lovemaking was insistent and laced with mutual craving, yet at first Roger was tentative in his explorations as if she could shatter like a thin crystal goblet at any moment. He abandoned any semblance of cautiousness, however, when she circled him with her legs and rolled on top of him. The brief stab of pain she felt in her abdomen—*whoa! haven't used those muscles in a while!*—evaporated amidst the waves of passion.

She snuggled into his arms and began to trace a spiderweb on his chest with her fingertips. The amount of dark hair on his upper body was perfect, she thought: not so much that he looked like a Neanderthal, but not like a naked mole rat either. In a few minutes she heard his breathing slow to deeper sighs, and her own eyes fluttered and closed.

Sometime in the middle of the night she opened her eyes, kissed him into wakefulness, and they made love again, this time slowly and rhythmically, allowing their bodies to become attuned to one another.

Hours later, Tess awakened to the caress of sunlight on her face and turned to see Roger watching her. He smiled and took her hand. "Like you said, that was good. Better than good."

"Yeah, it was."

"Did you know you're a beautiful woman?"

"Ahh, not so much. I won't win any Miss America contests, but I'm not like the bearded lady at the circus either. Somewhere in the middle. Hopefully leaning more toward Miss America than the other."

He laughed and shook his head. "You don't give yourself enough credit, Tess. You're gorgeous. And I'm not the only one who thinks so."

"Oh, yeah? You and what army?"

"Not necessarily an army, but darn near every man in the hospital was half in love with you by the time you left. I could see it on their faces."

"Nah, it's just my animal magnetism," Tess joked, gently raking his face with her fingernails.

"Well, that too."

They laughed together, then Tess threw back the covers. "Okay, I need to head to the bathroom. You know, I always think it's so weird how they portray this in the movies: there's no way a woman could get up from sex and put on clothes right away, because she'd be standing in a puddle. What the hell do they think happens to all that ejaculate? It just disappears into some cosmic black hole, leaving her fresh and dry as a flower in May?"

Her comment caught Roger completely off-guard, and he burst into booms of laughter. That got Tess laughing, leading to her involuntary snort, which made them both laugh even harder. She bolted from the bed and scampered into the bathroom, accompanied by Roger's continued laughter.

The following week's darknet email from Anton was disturbing.

> Y has fled his home in Odessa without tripping my security alerts. I am deeply sorry, I have failed you.

Tess hesitated before responding, not wanting to multiply Anton's obvious guilt at losing the man.

> *You have not failed me. Yevtushenko is more ingenious than we thought. You did your best.*

> I shall not rest until he is located.

Tess could almost see Anton's fury.

> *Where do we go from here*?

> I have people I can speak to. They may be able to help. I shall let you know.

Tess tried her best to heed his words. The idea of Yevtushenko in the wind wasn't terribly reassuring, but it was out of her hands. She knew Anton would do everything in his power to find the man, and based on the rabbits he'd pulled out of the hat since she met him, it wouldn't surprise her if he succeeded.

Meanwhile, she was absorbed in trying to put together her story for the magazine, even though she wasn't sure what kind of resolution it would have. If nothing changed, not much of a resolution at all. But then, not every story has a slam-dunk, put-a-lid-on-it conclusion. Sometimes they just hang there like the wisp of a summer's spider web, stuck in that narrow atmosphere between earth and sky.

The following Saturday she sat down with Roger over a dinner of linguini with chicken sausage, spinach and a sauce of fresh tomatoes, and told him the entire story, from beginning to now. If anything was going to make him bolt, it would be knowing what she was involved in, and she'd rather it happen sooner than later. She finally finished as they were sharing a dessert of fresh strawberries and a light Riesling.

He was silent for a long while, then reached out for her hand. "Well, I knew some of the story, of course: it isn't every day that a Pulitzer prize winning reporter ends up in our ER with two gunshot wounds, gets attacked in her hospital room, and then has the added benefit of an armed guard. You told me bits and pieces over the past couple of months, but I'm glad to have the whole picture."

"Unfortunately, I wish I could say it's over but I'm not sure it is. Not with Yevtushenko on the loose. And the FBI on my ass. And God knows who else. If you feel like this is all just too heavy, that it's all just too much drama and chaos, I absolutely understand. It's a lot to handle. Like someone once said to me, you didn't sign up for this."

"Maybe not, and maybe so. I said I had a feeling you'd

be trouble for me, Tess, though I'm not sure I expected it to be a life-and-death kind of trouble," he added wryly. "Regardless, you trapped me in your web, you wonderful witchy woman, and in case you haven't noticed, I'm not struggling to get out."

"Not now, maybe... "

"I'll let you know if it gets to be too much. Deal?"

Tess stared at him long and hard over her glass, then took a final sip. "Okay, deal."

Later, they sailed through the night together on a cloud of sheets, whirling away from the dark that lingered just over her shoulder, just beyond reach.

PART SIX

Even in the mud and scum of things,
something always, always sings.

~ Ralph Waldo Emerson

Long is the way, and hard,
that out of Hell leads up to light.

~ John Milton
Paradise Lost

24

She was startled by the soft chiming of her bedside phone. Was she dreaming? Or was it a vision? She glanced at the clock, registering the time as only 4:15. Who would be calling at this hour? Her stomach clenched, anticipating terrible news, and picked up the receiver.

"Yes...hello?"

"Ms. Alexander, I'm terribly sorry to ring you at such an abysmal hour." Tess instantly recognized the slight brogue of Chief Superintendent Marley.

"That's quite all right, Superintendent Marley. I'm presuming something has happened."

"Indeed. I hesitated to call so early, but I felt it really shouldn't wait. This morning, I traveled to Pentonville Prison to meet with Ulrich Flemming. He sent me a post indicating that he wanted to speak with me about the case, and asked me to come to the prison. I'm not in the habit of calling on prisoners, but Flemming—well, he's another story. I hoped he might have changed his mind and been willing to provide us with some information on the trafficking ring."

"And did he?"

The officer hesitated. "Yes and no. He's willing to talk,

but not to me. To you."

"Me?" Tess was flabbergasted. "Why me? He doesn't even know me." Aside from the fact that he likely ordered her execution in both Crimea and California, of course.

"I wish I could provide you an answer, but I can't. That's all he would say: that he wishes to speak with you. Now, my one concern is that it's just a ruse to get you here and to…well, I don't know why. To taunt you, perhaps? To bribe you? To intimidate you into not publishing your story? I honestly haven't the vaguest notion."

"Nor do I. It just doesn't make se…"

"I have a greater concern, however," Marley broke in. "And that is for your health. I know that your injuries were extremely serious, life-threatening, in fact. I wasn't even sure if you'd left hospital until I spoke with Detective McKittrick."

"I've been home for a month, Superintendent, and the month before I was in private rehabilitation. So I'm well on my way to being back in fine fettle."

"Even if you weren't, I expect you'd say you were," Marley grumbled. "Are you under a doctor's care?"

Tess blushed in spite of herself. "As a matter of fact, I am. And he even makes house calls."

"House calls? Most doctors say they've not got the time, at least here in the U.K.. And with the miserable state of health care in the States, I'm surprised…" Marley stopped and coughed self-consciously. "I apologize, Ms. Alexander. That was ill-mannered of me."

"No need to apologize, Superintendent. The health care system in the U.S. *is* miserable, and has been for decades. The irrational fear of anything that smacks even remotely of 'socialized' medicine has kept us pretty much in the Dark Ages; I have no idea if we'll ever be able to claw ourselves out the swamp we've created for ourselves. But to reiterate, I'm perfectly fit for travel. What are the procedures for getting me into the prison?"

"I can handle the particulars for you, Ms. Alexander. Since you'll be going through official law enforcement channels, you'll have much greater leeway than if you were a civilian visitor and we can make the arrangements much more quickly. You'll need to fax or email me a copy of your passport and one other form of photo identification, the sooner the better."

"I'll do it today. Then I'll make my travel arrangements and let you know. Are there certain days and times for visiting?"

"Yes, but that won't apply in this case. I'll send an official escort to take you to the prison, which will save you from having to go through the prison visitor's procedures."

"That's very kind of you, Superintendent. But since I'm presuming you'll want to interview me as soon as possible afterward, how about I just order a car when I'm finished at the prison and come by the station?"

"That would be ideal."

"Good. I'll be in touch as soon as I have my flight and lodging settled." She paused, deciding whether or not to tell Marley about Yevtushenko. "I don't suppose you've been in touch with Anton in Odessa?"

"As a matter of fact, I have. He reached out to me a few days ago to say Yevtushenko disappeared. Too bad. He's a devious character, that one."

"Yes, Anton feels he let me down. He really wanted to see that bastard caught and behind bars with Flemming."

"Perhaps he still will, Ms. Alexander. Perhaps with any luck… "

Ahh: there's my wonderful "hope springs eternal" again.

"I must admit, Superintendent, that I'm intrigued by why Flemming wants to meet with me. It'll be interesting to see what happens."

"Interesting, indeed," replied Marley. "I shall await your communication. And once again, pardon the early morning intrusion."

"Perfectly okay, Superintendent. I'm glad you called."

Tess sat on the edge of the bed and tried to wrap her head around this strange new development. What the hell could Flemming want with her? *Was* it just a ruse, and if so, what was the end game? She couldn't imagine she'd be in danger: much as she hated going into them, prisons were probably one of the safest places for an outsider to be. Plus, she had Marley watching out for her. The thought helped calm the wild thrumming of her heart.

She scheduled a flight out of Sacramento for the following day and contacted Mrs. Kitchen to ask about reserving a room at the Elsinore. The woman was delighted to hear Tess's voice, and said that even if it meant throwing out another guest she would find a room for her. After scanning and emailing her ID and flight information to Marley, she braced herself for a video chat with Roger.

His reaction was predictable. "Tess, this is insanity. You're in the middle of recovering from an attempt on your life, and now you're going to travel over five thousand miles to talk to the man who was probably behind the *first* murder attempt? Do you know how crazy that sounds?"

"It may sound crazy, Roger, but it's my job..."

"Your *job* is to stay alive," he interrupted, glowering. "To stay safe. And I just don't believe you'll be safe, doing this. You just can't go."

"*Can't. Go??*" She spoke the words slowly, with rising volume. "I hate to be the one to inform you, but this is *my* life, not yours."

"I know that, Tess, and you've managed to live it quite well up to now. Well, up to a few months ago. But you're simply in too much danger, too much..."

Now it was her turn to interrupt him. "Roger, we're not doing this. I realize you're coming from a place of caring, but you need to back off." *What I really want is to scream that he has no right to tell me what to do.* She took a deep breath and dropped her voice. "I'm not some crazy-ass adrenaline junkie with a death wish: in fact, I have a pretty well-honed sense of survival and by and large I know how to keep myself from harm. I don't do stupid things, which isn't to say I don't take some risks—but shit, life is a risk. Getting out of bed every morning is a risk. Driving down the damn street is a risk. My job *has* always, and *will* always, entail a certain amount of risk, but I do my best to mitigate it by being careful and sensible and calling on other people for help when I need it. I'm sorry, but this isn't up for discussion."

About halfway through Tess's rejoinder the doctor began looking down and pursing his lips, and now sat forward in his chair as if he could reach her through the screen. "No," he admitted sheepishly, "*I'm* the one who should be sorry. I do that sometimes: come off like a controlling jackass with some inalienable right to dictate someone else's life terms. Which I don't have.

"I realize this is your profession, and that it comes with a certain degree of danger. That doesn't thrill me because I care about you, but you've been doing this a long time and survived thus far. Well, except for almost *not* surviving a couple of months ago. I can't help but wonder how many other close calls you haven't told me about..." he added, almost to himself.

"But all that aside, you're a grown woman, and I have to trust that you're not going to take any foolish chances. I know you want to find resolution here, to bring some measure of justice to these women. That's part of who you are: I've known that from the very beginning, and if I couldn't honor it I shouldn't have gotten involved with you in the first place. Just do me a favor?"

"If I can."

"Please be careful. And come home to me, okay?"

Tess blinked in surprise at that last sentence, then grinned. "You betcha, doc. I promise you a memorable homecoming."

They say August is one of the best months to visit London, and as Tess's plane descended over the city, she agreed. The day was nearly cloudless, and the sea sparkled in the dipping sun as if some magical deity had tossed huge handfuls of diamonds on its surface. Sunlight glanced off the thousands of city windows, cathedral spires, and the gilded dome of the London Central Mosque, creating an almost fairy-tale panorama worthy of a Harry Potter novel.

Since she only planned on staying three nights, she crammed everything into a large carryon bag to avoid the hassle of the baggage claim, so headed directly to the front of the terminal to hail a cab. Arriving at the Elsinore, she spotted a familiar deep blue Audi parked in front. Once she knew her schedule she had contacted Anthony, inviting him to join her for dinner that first night in town.

She opened the door, and was almost instantly engulfed by a white tornado in the form of Harvey, yipping and bouncing in a tight circle around her feet. She dropped her bag and knelt on the floor, allowing herself to be bathed in joyful dog-kisses. A white-hot lance stabbed her heart as she slipped back and forth between the delight of Harvey's adoration and the anguish of Dancer's loss. Before the dog could lick away Tess's tears, Mrs. Kitchen touched her on the shoulder.

"I heard about your beautiful boy, my dear. I'm so, so sorry. I lit a candle for both of you at Saint John's, I hope you don't mind."

"Of course not. That's very kind of you."

Mrs. Kitchen took Harvey firmly by the collar and said, "Okay, Harvey: that's enough. Calm down or you're like to kiss the lass to death."

Tess stood, and after she and the innkeeper shared a warm hug, she spotted Anthony standing near the couch. "Sure didn't expect to see you again so soon."

They hugged and he patted her lightly on the back. "We were all pretty worried about you, Tess." He reached down and ruffled the dog's fur. "Even Harvey."

At the mention of his name, Harvey started to prance again.

"Uhh-uhh," scolded Mrs. Kitchen with a smile. "Settle." The dog did as he was asked and spreadeagled himself at Tess's feet.

"May I go freshen up before we head out for dinner, Anthony? I won't be but a few minutes."

"Sure, there's no hurry." He looked at his watch. "Our dinner reservations aren't for another hour. Hope you like Italian."

"Love it. Mrs. Kitchen, can you tell me where my room is?" Tess picked up her luggage and walked to the foot of the stairs.

"Same one you were in last time, dear. Luckily, the

guests who were there moved out this morning."

"That's perfect. Can Harvey come up with me?"

"Aye, all right. I'll even let him sleep in your room if you'd like." She giggled lightly. "As if you'd object."

"This means a lot, Mrs. Kitchen." Her voice thickened as her eyes began to mist. "Thank you." She gathered herself, looked at the dog and called, "Come on, Harvey!"

The big white retriever jumped up and shot to Tess's side, then looked expectantly at his owner. "It's okay, Harvey," she said. "You can go with her."

Tess came down ten minutes later, Harvey at her heels, and she and Anthony walked outside into the lukewarm late summer air. They chatted casually as he drove to the restaurant, a steel and glass neo-modern structure perched on the bank of the Thames. Their corner table with a view of the river was ready, and as soon as they sat down, Tess brought Anthony up to speed.

She wrapped up the story just as their dinners arrived, ending with the early-morning call from Marley.

"So, you're heading out to Pentonville to see Flemming tomorrow?"

"Yep, even though prisons give me the heebie-jeebies. But I'm curious about why he's insisting on talking only to me. It doesn't make a lot of sense."

"At least we know he can't get to you in there. Judging by the way he looked at you that day in the Met station when he was arrested, you're not on his Top Ten list of favorite people."

"Which makes his request even stranger and harder to figure."

"That it is for certain." Changing tack, he asked, "What about Yevtushenko? Any word on where he might have gone?"

"Nope. He just vanished into the night according to Anton. Which *also* doesn't make sense: he was fairly safe in Ukraine and surely had no problem controlling his organization from Odessa. I have to wonder, though, if he decided it would be even safer in Russia? After all, Vyacheslav Mikhailovich is still running free there despite the fact that both Europe and the U.S. say he's one of the most dangerous crime bosses in the world, and most likely the ugly head of the Russian-Ukrainian sex trafficking octopus. Sure wouldn't mind seeing *that* head sliced off."

"Which will probably never happen," said Anthony with a shrug. "He's so well-protected, so insulated, that it would take a nuclear bomb to take him down. Of course at his age he could die."

"Any hints about who's next in line to assume the throne whenever he does shuffle off this mortal coil?"

"Not that I know. Not that anyone knows, from what I've heard. Say, do you want some company at Pentonville? I could cut loose from the meeting I have scheduled."

"No, no, that's not necessary, Anthony. I'll be fine."

"Will you let me know how it turns out?"

"Of course I will."

The police car pulled up in front of the B&B at eight the next morning. Mrs. Kitchen gave Tess a travel mug of coffee and two raspberry scones: one for her, one to share with the driver. He eagerly devoured the warm, crusty delicacy before they'd even gone a half-mile, then concurred with the late Mr. Kitchen's verdict that these were without a doubt the best scones in East London.

They drove west, over and alongside the idyllic

Regent's Canal, originally built in 1820 to link the Grand Junction Canal with the River Thames, and even on this summer early morning was already dotted with blue and orange narrowboats.

Crossing the canal once more, they turned north onto New North Road, past Canonbury Gardens and over the New River Path, then west again at Canonbury Square Garden until veering onto Liverpool Road. By now, Tess felt as if she were on a motorized chessboard: first left, then right, then left again until she ended up with no idea whatsoever which direction she was traveling. Unfortunately, she'd neglected to bring along either meclizine or a scopolamine patch, and was getting a bit woozy by the time they finally turned onto Caledonian Road where the hulking prison crouched.

The four-story, decaying redbrick facility was surrounded by twenty-foot high whitewashed walls and row after row of evil-looking razor wire. One of the first "modern" prison designs in Great Britain, it featured a central hall with five radiating wings and cells on both sides. It was designed to hold 520 prisoners in single-man cells, but thanks to a chronic state of overcapacity most of those seven-by-thirteen-foot cubicles now housed two prisoners.

Since she was in a police vehicle they bypassed the regular visitor's entrance, instead driving under the automated crossing arms near the north wall gate used by staff. Her driver, a friendly young sergeant by the name of Billy York, walked her through the doors and to the area where she needed to check in with the prison officials, making sure all her paperwork was in order before he left. He thanked Tess again for the delicious scone, then walked out the way they came.

Tess's nerves were as jumpy as if they were attached to electrical wires. She really hated jails and prisons, but this one was worse than any she'd ever seen. Pentonville, one of the few remaining prisons from the Victorian era, first opened in 1842, and from what she could tell, hadn't seen many upgrades since except to move from gaslight to electricity. From the turn of the twentieth century until 1961, Pentonville even featured execution cells and a gallows, actually serving as a training facility for the nation's executioners.

The few reports she read on the prison were beyond grim, describing severe overcrowding, lack of prisoner access to essentials such as bedclothes and pillows, infestations of roaches and rats, water and sewer leaks, mounds of rotting garbage in the cell and common areas, generally squalid conditions, and an overwhelming prevalence of illegal drugs.

As she waited for her identification to be validated, a cleanshaven, heavyset officer in a short-sleeved white shirt with black shoulder epaulets, black tie, and ill-fitting black trousers approached her. His rank insignia identified him as a Supervising Officer, and his small black badge read Troy Blackbourne.

Tess extended her hand, and he shook it genially. "Welcome to Her Majesty's Prison at Pentonville," he said. "You must be Tess Alexander."

"Yes, I am. Thank you, Officer Blackbourne, and to Governing Governor Outterridge, for extending me this courtesy, even though I'm totally puzzled by your prisoner's demand to see me."

"Indeed, Chief Superintendent Marley explained the reason for your visit, but quite honestly, Flemming's request has us all in the dark."

"Hopefully in short order I'll be able to shed some light."

The woman behind the plexiglass window handed back Tess's passport and Blackbourne escorted her to the doorway that featured a metal detector. Before she passed through, a female officer approached and patted Tess down.

"I apologize for this, Ms. Alexander, but it's protocol for everyone coming into the prison, no matter who they are."

"No need to apologize. I fully understand."

She walked through the detector's passageway and Blackbourne met her on the other side.

"We've set aside a somewhat private cubicle for you that is usually reserved for solicitors to meet with inmates. Please, follow me."

They walked down a narrow hall past a warren of rooms where uniformed officers and civilians worked at desks, computers, printers, file cabinets, and talked on spiral-corded telephone handsets. The mingled smell of mustiness, sweat, and aftershave hung in the damp air. Then into another hallway, and another, until they reached a large room, obviously the visitor's center, filled with small tables with chairs on either side. Prisoners' artwork covered the walls, some of it remarkably good. That didn't surprise Tess, as she'd once visited a prisoners' art show at California's Folsom Prison and picked up a dazzling watercolor of roses in bloom. Just because a man was a serial killer didn't mean he couldn't also be an exceptional artist, although the juxtaposition was jarring.

From there Blackbourne led her to a series of small compartments along one wall separated from the main visitor's area, directed her to a chair, and walked out through a security door. Directly across from Tess on the other side of the small table sat an empty chair. Realizing she was holding her breath, she closed her eyes and tried to relax. Useless. She just needed to hear what Flemming had to say and get out of there. *Then* she could relax. Or throw up.

A door opened on the far wall and Flemming walked through, handcuffed and shackled. His black hair was no longer slicked back from his face, but hung limply at his chin. His face bore a two- or three-day stubble and his formerly neatly-manicured fingernails cried out for the services of a esthetician. What hadn't changed was the look of arrogance and hostility on his face as he regarded Tess.

"So we finally meet, Ms. Alexander."

"Why did you want to see me?" Tess dispensed with any niceties.

"What, no foreplay?" Flemming asked in mock offense. "Come on, relax a little. Let's get to know each other."

"I have no interest in getting to know you, Flemming."

"But what if *I* want to get to know *you*?" he smirked.

"So Google me."

"Oh, aren't we the little bitch today? What's the matter? That time of the month?"

Tess simply stared at him, refusing to allow her disgust to show.

"Okay, okay, I'll play nice. I guess you want to know why I said I wouldn't talk to anyone but you, right?"

"Right."

"Let me ask you a question: why do *you* think I wanted to see you?"

"I have absolutely no idea. And if you're not going to tell me, I have much better things to do with my time." She stood up and started to move away.

"Hey, don't be so thin-skinned, little miss. Sit down, and let's be reasonable."

Tess's strategy of threatening to leave worked. Now the key would be getting him to talk.

"I'm being reasonable, Flemming. It's you who's being the asshole."

He put his hands over his heart and his face took on a fake pained expression. "Ouch. That hurts." Then he gave her a greasy smile and said, "All right, you win. Vanna, let's tell the little lady what's behind Door Number Two."

Tess waited, silent as the Sphynx.

"I understand you've lost our good friend Dragos."

Tess flinched as the tiny hairs on the back of her neck stood up. *How the hell could he know about Yevtushenko? And how could he know we had him under surveillance?* Her mouth went dry in fear, but she willed her face not to show anything. "Sorry. Don't know what you're talking about." Maybe he would say more if she professed ignorance.

"Sure you do, Tess. You don't mind if I call you Tess, do you? Anyway, you absolutely know what I'm talking about. But you'd probably like to know how I know."

"Go on."

"Call it a 'network' that operates to keep certain people informed. Unfortunately, there was a crimp in that network when the *gendarmes* arrived at my home in Surrey, but those responsible for the obstruction have been dealt with, and the system summarily enhanced. Witness my knowledge of dear Mr. Yevtushenko."

Tess reasoned that revealing her curiosity would only entice him to further toy with her. "So?" She stifled a yawn. "Sorry, this is becoming tedious."

Flemming's eyes snapped in fury, then instantly

calmed. He was nothing if not the master of his emotions. "Far be it from me to bore you, my dear. Let's see if I can't spice things up a bit: I have only recently—yesterday noon, in fact—been in contact with Dragos." He fixed Tess with a direct stare. "Hmmm: do I detect a hint of surprise on your pretty face? Well, as you Americans say, you ain't heard nothin' yet. He has, in fact, returned from the wilderness and already begun revitalizing my ground operations here in the land of the Brits. You *do* recall what those operations are, don't you?" he added, his lip turning up into a sneer.

"So far, I haven't heard a thing I didn't already know." She was lying, of course.

"Right-o. That being said, his position is merely interim until my release is accomplished. Which should be within a fortnight."

Tess barked a hard laugh. "Oh, really? What gives you that idea? They've got you on so many charges you'll need two lifetimes to live out your prison term. Then there's that little matter of the statute allowing for life sentences for sex trafficking. If anyone deserves that sentence, it's you."

Flemming's eyes narrowed, but an insipid smile remained pasted to his face. "As I recall British law, there's this strange requirement for something called evidence, and in this case that evidence appears to be evaporating with each passing day. You remember my house-manager Duncan Ceannaideach, on whom you made such a strong impression in your fair-haired fashion-icon disguise, and the young man Grigory Chaykovsky who managed my London home? Well, after both of them lied shamelessly to the authorities about me in order to obtain deals, each made bail and have apparently disappeared. I suspect Duncan returned to the wild highlands of his native

Scotland, while Mr. Chaykovsky is most likely in his Russian motherland. I'm always so happy to see people return to the lands of their birth. Makes one's heart warm, doesn't it?"

"There's a lot more on you than just the word of those two trolls."

"Oh, yes: sweet little Raisa from Chechnya, who used such ugly words about me and my dear friend Ludmila. I hear she missed her family and loved ones so badly that she too returned to that war-torn region. Such a beautiful girl. I cannot imagine she will survive for long there, amidst all those pitiless Russian soldiers."

Tess felt sick to her stomach. Had Raisa really disappeared? Was the case against Flemming really in the process of disintegrating? Why hadn't Marley told her?

"I also understand that some of the supposedly-incriminating records seized, illegally, I might add, from my Surrey residence were unfortunately subjected to water damage during one of our winter storms. It's a crime, the sad state of our municipal buildings these days."

It was clear that Flemming's allies were everywhere, ready to do his bidding with the flick of a finger. While Tess didn't mourn the probable killings of Ceannaideach or Chaykovsky, she was deeply remorseful that Raisa also may have paid with her life for speaking against Flemming. As for how he knew that Raisa talked, Tess could only guess that one of the other women in the house, too inculcated into that life to give it up, got word to her former overseer. Tess knew Raisa's death, like that of Paul Collingwood, would haunt her for the rest of her life.

Flemming continued, unable to contain his conceit at defeating the system. "My solicitor is quite confident that the case against me is increasingly shaky and will soon collapse under its own weight." His smile widened, reminding Tess of the title character in the old black-and-white horror film, *Mr. Sardonicus,* that she and her college roommate Jody watched. "And as for your spy, the mole who infiltrated Mr. Yevtushenko's home in Odessa? I have it on good authority that he met an untimely end a day or two ago when the security staff took him for an intruder, and rightly so. I believe they left his body there in the empty residence."

Anton. What have I done? It took every muscle, every fiber of her being, to stay composed and inexpressive, even as she felt the walls closing in and the room spinning.

"Oh, my dear, have I upset you?" Flemming's unctuous smile never faltered. "Do you need some air? A glass of water? On the other hand, I wouldn't recommend the water here: it's not exactly tasty. Perhaps a soda. Officer! Come assist this woman!" he called loudly, still grinning.

"Screw you, Flemming," Tess growled, then held up her palm to the approaching guard. "It's fine, officer. I'm fine."

She turned to Flemming, wanting more than anything to simply rip his eyes out. Instead, she just smiled. "So you think you've won? You think the Met and Interpol won't be able to dredge up anything else that will keep you in Pentonville, or someplace even worse, for the rest of your miserable life? Dream on.

"I guarantee you, Flemming: Superintendent Marley, his staff, and the whole of Scotland Yard are even this minute knee-deep in examining every record, every slip of paper, every byte of computer data, that you've ever breathed on, that has ever come within a hundred miles of you. School records, driver's license, car registration, credit cards, property records, loans, taxes, voter registration, bank records, financial transactions, plus every person who's ever known you, liked you, hated you, slept with you, passed you on the street. Hell, if they can find your fucking grandmother, they'll put *her* under the microscope. And when they're done your face won't be wearing that repulsive smirk and your precious 'operations' will be nothing but a distant memory, to you or anyone else."

Flemming was rattled by Tess's furious monologue, but then composed himself. "You're forgetting about Dragos."

"Hardly. The authorities will capture him one way or another."

"Before or after he finally succeeds in killing you?"

So it was *Yevtushenko who was behind her attacks. At least the latest one.* "He hasn't had much luck up to now, and I can't imagine that the passage of time will change that. Judging by their botched jobs, the jackbooted troglodytes he hires to do his bidding aren't exactly candidates for Mensa. You included," she added with a smile.

Now it was Flemming's turn to flinch, and his face grew dark. "You have seriously underestimated me, Ms. Alexander. And I warn you: those who underestimate me usually come to a very bad end."

"Like I'm worried." Except, of course, she was.

"Let me share with you a little secret," Flemming spat, leaning across the wooden table. "Dragos Yevtushenko may be a powerful man, but that power is restricted to one very poor, very insignificant, country. Who cares what happens Ukraine? How far is that nation's pitiable reach? While Dragos is a friend and ally, it is *he* who reaches out to *me* for guidance, even in my present situation. In fact, we even saw ea…." He cut himself off in mid-sentence.

"I'm glad he cares, because he's the only one who does. Everyone else can't wait for the day when you're closed off in some rat-infested prison dungeon for good. Then we can all proceed to forget about you." Tess had guessed the gist of Flemming's censored sentence, but didn't want him to know it. She would walk out with some significant information, the most valuable being that somehow, Yevtushenko was in the U.K. and managed to get into the prison to visit Flemming.

She stood up, signaled to the officer, turned her back on Flemming and began walking away. She knew that his massive ego hated not having the final word, so she expected one last surly comment to come flying in her direction.

And here it was. "Enjoy your visit to the U.K., Tess. It's going to be your last."

25

Sitting in Superintendent Marley's office late that morning and recounting what she'd heard, made it all feel hideously real. As tough and resilient as she was, she was feeling the effects of spending time with Flemming. It started with a trembling in her hands, then as she spoke about the deaths of Raisa and Anton, the jackhammer hit her midsection.

"I'm responsible for their deaths," she choked out. "These people only wanted to help, and it got them killed."

Marley stood up from his desk and came around to the side of her chair, placing a hand on her shoulder. "No, Tess," — this was the first time he'd used her first name — "I don't believe that's the truth. The deaths of these fine people are *not* on you. You're right that they wanted to help. That is their legacy. And it's a fine one. You cannot take the blame for the inhumane acts committed by others who lack that humanity."

Tess sat quietly and tried to regain control of her shivering body. Finally, she cleared her throat and spoke. "Is Flemming right about the case against him coming apart?"

"No, he's *not* entirely right, although it was a blow to hear from you today that three of our strongest witnesses are probably dead. But we have other evidence, and what he doesn't know is that Interpol's forensics unit and our own team of computer experts are just millimeters away from cracking the encryption on his laptop. The phone is another story: as yet we haven't been able to get the manufacturer to provide us the key. Perhaps telling them that Flemming ordered at least four people killed to protect himself will help convince them.

"As well, he's not completely up to date about the water-damaged documents: yes, there was an unexplained leak in the roof of the evidence room and several key documents were spoilt. However, again thanks to modern technology, the experts at the British Museum have been able to reconstruct most of them to a point where they're decipherable and can be used as evidence."

"Is the case against him going to hold? Enough to keep him in prison?"

"We'll push for life imprisonment on indictment." The superintendent returned to his chair and sat down heavily. "But now with your new information about Raisa and the others, the Crown Prosecutor will have her work cut out for her and will likely need to regroup. But," he added with a smile, "she's extremely experienced and knows how to poke into dark corners to find what may be lurking there. I have great faith in her."

"What about Flemming's slip that Yevtushenko is in the U.K. and has actually gotten in to visit him?"

"Yes, that is extremely troubling. I will contact Pentonville's Governing Governor Outterridge and have him carefully inspect the visitor logs and video surveillance. There's bound to be something there, even if they have to search twenty-four hours a day until they find it. We absolutely must know when, and if possible, how,

Yevtushenko managed to get inside the prison."

Tess took a deep breath. "One other thing, maybe the most important. What do we do about Anton? If his body is still in Yevtushenko's house, we can't just leave him there."

"I will contact Interpol right away, Tess, but you need to be prepared for the likelihood that Yevtushenko's henchmen have removed Anton's remains. Either way, trust me: if he is not there, we will do everything we can to find him."

"I know you will, Superintendent. Can you please let me know?"

Marley nodded. "Yes, of course we could do that. May I ask when you were planning to fly out?"

"I don't have a set flight because I didn't know what might come of this visit with Flemming, so I can extend my stay for another day or two. However long it takes." Tess stood, and realized she needed to support herself on the back of the chair. The events of the day had taken more out of her than she realized.

Marley saw her slight wobble and rushed to her side. "Let me call you a car to take you back to the Elsinore. You just rest here until it arrives."

"No, I'll wait in the outer office. That way, you can do whatever you need to do without me bothering you."

"All right: I'll have my secretary let you know when the car arrives."

Tess fell into bed without eating lunch, even though Mrs. Kitchen volunteered to fix her something. "You look like death warmed over, dear," she said when Tess walked in the front door, alarmed at the dark streaks under her eyes and how pale she was.

When she woke later that afternoon, Harvey was stretched out beside her, snoring softly. She reached out and stroked the dog's silken fur, thankful for his presence but wishing it were Dancer. The fierce and constant ache of loss lessened over the intervening weeks, but there were times....

Just then, her phone buzzed. It was Marley.

"Yes, Superintendent."

"Interpol will search the house tomorrow morning at ten o'clock, Odessa time. I can let you know as soon as their findings are confirmed. Also, the prison logs established that someone else visited Flemming apart from his solicitor and you. The man was wearing a wig, false moustache, and shabby street clothes when we ran the surveillance video, but it was undoubtedly Yevtushenko. He signed in under an alias, and of course provided unassailable documentation to back up the false identity."

"When did he visit?"

"Yesterday."

Tess sucked in her breath. "Well, at least we know I was right in my guess about Flemming's slip of the tongue, although the fact that Yevtushenko really is here in England won't help me sleep better tonight. Thank you for letting me know all this. I'll wait to hear from you."

She was still exhausted, but knew sleeping would mean she'd be awake all night. Maybe a shower would help. That's where she was when the darknet email arrived, but she didn't think to check her messages until later that night after dinner.

Seated on the bed next to the everpresent Harvey, Tess was taking off her shoes when she realized she hadn't even opened her computer since leaving California. Tempted by her fatigue to wait until morning, she reluctantly pulled out the little tablet and lay it on the bed while she finished undressing and tugged the nightgown over her head.

"Okay Harvey, let's see what the world across the pond has been up to."

Once she opened the computer, she saw the flashing icon informing her of a darknet email. "That's weird," she said absently, and Harvey lifted his head to look at her. "Wonder who's communicating with me through this address?"

She logged onto her account, opened the email program, then inhaled sharply when she saw who the sender was.

Anton.

And the message was sent only this morning, just as she was traveling to Pentonville. How was that possible? Only an hour later, Flemming would be telling her about Anton's murder.

> There has been a development. My associate observing Y's house has been killed. After Y fled, he entered the home hoping to determine Y's destination, but did not know a guard had remained behind. However, after that I learned something that could lead me to Y. I shall inform you.

Stunned, Tess found it hard to take a breath. Was Flemming misinformed about Anton's death, or it was all just part of his twisted ploy to break her? No matter: she now knew what he told her wasn't true.

Tess picked up her phone, dialed Marley's number and left a voicemail, even though the man wouldn't get the message until he got back to his office in the morning. Then she typed a response to Anton.

> *I'm incredibly happy to hear from you, but so sorry about your associate. We thought it was you who'd been killed: it's a long story, but I'm here in the UK & saw Flemming this morning at Pentonville Prison & he said Y's men murdered you. Marley has Interpol raiding the Odessa house tomorrow morning to recover the body & gather evidence. Also, Y is in the UK & visited Flemming at Pentonville under a disguise & false name yesterday. I'm very glad you're alive.*

It was late, but in her current state of excitement Tess knew sleep would elude her for a while, so she pulled on her robe and tiptoed downstairs. Entering the spotless kitchen, she opened the refrigerator on the off chance there might be an opened bottle of wine there, and found a half-full magnum of French Pinot Blanc. She was sure Mrs. Kitchen wouldn't mind, and poured herself a small glass.

She sat on the couch in front of the dying fire, Harvey at her feet, and tried to make sense of everything. Anton being alive put a new spin on things. First, it meant that Flemming's communication channel was flawed, which opened a whole realm of possibilities regarding the other information he gave her. *Perhaps there's even a remote chance that Raisa is still alive.* And what about Flemming's claim that Yevtushenko was reviving the British slice of the sex trafficking operation? Was that just a flight of fancy, meant to unbalance her?

He'd obviously been telling the truth when he almost let it slip that Yevtushenko visited him, but what did that mean? *Why* would Yevtushenko, one of the most powerful crime bosses in Ukraine, stoop to wearing a phony costume and risk being caught just to see Flemming? Sure, they were colleagues, along with Ludmila Zhuravlyov and the still-no-last-name Radic, but what was so important that it necessitated a wanted fugitive making a surreptitious trip to a high-security British prison? Even considering Flemming's boast that he, not Yevtushenko, was the power behind the trafficking ring, it made little sense.

Then there was Marley's revelation about Interpol being close to cracking the passcode on Flemming's computer and the British Museum team's success at resurrecting the water-damaged documents seized from Flemming's safe. The man was obviously unaware of either development, pointing to further cracks in his network.

Tess wondered idly if she should head back to the States the next day as she initially thought she would, but decided to wait until the dust settled and hopefully, more information emerged. She was pretty sure Marley would disagree, but she might even be able to help.

Her laptop blinked brightly with a darknet email alert at 4:30 the next morning. It took a while for the light from the screen to awaken her, but eventually it did. She'd intentionally left the program open just in case Anton responded.

> I am sorry you were informed of my death, but glad it was a falsehood. Knowing that Y is in the UK where you are as well is troubling. Also that he slipped into the prison is a concern.

> *I too am glad the news of your death was false. I failed to tell you that Flemming claimed that his assistant in the London*

brothel & the house-manager of his private home in Surrey are dead, along with one of the women I interviewed from the house in London. I have no idea if this is true, but he had nothing to gain by telling me, unless just to rattle my cage.

She was surprised when a response came from Anton right away.

Rattle your cage?

Sorry. Distress me. Knock me off balance emotionally.

Oh. I would not be shocked to learn that he ordered them killed. If true, he will probably never be found out.

But he made a big mistake by telling me. His huge ego & the fact he sees himself as invincible may be his downfall.

How long are you to be in London?

Tess replied that she wasn't sure, but would probably stay at least another day or two. Anton responded, asking for her disposable cell number in case he needed to reach her quickly.

After she logged off, Tess reached down to pet Harvey. "So what the hell do we do now? I feel about as useless as tits on a frog." She climbed the stairs and got back into bed, patting the sheets beside her. Harvey happily jumped up, circled, and lay down with his head on his paws. She didn't think she'd be able to fall back to sleep, but surprised herself by drifting off within minutes.

Summer appeared to have abandoned London. There was no fog, but the lead-colored clouds hung thick and suffocatingly low. The television anchor said temperatures wouldn't budge above 13° C all day—about 55° F, Tess quickly calculated—falling from the last two days' balmy highs in the low seventies. Humidity would near sixty-five percent, he intoned, as if delivering a funeral eulogy.

"What have you planned for today, dear?" the affable Mrs. Kitchen asked as she poured Tess another cup of coffee and dropped another spoonful of clotted cream onto her scone.

"Mrs. Kitchen, I'm going to go back to the States ten pounds heavier if you keep feeding me like this!" she teased, savoring every bite of the delectable pastry.

"You need to get some more meat on those bones after your 'accident.' And," she added, her voice lowering to a near-whisper, "wouldn't I just love to get my hands around the throat of the villain who did that to you, and your golden Dancer."

"You and me both." Tess picked up the last crumbs of the scone with her fingertips, considering what she should do for the day. "I need to wait for a phone call this morning, but afterward I may just hail a cab and go shopping in SOHO. Do something enjoyable for a change."

"That's a capital idea! Go out and have fun even if the weather has turned sour. They say tomorrow will be better, but with London you never know."

Marley called around ten o'clock to say Interpol found nothing in Yevtushenko's Odessa home. No body, no blood or evidence of foul play, no nothing. Not even a stray slip of paper. It was a dead-end.

Tess was disappointed, but not surprised. The trafficking ring didn't survive this long by being sloppy. Yevtushenko would probably sell the house through a proxy, launder the proceeds, and buy himself another mansion in Ukraine. All perfectly legal and above-board.

With no further word from Anton, she called a cab and resolved to hit the shops in SOHO. Harvey looked like he was losing his best friend when she told him he had to stay behind, but she knew that once she was out of sight he'd happily return to his beloved human's side without a second thought.

She asked the driver to drop her off at the luxurious Liberty London department store on Great Marlborough Street, where she roamed among the Hera silk scarves, Dries Van Noten cocktail dresses, Bruce Lepere vintage rugs, and Fornasetti ceramics. After stopping for a light lunch at Patisserie Valerie, she meandered through a dozen or more quirky SOHO shops showcasing everything from clothing to musical instruments to tattoo artists to gourmet chocolate, then spent the better part of two hours browsing through Foyles, the five-story Charing Cross Road bookstore, a London fixture since the dawn of the 1900s. While she was there, she picked up a copy of the book, *A Cabinet of Ancient Medical Curiosities: Strange Tales and Surprising Facts from the Healing Arts of Greece and Rome* for Roger. She could pretty much guarantee he hadn't already read it.

It was almost five o'clock by the time she made it back to Regent Street after stopping at Paul Smith, where she tried on several of the iconic British jeans until she found a dark indigo slim-cut pair that fit perfectly. She picked up a three-quarter sleeve forest green t-shirt with subtle lace trim at the scoop neckline, and added a set of faux-malachite drop earrings that matched perfectly.

She didn't realize just how tired she was until she settled into the back seat of the cab for the short drive back to the Elsinore House. Barely five minutes into the thirty-minute ride she fell asleep, her head lolling on the seat back.

A blood-red ocean appeared before her, churning and beating against the shore in a paroxysm of violence. Someone approached behind her, and she knew with absolute certainty that her life was in danger. Prepared for the assault, she turned swiftly and raised both hands, palms toward her attacker in a blocking gesture. Astonishingly, he stopped as if she'd thrown up an invisible force field. She couldn't make out his features, but blood seeped from a deep cut on the side of his face. As he tried to move toward her, she looked down at his feet and saw they were shackled with rusty iron chains. With a thunderous, guttural roar, the man bent down, grabbed the shackles, and the corroded links splintered in every direction, one impaling itself in her left arm. A venomous grin spread across his face, revealing barbed-wire-jagged teeth, one of them a bright gold. He oozed toward her.

"Miss? Miss?" The cab driver's clipped query jolted her into awareness. "You're at the Elsinore, miss."

Tess took several breaths to calm herself, then tossed the driver two twenty-pound notes, gathered her shopping bags, and sprinted to the front door through a sudden downpour.

She slammed the door behind her and leaned against it, trying to figure out what she'd just seen. Was it just a dream? Another of her premonitions? If so, what the hell did it mean? Just then, Harvey dashed from the back of the house to greet her, and Tess couldn't help but smile. "Hey, big boy! You miss me?" She was surprised at the quiver in her voice when she spoke.

Harvey danced in a circle near her feet, his tail whipping back and forth so ferociously it seemed in danger of flying off. She bent down and kissed the top of his head, then started upstairs.

"Tess? Is that you?" Mrs. Kitchen's Irish lilt wafted from the rear of the house. "Wait, dear. A call came in for you while you were out."

A call? Who would be calling her at the Elsinore?

The woman toddled in through the kitchen, looking down at a note. "He said his name was Anton. He had quite an accent, that one, I found it hard to understand him. He said to tell you he was alive, which I thought was very strange, and said it was extremely important that you meet him tomorrow afternoon at one o'clock under the east-bound line clock inside the Bethnal Green tube station."

Tess stopped in her tracks and turned to the innkeeper with a stunned expression on her face. "What? I'm sorry, I'm not sure I understand. Anton *called* you? Here?" Her brain was desperately trying to track and make sense of what Mrs. Kitchen said.

"Yes, my dear. Here's the note I took so I wouldn't mix anything up." She handed Tess a piece of paper, handwritten on the Elsinore House stationary.

Tess read it, looked up, then re-read it. "And you're one hundred percent sure he said his name was Anton?"

"Absolutely. I even asked him to spell it. He spoke English very well, but as I said, his accent was heavy. Maybe Russian? I don't know for sure."

"Well, thank you, Mrs. Kitchen. I appreciate it."

"You're welcome, dear. Will you be going out again this evening? Looks like it's really tipping down, and you haven't a 'brelly or Macintosh."

Tess smiled at the British colloquialisms. "I'm not sure right now, but if I do I may need to borrow your umbrella. I just didn't think to pack one on this trip."

"Of course. Just ask."

Ultimately, Tess decided to order in a pizza from the neighborhood pizzeria she discovered on her last trip, and invited Mrs. Kitchen to share it. They sat together in the small breakfast nook that looked out over the late summer garden, now wet with rain, while they ate and chatted and enjoyed a glass of wine from the bottle of Pinot Blanc that Tess purloined the night before.

When she got back to her room, Harvey glued to her side, she had a much clearer picture of what was going on and what she needed to do.

She picked up her phone and called Marley.

26

Tess had never been to the Bethnal Green Underground station, but since it was only a half-mile away and the day had turned clear and bright, she decided to walk. It would give her time to think about the upcoming meeting, even though she'd already run it over in her mind a dozen times.

The evening before, Mrs. Kitchen told Tess about the tragic World War II disaster at the station that crushed to death 173 people after a false air-raid alert caused crowds to surge into the narrow, poorly-lit staircase leading to the underground shelter. After almost 75 years, a memorial to the victims called Stairway to Heaven was erected at the site.

Within minutes, the outline of the tall memorial came into view. It stood in Bethnal Green Gardens only yards from the entrance leading down into the former shelter, now the Underground station. The long, jagged marble base featured bronze markers with the full names of each victim and a dozen or more plaques with individual survivor accounts. As Tess read their stories, she was shaken by the depth of the tragedy that had hit the destitute East End, already so devastated from the German bombings. Atop the marble plinth was a massive inverted stairway of reclaimed teak with the surnames of the victims carved into its sides.

She glanced at her watch. *12:40.* She wanted to get to the meeting spot ahead of time, so started down the eighteen steps, conscious of the brass handrails that weren't there in 1943 when the 173 people perished. Turning left, she walked another hundred feet and went down several more stairs to the ticketing area. Although she wasn't planning to use the subway system, she still needed to pay to get through the gate. She swiped her card across the electronic reader and waited for the green light. Her pulse quickened as she took the down escalator into the bowels of the city.

The problem was, she didn't know whether to go left or right on the platform to find the distinctive hanging clock, one of only a tiny handful in the Underground system that featured a brass surround and on the facewhat, twelve small gold roundels instead of numbers. As she stood and peered up and down the track, she felt a tickle at the back of her neck and intuitively turned left. *Yes, this is the way to go. It'll all be resolved soon, one way or the other.*

She saw the remarkable ivory-faced clock just ahead. The hands pointed to 12:51 or :52, although with analogue clocks it was hard to be precise from a distance. Now, all she needed to do was wait.

So she waited, immobile under the peculiar clock as the lazy stream of late-day commuters and travelers flowed toward and around and away from her: mothers and fathers pushing strollers and clutching toddlers, men in high-fashion suits and ties with briefcases in hand, nose-ringed teens ambling aimlessly to nowhere, elegant anorexic women in Armani jackets and pseudo-grunge-rocker jeans, shabbily-dressed housewives and retired blue-collar workers, machinists and manicurists and mail clerks and models and musicians and the whole range of humanity, sauntering and trudging and scurrying to get from here to there on a summer London midday.

12:56. She waited as a homeless veteran shuffled by with a musty sleeping bag on his back, as a blind man with his service dog sat down on a nearby bench to adjust his socks, as a frazzled mother tried to placate her little girl who was screaming *Mummy I want a chocolate*, as a college student weighed down with a backpack argued with his girlfriend as they stood on the platform. Here and there she caught someone's eye and smiled, or an elderly gentleman tipped his hat, or a baby giggled up at her.

12:58. There was a panhandler holding tight to a cardboard soup bowl, here was an artist with his paints and palette, and somewhere out of sight a busker playing *Norwegian Wood* on a viola. A few feet ahead and on her left, she saw a bearded man with long blond dreadlocks and rimless glasses, dressed in jeans and a baggy yellow sweater, and carrying a guitar case on his back. As he strolled toward her with the thinning crowd, he pulled a cell phone from his pocket and put it to his ear. *Yes*, she overheard him say, and caught a glint as he smiled. *I'm on my way. Love you too.*

Then in a lightning-fast move, both the phone and the guitar case went crashing to the concrete as the man turned suddenly to his right, clipping an unsuspecting young woman wearing chartreuse earbuds and sending her careening toward the wall. At that moment, pandemonium exploded. Shouts boomed out from almost every direction, a chorus of shrill whistles sounded, and people all along the platform found themselves roughly pushed aside by either burly men in everyday clothes or ones in dark blue jackets and helmets adorned with official coats-of-arms. Screams, profanities, and heavy footfalls echoed in the subterranean cavern. Nearby a man lay face-down on the platform, blood pooling around him. Surrounded by a half-dozen police officers with batons and Tasers, one of them turned him over and saw a knife buried up to the hilt in his right chest. A skull-shaped thicket of phony straw-colored dreadlocks lay a few feet away, knocked off in the scuffle.

Tess felt herself lifted off her feet and carried, by whom and to where she didn't know. She was extraordinarily lightheaded and a dribble-trail of bright blood marked her passage along the platform, up the escalator and flights of stairs into the bright sunlight and into a waiting car, which sped off almost before the door clanged shut.

It was all part of the plan hatched by Tess and Superintendent Marley the night before. The minute she heard that "Anton" called the Elsinore, she knew something wasn't right. He would never have called the B&B, and would never have left his name with someone he didn't know. Besides, she reasoned, why would he want to endure a six- to eight-hour flight from Odessa to London to meet with her when they'd settled everything by email two days before? If he need to tell her something new, he would have either emailed or called her.

But of course, what Yevtushenko didn't know was that Tess already knew that the man killed in the Odessa house wasn't Anton. There were two possibilities as to why he thought the ruse would work: either he really believed the dead man was Anton, or he knew the man was someone else and wanted to lead her astray. Either way, he needed to plant the idea in Tess's mind that even if she believed Flemming's claim that Anton was dead, he was in fact alive and well and needed desperately to meet with her. It might have worked, if Anton hadn't reached out to Tess that night.

The idea was to catch Yevtushenko before he could get to Tess waiting under the subway clock. Thanks to Superintendent Marley, the Met sprang into action astonishingly fast, setting up for the capture in just hours. A squad of police, many undercover, were posted in various spots within the station and along the eastbound platform, each with a description of Yevtushenko and a still image of the man pulled from the prison's video surveillance. The unknown factor was what sort of disguise he might be wearing, although the hope was he'd employ the same masquerade as he used at the prison.

Yevtushenko, however, taking no chances that he might be spotted, altered his appearance again, successfully confounding many of the bobbies and detectives who weren't looking for a guitar-carrying middle-aged hippie.

Until he made his move, but by then it was almost too late.

Tess sat on the hospital gurney, her left arm wrapped in thick gauze and talking intently with the police superintendent. Marley had finally collected himself after the near-assassination, but kept apologizing that his team wasn't quicker to identify Yevtushenko and reach her. He also kept asking if she was sure she was all right.

Tess smiled. "Superintendent, I promise I'm fine. Yevtushenko was unlucky that I figured out who he was right as he was finishing his fake phone call, and I turned sideways the instant before he reached me. Otherwise he'd have probably sliced my carotid artery instead of my arm, and I wouldn't be sitting here having this conversation."

"I was terribly distressed when I saw the blood trail as you were being carried away." Marley's voice cracked. "I must admit, I feared the worst."

"I think I did at first too, especially after I almost passed out in the car heading here. I was vaguely aware of the siren and a man next to me saying to hold on, but everything was blurry, as if there were a scrim over the whole scene. It wasn't until I reached the hospital that I saw he only sliced my arm, and that I'd live to fight another day."

"But tell me," asked Marley, "how did you recognize Yevtushenko? He was extremely well disguised."

"I didn't at first. I actually looked at him then glanced away. But he smiled a little as he said 'Love you, too,' and his gold incisor caught the light."

"Gold incisor? How did that help you identify him? We have no photos of Yevtushenko smiling, and the only thing to go on was his facial scar, which he covered with the false beard. And you'd never seen him in person."

Tess hesitated, then half-explained. "I had a...dream the day before of a threatening man with a scar on his face and a gold tooth. The image stuck in my head, and when I saw him I had an instinctive reaction. I can't explain it, but I'm grateful for it."

The truth was, Tess *couldn't* explain it. She'd never been able to. By the time she was a teenager, she'd come to simply accept her enigmatic gift as a normal part of being Tess Alexander, for better or worse. This day, it was definitely for better. As Marley regarded her silently, Tess recalled that part of her vison on the cab ride back to the Elsinore that day included her arm being impaled with a shard of metal. She wisely decided not to mention that to the scrupulously pragmatic superintendent.

"I don't believe you know this yet, but Dragos Yevtushenko is dead."

"Dead? How?" Tess was astonished and enormously relieved at the same time, even though it felt somehow immoral to be glad for someone's death.

"Apparently he fell on his own knife in the fracas with my officers, and it pierced his heart." Marley hesitated, then added, "Can't say I'm sorry."

"Nor am I," said Tess with a small smile, "even though it makes me feel like a dreadful person. Will his death have any impact on the case against Flemming?"

"Not at all. And thanks to those computer wizards who've cracked both Flemming's laptop and phone, we now have sufficient evidence against him to cobble dogs with."

Tess laughed in spite of the deadly serious subject." Uhh, 'cobble dogs with'? That's a new one on me."

Marley grinned. "It's an old-fashioned expression that means you have more than enough of something. I doubt most people outside of north Lincolnshire know the adage."

"Since I have a recording, can anything Flemming said to me in Pentonville be used against him?"

"I'm fairly certain the High Court will allow the recording to be admitted into evidence, but they may need you to testify to its veracity. That's a a bit far off in the front-view windscreen, however, and not something you need trouble yourself with."

"Well, just know that I'll happily to return to the U.K.

to testify if need be."

"I hope that won't be necessary: once his solicitors have examined the new and resurrected wealth of evidence we have against him, I believe they'll be convinced to accept a plea deal from the Crown Prosecutor rather than risk a trial where the jury would surely be horrified at his crimes. Either way, I expect he will face a life sentence under our Modern Slavery Act."

Tess nodded. "It's just too bad you couldn't grab Ludmila Zhuravlyov or identify the mysterious Radic."

"But we've pinched off the head of the scorpion, which is good. Unfortunately, there are always more where they came from."

"Like Vyacheslav Mikhailovich," Tess added, eyes narrowing. "Now, *that* would be one hell of a scorpion to crush."

"That's not likely," Marley responded dourly. "Better men than I have tried over the decades to entrap him, but he's far too well protected by his criminal cohorts, not to mention puppets inside the Russian government. We must be satisfied with what we have."

"I suppose so." Tess let the comment hang in the air for a moment, then touched Marley's arm. "Superintendent, I can't begin to thank you enough for everything you've done over these past months, not just for me but for the victims of these two inhuman beings. I still grieve deeply the loss of Inspector Collingwood as well as Raisa, but without your willingness to put everything on the line, the ending to this story would be far different."

He put his hand atop hers and squeezed it. "Tess, it is I, all of us, who owe *you* the debt of gratitude. Without you, these two men would still be plying their wretched trade, their victims would remain in bondage, and women like your Galina would never have a chance to see the light of justice. I am truly in awe of your courage and determination to expose these terrible crimes. Even if you *did* drive me barmy from time to time," he laughed.

Tess reached out, and they hugged warmly, Marley patting her affably on the back as Anthony did before. *Maybe it's a British thing.* The gesture was both comforting and amusing, a sign of the genuine friendship between the two dissimilar, metaphorically sword-wielding advocates for justice. As he strode down the hospital corridor, Tess hoped they would meet again.

Maybe just not under such perilous circumstances.

AFTERWORD

Hope always transcends experience.
~ George Schaller

Both Detective McKittrick and the FBI's agent Jephson were more than happy to close their respective cases centering on the attempted murder of the obstinate journalist, even without a suspect under arrest. Each man concurred with the premise that whomever the would-be assassin was, he was likely dead, a casualty of his own abject failure.

The Metropolitan Police Department was no closer to solving the murder of Paul Collingwood, and privately Tess wondered if they ever would. This type of low-level killer almost always eventually ran afoul of higher-ups, who feared that one day in some drunken bout the man could say too much to the wrong person. Not unlike his compatriot in America, he was probably at the bottom of the Thames or buried on some desolate Irish moor.

Once Tess received word from Superintendent Marley that Flemming would spend the rest of his life in a British prison, she called Katia and asked if she could drop by the house to deliver some news. And I'd like Elliott to be there as well, she said.

As it was the last time she was there, winter was descending on Auburn and the Sierra mountains. The huge cedar and oak trees that lined the town's streets leaned against the wind in denunciation of its supremacy, and fallen autumn leaves churned in multicolored whirlpools along the sidewalks.

Inside the Palmer's home, the mood was again calm and welcoming. A fire burned in the great stone fireplace, and the smell of freshly-brewed coffee and baking muffins filled the air. Katia welcomed Tess with a friendly handshake, which came as a surprise considering the woman's former reluctance to make physical contact. Maybe that was changing, the more comfortable she became with her new life, Tess thought.

"Please to sit down," Katia said. "Is Dancer not with you?"

Oh, God. She didn't know what happened.

"I'm so sorry, Katia, but..." Tess swallowed, then continued. "But Dancer died this past summer." She didn't want to tell Katia how it happened for fear she'd feel some responsibility for it.

Elliott moaned "Oh no," as tears sprung to Katia's eyes. They trickled down her cheeks as she spoke. "Oh, oh...I am so sorry. He was such a beautiful, wonderful dog. I do not believe I could have told you what I did if he was not here beside he, giving me courage. That is so heart-breaking."

Tess smiled weakly. "Yes, it really is. My life has been quite empty with him gone."

"I'm terribly sorry, Tess," added Elliott.

Tess wanted to sidestep any questions about what happened, since they would find out once the story went public in *Panorama,* so she spoke up. "Katia, I have some news for you and Elliott. Some very good news. Ulrich Flemming was arrested in Great Britain and sentenced to life in prison. And Dragos Yevtushenko is dead."

Katia's eyes widened and her mouth went slack. For a few moments, the only sound from her was a series of rapid breaths. Then she burst into a torrent of tears, rocking back and forth and hugging herself tightly. Elliott kneeled next to her and cloaked her in a protective embrace as she sobbed.

Finally, she quieted and gathered herself, fixing Tess

with an incredulous gaze. "How…did…what…I don't…I'm sorry. Please tell me. Everything."

"Katia, the story is very long, and parts of it are very ugly…"

"I do not care how ugly it is," she interjected. "It cannot be any uglier than my life before was. Please to tell us."

"Wait, my dear," said Elliot, standing again. "Perhaps we could all have some coffee or tea, and one of your wonderful apple muffins warm out of the oven? That will give both of us a chance to absorb this news, then listen to Tess's story."

"Of course," said Katia, jumping up from the couch. "I am ashamed at my lack of courtesy. Please, Tess, I shall bring you coffee and a muffin. I confess that they are very good."

For the next two hours, the three sat in front of the crackling fire while Tess recounted the events of the last many months. Some details, like the murders of Raisa and Paul Collingwood and the truth of Dancer's death, she intentionally left out to spare Katia any more pain. She would learn about it all soon enough. The most important thing was that she be unreservedly assured that two of her captors—without a doubt, the two leading impresarios of their perverted cabal—would never be free to pursue their vile trade again.

Katia barely moved and said nothing during Tess's recitation. When it was over she got up and walked to where Tess was sitting. She held out both hands, Tess stood, and Katia put her arms around her. When she pulled away, each woman's face was coursed with tears, but each was smiling. Words were unnecessary.

The next morning, Tess's doorbell rang and a delivery driver held out a bouquet of two dozen roses. They were, of course, from Katia and Elliott. The card read, *You have changed our lives forever, and changed the world as well.*

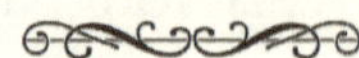

Just after Valentine's Day, Tess got a call from her good friend Jan, a volunteer with Homeward Bound Golden Retriever Rescue. They just got a dog, she said, that might be perfect for Tess. How about they drive down to the ranch together and see her?

At first Tess resisted, not sure she was ready to bring another dog into her life. Her relationship with Roger Holland was wonderful, she was almost completely healed from the attack in Monterey and only a faint scar remained from the London stabbing, she'd finished and submitted the three-part article to *Panorama,* and life had settled into a fairly peaceful equilibrium. Why upset things by adding in another responsibility?

"Because," Jan countered fervently, "you need to have a dog to share your life with. As great as Roger is, and as well as things have been going with him, you know it as well as I do: you simply need a furry heartbeat in your house."

Tess gave in. It didn't take much to convince her.

The next day, she walked into the kennel area with Jan when her eyes locked with those of a gorgeous, snow-white English cream golden retriever standing in rapt attention. She had, Tess thought, the deepest, kindest brown eyes she'd ever seen. Even before she took the dog out for a "test-walk," Tess knew she'd be bringing the beautiful girl home. Just forty pounds and not quite full-grown at probably not more than a year old, she'd belonged to a healthy 50-year-old runner in the Santa Cruz area who suddenly and inexplicably died in his sleep. His family couldn't take the dog, so they called Homeward Bound. Which is how Luna came into Tess's life.

That weekend Roger arrived for his weekly "visitation," which most of the time stretched into three days rather than just the weekend. In the past few months, he had talked more and more about resigning as Chief, taking an early retirement and starting a practice with a good friend from medical school who lived in the foothills of the Sierra just a few miles east of Sacramento. Even though Tess didn't want to get her hopes up, she admitted that the idea of having the handsome doctor closer was nice. Better than nice.

Luna fell in love with Roger instantly, and the feeling was mutual. She adapted beautifully to being with both of them, and in fact acted as if Tess's was the only home she'd ever known. She was a near-perfect companion, although like most goldens wasn't much of a guard dog, more likely to invite a criminal inside and show him where the good stuff was. But she was excellent on a leash, friendly with other dogs and their humans, and knew how to use the dog-door. She drove Tess crazy sometimes with her squeaky-toy obsession, but if that was the worst of it, it was pretty wonderful.

Saturday night all three of them pigged out on popcorn as Tess and Roger watched the classic 1957 love story, *An Affair to Remember* with Cary Grant and Deborah Kerr. As the final scene played, a tear trickled down Tess's cheek, which happened every time she saw the film. It never got old.

Trailed by Luna, they walked hand-in-hand up the stairs to her bedroom, Roger with a bottle of Russian River Iron Horse Vineyard Classic Vintage Brut and two champagne glasses. Tess didn't know what they were celebrating, but wasn't about to refuse a glass of elegant sparkling wine.

When they reached the room, Roger placed the bottle and champagne flutes on the marble stand next to the bed and lowered her onto the mattress until they were both lying face-to-face, gently intertwined together.

"I have something to tell you, Tess." She looked over at him with eyes half closed. "Mmm-hmm."

"I'm leaving the hospital, and Sean and I are opening our practice in Auburn."

Tess's eyes flew open. "When?"

"I'm actually quitting next month, but it'll take a while to get the practice set up, though Sean's already found office space in Auburn. Like I've said before, this is something I've wanted for years, and now's a perfect time since I have enough years in at Stanford to have a decent retirement income. I'll find a place to rent somewhere around Auburn and finally get to enjoy a slower pace."

Tess smiled, and reached up to touch the crinkled laugh-lines around his eyes.

"Finding you has pretty much rocked my world, you know," he said. "Not only are you incredibly kind and compassionate, you're one of the most idiotically, doggedly, outlandishly courageous people I've ever met, even though you're terrified of tarantulas. I mean, what's to be terrified of? They have such cute little bug-eyes, fuzzy legs and bodies…"

"Quit it!" cried Tess, laughing and cringing at the same time.

Laughing along with her, Roger kissed Tess's nose. "Anyway, my Tess, having you in my life has opened a whole new dimension for which I'm more grateful than you can imagine. And there's one more thing."

"What's that?"

"I happen to be in love with you."

For what may have been only the second or third time in her life, Tess was speechless.

He kissed her tenderly on the forehead then moved his lips softly down her face to her outstretched neck. While deftly unbuttoning her teal silk blouse, his mouth continued the exploration of Tess's throat, then back to her open lips. They kissed, sweetly at first and then with more urgency.

Tess opened her eyes and saw the silvered moon standing full and round in the sky, adorning the room with its lustrous glow. Roger caught her gaze, and for a moment they both lay still, entranced as one with the magnificence of this otherworldly object. Then she pulled him down to meet her open mouth, and the moon flew away.

Afterwards, Luna jumped up and stretched out at the foot of the bed. Roger reached across to the table, filled each glass with the bubbling, gilded wine, and handed one to Tess. They touched the crystal flutes together and drank, letting a comfortable silence fill the room.

Then Tess took both glasses, set them back on the table and gently pushed Roger down onto the pillow. Raising up on one elbow, she gazed at him tenderly, the remnants of moonlight caressing his face.

She bent down to kiss him, then stopped and smiled. "You know doc, it's like someone once said: I do believe this is the beginning of a beautiful friendship."

ABOUT THE AUTHOR

A Just Reckoning is Joan Merriam's first book in the Tess Alexander mystery series. ***A Fine Oblivion*** will be published in mid-2021.

Joan admits to being one of those bewildered baby-boomers who couldn't decide what she wanted to be when she grew up. Her careers have ranged from real estate sales to political organizing to directing a child abuse prevention agency to running her own business, and more.

Today, she is a college instructor and freelance writer. Author of the nonfiction book, *Little Girl Lost: A True Story of Shattered Innocence and Murder,* she currently writes a syndicated newspaper column on life with dogs.

She lives in northern California, in the historic Mother Lode region of the Sierra Nevada.

Visit her website at www.joanmerriam.com, or on Facebook at www.facebook.com/JoanMerriamAuthor

www.ingramcontent.com/pod-product-compliance
Lightning Source LLC
Chambersburg PA
CBHW051530100726
47898CB00005B/1645
9781736563205